THE FIDDLER OF KILBRONEY

Brandon Originals

The
Fiddler of Kilbroney
Kathleen O'Farrell

Do Thomáis

le mìle grá

o Caitlín Dic Fhearghaile

18. 5. 94.

BRANDON

First published in 1994 by
Brandon Book Publishers Ltd
Dingle, Co. Kerry, Ireland

British Library Cataloguing in Publication Data is available
for this book.

ISBN 0 86322 177 7

This book is published with the financial assistance of the
Arts Council/An Chomhairle Ealaíon, Ireland.

Front cover paintings: *Self-Portrait in a Black Feathered Hat* by
Joseph Wright, reproduced by permission of the Derby
Museum and Art Gallery; *The French in Killala Bay* by William
Sadler, repro-duced by permission of the National Gallery of
Ireland.

Typeset by Koinonia Ltd, Bury
Cover design by The Graphiconies, Dublin
Printed by ColourBooks Ltd, Dublin

'There exists in this Kingdom a traitorous conspiracy by persons calling themselves United Irishmen.'

Lord Camden 1797

Dedicated to Liam, Bríd, Jack and Katie Farrell
who now live at the Crag.

Contents

Author's Note

KILBRONEY LIES IN the foothills of the Mountains of Mourne in the southernmost part of County Down. Long regarded as a place of healing, it is reputedly the only part of Ireland to have escaped disease during the Great Famine.

My story begins in 1790, just as Ireland is emerging from the dark years of the Penal laws and the threat of a Jacobite uprising. Yet the new-found peace is uneasy, for the British surrender to George Washington in 1781 had been only the first in a series of events to shake the kingdoms of Europe. The Bastille fell in 1789; in 1790 Edmund Burke wrote his *Reflections on the French Revolution* to which Tom Paine replied in his seminal work, *The Rights of Man*.

In the words of Wolfe Tone, leader of the United Irishmen, 'oppressed, plundered, insulted Ireland' was electrified by the changes happening beyond its shores. Schoolmasters, innkeepers, tradesmen and peasants found common purpose in the new radicalism which united people of all creeds and classes. In the prosperous linen ports of Ulster, Presbyterian merchants reached out to their Catholic fellow countrymen in a spirit of equality and fraternity. These were euphoric years, undiminished by bigotry. These were the years of the United Irishmen.

My father and mother told me stories of the people and events of those times; some of their tales had come down from Johnny Fearon, known as '*Leath-láimh*' or 'One-armed Johnny', who was my grandfather's great-grandfather. Many of the people who feature in this book once lived. Tom Dunn was leader of the United Irishmen in the area and Kilbroney still honours his memory; Ruth, the dark woman, is based on a real character as is Owen MacOwen (Eoghan MacEoghan), the last of an ancient sept and Keeper of the Staff of Bronach. John Mercer, the East India merchant, resided at Arno's Vale, while the Hall family still live at Narrow Water.

They say that people in the north have long memories, but in such a rich and ancient place two hundred years can seem like yesterday. I wish to acknowledge the help of Fr Raymond Murray, whose research on Mercer and the French trade expedition inspired that element of the story. My thanks also to local historians Fr Anthony Davies PP, Dromara, and John Joe Parr, and particularly to my brother, Dr W. J. Farrell, for his considerable help with the manuscript.

October 1788

THE *ST GENEVIEVE* HEAVED and groaned as the waves lashed its decks. The ship had lain becalmed for some ten days before a gentle breeze had coaxed it northwards into the unpredictable waters of the Bay of Biscay. Now the few fare-paying passengers huddled below as the vessel, laden with a cargo of molasses, tossed and lurched towards the south-west coast of Ireland.

On the open deck a woman crouched in the darkness, too scared to move. She watched in fright as the sinister figure of the ship's mate advanced towards her child. The little boy clutched at the rigging and began to climb.

'Watch out,' she screamed, 'you'll fall!'

'Come down, you thieving little bastard,' sneered the mate. 'You heard your mother. Come on, you'll be safe with me!' The boy glanced down at the grinning face and began to pull himself further up the ropes.

'Come down, Michael, I'll not let him hurt you.'

The boy hesitated. The world around him was black and terrible and his grip was weak. The momentary pause was chance enough for the mate, who grabbed the child's foot. The little boy writhed and squealed as he felt himself being dragged down. He kicked out as hard as he could at his assailant's face and heard a roar of rage.

'I'll kill you! I'll bloody well kill you!' The mate drew his knife from his belt.

'No,' pleaded Ruth, 'please, no!' The boy kicked again, bloodying the mate's nose. He pulled his other foot free and began to climb once more. The mast swayed as Michael's cold fingers grasped the ropes. The mate was gaining ground, his huge, whiskered face convulsed in anger. Suddenly a loose boom swung around dislodging both climbers and they fell on to the deck. The boy slithered towards the capstan, to the safety of the shadows. Ruth, spurred into action, grabbed the mate's dagger. She placed herself between him and her son.

'I'll thankee to return my weapon.' The mate scrambled to his feet, wheezing heavily. He lurched towards her, huge but clumsy. She struck out in fright with the knife and felt it slip into his body; she struck again, and again.

After he fell she continued to stab him in fear he might still rise up. She could hear her little boy's hysterical weeping. The mate was heavy but a sudden lurch sent his body rolling and sliding towards the rails, and with one heave Ruth pushed him into the black waters below. Rain and crashing waves removed all bloodstains from the deck, and with them the evidence of a violent deed.

When the mate's absence was discovered the following morning several crew members reported hearing a loud cry: in such a storm it had not seemed unusual. He had too much rum in his belly, some said. Ruth was questioned. Yes, she said, she had witnessed the accident: the man had lost his footing. She had been too frightened to call for help. The captain recorded the mate's sudden disappearance in his log. With Ireland only a few days away one crew member less made little difference. The mate was a heavy drinker who bullied the young lads and cheated at cards. No tears were shed for him.

Once on land, Ruth sought directions to the north. She felt weak and ill after the ocean voyage but her journey was not yet complete. The pair's dark skin, however, earned them an uneven welcome. Some helpful folk directed them on the way, but they were stoned as they passed through a quiet Tipperary village and afterwards were more careful about talking to Irish folk, no matter how ragged.

After a time a roving fiddler took them under his wing. His name was O'Cassidy, and he told Ruth that there was a living for his like around the linen ports of Ulster, where flax made men rich and whiskey made them generous.

'We'll stay clear of Dublin,' he advised, 'for they'd murder a man there for less than a few strands of catgut.' Ruth had not met with much kindness in her life and trusted few men, but she had little choice.

'To the north then,' she said.

Dargan Butler packed his bags swiftly. The embers smouldered in the grate and outside the night was silent and moonless. This was his opportunity to leave without paying the innkeeper for his three weeks' lodgings. It was not as if he were unable to pay, for he had soundly thrashed a retired naval officer in a card game that evening. Unconsciously he patted his purse, and winced at the noise jingling in the quietness of the night. He remained still for some moments until satisfied that no one had heard him. Yes! The evening had been richly rewarding, and if he did leave the old salt penniless it was no more than he deserved for telling one boring yarn after another. Ridiculous stories of mermaids and men who ate each other; a tale of a dark sea witch who had lured a sailor to his death and now roamed the land of Ireland. He laughed to himself as he straightened his hat in the looking-glass. Perfect white teeth smiled back at him. The flickering candle emphasised the fine cheekbones and skin smooth as a young boy's. Only a few fine lines around the mouth reminded him of his own mortality.

'I think 'tis time,' he said to himself, 'I got myself a wife.' And, lifting his bags, he blew out the candle and was gone.

Mistress of Kilbroney

WITH A FINAL flourish of the quill, Grace O'Lochlainn stepped back to admire her handiwork. Long elegant letters spelt out the details of a tenancy agreement, which would act as a model for other such documents. Tom Dunn listened carefully as she read, his pipe between his teeth. Now and then she paused, waiting for his agreement.

'Fine work, Grace. You have a better way with words than many a wise professor. But you know that the courts will not recognise such contracts.'

'I'm sure Madam Valentine will. She's a woman of honour, whatever about the rest of her breed.'

'Fanny Valentine will not be here forever. If a new landlord comes to Kilbroney, what then for your tenancy agreements?'

'She has a few more years left in her,' Grace replied as she rolled up the parchment, 'and by that time we may have changed the law. At the very least, more people will be able to read and write their signature. Just like I learned my letters,' she added smartly, 'at your school.' She stood up to leave, wrapping up warmly against the bitter December wind which battered the shutters of the house on Dunn's Hill.

Dunn smiled as he contemplated the confrontation she would have with Fanny Valentine's land agent, Crampsey. Grace had a sharp tongue.

'Don't be too hard on the man,' he called after her.

'Grace takes matters too seriously,' said Annie Dunn as she wiped floury hands on her apron. 'Crampsey won't like being ordered around by a woman. He'll make difficulties for her.'

'Crampsey always takes the easy way out. Believe me, Annie, I know him.' Dunn stretched his legs and took a long draw on his pipe as his wife tidied the quills into a neat bundle. In a short time some of his senior students would arrive at the barn where he now conducted his lessons.

More than a score of years had passed since the first batch of pupils had met among the ruins of the old monastery where the memory of ancient scholars and the shelter of crumbling walls encouraged diligent study. Grace had been the only girl, a skinny, flaxen-haired nine year old accompanying her brother, Sean. They were the children of Thady O'Lochlainn, a poor cottier facing eviction from the Close where his family had lived for generations. Dunn, a respected lawyer, had helped the O'Lochlainns through that difficulty, and had gained their life-long loyalty and friendship.

The hedge-school had been small then, an occasional diversion from his legal work, but such had been the needs of the Poorlands children that Dunn had found himself gradually devoting more and more time to teaching. Annie had taught the very young children. They squatted around her kitchen fire in the bleak winter months, and in the late summer evenings when the work was done they gathered on the sward behind the house to hear stories of Hector and Achilles, Cuchulainn and Owen Roe. They were thin and ragged but hungry to learn, and the ablest boys progressed to Master Dunn's class where they learned Latin, Greek, history, mathematics and English, the language of commerce. The older students repaid him by teaching their younger fellows and several now held their own classes in the more remote parts of the Poorlands and even further afield.

'Don't be keeping those lads for long now,' Annie Dunn scolded her husband, 'for the barn's too cold at this time of year.'

'Maybe I could bring them in here if there are not too many,' said Dunn. 'Don't worry, I'll make sure they wipe the clabber from their feet.'

The day's class squeezed into the kitchen, some of them sitting in the loft. They were all boys from the Poorlands, the mountain wilderness and forested slopes of the southern Mournes. They spoke in Irish and for the most part had little contact with the cosy village of Rostrevor which nestled in a sheltered valley on the shores of the lough. There the English-speaking weavers, scutchers and bleachers who inhabited the tidy limewashed cottages sent their children to a church school, administered by the vicar and supported by the Valentines. These children were instructed in the Reformed faith and a curriculum approved of by Madam Valentine herself. Tom Dunn's 'bog school', as the Agent Crampsey called it, was an object of ridicule among many of the gentle people of Rostrevor, but to the people of the Poorlands it restored long-forgotten feelings of hope and dignity.

Grace O'Lochlainn made her way homeward. The Agent had blustered and protested at her tenancy scheme, but she was not deterred. She knew enough of the language of the law to deal with tougher opponents than Crampsey. She laughed aloud as she recalled the way his face had twitched as she read to him. It was beyond Crampsey's comprehension that a woman should want to read, least of all a peasant. In her drab grey gown Grace would certainly never pass for a lady of quality, nor did she want to. Yet even she was aware that people listened when she talked, and that men's eyes turned to her when she entered a room. Her strength and confidence won people's admiration, and had inspired love in a man who paid for his devotion with his life.

Grace helped out at the school regularly now, but her life had followed a very different course from any of her contemporaries. Well educated, she had travelled widely and mixed with men of power and influence. Since she had returned to the Poorlands she had assisted Tom Dunn with his legal work on behalf of the poor. Her ability to master languages both ancient and modern would have gained her a place in any educational establishment, but she chose to stay and work among her own people. Yet many still treated her with distrust and suspicion. After all, she had been the landlord's mistress, or, as some still whispered, 'the planter's whore'.

She climbed the hill towards home. Passing the dilapidated Mass House she met Mick the Fox and exchanged a brief greeting. Mick enquired about her father's health.

'No word of your Sean, then?' he added slyly. 'I suppose he'll be saying Mass here one of these days.' Grace was well used to such barbed remarks. Mick knew very well, as did most of Kilbroney, that Sean would never say Mass. Her father, Thady, had been so proud when Sean had left for the seminary in Paris, and then so bitterly disappointed when news came that he had abandoned his vocation. That had been many years ago, and still the pious Kilbroney folk gossiped about what had become of him.

'He must be dead,' Thady had decided, 'or he'd try to let us know if he's alive.' He rarely spoke about his lost son now.

'Maybe he can't,' Grace would answer, knowing the difficulty of communicating over land and sea. Soldiers disbanded from the Irish Brigade or priests returning to minister in Ireland often carried letters and messages from exiles to families, but it seemed that this option was not open to Sean. Grace worried about her beloved brother, for she knew that he would return home if he could, if only to reassure his parents of his well-being.

As she made her way up the valley, past the shelter of the woodland, the landscape become bleaker and more lonely. To her left, on a rocky elevation just above the Owenabwee river, stood the ruined medieval monastery beneath which her three younger brothers lay buried. She blessed herself. An inner sense told her that Sean was alive, but in great danger.

''Tis this place,' she told herself brusquely, 'so full of ghosts, and not only of the dead.' She lengthened her stride for a gloomy December dusk was settling over the mountains.

The Cobbler's children were playing around their tiny cabin and waved to her as she passed. Their father's bearded face appeared in the doorway.

'Will you step in for a draught of buttermilk?' he called.

Grace declined the offer, wishing to be home before dark. The Cobbler, she thought to herself as she went, is one of the many who should benefit from a tenancy agreement.

The Valentine family had been the landlords of the greater part of Kilbroney parish since their illustrious ancestor

Colonel Whitechurch, the priesthunter, had taken possession from the clan MacAongus. Along with the mountains and bogs, forest and meadow, they had inherited a hostile and suspicious tenantry. While the worst of the Valentines had squeezed the last breath of life from their estate in order to finance excessive lifestyles in Dublin and London, the best of them had been indifferent, trusting their agents to administer the land. The present encumbent of Kilbroney House was Fanny, the daughter of the late George Valentine. Following a short, uneventful marriage to Frederick Ward of Armagh, she had returned as a young widow to live with her brother Henry Valentine, and on his death had inherited the estate.

Fanny's county friends were concerned about her. Since the death of her brother she had become a social recluse, preferring the company of common merchants and tradesmen. It was a matter of some particular distress to her friend Madam Hall of Narrow Water, an estate in the neighbouring parish of Clonallon. Involvement in commerce scarcely became a gentleman, much less a lady, she considered.

Fanny's decision to revert to the use of her maiden name had caused great offence to members of her late husband's family, and her tastes, it was whispered, were nothing if not vulgar. Yet many eccentricities could be excused in a woman with a fortune as large as Fanny Valentine's. Her confined circle of county friends were in agreement that the mistress of Kilbroney was a warm, generous and likeable person, well connected on her late mother's side, who deserved better than to spend the rest of her days in that little outpost of the realm where the king's law could be firmly enforced only as far as the edge of the forest.

On St Stephen's Day Madam Hall, having seen the rest of the house party off on a hunting expedition, tackled the difficult subject of Fanny's social life. As the servants discreetly withdrew, she served afternoon tea by the cosy log fire. An expensive luxury if bought in Dublin, her own personal brew was procured at a reduced price from an East India merchant who had set up business in Newry, a prosperous port at the head of the lough, only five miles from Narrow Water. A talented town artisan had crafted an elegant caddy in the fashionable mode, and Madam Hall regarded the daily ritual as the essence of gracious living.

'So, Fanny, what are we going to do with you?' she asked, while busying herself with the tea paraphernalia.

'I beg your pardon?' Her guest lifted a cool eyebrow. Her mind had been on Grace O'Lochlainn's latest crusade for the poor of Kilbroney, not on Madam Hall's genteel ritual. Her friend misunderstood her distracted manner.

'Now don't start huffing with me. We are old friends, are we not?'

'And I hope we will remain so.'

'Savage and I...' began Madam Hall.

'So, I am outnumbered already?'

'Nonsense. We think only of your well-being. We both agree that you should get out and about much more. Look at yourself! Your figure is still trim and elegant; your hair is not yet completely grey; and I am certain a little French rouge and some lip salve will do wonders for your complexion. You are taking these duties of yours much too seriously.'

'And I thought the Squire disapproved of neglectful landlords.'

'Yes! Of course he does, but you are a woman!' Madam Hall realised that she had lost ground on the subject, so she quickly changed tactics. 'Of course, I don't know what goes on in the male mind, and my dear husband is always so busy that I long for some female companionship.'

'Even mine?' Fanny replied.

'You know what I am trying to say. Stop making it so difficult for me. I would like you to join us next week when we go to the playhouse in Newry,' Madam Hall continued in measured tones. 'A commonplace entertainment among common people!'

'Certainly, I'd be delighted to go.'

'Splendid! I knew you would like the theatre.'

'I don't like the "theatre", if that is what you call it, but I do like common people – as long as they keep their distance.'

The party from Narrow Water set out in a gay mood, having enjoyed an excellent supper of partridges and ox tongue. Savage Hall, known as 'the Squire', had been persuaded to join them, much against his better judgement. He growled something about snow on the mountain and what would they do if caught in a blizzard, or if the coach lost a wheel and they were attacked by cut-throats, but his wife assured him that once in the playhouse he would enjoy himself just as much as the rest, and warned him not to be a spoilsport after all the inconvenience to which she had put herself. At least, she consoled herself, the younger members of the party were in high spirits.

The carriages took the old road high above the lough, the horses' hooves carefully muffed as a protection against icy surfaces. The moon rose over the mountains of Cooley, and if the ladies within were ecstatic about the sight, the frozen coachman could only curse the necessity to be out at all on such a winter's night, let alone for something as inconsequential as a play in Newry. His ire might have increased had he heard their conversation, and Madam's vow to return the following night in order to record the rapturous scene in her sketchbook.

On arrival at Newry the entourage came to a halt outside

an imposing edifice in Hill Street, with the grandiose name of the Theatre Royal. Fanny's last such visit had been to the smaller playhouse beside the Pope's Head tavern, and she hoped this one would be as much fun. Hill Street was buzzing with life as labourers from the sugar refinery across the river rubbed shoulders with the honest burghers of the town and their families. One or two merchants from the White Linen Hall paid their respects to Madam Valentine, expressing their delight at seeing her in their midst once more. As the crowd milled around the playhouse entrance, a few limbless army veterans with begging bowls were shooed away, on the instructions of the theatre management. A street fiddler played a merry hornpipe for the benefit of the townspeople who, having ventured out of their homes to be entertained, were generous with their money. The fiddler knew he would receive little coin from the gentry.

Latch, the theatre manager, welcomed the Squire and his party effusively, assuring Madam Hall that he had reserved her favourite chair in the gallery. The same chair had, just five minutes earlier, been occupied by a town matron of ample proportions and had been vacated at considerable personal expense to Latch, who nursed a red ear while the Narrow Water party took their seats. A pair of gangly youths were dispatched with candle extinguishers and the orchestra struck up a loyal tune. A hush descended over the audience as the curtain creaked slowly open to reveal a limelit Arcadian scene. Madam Hall circulated bonbons among her party.

A local thespian had just begun to speak when Fanny's attention was drawn to the arrival of a stranger. He was garbed in the height of Dublin fashion, his tight silk breeches and crimson velvet waistcoat surmounted by a snowy jabot adorned by a single diamond pin. His beautifully tailored coat displayed an elegant figure, and he had an ease of manner to which one could only be born. His languorous expression and stifled yawn implied that he was used to mixing in better circles. He was one of the most handsome men Fanny had ever seen.

Madam Hall, who had followed her friend's gaze, turned to her husband, nudging him to look.

'If he's as grand as you say,' muttered the Squire, 'what in the hell is he doing in Newry?'

Fanny beckoned to Latch, who was hovering around the footlights, to make discreet enquiries as to the identity of the stranger, who was now attracting more attention than the actors on stage. As the manager whispered in his ear the stranger turned his eyes from the stage to look at her, and Fanny smiled. The manager came sidling back to them.

'Well, Latch. Who is he and what is he doing here?' asked Madam Hall.

'He is here,' replied Latch grandly, 'because he is interested in the theatre.'

'Poppycock,' the Squire butted in. 'You don't call this a theatre? More like a henhouse! Tell me his name at once, Sir!'

A hush descended on the auditorium as the audience switched its interest to this new drama. The handsome stranger now took the leading role. Making his way to Madam Hall's seat, he bowed in a most courteous manner before introducing himself.

'I think you know my cousin, Dr Ulick Butler,' he began. Latch, however, was not going to be deprived of his big moment.

'Ladies,' he declared, 'allow me to present the Honourable Dargan Butler.'

Madam Hall, on finding that the Honourable Dargan Butler was in temporary lodgings in Hill Street, wasted no time in inviting him to reside at Narrow Water for the duration of his stay.

'It is really too bad of Polly Butler. She might have written to say you were coming!' chided Madam Hall.

'Dear Polly was unaware of my intention to visit Newry. Indeed, they both speak very highly of Narrow Water.' Dargan smiled disarmingly at Squire Hall, who had not tried to disguise his suspicion of the stranger. 'I think Cousin Ulick would dearly love to visit the north again.'

Savage Hall choked in disbelief. 'What happened then, has he actually become sober? The last time I saw him he was speeding towards the Gap o' the North as if the hounds of hell were on his scent,' he declared.

'Oh, nonsense, that was a long time ago!' Madam Hall was much impressed by the charming young man. It was not often that an honourable gentleman of such breeding, one who was still unmarried, had occasion to visit Newry, and Madam Hall felt pleased to have gained a march on the other local hostesses.

Fanny Valentine made an appearance at every afternoon party and soirée of the season. She danced into the early hours and was clearly entranced by Dargan Butler. Madam Hall, delighted with having coaxed her reticent friend from her shell, persuaded her to have her gowns remodelled, and had delivered to Kilbroney House some illustrations of the most fashionable London attire. Kilbroney House itself was thoroughly spring-cleaned and dust covers were removed from long neglected rooms. Even the servants were treated to new liveries as Fanny threw herself into a frenzy of social activity. As spring gave way to summer, she delighted in entertaining her friends with lavish picnics in pretty woodland glades and in taking evening strolls with Dargan along the shore of the lough. The county folk of south

Down, fondly recalling the hedonistic George Valentine, declared their pleasure in having Fanny grace their ranks once more.

The Lord Lieutenant's Assembly

'I DON'T CARE what you say. I have never seen Fanny so happy before in my life. Besides, you yourself have always said that she involves herself too much in men's affairs!' Madam Hall allowed a footman to escort her up the steps of Dublin Castle, while giving little moues and waves to familiar faces.

The Squire decided to let the subject drop for the moment. His wife was an incurable romantic who failed to see that her middle-aged, countrified friend was making an utter fool of herself, mooning around a young buck fifteen years her junior. The fact that he was well connected with one of the oldest Anglo-Norman families in the country made the Squire all the more certain that he was only playing games with the poor woman's affections, and that he would abandon her for younger, prettier quarry at the drop of a hat.

The well-born and the wealthy gathered at the Castle's assemblies twice weekly, and Madam Hall was keen that her reticent spouse should be seen there. Resplendent in a new green satin gown cleverly fashioned by her Clontafleece seamstress at a fraction of the cost of a Grafton Street model, she pushed her way through the throng, holding on tightly to her reticule. The rest of the week would be taken up with operas, concerts, balls and suppers, but it was essential to be seen occasionally in the company of the Lord Lieutenant, a distant cousin.

'Upon my soul, look who it is. Why, Dr Butler!' called Madam Hall gaily.

At his wife's insistence, the master of Narrow Water took a deep breath and approached the supper table where Dr Butler was gorging himself with a veal jelly and an assortment of delicacies. His stomach had doubled in size since he had last visited County Down, and he had acquired an extra chin.

'By Jove, if it isn't Hall. And how are things up in the wild north, eh? Still awash with brigands and bandits, eh?'

The Squire answered with magnificent restraint. 'No, the country is quite peaceful now, and will remain so until some blackguard stirs things up again.'

'All the same, you'll not see me up that way again. Oh no. Beyond the Styx, what?'

'That is indeed a pity! Yet a certain member of your family has been making himself quite at home with us this past year. He is, I gather, something of a ladies' man?'

Dr Butler moved to a sideboard, where he proceeded to relieve himself into a porcelain chamberpot kept there for such purposes. 'A kinsman of mine, you say?' he enquired amiably.

'The Honourable Dargan Butler,' replied the Squire.

'Honourable my arse!' guffawed the doctor, spraying his companion with sparkling, yet pungent, dewdrops. 'I will advise you, Hall,' he confided loudly, 'to lock up your wife

28

and daughters, for that bastard excels at getting under the densest of skirts. And mark my words, Hall, you'll be the last to know. He may have made a cuckold of you already!'

'When you mention the word, bastard, were you...?' the redfaced Squire probed.

'Telling the truth. His mother was the greatest whore in Ireland, even though she was my own sister-in-law. God knows who his father is. Some pox-ridden hireling, I suspect. Oh, he calls himself a Butler, but you can see that the breeding is just not there!'

'And how is my dear godchild?' Madam Hall enquired of Dr Butler's wife.

'Letitia? Expecting her second child. She is so fortunate in finding such an understanding husband in Sir Vesey, even though he is forty years her senior, but as it happened,' Madam Butler leaned forward, her outsize fan giving the ladies a degree of privacy, 'after her fiancé's untimely death, dear Letitia was inconsolable. Oh, plenty of young men came calling; she is a very wealthy woman in her own right you know.'

'Indeed?' urged her eager listener.

'Well, my dear Bessie,' sniffed Madam Butler, 'who should come along but a scoundrel of the first order, without a copper to his name. Dr Butler ordered him to stay away, but the fellow threatened to rob her of her virtue if we did not pay him five hundred pounds – on the spot! You see, Letitia was already madly in love with him, and threatening to elope at the first opportunity.'

'Surely you didn't pay the blackguard?'

Madam Butler looked affronted. 'Of course not, Bess. Ulick just said: "She could have lost her virtue already, for all I know, but five hundred pounds is five hundred pounds!" So the next thing was, poor Letitia was expecting his child, and we had to marry her off to old Sir Vesey, who could not tell you what colour his own beard is. The strange thing is, he and Letitia are very happy!' Madam Butler concluded in floods of tears.

After procuring the smelling salts from her reticule, Madam Hall made comforting noises. 'My dear Polly, if I were ever to set eyes on this chap, I swear I would have Savage run him through.'

'Oh you won't, for he has gone off to foreign parts, where no doubt he is deceiving some other innocent. And the worst of it all was,' Madam Butler sniffed, 'it was her own cousin: Dargan Butler.'

'You are entirely to blame for this, Bess, no one but you.'

The carriage trundled through the night towards the north.

'And how was I to know? You yourself thought him a fine fellow.'

'I thought him a popinjay!'

'Hindsight is a fine thing, Savage.'

'For goodness sake, my dear, let us get things into perspective. Fanny Valentine is nothing if not a sensible, down-to-earth woman. What's a broken heart to her? And anyway, she is too old for a lump in the belly.'

'What a vulgar expression.'

'Pardon me, being in Ulick Butler's company has that effect on one. All I am saying is, there is a limit to the damage this Dargan chap can do. 'Twould be quite different with an impressionable young virgin, which Fanny is not.' Then, remembering Dr Butler's warning, he cleared his throat and continued. 'Er, you didn't think the scoundrel in any way attractive, did you, my dear?'

'Me? Of course not!'

The Squire wondered uneasily at the hesitation in her voice, and remained silent for the rest of the journey.

After a short night in an uncomfortable Drogheda inn, the Halls resumed their journey. The Squire was in even worse form than before.

'Why you have to drag us back on this wild goose errand, I just do not understand. You usually hate the country at this time of year.'

'Think of the number of nice county people with young daughters to whom you introduced this man. Surely we must bear some responsibility for giving him credence.'

'We were taken in as well; at least you were.'

Madam Hall sighed and wished their carriage would move a little faster.

It was late afternoon before they reached Narrow Water, fatigued and thirsty, yet the coachman was given instructions to continue to Rostrevor. If dear Fanny must hear bad news, they might as well get it over and done with.

'Leave it to me,' Madam Hall instructed her husband. 'I do not want you to go barging in like a raging bull.'

Darkness was falling as they made the last of the journey up the tree-lined avenue of Kilbroney House. The mistress of the house came out to meet her callers.

'This is an unexpected pleasure,' Fanny called. 'We were not expecting you back until the end of the season!'

'Fanny, dear,' Madam Hall bustled out of the carriage, 'I must speak with you urgently.'

'And I have something to tell you, too,' replied Fanny coyly, 'only I'm not plain Fanny Valentine any more. I'm the Honourable Madam Dargan Butler!'

Dargan Butler was well satisfied with his triumph. To be sure, a younger, richer, better bred woman would have been better, but there were precious few of those around. It was fortunate that his reputation – in his view undeserved, and put about by vengeful relatives – was not generally known north of Drogheda. Now he had a pliable, loving wife who adored him, and who had the means to support him in the manner to which he aspired. Fanny was cloying, past the age of child-bearing, and incredibly gauche in her ways. Yet he was confident that he could persuade her to ease her grip on the purse strings, and could take complete control of her fortune eventually. As he walked up Hill Street a month after his wedding, he stopped to look down over the town of Newry. It was unsightly and smelly, but very wealthy: here he would make his fortune. He whistled as he turned into one of the back-streets, and picked his steps over rotting fish. A scented handkerchief pressed to his nostrils masked only some of the stench, but he was in buoyant mood and even stinking entrails would not dampen his spirit. He had virtually all he ever wanted: money, position, and a deliciously dark mistress who should at this minute be awaiting his arrival.

Johnny's Return

A s THE FIRST flakes of snow floated over the Poorlands, Johnny Fearon added an inch to his stride, his thinly clad body shivering as the threatening sky merged with the bogland before him. He stopped for a moment to find his bearings, for the familiar mountain skyline had faded into the gloom. Johnny's threadbare coat offered little protection against the biting wind and his shabby boots were soaked through. He pulled his hat down as far as it would go and ineffectively tried to raise his collar to meet it.

The Quaker woman who had provided him with a decent shirt and breeches had also insisted on shaving and delousing his head with pitch and lard. 'Thou wilt feel the better for it afterwards!' she had assured him stoutly. Johnny had been grateful for the clothing, but he wished now that he had his hair, lice and all, to ward off the cold. Mile followed mile of desolation, with not a tree or ditch to give shelter, and Johnny, given the choice, would have wished himself back in his cell were it not for the thought of a warming draught and a welcoming hearth at the end of his journey.

It was many years since he had left Kilbroney, and he hoped the Widow would recognise him. Few folk in Kilbroney did not know the Widow Fearon, a lively old vixen with whin-dyed hair and an ample bosom, for she did everything from delivering babies to laying out corpses. She had been the wife of his late uncle, Hugh Fearon, and Johnny looked forward to his reunion with her. She was the closest to a mother he could remember, although he had not seen her since he was eight years old and the Poor Law men had come to take him away. That was the day they had hanged his father.

Casting aside this bitter memory he concentrated his mind on the future, and forced himself onwards, his feet and hands numbed with frost. The half light was turning to dusk and a bitter north wind whirled between the two mountain peaks above Levallyclanowen. He started in recognition as the dark rocks of Slieve na Broc loomed to his left. He would soon be resting in the Widow's cabin.

The snowfall was heavier now and a thick sheet already shrouded the ground before him. A few sparse trees, which acted as a windbreak for the meagre cabin built into the side of the hill, were the first sign of human habitation he had encountered for miles. Like many wanderers before him, Johnny found the last few yards to the door the hardest. He called out plaintively:

'Aunt! 'Tis myself, wee Johnny. I'm home, so I am!' He stopped to listen, and summoned up some additional volume. 'Are you there now? I'm not a stranger come to rob you. 'Tis me, I'm let out of gaol!'

No answer came, only darkness and the howl of the wind through the thatch. Some ragged garments draped over a thorn bush reassured him that the old woman must be still alive: there were plenty around Rostrevor who would soon find a use for abandoned clothes, be they even a corpse's shroud. The hurdle in the doorway swung on one rope hinge as he gingerly stepped into the cabin. It took some moments for his eyes to adjust to the gloom, and although there was no one there he was reassured by the scent of wild herbs and shrubs, a stock of which the Widow always kept through the winter months. Throwing his pack on a bundle of rags in the corner, he surmised that his aunt must have bedded down in a neighbour's house, rather than walk home through the snow. Whatever else about the Fearons, the saying went, they could fend for themselves.

Before settling down for the night he opened his tinder box and set about kindling a fire to warm the cabin and dry his clothes. Some of the Widow's collection of dried plants were first sacrificed to the flames, followed by a few sods of turf and twigs he found at the back of the cabin. A fire was soon smouldering, filling the damp cabin with a smoky glow. Johnny peeled off his wet boots, sniffed around the various jars and pitchers in the corner, sampled a liquor, and fell fast asleep by the hearthside. It was not the homecoming he had expected, but the reunions could wait until tomorrow.

As Johnny Fearon was settling himself down for the night, other creatures wandered abroad. On the leeward side of Leckan, a small boy picked his way over the mountain pad, not yet obscured by the snow. 'O'Lochlainn,' he repeated to himself, 'O'Lochlainn.' So she had told him. Now she was asleep, and he would do as he was bid but, here, out on a strange hillside in a strange, cold land, he was alone and helpless. The dark shape of a cabin loomed to his right and he regarded it timidly. Folk had not always been kind to his mother or himself, and he was reluctant to approach. A dog barked and the boy retreated in alarm. A small girl appeared from the cabin.

'O'Lochlainn?' the boy carefully repeated his mother's words. The girl looked at him curiously, then pointed in the direction of a few dark shapes, the barely recognisable outlines of cabins.

'O'Lochlainn's Close,' she said.

'Murren,' yelled a cross voice. 'Come in here or I'll skelp your backside!'

The boy did not linger.

'You'll not go back to Arno's Vale tonight,' Tom Dunn advised, as falling snow obliterated his view of Rostrevor village in the valley beneath Dunn's Hill.

'Mistress Dunn can do without the vexation of a stranger in the house,' Marcas MacSorley replied, emerging from the sickroom where Betsy Dunn was recovering from influenza. The epidemic in the parish had claimed more than a few victims, and not only the very young and the aged. Red-haired Betsy, the fifteen-year-old pride of the Dunn household, was putting up a brave fight, and the physician had every confidence that she would soon be back on her feet, breaking the hearts of all the young men in the valley.

'You need worry no more about Miss Betsy,' he continued, 'but constant nursing is taking its toll on her mother. She needs to rest.'

'My woman? She may look like a sparrow but she has the strength of a hawk,' laughed Dunn. 'And she thinks more of you than the rest of us put together; she'll not let you out the door this night.'

'For shame, Tom Dunn,' scolded a tiny woman, who was already delving for clean bed-linen in the dower chest. 'You know that physicians would venture out whatever the

36

weather, although,' she turned to the visitor, 'you're more than welcome to bide here, for our Harry's bed's empty, and I'll warm it through with hot bricks.'

'I told you not to mind Annie.' Dunn ushered his friend to a chair and produced a pair of tankards. 'She'll sleep well tonight knowing that we have a physician under our very own roof.'

Dr MacSorley, in truth, needed little persuasion. The aroma of rabbit stew wafted from a pot simmering on the hearth and the kitchen had a warm, cosy glow. A tall, lean man, some years past his youth, he had spent too many years travelling not to appreciate the comfort of a well-kept house. The snow without, and the warmth within, made him falter.

'If you're certain that I would not be of any bother,' he began. Tom Dunn was already filling the tankards.

'Shake off your boots, man! No right-minded soul would step out on such a night. This is the time for storytelling.'

The following dawn found Kilbroney silent as a pale sun rose on the snow-covered valley. A mile or so from the Widow's cabin, Grace O'Lochlainn donned her sturdy greatcloak and boots to venture forth. Her little stone cottage was dry and comfortable, and she had stacked up a retaining fire for the day. She was concerned about her elderly parents whose cabin further up the mountain was, she could see, almost submerged in snow. Thady, in spite of his daughter's wishes, had stubbornly refused to budge from what had been his grandfather's home, declaring to the world that he would die in the bed in which he was born. He turned a deaf ear also to Eily's protests that the bed in question had been burned years ago, along with half the house, when his doting old mother had dropped her candle on it. Such truths were easily dismissed by Thady, stubbornly moulded to the ancestral hearth. Grace had accepted that her father's determination to stay put would have to be broken down by subtler means. Loyalty to the memory of one's forbears was all very well, but not at the price of comfort.

Eily watched her daughter approach from the distance. Grace was their lifeline with the outside world, for Thady had not been fit to leave the cabin since October last and, much as she loved the comfort of her daughter's fine house, she had little choice but to stay by her ailing husband. She had once given voice to a secret dread that Thady might emulate his mother and roast them as they slept.

'I wondered if you would come,' Eily scolded. She said this every morning, for no particular reason, and an onlooker would be forgiven for thinking that hers was a neglectful daughter.

'How is his lordship today?' Grace enquired, as she always did.

'Up all night with the cough. He has himself worn out trying to spit up the phlegm,' Eily replied. 'Not that I got much sleep myself!'

'If you like, I'll sit by him and you can sleep.'

'And how could I sleep with a cough that would rouse half the graveyard?'

Grace winced as a rasping hack came from within, as if to punctuate Eily's remark.

'What about the Widow's elixir?' she asked. 'Has it helped him at all?'

''Tis gone, every last drop of it.' She looked at her daughter. 'To be truthful, I let it spill, and the curse of it is he never needed it more.'

Before setting out again Grace reassured herself that the old couple had enough to sustain them for the day. The normally draughty cabin was warm and cosy, as the drifting snow had formed a thick protective blanket around three walls and the roof.

'Why, you're as snug as a wee mouse in a haystack,' she told her father as she fixed the fleece around his toes.

'As long as the beams hold and the thatch doesn't give under the weight,' replied the pessimist. 'We may every last one of us be buried alive by the time you make your way back.' Grace smiled at her father's ability to make two people sound as though they were a multitude.

'I'm off to the Widow Fearon's,' she called. 'I'll be back with your bottle before nightfall.'

Owen MacOwen yawned as the first shaft of daylight roused him from slumber. His home was little more than a booley hut built defiantly near the top of Leckan Mountain. His family had been evicted from the townland in the glen below and now all that remained of the MacOwens was the name: *Leath Bhaile Clann Eoghan*, or Levallyclanowen, and the ruins of the Healing House where generations of the ancient sept had lived and died. Not a day went past when Owen did not look down from his mountain eyrie and swear to recover his hereditary lands and, more importantly, the respect that went with it. He was the hereditary keeper of Saint Bronach's staff, only a few broken shards of which remained.

The land, glistening white and still, lay spread out below him. The motionless waters of the lough mirrored the dazzling snow-capped peaks of distant Cooley, and the tiny dwellings in the valley were hidden from sight. The only movement was the black-cloaked figure of a woman labouring across the snow.

'Grace O'Lochlainn,' he guessed. 'The old man must be bad again.' Out of concern for the safety of the schoolmistress Owen yelled a warning. 'Mistress O'Lochlainn,' he shouted. 'Have a care for yourself and keep to the beaten pad!' From above he could trace the path of the hidden track. If Grace were to stray she could end up buried in a drift.

The woman looked up towards the figure of Owen, and gestured that she was quite safe. She pointed towards Levallyclanowen, confirming that she was bound for the Widow Fearon's cabin. Did she not know that the Widow had gone to Clontafleece the previous day and would not return until Friday? It was then he noticed a thin spiral of smoke curling from the roof of her cabin: the old woman had returned earlier than expected. The door, now hidden from sight, was almost completely sealed by the drifting snow. Lifting his shovel, Owen started down from Leckan like any dutiful son, hoping that in return for digging her out the Widow would supply him with a good bowl of oaten gruel. Since his mother died, she had fed him when he was hungry and kept him out of the workhouse, and there was a strong bond between them. He waited for Mistress O'Lochlainn at the foot of the hill, enquiring courteously after her father.

'I'd say this winter will be the finish of him,' he added in the same concerned tone. Owen was not known for his tact.

When they reached the cabin, Grace stood aside while Owen began to dig.

Johnny Fearon stirred in his sleep. He was warm and dry but very hungry. As he wondered if the Widow had any food stored away, he became aware of mumbling voices from outside the cabin. Momentary panic overcame him and he had scrambled to his feet before he realised he had little to fear from either warders or troopers, for he was a free man again.

A man's voice called: 'Are you asleep, Widow Fearon, or have you some old boy under the sheet with you?'

'I've nobody under the sheet save myself, and I'm not Widow Fearon, I'm Johnny Fearon.'

The door burst open with a sudden rush of cold air and a spray of snow. The two men stared suspiciously at one another.

'She did not tell me you were coming. I've never heard tell of a Johnny Fearon,' growled Owen.

'When it comes to that, why, I've never heard of you either,' answered Johnny, wide awake now and raising his fists.

'Johnny Fearon!' Grace spoke sharply, "Tis that kind of foolish behaviour that put you in gaol in the first place. You are surely not eager to return so soon?'

'Mistress Grace O'Lochlainn; and me thinking I'd be forgotten after all these years,' Johnny said with delight.

'You are welcome home, Johnny, and if you pick a fight with every man you meet, folk will soon remember you.'

'She never told me she had a son,' Owen put in. 'I came to see if she needed help. Had I known,' he continued, throwing his shovel at a startled Johnny, 'I would have let you dig your own snow.'

'She has no son that I know of, and I'm glad to know that my aunt is so well taken care of,' replied Johnny graciously, proferring his hand.

'She would have told me she was expecting you...' Owen was still doubtful.

Grace laughed. 'I wonder how long it is since she's had two grown men fighting over her? I am sorry we disturbed your slumber, Johnny, but Owen meant well. I came in search of some cough elixir.'

'She keeps it among her potions there in the corner,' said Owen and he indicated the motley collection of brews.

'I helped myself to this last night to keep out the cold,' Johnny confessed, holding up an empty flagon.

'No harm done,' Owen remarked smugly. 'It will cure any warts you might have. This bottle is what Thady gets; can you smell the garlic?' Grace recognised the pungent odour only too well. Reaching for the bottle, she lost her footing in the gloom.

'*In ainm an Diabhail!* Are you all right, Mistress?' asked Johnny. 'Did you fall on my pack?'

"Twas not your pack that made me trip.' Grace knelt down, carefully lifting a few rags, then straightened up with a gasp.

'May the Lord have mercy on the poor soul. She must have died of the cold.'

'Widow Fearon!' cried a horrified Owen, rushing to her side. Johnny stood rigid as the others turned over the body.

'Merciful God, I never knew,' Johnny whispered. 'She lay there all night long and I never knew.'

Owen's reply caused another jolt. 'Well, whoever she is, she's not the Widow Fearon.'

Struggling to overcome the shock, Johnny gazed on a face such as he had never seen before. It was a beautiful face, tranquil in death as an angel. It was the face of a young woman of dark complexion.

The Dark Woman

FTER ENJOYING A good breakfast of bacon and oatcake, Marcas MacSorley pulled on the boots which Mistress Dunn had been warming by the fire. His mare had been fed and watered and stood waiting for him in the yard.

'You should be less busy from now on,' Tom Dunn remarked as he helped him mount. 'The old people will tell you that it takes a good fall of snow to clean the air, and they are not often wrong about the weather.' He watched with a smile as some of the neighbouring children flew down the hill on a hurdle, one young boy taking an unexpected tumble.

'Pick yourself up there, lad,' called Dunn. 'No tears, mind.'

'One epidemic follows another,' MacSorley sighed. 'I foresee a trail of broken limbs and bruised joints all the way from Kilbroney to Hill Town!'

His attention was drawn to the figure of a woman, approaching from the direction of the mountains. He saw that she wore the garb of a peasant except for a dark flowing cloak, the hood of which had fallen back to reveal silvered hair. She was not a young maid, but neither did she bear the signs of toil and matronhood which were the inheritance of the peasant women. Her finely chiselled features were cool and aloof, and it was only the slight flush on her cheeks and the urgency of her gait which suggested that she was in need of aid.

'Mistress Grace O'Lochlainn,' Dunn answered Mac-Sorley's question. 'One of the loveliest women ever born. And one who has paid the price of having beauty without high birth.' He strode towards her, smiling a welcome.

'Master Dunn,' she forestalled his greeting, 'your help is needed.' Without further explanation she turned on her heel, retracing her steps along the ditch which marked the track towards Levallyclanowen. To the physician's surprise, Tom Dunn followed her without question. Curiosity, and a vague wish to know more about the woman, caused MacSorley to accompany his friend.

'Perhaps I can be of service,' he called as Grace turned once more in vexation.

'A renowned physician,' explained Dunn. 'Dr Marcas MacSorley.'

'I fear your services will not be necessary,' spoke Grace. 'No physician, however respected, can bring back the dead.' She reassured Master Dunn that she spoke of neither her father nor the Widow Fearon. 'The poor woman is unknown to me, but it seems she was done to death in a most cruel way.' She shivered, and MacSorley expressed his concern in an unintentionally curt tone.

'Mistress O'Lochlainn. You will avoid yourself further distress by remaining at Dunn's Hill. Women should not involve themselves in these matters.'

'I will do as I choose, Dr MacSorley,' she replied frostily.

Dunn, already breathless from their laboured passage through the snow, tried to placate her.

'Dr MacSorley is thinking only of your welfare. That's so, is it not, Marcas?'

The physician attempted an apology, but Grace, as she scrambled over a march ditch, appeared not to heed him.

A small crowd of onlookers had gathered outside the Widow's cabin and stood murmuring to themselves. Not for the first time Dunn marvelled at the way news could spread in the parish of Kilbroney. Stopping to recover his breath, he watched as MacSorley pushed his way past the curious faces, stepping ahead of Grace into the cabin. Dunn made to follow him.

'A black woman, Master Dunn,' said a man. 'The first I ever saw.'

After the brightness of the snow, it took Dunn's eyes some time to adjust to the murky cabin interior. As he blinked, he became aware of the presence of two other men, Owen McOwen and a pale, frightened young fellow of seventeen or so. They watched as the doctor bent over the dead body.

'I cannot at this moment say how she died,' Marcas MacSorley said grimly. A few neighbours had gathered in the door, shaking their heads in disbelief.

'A poor travelling woman from the west?' someone offered. 'They often turn up at the hiring fair.' A round of comment followed this suggestion. It was possible that there were black faces in the province of Connacht, where none had ever ventured. Curious bystanders endeavoured to get a peep at the corpse.

'It would suit you all better if you said a prayer for the poor soul,' Grace remonstrated, to the offence of some black-shawled women who muttered that the 'Lochlainn woman' was in no position to lecture anybody on morality.

'There is as yet no evidence of foul play,' Tom Dunn

explained to the knot of people at the door, 'although there are many unanswered questions concerning this death.' All agreed that the cabin should be locked while somebody with a good command of English reported the death at the village barracks.

As the onlookers filed out of the little cabin, Dr MacSorley made a further brief examination of the body. Under her customary black shawl, the dead woman wore a strangely exotic costume, an ill-fitting gown of crimson and blue which was now stained and dishevelled. There were some ugly bruises and lacerations on her neck and chest.

'The gown looks as though it once belonged to a lady of quality,' he remarked to Dunn.

'Could she be a lady's maid? Perhaps it belonged to her mistress?' Dunn was equally puzzled.

They turned to Johnny Fearon.

'You understand,' Tom Dunn spoke grimly, 'that this death must be reported. Otherwise, if a crime has been committed, everyone here will be implicated.'

'I slept the night there by her side, God rest her soul,' whispered Johnny. 'I was so weary...'

'This is Johnny Fearon. Hugh Fearon's lad,' said Grace protectively. 'Where else would he go but to his aunt's cabin?' Tom Dunn looked at the young man, taking in his sunken cheeks and wan features. He could see the problems which lay ahead for the youth: a newly released convict made a convenient scapegoat. He felt some pity for the lad, and thought a good sup of hot broth was what he most needed now. He called McChesney the Cobbler.

'Take him to Dunn's Hill and my Annie will feed him. Stay with him until I return, and for the life of you don't let him bolt.'

'You think he's a murderer, then?' McChesney asked dubiously.

'No, I surely don't. But if he is tempted to flee from this problem, God only knows what a magistrate would think of it.'

'You think he'll have to face a magistrate?'

'He might have to look a circuit judge in the eye, and we know what merciless fiends they are.'

'So much for my errand. I thought I'd find a good strong elixir for my father,' said Grace. Master Dunn, noticing the woman's careworn face, insisted on escorting her home.

'Is Thady poorly again?' he asked gently. Grace was like a daughter to him, and he often wished for her a better future than life in a lonely mountain cabin. 'Don't fret yourself, Grace. Haven't we the best physician in Ireland at our service? If he can't cure Thady, nobody can.' MacSorley, aware that he had already caused offence to Mistress Grace, nodded in agreement.

Grace knew that her father had more faith in the Widow's potions than in strange physicians, yet she was glad of the company, for the O'Lochlainn Close was quite isolated and the sight of the poor dead woman had distressed her more than she cared to admit.

'To come from a far country and die unmourned in a lonely mountain grave.' She shivered.

'Maybe not unmourned. Who is to know?' MacSorley resisted the temptation to put a comforting hand on the woman's shoulder.

They retraced Grace's tracks leading to the O'Lochlainn Close, with its cabin, small byre and a few rough peat constructions huddled into the mountain, almost invisible under the snow. The young river, the Owenabwee splashed its way over the stones some distance from the Close, and there, on a rocky outcrop, stood Grace's solid little stone cabin. MacSorley looked around him; he had been in many parts of the world, and had seen its divergent splendours, but

47

the white-cloaked Mournes held an enchantment all their own. He doubted if the poor mountain dwellers toiling the frugal earth would be too concerned with this observation. Certainly the woman yelling from the cabin had more immediate concerns on her mind.

Eily O'Lochlainn grimaced in annoyance as another spasm of coughing overtook her husband. 'Wheesht a while,' she urged. Surprisingly, he stopped immediately.

'What is it you hear, woman?' They both listened in silence.

'Do you hear it now?' she whispered.

'How can I hear anything when I don't know what the hell it is I'm supposed to be listening to?' Thady roused himself out of bed.

'What do you think you're doing?' Eily asked in alarm as Thady lifted a heavy staff from the corner.

'Stand aside, woman,' he commanded, 'for devil the chance of me being murdered in my bed. Not without a fight anyway.'

'Will you lie down or you'll die on your feet,' Eily cried as he pulled open the door. A shaft of strong sunlight belied the bitterness of the cold. Her sharp eyes picked out three approaching figures.

'Grace,' she screeched. 'Come quickly, 'tis your father; he's gone mad!'

The wizened old man pushed her aside and stood defiantly with his staff.

'Unhand the maid,' he roared, 'or ye'll answer to this!'

'Put that down and get back to bed,' Grace scolded, running the last few yards of her journey. 'I have brought Master Dunn to see you.'

Dunn supressed a laugh at the sight of the diminutive figure wielding a cudgel. 'We come unarmed,' he said sternly, and made a mock military salute.

'Oh, 'tis yourself, Master Dunn. I don't have to show you the way to the hearthside. Come in, you and your companion, and shake your boots off.'

'Oh, Master Dunn, thank God you came. We thought we were all going to be murdered alive,' cried Eily, bursting into tears. 'There's something lurking round the back!'

'And you are sure the noise came from in here?' asked Dunn, looking towards the little byre.

'Listen for yourself,' Eily said nervously. From within the barn came the sound of soft whimpering.

'Rest assured, Mistress O'Lochlainn, it can be no more than a poor strayed beast taking shelter,' Dunn reassured her as he and MacSorley began to clear the snow which blocked the entrance. As the two men ventured into the byre the noise stopped. They peered into the darkness.

'Who is it?' MacSorley said softly. 'We have no wish to hurt you.'

A small figure sprang from the corner and made a dash for the opening.

'What is your hurry, lad?' Dunn grabbed the fugitive. They looked in surprise at the boy's dark hue, and the deep brown eyes which stared at them from a tearstained face. He was clad in layers of wool and linen, topped by a greatcoat twice his size, and a pair of stout brogues.

'Someone made sure you were dressed for the weather,' said MacSorley as he carried the struggling child into the cabin. 'This is your ghost, Mistress O'Lochlainn.'

'The poor wee mite, out in the cold by itself,' clucked Eily. 'Bring it over to the hearth to warm its toes.' Grace's eyes sought Tom Dunn's and Marcas MacSorley's, their exchanges acknowledging the connection between the dead woman they had just left and the tiny waif with his black curls.

'Who are you, lad? What name have you?' coaxed Eily as she ladled some porridge into a wooden bowl. The child did not respond. 'It can't talk,' the old woman decided. 'The poor soul.'

'He may be in shock and unable to speak,' MacSorley spoke quietly to his friend as they left the Close, 'or maybe he speaks another language.'

'Goodness knows,' Dunn replied, 'I didn't know there were any others. Between Grace and yourself, you must have tried them all. Another possibility is that he will not speak. Perhaps he has little reason to trust strangers.'

'Was it right to leave him there with the O'Lochlainns?' MacSorley asked as they retraced the path down the mountain. 'The poor mite looked petrified.'

'You may be certain that the O'Lochlainns will look after him well,' Dunn assured his companion. 'They are old and valued friends of ours. The bit of excitement will shorten the winter for Thady,' he added. 'I have never known anyone like the master of that house to thrive so much on adversity. I venture to guess that his cough will have disappeared by now.' They walked on in silence before he spoke again.

'All the same, 'tis a strange affair. An unknown foreigner found dead in the Widow's cabin; a small boy lost on the mountain. Perhaps when the old girl returns she will have an answer to the mystery, and maybe clear poor Johnny Fearon's name.'

Marcas MacSorley was thoughtful. 'Was the dark woman running from someone? She must have been desperate to venture out at such a time to a strange place. Tell me, Tom, did you notice those marks on her face, around her lips and eyes?'

'Bruises left by her assaulter.'

'I wonder,' MacSorley murmured to himself.

Annie Dunn was feeding the ducks as Johnny and his escort arrived in the farmyard. Any thought of making a bolt for freedom had evaporated on the sight of the Cobbler's cudgel and Owen's boast that he was the fastest runner in Kilbroney. Johnny's legs still ached from the previous day's journey, but there was a forlorn feeling also that he had nowhere to run to. During his years in prison he had dreamed of returning home to a hearty reunion with his old neighbours. Now, it seemed, no one knew him, save Grace O'Lochlainn. Even Master Dunn, whom he remembered from childhood, looked on him as though he were only some inblown wrack that the tide might sweep in.

He took some comfort from the sight of Dunn's Hill, which was just as he remembered it. Mistress Dunn was puzzled as the Cobbler relayed Tom Dunn's instructions. 'He may thaw himself by the fire, the poor lad,' she said, dismayed by Johnny's emaciated condition.

'But he might be a murderer,' protested Owen.

'Johnny Fearon?' replied Annie. 'Not the wee Johnny I used to know.'

Johnny felt a wave of relief at the sight of a crock hissing gently on the fire; the kitchen, too, was warm and welcoming. He eased his bony feet out of his sodden boots.

'Get back to bed, Betsy, or I'll take a stick to you!' scolded Annie, as the curious freckled face of a young girl clad in a linen shift, her red hair tumbling freely around her shoulders, peeped around the corner. Johnny tried to struggle to his feet as the woman of the house thrust a bowl of stew into his lap.

'Get back to bed, you young vixen, or you'll get another dose,' barked Annie at the retreating figure. 'Sit down there, Johnny, and pay no heed to my bold Betsy,' she said, poking up a blaze. The stew was hot and nourishing, and made all the tastier by the impish grin of a pretty girl.

Johnny's Dilemma

THE WEATHERWISE OF Kilbroney had predicted a bleak baptism for the new decade, and January of 1790 fulfilled their gloomy prognostications. Snow and biting frost stalked the landscape, from Slieve Ban to Ruaslieve, and several old folk had to be dug out of their hovels and moved to temporary accommodation with kinsfolk further down the valley. For many, the worst fear was that they would die unshriven, for the ailing priest was not fit to venture out.

The gravediggers had a busy month and complained about the difficulty of cutting through snow and frozen earth, but there was nothing much to be done about it except to commandeer extra manpower; no one was so old, so alone or so forgotten that they did not have someone to give them a decent burial. Family quarrels were temporarily suspended as folk faced the common enemy together. Most mountain dwellers had taken heed of the warnings of bad weather and had made sure of a supply of turf and potatoes as would see them through to Brigid's Day, when a thaw could be expected.

The Buller, Thady's nearest neighbour and most frequent visitor, was one who enjoyed the long evenings by the hearthside, especially, Eily often remarked, if it was somebody else's hearth. A skilled storyteller, the Buller made use of the inclement conditions to refine his art. Yet for several weeks the main topic of conversation was a story which surpassed all the Buller's inventions: the finding of the body in the Widow Fearon's cabin and the arrest of her nephew, Johnny. There were those who contended that none of the Fearons were up to much, and the young fellow was likely as not to end up dangling from a rope sooner or later, but most were sympathetic, if not for Johnny, then for the poor old Widow who deserved better after a lifetime of helping other folk. Thady O'Lochlainn stoutly opined that Master Dunn would see that no harm came to the lad, and brushed aside Tom Dunn's own well-justified doubts.

Johnny Fearon huddled in the corner of the barrack gaol, nursing his misery. He blamed everything: the troopers, the gaolers, his aunt who wasn't there when he needed her, his own luck; he blamed the unfortunate woman for dying where she did and Grace O'Lochlainn for finding the wretched body. Most of all he blamed himself and his own stupidity. How on earth could he have spent the night in a tiny hovel with a corpse and not known it was there? Had he been an hour or so earlier, he might have saved the poor woman's life and then he would have been a hero! Or he could have taken off and no one would have known he had ever been in Levallyclanowen that night. But where else could he have gone without freezing to death? The workhouse matron was right all along. He was destined for the gallows, just like his father before him.

A rattle of locks and bolts aroused his attention as a shrill voice made itself heard. Johnny assumed it to be another drunkard put in to keep him company for a night or two, but instead he saw a plump little woman with piercing eyes and the most shocking head of whin-dyed hair. Hair like that, which owed nothing to nature and even less to art, he had seen many years ago, but on a thinner, younger woman. His heart gave a leap, for she was still his aunt, the indomitable witch of Levallyclanowen, the Widow Fearon.

Tears of joy and sadness accompanied her greeting along with many questions, none of which he had a chance to answer. She remarked on his size, just like his grandfather, and his soot black hair, a gift from his mother, and his pale face, to be blamed on the wretches who had kept him locked up, suitable candidates for a reliable curse she had on her person. She reassured Johnny that it would not kill them, nor turn them into hedgehogs, but would leave the whole lot of them impotent for a month. They would never talk about it because they would be too ashamed, but Johnny would know. The Widow could certainly cheer a body up, Johnny thought. When the opportunity finally arose, he questioned her.

'Who was she? What was she doing under your roof?'

'You may well ask, but I have no answer to offer you.'

'Surely to God somebody would have noticed her? A black woman? And it snowing?'

The Widow shook her head helplessly. 'Master Dunn keeps asking the same question. Says he: "'Tis only a matter of time before somebody or other comes forward."'

'And by that time I'll have the neck stretched off me, if I'm not already sleeping in my bed of lime.'

'Whisht, Johnny!' said the Widow, showing her distress. Her sharp little eyes welled with tears, for the memory of the lad's father's execution was all too fresh.

'I would say we can do worse than put our faith in Master Dunn. He knows about such matters better than we do.' Johnny spoke with sudden bravado, but there was not much confidence in his heart.

John Mercer, a stout man of medium height, with greying locks around a bald and weatherbeaten crown, sat at his desk overlooking the lough. The snow around Arno's Vale was beginning to thaw, although it would grace the mountain peaks for several months more. The clearing between the house and the shore was already revealing portents of spring where tiny snowdrops peeped through. An East India merchant, Mercer never settled for long in any one place. He had rented his present residence, a handsome stone farmhouse of English proportions, from Madam Butler shortly before her marriage. Her new husband, who had taken over the running of the estate, had recently tried to increase his rent, but Mercer, himself a shrewd businessman, had taken the precaution of having a water-tight tenancy agreement drawn up.

Mercer applied some sealing wax to the letter he had just written and turned with interest towards his friend, Marcas MacSorley, who stood warming his rump by the fire.

'No, Mercer, I have no more news, not this evening at any rate.'

'Nothing more to relate?' replied the host, feigning disappointment. 'My original assessment of this place was correct. It is excessively dull.'

'Your thirst for mystery, my friend, far exceeds my capacity to provide it. Unless, that is, you find Mistress Lightbody's sprained ankle of interest. She acquired it, I'm told, while descending from the loft, yet her house has neither loft nor ladder.'

'Obviously the woman has designs on your person and

will go to any lengths to get your hand on her leg. Tell me, had you a chaperone?'

'Well, yes.'

'There's your answer. You would have been in trouble had the two of you been alone. Improper advances! Say no more.' Mercer, pleased with this piece of deduction, went on. 'Any more bodies of dead black women? And what about the young rascal in prison. Is he truly guilty? Will we have a hanging soon to enliven the winter?'

'I cannot say,' MacSorley replied more gravely. 'I feel somehow responsible for his misfortune.'

'You?' declared his surprised host. 'What had you to do with it? Your only role was to examine the body.'

'I'm afraid that, in the darkness of the cabin, I assumed from her wounds and bruises that she had died from a beating. When I examined her for the second time, in the barracks, I could see that her injuries were not recently inflicted. Indeed, there were so many different hues of bruising, she must have been beaten over a period of several months. Yet she had other, unusual disfigurements. I dare not comment on them.'

'There now! The young convict must be innocent.'

'Oh yes, of that I am quite sure. The poor woman was fleeing from something – or someone. I would say she died of exhaustion.'

'So she was not murdered?'

'That would be a question for the lawyers. For my part, any woman frightened enough to brave the mountain snow to escape her pursuer must surely have feared for her life. Perhaps for her son's also.'

'So why are you downhearted, MacSorley? Clearly you've exonerated the young man.'

'Because at first the sergeant seemed to accept my opinion. Oh, he explained very properly about the formalities which would have to be considered. I thought that that would be the end of the matter, but...'

'I see,' mused Mercer, 'the scapegoat is altogether too convenient for them.'

'The magistrate would not listen to my opinion on the matter,' MacSorley sighed ruefully; 'thought I had been in the sun too long to know a murder when I saw one. He said he would accept instead the evidence of some quack who would swear that the injuries were caused only hours before the finding of the corpse.'

MacSorley settled himself in a solid armchair by the fire and looked at his old friend. They had been on many voyages together, and had visited tropical islands and sun-soaked lands where no white men had ever been. They came not as invaders or missionaries but as traders, and took nothing without leaving something of value in exchange. MacSorley was a scholar of tropical medicines and diseases, and had studied with interest the treatment given to malaria, yellow fever and leprosy. John Mercer himself had fallen victim to malaria about a year previously, on the homeward journey from the Cape of Good Hope. The physician had at first despaired of saving his life, but such was the strength and determination of Mercer that he had pulled through. Afterwards, MacSorley had managed to persuade his friend to take a long break from the sea, and suggested a period of recuperation in Rostrevor, a handsome village on the shores of Carlingford Lough with a reputation as a place of healing. It was only ten miles or so from the port of Newry, so Mercer could keep in contact with his trade, and equally near to Bannvale House in the parish of Clonduff, home of MacSorley's uncle, John O'Neill of Clannaboy. Mercer was used to a life of excitement and did not settle easily to a diet of goat whey and chicken broth, but the clean mountain air and the care and attention of his housekeeper, Mistress Hanratty, had cleared the pasty yellowness from his skin. He also thrived on the company of his ten-year-old daughter, Charlotte, his only legacy from a short marriage and a tonic in her own right.

'You are hungry for a little excitement, my friend,' Mac-Sorley told his host. 'May I suggest that you invite Master Tom Dunn and his lady to join us at supper tonight. Then we can indulge in some informed and learned discussion on the mystery of Levallyclanowen.'

Marcas MacSorley was pleased with himself for having found an excuse to visit Dunn's Hill. It would give him an opportunity to enquire after Thady O'Lochlainn. He had treated many sick old men in his time, but not all had such lovely daughters as Mistress Grace.

Soon after the arrest of Johnny Fearon, a soberly garbed clerk arrived at the O'Lochlainn Close with a military escort to interview the little boy who had taken up residence there. On finding that he understood neither English nor Irish, he dismissed the boy as an imbecile, unable to help with their inquiries. Thady took this assessment as a personal insult but was restrained by Grace, who explained later that they might have taken the child away if they thought he had any intelligence.

Eily O'Lochlainn was intrigued with her new charge. The frightened little fellow had given them all cause for concern: he had refused to eat and he would not speak; by night his sleep was disturbed, and he cried out in some strange tongue. This frightened Eily, who began to think the boy might be possessed. Thady, however, thought he saw a flash of recognition in the boy's expression from time to time. 'He knows more than he's letting on,' he told his wife.

An object of great curiosity to the denizens of Upper Kilbroney, the boy attracted many callers, who arrived in the

O'Lochlainn Close on the flimsiest pretext.

Eventually Grace persuaded her parents to let her take the boy to her cabin for a few days. Eily worried about what folk would say when they heard that a spinster woman had acquired a child, but Grace brushed aside her protests.

'At my age, all that could be said has already been said. Besides, I wouldn't want the little fellow to end up in the workhouse, or dressed up as an ornamental blackamoor in some planter's residence.'

It was to Grace that the boy spoke first. She had made him a little brown linen shirt, and he tried it on and inspected himself critically. He gave a little cry of delight and threw his arms around her neck. Grace, returning the embrace with a warm smile, took his hands.

'Who are you? Can you tell me?' she asked gently. 'From where have you come? Not that it matters, you are welcome to stay here.' His unexpected reply puzzled her.

'Michael.'

'Michael?'

'Michael O'Lochlainn!'

Grace looked into the brown eyes for some time. The hunted, shadowy look had been replaced by one of trust. 'Michael O'Lochlainn? Why, that's a fine name. Did you choose it yourself?' The boy shook his head. Grace felt a surge of excitement that she had uncovered part of the mystery: Michael understood Irish as well as some words of English.

Thady O'Lochlainn, to no one's surprise, made a stout recovery. Eily was effusive in her praise of the saintly physician who had braved the snow to place his healing hands on the chest of her Thady, and she sang his praises throughout Upper Kilbroney and the neighbouring townlands. Grace maintained a different explanation for her

59

father's well-being. He thrived on excitement, and the recent events, along with the frequent visits from the lamenting Widow Fearon, had taken his mind off his own problems. Most of all, he delighted in the presence of little Michael and was very taken with the idea of his calling himself an O'Lochlainn. No cleverer child, he maintained, ever walked the earth.

While the snow lasted there was not much to be done on the land, except to make sure the donkey and the fowl were fed and watered and the fire did not go out, so Thady began instructing young Michael in the art of weaving a new set of creels for the ass. He was amazed to find how quickly the lad could learn.

'He's a wonder,' the Cobbler remarked. 'He must have learned that art wherever he came from. Does he say naught else about himself? Does he mention the dead woman?'

'He says naught. Maybe he's biding his time.'

The Cobbler arrived up one day with a dog for Michael, a sheepdog cross. Eily, though blanching at the thought of another mouth to feed, warmed to the little boy's pleasure and raised no objections.

'What do you call him?' asked Thady, stroking the animal's head.

'Pup,' replied the Cobbler drily.

'Pup?' echoed Michael.

'Aye, that's what I called him when he was young, and it stuck.'

'At least neither of the pair of them will get lost in the snow,' said Thady with confidence. He noticed an elderly man making his way up the valley towards the Close.

'Where could thon boy be heading in this weather?' he wondered aloud. 'He must have lost his bearings, the poor devil.'

'You know him as well as you know me,' answered the

Buller. 'MacVeigh the fisherman! Old White Matty.'

'White Matty? I haven't laid eyes on him this years. I mind the time he used to come into Rostrevor to sell his fish. "Herrings alive!" he would shout and maybe them dead and salted for three months or more. Mind you, there was folk that had nothing else to eat that were glad of them, and he would say to many a poor woman, "You can pay me when himself comes home from England." I'd say he's still waiting for some of his debts. Call him in for a sup there.'

Michael was off in a flash, like any son of the house to do his father's bidding.

'I'll give him a hand with his belongings,' said the Cobbler.

Resting by the fireside with a much welcome draught, White Matty related his sad story. The new agent had paid him a call a few weeks earlier and had doubled the rent, without explanation of any kind. His son, Jimmy Bán, had helped him meet the cost, even though he had a young family of his own to support.

'And why would he want to double the rent? Sure you haven't room to scratch yourself down there.'

'The size of a few poor drills, nothing more,' agreed White Matty. 'Then a week ago he came looking for the next quarter's rent. Well, you can see the struggle Jimmy would have putting to sea this past month.'

Thady, mountain born and bred, held anyone who would venture on the sea, winter or summer, in the greatest respect.

'Then, as if things weren't bad enough, what did they go and do but double poor Jimmy's rent as well. Eviction was staring us all in the face, and starvation for the children, for we have no other trade but the fishing and, without the cabins by the shore, how can we fish? I tell you, Thady, my heart is broken, for I learned my trade from my father's father, and he from his father before him. And all that I knew

61

I passed on to Jimmy, with a glad heart, and a great fisherman he is too.' The old man paused for a moment. 'Then Jimmy said he wouldn't hear tell of me being evicted and that we had more right to be there than anybody.'

'Your Jimmy's a sound man,' the Buller affirmed.

'But the fear of God was in me that Jimmy would take to the sea in search of a catch, and the waves are mountainous past the bar. So this morning I packed my belongings and told Jimmy's wife that I was off to stay awhile with our Molly in Clonduff,' Matty concluded, 'and that's where I'm bound this day. I'll be on my way again before dark.'

'You'll bide here the night and be done with it,' Thady insisted, but the old man was equally stubborn.

'I'll be a burden to none, least of all generous folk like yourselves.'

'You'll not get past the Lonely Gap,' the Cobbler warned him. 'I had a pair of boots soled for a farmer past the Bolie, and damned if I didn't have to turn back and me within a wink of his Close.'

It was with marked reluctance that White Matty agreed to stay put, for easy graciousness was a skill not usually required by a good fisherman.

Fanny Valentine had been a good landlord 'in as far as the breed went', Thady liked to qualify, and evictions were a rare phenomenon. Yet there had been rumours of rising rent in the houses around the village.

'But why old White Matty's?' he asked Grace the following morning. 'Who else would want to live in a lonely hovel by the shore that's forever damp and stinking of fish?'

Grace was perturbed that her mother should have the inconvenience of another man in her home and, not for the first time, regretted her father's impulsive generosity. 'I'm sure the Cobbler would take him under his roof,' she scolded.

'How could I ask a man with a wife only dead to take in a dirty old beggar?' Thady looked affronted.

'Why is it always our house that has to take in the waifs and strays?'

'Ah, for a wee woman she has a great heart, your mother.'

'I will pay a call on Madam Butler,' Grace said firmly. 'I cannot see how she would countenance such treatment of her tenants.'

Conclave at Arno's Vale

CHARLOTTE MERCER LOOKED out from her bedroom window as first one and then another man on horseback arrived at Arno's Vale. To her disappointment, there were no finely dressed ladies. Since her father had taken her away from her Dublin boarding school she had seen very little of what fashionable people were wearing; her father did not associate with fashionable friends, and from what she had seen of the residents of Rostrevor village, their garb was designed for comfort rather than elegance.

The door opened and Mistress Hanratty stood there with a supper of hot curds. 'You must keep away from the window, Miss Charlotte,' she scolded. 'There are many plagues and ailments in the night air all waiting to get in.' The stout little housekeeper brusquely drew the curtains and tucked her charge into bed. The room was warm and cosy with a beautiful French embroidered counterpane, a legacy from the little girl's mother.

'Who is visiting Papa?' she asked. 'I saw Master Dunn and Dr MacSorley, but I could not recognise the third caller. Was it a lady?'

'Nonsense! That is Dr William Drennan, an eminent physician who practises in Newry. There, I've told you too much already and your little mind needs its rest. Have you eaten your curds? That's the girl. Goodnight, my dear,' she cooed, and blew out the candle.

Below in the dining room John Mercer produced the pride of his cellar.

'Port wine, Dunn?'

'You keep a most generous table, my friend. And I thought MacSorley here enjoyed his rabbit stew,' smiled Tom Dunn.

'I certainly did,' protested Marcas MacSorley, 'and your mulled ale was like the nectar of the gods on that particular evening.'

'His compliment is sincere,' Mercer assured Tom Dunn. 'He talked so much about the excellence of Mistress Dunn's cooking, I declare I envied you your married state, if only for a moment!'

'There speaks a man who relishes his freedom,' said William Drennan, 'if we are to take him at all seriously, that is.'

'I enjoy the freedom to employ an excellent chef.'

All concurred that, if the meal they had just eaten was anything to go by, Captain Mercer was indeed a fortunate man. 'But you did not call us here just to praise your table,' said Dunn. 'What is the news from France?'

As Mistress Hanratty removed the supper dishes, Dr Drennan began to speak of the recent uprising in Paris. The housekeeper had heard about it herself while shopping in the village, and had been shocked by the outrageous tales of ravaged women and babies sold as butchers' meat. Yet here was the doctor talking about a revolution and queer notions such as 'the will of the people'. The king and queen had abused their power, he said, and thus forfeited their right to rule. And the Captain was just as enthusiastic, declaring that he would do all in his power to help the republican government, though he was sure the king and queen would not be executed. But it was only a matter of time, he declared forcefully, before the same thing happened nearer home.

The housekeeper prayed silently. Protestant gentlemen had strange ideas, she told herself.

'I hope I haven't startled your servant,' said Drennan. 'She looks rather upset.'

'She always looks upset,' Mercer said cheerfully, 'but she knows better than to talk about what she hears in this house. But tell me, Dunn,' he went on, 'what do our peasants think of the revolution?'

'At the moment,' Dunn replied, 'the only topic of conversation amongst them is the innocence or otherwise of Johnny Fearon.'

'A local mystery in which Dunn and myself have become involved,' Marcas MacSorley explained to the table.

'Why don't you tell Drennan the tale?' Mercer invited him. 'Start with the finding of the body.'

'I will, with one indulgence. I should start with the execution of Johnny Fearon's father.'

Some twenty minutes later he concluded his story, and allowed a few moments silence while Drennan pondered on the tale.

'If your diagnosis of how the woman died is not accepted, as an independent observer I would say that Fearon is in a difficult situation. He has, you tell me, served a lengthy prison term for attacking one of his benefactors while in the workhouse. Was there any reason why he was not hanged for that alone?' Drennan wore a perpetual expression of disapproval. Those who did not know him might have thought he was one of those dour preachers who appeared at the crossroads dances, but his friends knew him to be a compassionate and caring man.

'I spoke on his behalf at the time, pleading his extreme youth. He was not even ten years old,' Dunn explained. As a lawyer, he had been asked by the Widow to do his best for her nephew.

'Yet it is on his record that he has, in the past, committed an act of agression against an innocent person; according to the law, that is, for we have no way of knowing what vile deed may have provoked the poor lad,' admitted Drennan. 'And we must also consider his father's past record. Like father, like son, I can hear it being said.'

'Yes,' Dunn agreed, 'and there is nothing more dangerous than folk memory. People, with no particular intention of malice, will recollect stories about some great-uncle or other distant relative which underline the young man's guilt.'

'Tell us some more about the garments the victim was wearing,' Mercer asked. 'They were not the usual peasant homespun, from what I've gathered. Could she possibly be identified by her mode of dress?'

'I hardly think so,' Drennan was discouraging. 'Gentlewomen's discarded garments usually pass to poor relations or to their servants, but I would think that many find their way to the charitable institutions. What did you think, MacSorley?'

MacSorley was not concerned with the victim's mode of dress, however; he was still perturbed that his professional opinion had been overruled by the authorities. 'My evidence has not been accepted. Perhaps only Doctors of Physics from Trinity or Edinburgh can tell the living from the dead.'

Drennan, himself a graduate of Trinity, bristled. 'You take

things too much to heart, MacSorley. Maybe they think you've been away too long.'

'Maybe they're right,' Marcas MacSorley said sourly. Orphaned from infancy, MacSorley had followed the trail to the continent and was a graduate of the University of Paris and the celebrated medical school of Leyden.

'It seems to me that the little boy must give evidence,' Mercer suggested, seeing his friend in low spirits. 'His testimony as a child may not be accepted but, surely, if he met young Fearon face to face, we could at least tell if there was any sign of recognition on the part of the child.'

Drennan looked doubtful. 'I have my suspicions, too, about the involvement of this Grace O'Lochlainn.'

'Say naught about Grace! I'd trust my life with her,' Tom Dunn defended the Kilbroney woman.

'Whatever good opinion you might have of her, Tom, Mistress Hanratty informs me that she was for many years the late landlord's mistress,' declared Mercer. 'That's true, is it not?'

Marcas MacSorley looked up sharply at this revelation and shortly excused himself from the company.

The Master of Kilbroney House

SINCE THE DEATH of Major Henry Valentine, Grace O'Lochlainn had maintained an amicable relationship with his sister, Fanny. Henry had never married, but Fanny had grown to respect, even envy the strength of his love for the peasant girl with whom he had lived for so many years. Their paths rarely crossed now, for Grace had turned her back on the life of the privileged classes and refused financial help of any kind from Fanny. The two women bore many common characteristics, not least a strong, independent spirit, so it was with some dismay that Grace had noticed a change in her friend since her marriage.

As she was ushered into the drawing room of Kilbroney House, painful memories flooded back of happier times. She caught a glimpse of herself in a looking-glass. Her pale flaxen hair, caught in a twist at the base of her neck, was turning to silver at the temples. Her eyes were the same grey, only sadder and wiser than those of the fourteen-year-old girl who had come to the house as a scullery maid all those years ago. She wondered if she had made a mistake: perhaps she should not have come. Her recollections were interrupted by a light footfall. Turning, she fell under the gaze of a tall man with wavy blond hair, blue eyes, and skin as flawlesss as any woman's. He approached her and lifted her hand to his lips; it was clear that he approved of her appearance.

'My dear Grace, I am so glad you have come. Is he not wonderful, my husband?' And Fanny, her eyes blind to all else, rushed into the room to stand by Dargan Butler's side.

'So it is true what they say about him?' Annie Dunn had listened, enthralled, to Grace's description of her visit to the Big House.

'A dandy, for certain,' said Grace wryly. 'I was almost falling for himself myself. Imagine! A spinster of my age.'

'I wish my looks had improved with age as yours have,' her friend responded loyally. 'But I do pity Madam Butler.'

'Strangely, she thinks herself to be the most fortunate woman in Ireland, and who are we,' Grace continued, 'to question her judgement?'

'And when you asked about old White Matty?'

'She did not know anything about the case. She said that her dear husband would not dream of involving her in estate matters. And, more worrying still, she did not seem to care.'

Young Betsy Dunn breezed into the kitchen with a box of fresh down, her eyes aglow. 'Tell me, Grace,' she cried gaily, 'what do you think of the new master of Kilbroney? Is he not handsome?'

'Enough of that, young woman!' her mother warned. 'It would suit you better if you paid more attention to your lessons.' Betsy departed as quickly as she had arrived, the scolding disregarded, leaving her mother to lament over the girl's precocious behaviour.

'I thought she was beginning to grow up when she began insisting on attending the Mass House above the village. You know, of course, that having been brought up as a Presbyterian my personal instinct has always been to give my children and grandchildren the freedom to choose whether to attend or not, as their consciences dictate. I was pleased to see that Betsy had other things on her mind than flirting with young men: then I caught her batting her eyelids at MacCormac the blacksmith during the sermon. Thank God the parish priest is as blind as a bat.'

'Are you sure it was not the other way around? Do not underestimate Betsy's charm.'

'Or her cunning! She went out of her way to captivate that unfortunate young Fearon. I could almost think he's better off in prison.'

Annie and Grace began stuffing pillow cases with the goose feathers which Betsy had brought in. They were interrupted in their task by the arrival of the master of the house in the company of Marcas MacSorley. Annie regarded her husband, tall and broad shouldered even in his late fifties, his silver hair tied neatly with a black ribbon. He was the most handsome man that ever walked, she thought, surpassing any Dargan Butler.

'Why, Tom,' she said to him, 'I have been listening to Grace's description of the new landlord. She is quite bedazzled by him.'

'He must have some special qualities if he can capture your heart, Grace,' said Dunn.

The women laughed; MacSorley allowed himself a thin smile. How aloof, Grace thought, and continued stuffing her pillow.

'Young Fearon,' said Annie anxiously. 'Is there any news of the lad?'

'There is no change in his situation,' her husband replied,

71

easing himself out of his boots. 'He will be tried at the spring assizes in Downpatrick. Who knows? The circuit judge may not consider the death of a poor black woman worthy of the death penalty.'

'Tom!' Annie stood affronted.

'For a change we must rely on man's intolerance to man. The only other hope lies in Dargan Butler.'

'Butler?' enquired Grace.

'He has been appointed to the County Grand Jury. He will be sitting with the judge and, perhaps, can be persuaded to speak in Fearon's favour. Perhaps you can use your influence, Grace.'

'Me? Why, I...' Grace was unprepared for the disapproving look cast in her direction by MacSorley. Anger surged within her. He has already tried me and found me guilty, she thought.

'Of course I'll speak on Johnny's behalf,' she said.

Inblown Wrack

THE SPRING OF 1790 came in a blaze of whin blossom and red-coated troopers in the valley. Few had time to take notice. The laborious toil of turning the sod had begun, and the stony ground of Kilbroney resisted the spade with a vengeance. Turlough MacCormac, the blacksmith who had taken over Murtagh Fegan's forge, laboured day and night to keep abreast of the broken ploughshares and blunted spades. Further down the valley, seed potatoes which had been sown just after Patrick's Day were already sprouting green shoots. At Arno's Vale, John Mercer felt well enough to oversee the ploughing of his fields. There were times when he enjoyed this close contact with his native earth, in the safe knowledge that he was within spitting distance of the sea.

There were stirrings of discontent in the valley when Dargan Butler's land agent, Crampsey, announced a general increase in rents and a declaration that no excuse for tardy payment would be accepted. The Kilbroney tenants realised that this was no idle threat, for the many dispossessed families who had migrated from other parts of Ireland in search of a living would gladly take over any vacant plots. Destitute when they reached Kilbroney, many found that they could go no further and took their chances with the seasonal work offered in the flax fields and linen mills. Few paid heed to the arrival of a roving fiddler with the gaunt look of a man from Donegal. He made his home in a rude woodland shelter above the Clasha, a clearing in the old forest. Cobbler McChesney advised him to move on to Newry where he would find customers at the docks.

'They won't have much to spend,' he said, 'but what they have they're happy to throw away on the services of a fiddler.'

Oran O'Cassidy thanked him politely for his advice, but insisted he wanted to stay in the parish of Kilbroney.

In Levallyclanowen the Widow Fearon dealt with the usual crop of spring confinements, including a set of red-haired twins in Knockbarragh. The ecstatic father, when he sobered, offered the Widow the pick of his sow's litter which had arrived a week earlier. To everyone's surprise she refused this token of gratitude, saying that by the time the first cut of bacon was cured she would be pushing up the weeds from below, for she had not much time left. The old woman, distressed at the thought of Johnny's being convicted, regressed into religion, confessing sins to the confused parish priest which far surpassed the scope of a woman of her years. Her usual indelicate turn of speech was replaced by a constant litany of saints long forgotten, if they had ever existed at all.

Having decided that the local saint, Bronach, was only good for curing pussed eyes, she undertook a painful barefooted pilgrimage to the hill of Saint Patrick at Saul in the north of County Down, where the saint had wrestled demons when he was not tending swine. The Widow then returned by way of the town of Downpatrick, the regional centre of justice which heard all capital cases. Her bizarre appearance attracted the taunts of urchins, and one stallkeeper set his hounds on her, but the indomitable Widow Fearon quickly called them to heel and they followed her like lambs up through the cobbled lanes to the courthouse. There she saw again the skulls of executed men, at various stages of decomposition; many years before she had carried one such skull back to Kilbroney for Christian burial. Not to be diverted by painful memories, she proceeded to impose a painful and irreversible curse on the judges, the warders, the hangmen, and any who would lift a finger to harm her Johnny. The spell had to be irreversible, in case the priest compelled her to overturn it at her next confession.

As the day of the hearing at the assizes approached Tom Dunn made several attempts to question Michael, but without success. Eily was uneasy about having the young boy relive such a horror, and expressed her fears to Dunn.

'He may be the only hope we have left to clear young Fearon,' the lawyer told her, 'and 'tis a slim expectancy at that. He may not be able to distinguish one white face from another.'

'Our lad,' Thady challenged him, 'is the smartest boy ever came into Kilbroney. Our girl says he's picking up his letters as though he knew them all his life.' Thady's girl, Grace, had taken over the tuition of the older students of the hedge-school for a while and Michael would not join Mistress Dunn's group of younger scholars, preferring to stay close to his patroness.

75

Tom Dunn marvelled at the new life in Thady since Michael's arrival. He went about his tasks with the energy of a young man, and in the evening took delight in teaching Michael chess on Sean's old chequered board, using pebbles for the missing pieces.

It was Grace who gently, persuasively, coaxed the child to talk about that traumatic night which had so changed his life. He sat on her lap and leaned his head against her as he talked about his memories of sun and palm trees and a long voyage by ship through stormy seas. His story was a confused one; of perilous journeys and strange, unearthly faces, and dark rooms with covered windows. Grace could only imagine his mother's terror of losing her child to slavery, and she hugged him protectively. Then he spoke of the man who had beaten his mother, and how she had screamed and screamed. He was overcome with pitiful sobbing and buried his head in Grace's breast.

'Did you see this man?' she whispered softly. The boy nodded at first, then shook his head.

'The poor lad's tired!' Thady intervened anxiously, seeing the child's distress. 'Let him lie down for himself.'

'I'll take him home with me tonight,' said Grace, afraid to leave the troubled child for her parents to cope with. 'Come on with me, Michael. We'll be back in the morning to feed the hens.'

'Go on, lad,' coaxed Thady, 'and take my stick in case you meet a cut-throat on the pad.'

The following morning, as Grace was mixing his whey and potatoes, Michael brought up the subject on his own initiative.

'What happened to her?' he asked hesitantly.

'I saw her, Michael. She was lovely. She was at peace. No pain, no suffering.'

She explained to the boy about Johnny Fearon, and why

they needed Michael to confront him. She saw the fear that rose in him. He twisted off her lap and they did not see him for the rest of the day.

'You had no right to torment him so!' a worried Thady shouted at Grace. 'And what if Fearon is a murderer, or worse, that Michael thinks he is?'

Grace, ashamed of having so frightened the child, set out to look for him. She knew that he would probably be found in the direction of the Priest's Mountain, a place which seemed to hold some strange fascination for the boy, with its eery white rocks and sparse trees like rooted skeletons. Towards the summit stood *Carraig an Aifreann*, the Mass Rock, scene of a bloody massacre many years previously. Grace had surmised that Michael was drawn to the place because it bore some resemblance to his distant home. As she climbed up the slope he came to meet her, and they walked home in silence, Pup at Michael's heels.

'I would like to see this man,' he said. 'If he is the one, I will tell you.'

Fanny Butler found herself with more and more time on her hands. Haggling with Newry merchants or cajoling bankers being occupations regarded by her husband as unsuitable for a gentlewoman, her active mind instead sought employment in other, more domestic tasks. Fanny took great pleasure in her garden, which was in excellent condition, with the new terraces laid out to perfection, the spring borders well ordered and delicately coloured in accordance with fashion, and the orchards cut back to give way to another lawn which set off the southern aspect of the house to great effect. It was a handsome country residence, built in the days of Colonel Whitechurch, and many of the uglier features of fortification so necessary in those turbulent times had been modified and refashioned by the generations following. The Honourable

Dargan felt that Kilbroney House was old-fashioned, however, and more suitable for a prosperous farmer than a man of his rank.

Fanny was constantly trying to make little improvements in hopes of winning his approval, but he rarely seemed to notice them. Occasionally she would suggest that he invite his family or friends to stay, but he always demurred, implying that they would think he had married beneath him when they saw the size of the building, as all men of rank were judged according to the houses they kept. Yes, he admitted, the townhouse in Dublin was adequate, if understaffed, but Kilbroney House reflected poorly his position in society. When such remarks upset her he would scold her for her foolishness, put his arms around her and tell her that he loved her.

As she walked along the riverbank Fanny thought with satisfaction of her latest scheme to please him. The apiary to the south of the orchard had been established for many years and it was time she replenished some of the deserted hives. She had acquired a swarm from a Quaker shipping merchant called Neville who insisted that they should be considered a gift. This honey, he claimed, was second to none, and was prized even by London chefs. Dargan would certainly appreciate what was good enough for the English nobility and so, with his pleasure in mind, she headed for Willow Cottage, home of old Doubting Mooney.

A gentle old man whose eighty years would have passed for sixty, Mooney was an expert on the art of beekeeping. A shy individual, some said that he was more comfortable with the bees than with people, and that he could talk to the swarms in their hives of willow and wattle. Visiting gentry purchased his honey in the hope that it would keep them young, as it so plainly had the beekeeper. On the subject of bees Mooney had no equal, and Fanny wanted him to settle the swarm into their new quarters next to the native insects. The English bees were, she explained, from the castle of a viscount, and promised a fine yield of top quality honey. Doubting Mooney held strong, if private, opinions regarding the value of 'planters' of any species, but had survived to a ripe old age by suppressing his thoughts beneath a hive-shaped hat.

'I doubt I would consider it if I were you, Ma'am. Leave well enough alone where the swarm is concerned. How would you like it if a band of foreigners took over your home?'

'Nonsense, Mooney. I know you can manage it.'

On taking her leave of Doubting Mooney, Fanny mounted the rickety footbridge at the end of the lane leading to the shore, where she liked to watch the sailing vessels come and go. The little harbour was unusually quiet, and two wives, gutting the morning's catch at the water's edge, curtsied respectfully before scurrying indoors. She glanced overhead to see if this was a portent of poor weather, but the sky seemed clear. A few gulls screeched and squabbled over a bucket of entrails, encouraging Fanny to turn her back on the scene. Even the Garden of Eden had its serpent, she mused. Turning from the shore, she chose a secluded path through the woods where she once played truant with her brother, Henry. In those days the forest was considered highly dangerous, swarming with cut-throats and outlaws of all description, and yet Fanny felt safer there than she ever did in Newry or Dublin.

Everywhere was fresh and damp and very still. She stopped to listen to the familiar trickling water in the undergrowth and the twittering of nesting birds. She walked on, stopping again to listen. Another sound had joined with the soft woodland voices; it was very faint, almost inaudible, but seemed to be a violin. It appeared to come from further up the mountainside, where the woods were thickest. The lament was very sweet and sad. As she listened it faded and a sudden breeze rustled the leaves of the forest. 'I'm so lonely I'm imagining things.' Fanny spoke aloud, almost hoping that someone would answer, at least to affirm that other ears had heard the sound.

Returning via the footbridge she chose the little path past the Crag, a fortified stone house in which resided the officer in charge of the barrack and his wife. It was, she understood, quite a desirable appointment, usually given to well connected older officers, who could look forward to a restful retirement. Nothing much happened around Rostrevor and, if it did, the large garrison at Newry was only a few miles up the lough. Behind the Crag stood the little parish church of Saint Paul, a pre-Reformation building which, since Cromwell's time, had been stripped of any decoration which could be construed as Romish. It was, she had told the vicar, much too austere, and time the congregation had a new one. The Honourable Dargan agreed with her that such a meagre church did not reflect the true standing of the family, though by 'family' Fanny meant neither the Butlers nor the Wards, her late husband's people, but the Valentines, of which she was the last.

Fanny crossed the churchyard to the crypt where rested the bones of the Valentines, including those of her brother and father. Her mother, who had disliked Ireland, was buried by the side of her second husband in a comfortable Gloucestershire abbey. It was not in Fanny's nature to dwell for long on the subject of her own mortality, so having sympathised with the sexton on the low attendance at Sunday worship, she made her way home. Yet the sound of the fiddler in the woods continued to haunt her in the days following.

The Widow's Joy

'YOUNG FEARON? HE is guilty beyond a doubt. The scoundrel should have been hanged long ago,' said Dargan Butler to Tom Dunn, letting his annoyance be known. He considered the Kilbroney lawyer's interference an impertinence.

'I think we have evidence of his innocence at last.' Dunn had been anxious to speak with Squire Butler before his departure for the assizes in Downpatrick, and had been fortunate enough to encounter him leaving the Seneschal's house in Newry.

'Evidence?' Butler raised an enquiring eyebrow.

'An eye-witness!'

'Surely an eye-witness, in such circumstances, might be regarded as an accomplice. Why did this person not intervene to prevent the murder?'

'It was not possible in this case. The witness was a child, terrified and helpless. There was nothing he could do to protect his mother, but hopefully he will bring the guilty to justice, or at least save an innocent man.'

Butler's groom approached with his horse, a fashionable dapple grey gelding, and assisted him to mount.

'The circuit judge would never accept the child's testimony. I doubt if he would even be allowed into the public gallery.'

'I had hoped you could use your influence. I have already enlisted Squire Nedham's support: he can see the justice of the case.' The Nedhams were Newry's wealthiest and most influential family, responsible for the appointment of the Seneschal and most of the town's officials. Butler had been courting their approval since his arrival in Rostrevor, and could not afford to be seen in opposition to the Squire.

'This boy. Where is he now?' he said impatiently.

'In the care of Grace O'Lochlainn, the schoolteacher, one of your tenants.'

'Ah, Mistress Grace. Why, of course. An old family friend, no less.'

'If you care to see the child for yourself...'

Butler shuddered. 'A young negro? That won't be necessary.'

Dunn shrugged in annoyance. Such an attitude he might have expected.

'Send Mistress O'Lochlainn to me tomorrow,' Butler said. 'Perhaps I may be of some help. A court appearance may not even be necessary.' He rode off towards High Street, his groom following on foot.

'I cannot understand why he would wish to speak to me.' Grace peered at Tom Dunn over the rim of her spectacles. Hours of painstaking transcription of legal documents for him had taken a toll on her eyesight and she could no longer work without them.

'If I were you, I would wear those spectacles when you meet him,' he said, to her annoyance.

'I can see without them quite well, thank you,' she replied.

'They might go a long way to protecting your virtue. You look most forbidding!'

'Virtue,' Grace smiled, 'is an overrated quality. But,' she went on, 'I am flattered to hear you describe me in such a way.'

'Really, Grace,' Annie Dunn spoke from the corner, where she was nursing her grandchild. 'Don't be listening to him.'

'His virtue, at least,' said Grace, cleaning her quills, 'is beyond question, unlike mine! How do I look?' Grace pushed the spectacles onto the bridge of her nose and pursed her lips in a prim manner. 'Do I go into battle well defended, or ready for the attack?'

'I wish to speak with the Honourable Dargan Butler,' Grace informed a curious footman, who looked confused by her worn serge gown and haughty demeanour. He showed her into the drawing room, unsure about her status.

'Mistress O'Lochlainn. I was looking forward to your visit!' Dargan Butler entered the room to find Grace standing in the light of the late evening sun. Her hair shimmered silver in the glow. The same grey eyes which had captivated young Henry Valentine all those years ago now turned to him.

'I received your summons,' she said, 'and understand you wish to speak with me about the child in my care.' He was not listening to a word she was saying.

'No wonder Henry Valentine loved you,' he said at last. 'How could he have ever let you go?'

'It was my choice, not his.' Grace's gaze was unflinching.

'If you were my mistress, you would have no choice,' he murmured, moving closer to her. She was a tall woman, and their eyes were almost level.

'I am here to discuss young Fearon's trial, to see if Michael can help him,' she said sharply, breaking away from him. Her eyes met his, clear and challenging.

'What?' Even the whores of Newry put up a token demeanour of coyness. Her scent, of candlewax and sweet earth, was intoxicating, her dark gown more seductive than the current décolleté modes. Had she been any other servant he would have stripped her and taken her then and there.

'About young Fearon,' Grace was saying.

'Let Fearon hang!' he spat angrily.

'He will not hang,' said Grace, 'unless he is guilty, and only Michael can tell us if he is.' She turned to the door, then stopped as Fanny Butler came into the hall.

'My dear,' said Fanny, removing her hat, 'I trust my husband has been of some assistance?'

'Indeed,' replied Grace politely, 'he has been helpful.'

'Is he not wonderful?' whispered Fanny. 'I hope he'll like the bees.' She rushed off, leaving Grace to ponder on her friend's cryptic comment.

A few days later Tom Dunn and Marcas MacSorley brought Johnny Fearon back to Rostrevor. The Widow Fearon was waiting with open arms for her nephew, once more a free man.

'God bless Master Dunn,' she kept muttering, 'for he's a living saint!'

Annie Dunn had little time for saints, living or dead, but she shared in the Widow's delight. 'You may thank Grace,' she reminded the old woman. 'Her good offices with Dargan Butler certainly had its effect.'

The Widow laughed and danced a little jig of happiness. 'God bless Squire Butler for his good sense,' she cried, her eyes crinkling with merriment and distilled root spirit, 'and whatever other divilry caused him to let my Johnnie walk free.'

Even the most charitable of Dargan Butler's tenants were surprised when news spread that the Squire had intervened on Johnny's behalf, and there were more than a few whispers when Grace O'Lochlainn's intercession became common knowledge. Grace, hearing of the rumours from Cobbler McChesney, her unofficial champion, smiled thinly.

In fact, Dargan Butler had not acceded to her request that Michael should confront the prisoner, but instead agreed that Dr MacSorley's evidence should be heard. It was with some surprise that MacSorley received a summons requiring him to testify to the extent and type of injuries on the corpse. He confirmed that although the unfortunate woman had been constantly and brutally beaten over a period of time, there was no evidence that these injuries had directly caused her death; rather she had died of exhaustion and extreme cold. The court was forced to accept that no wilful murder had taken place, and that in any case the injuries on the body could not have been caused by the prisoner, Johnny Fearon. The magistrate, Dargan Butler, therefore ordered his immediate release.

Marcas MacSorley had been silent as he accompanied the Kilbroney men homewards. Tom Dunn noticed his mood.

'Tell us, MacSorley, were you holding back on some dark and dreadful secret? Perhaps she was murdered after all, and you perjured yourself.'

MacSorley drew a deep breath. 'God forbid that I should do such a thing. No, I expect that her full story will never come to light.' He gave a heavy sigh.

'Take my counsel, Fearon,' he turned to the young man, 'and put this behind you. We'll stop at the next alehouse and toast your liberty! That much is worth celebrating.'

That evening the party arrived at Dunn's Hill to a warm

reception. If MacSorley was disappointed by Grace's absence, no one noticed; they were busy making Johnny feel welcome. And chief among the revellers was Tom Dunn's daugher, Betsy.

Thady's Pride

'MAYBE NOW THE dark woman's soul can rest in peace,' muttered Eily as she shuffled in and out feeding the household fowl, a few scrawny chickens. Thady, puffing at his pipe in the doorway, was more interested in the antics of Michael and Pup. The dog was learning a new trick every day, while Michael was growing stronger and more confident in his new surroundings.

Thady's scrawny chest would swell every time he heard praise being lavished on his newly adopted son, and he revelled in the host of callers to the house, looking for the story first hand. Eily dismissed them with a sniff. 'If they'd quit poking into things that don't concern them, they'd be welcome,' she said, but Thady, who prided himself on being a magnanimous host, was delighted to receive so much attention.

'You know, 'tis like the old days back again!' he declared to the Buller, thinking of earlier times when he had had his sons Sean and Eamonn around him. Thady often pined for the company of his boys, and he took solace in the attention of his friends and neighbours. The Poorlands held a tightly knit community, struggling together to survive on the barren mountain soil. The O'Lochlainns' nearest neighbours were the Buller and Cobbler McChesney. The Cobbler had been evicted from his shop near the village forge when he had boldly declared that the Agent Crampsey's boots needed the hides of two bulls to make a pair. Crampsey, self conscious about the size of his feet, responded by banishing the widowed Cobbler and his brood to the wilds of the Poorlands, and replacing him with his cousin, a bootmender with less skill but more discretion. McChesney had difficulty making a living now, and relied on the custom of fairgoers at Hill Town and Waring's Point.

Michael was quickly assimilated into the community; indeed, Eily, while doting on the little boy, feared he would be spoiled by all the attention showered on him. She saw to it that he was properly dressed and shod each morning, but invariably he returned home barefoot and hatless. 'The young McChesneys haven't a boot between them! The lad doesn't want to be any different,' Thady reminded her.

Grace was concerned that Michael would be picked on because of his appearance, but Thady dismissed her worries. 'Aren't there plenty of odd-looking folk here already? What harm if he looks a bit dark? He could be one of those wee lads from the west that see more of the sun than ourselves. And look at the head of hair on him! There's many a boy around Rostrevor with curls like that, only it's red instead of black.'

Curiosity about Michael was not confined to Kilbroney. Captain Mercer himself was anxious to see the lad and asked MacSorley if he would bring the boy to Arno's Vale. Tom Dunn laughed and suggested that here was just the excuse for the doctor to visit Mistress Grace once more. He was surprised by MacSorley's curt response, and decided he had been mistaken about his friend's initial interest in her. It was a pity, he thought, for his Annie had been considering a match between the two. Marcas MacSorley, she maintained, was a lonely man who, having spent a lifetime at sea, should now be content to settle down with a good woman by his side. Yet Tom had a nagging suspicion that much as Marcas might need Grace, she did not need anyone.

Grace enjoyed the unconditional affection of young Michael, who was too young to appreciate her loveliness and too innocent to know about her past. The Cobbler McChesney, everybody knew, greatly admired her, and was much in need of a mother for his children; Mick the Fox also had approached Thady, saying that he was prepared to overlook her shameful carry-on with Henry Valentine and make an honest woman of her.

Grace held herself aloof from such incidents. She had to admit to some uneasiness, though, about her encounter with Dargan Butler. He was certainly handsome, one of the most elegant and comely men she had ever seen, and she did not wonder at Fanny's infatuation. She recognised, however, that this was a man who was self-indulgent and ambitious; his treatment of the fisherfolk suggested that he was capable of great ruthlessness. Yet he had shown mercy towards Johnny Fearon. Grace had seen enough of the world to know that he was attracted to her, and had wanted to impress her; but then, he had a licentious reputation. 'Like myself!' Grace smiled wryly. Perhaps Butler was not as black as he was painted and there was a certain wildness, a recklessness about him which she found compelling.

The French Expedition

ON A CHILLY evening at the end of April Grace received an invitation to Arno's Vale. She had just returned from a short visit to Newry, where she had helped a local shipping merchant cope with a visiting French trade delegation. King Louis was in prison and the old order had been overthrown, but the fledgling republican government was anxious that the world should know that business would continue under the new regime. If the loyal English ports were too nervous to be seen, officially at any rate, to condone the overthrow of a monarch, even a Papist monarch, the Irish seafaring towns, particularly the linen ports of the north, had no such scruples. Gold was gold, be it republican or monarchist. Ireland also had its liberals who lauded the courage of the French in overthrowing a tyrant king and a corrupt church. This combination of self-interest and egalitarianism had prompted the merchants of Newry to agree with John Mercer that a message of goodwill should be sent to General Robespierre on behalf of the town.

Mercer, having been charged with composing the message, was aware that his knowledge of the French language was confined to the vernacular of seadogs and corsairs, so, at Tom Dunn's suggestion, he sought the help of Mistress O'Lochlainn. He had to admit to a certain curiosity about her, too, having heard her name mentioned so often. The following morning Grace arrived at Arno's Vale, her cloak damp from an April shower and her hair bejewelled with droplets. Casting off her boots at the kitchen door, she accepted Mistress Hanratty's offer to dry her cloak and within a short time was at work in the cheerful front room overlooking the lough.

'Mistress O'Lochlainn is a non-pareil,' Mercer declared to MacSorley over dinner that night. 'She is so thorough in her work, and so engaging in her manner.'

Mercer was already formulating a new plan. 'We should really send a personal emissary to Paris. There is trade to be won, and who better to captivate those hard-nosed rebels than Mistress Grace. Why, she speaks French like a native, and she knows as much about the law as any man. She must, of course, have a worthy escort!'

'Forget this, Mercer,' MacSorley replied. 'You are not yet fit to return to sea, let alone visit a war-ravaged city.'

'Quite right,' replied his host. 'You must go in my place. A physician would surely be welcomed in the circumstances. And you are a graduate of Paris – you know the city well.'

'And what makes you think that Grace O'Lochlainn would be prepared to make such a journey?' MacSorley asked.

'I can but ask.' John Mercer shrugged and helped himself to the port.

'Yes, I will go to Paris, if you want me to do so.'

91

John Mercer had not expected Grace to concede to his request so easily. He had asked her to accompany him while he inspected a new addition to his dairy herd so that he might have time to talk over his plans.

'It will be important for the prosperity of this area to establish good relations with the republican French. For too long we have been subject to this ludicrous embargo imposed on us by the government. It will be broken soon, of course. There are reports that Belfast and Larne are casting their eyes in the direction of the French trade, but I am confident that Newry can be first. Indeed, we have collected a sizeable donation to present to General Robespierre.'

'And has this not upset the Tories?' Grace asked.

'Such is the wave of popular sentiment, they made but token opposition to the move. Why, my own wife was French, you know. Her father was imprisoned for many years for his outspokenness against the Bourbon regime. So,' he rubbed his hands briskly, 'we have good credentials.' He nodded towards a new-born calf. 'Look at that: a fine beast, isn't he?'

Grace smiled at his enthusiasm, but her mind was not on the calf. 'You have good credentials,' she said cautiously, 'but I have none at all.'

'You will not be at risk,' he began to reassure her but she stopped him.

'I have already agreed to go, Captain Mercer. I have reasons of my own for wanting to visit Paris.'

'I knew I could talk you into it.' He had been about to offer her the calf as an inducement and now was glad he hadn't. From what they said about Mistress O'Lochlainn, she might have responded quite badly to a bribe.

Grace's travelling plans were upset when Thady disclosed his intention of accompanying her. In spite of Eily's appeals and the Buller's ridicule, he ordered a new pair of travelling boots from the Cobbler and sold his pig to pay for them.

'I might have known he would take such a notion,' said Grace to Tom Dunn. 'I know he would dearly love to have news of Sean before he dies, but he's hardly fit to make it to Hill Town fair and back, let alone endure an ocean journey.'

'Your father's hardier than you think. Remember, he saw the worst of times in his youth, so a little hardship on board a ship will hardly vex him.' Dunn spoke reassuringly, but Grace was not to be mollified.

'Thady O'Lochlainn? He bathes his feet in the lough but once a year, on the Blessed Virgin's feast day, and then only to partake of the cure in the water. Why,' she reminded her amused listener, 'he wouldn't take White Matty's boat to Omeath to save his life.'

'Now Grace, 'tis only to take care of you that he wants to go. He is concerned for your safety,' Annie Dunn put in. This time it was Grace's turn to laugh.

MacSorley was called upon to dissuade the recalcitrant pilgrim as he readied himself for the journey of a lifetime. But Thady was determined to go, 'be it on the Devil's own barque,' and MacSorley emerged from the cabin after a prolonged but unsuccessful conclave. Grace looked at him in exasperation. 'Could you not have told him he wasn't fit to travel. Everyone can see that he's a sick old man!'

'Everyone but Thady,' MacSorley shrugged. 'And if he thinks he's well and able, who am I to deny him?'

'He could die on the ship.'

'He could die in his bed.' MacSorley and Grace glared at one another.

'He told me that to ignore such a God-given sign would be bad luck,' said MacSorley finally, 'and he has hopes of finding his son.'

'My father is ruled by luck and superstition,' sighed Grace.

'He frets a lot about his son.'

'Sean? There's barely a word about him. If anyone ever mentions the name he just pretends not to hear, or walks away.'

'He's still very much on Thady's mind, the poor old fellow.'

'I had four brothers,' Grace told him. 'Two died in childhood; Eamonn was to join the priesthood when he was murdered. When Sean went to France in eighty-one my father was broken hearted. He was accepted as a student at the Irish College on the recommendation of the bishop, and I can tell you in truth that he left Kilbroney with a light step.'

'Wanderlust. It strikes us all.'

'Even my father, at seventy-one years of age?'

'Especially at seventy-one years of age, when the furthest you've ever ventured from home is Hill Town. I take it,' MacSorley ventured, 'that your brother did not serve his full time at the seminary.'

'No. He never accepted authority gracefully. Sean was the disputatious type. He was always likely to be suspended, but before that he left of his own accord. We haven't seen him since.'

'A single-minded, argumentative fellow with a determination to travel.'

'Yes,' agreed Grace, 'that would be Sean.'

'I was not thinking of Sean. I was thinking about your father.'

Reluctantly, Grace left Eily and Michael in the care of the neighbours. Eily lamented their going, but Johnny Fearon promised Grace he would look in on her and take care of any heavy work around the Close. Grace accepted his offer with relief.

In preparation for the journey Marcas MacSorley, accompanied by Captain Mercer, paid a courtesy call on Dr Lennon, the Catholic Bishop of Dromore. A letter of introduction from a bishop would be useful also, even in republican France. The episcopal residence in Newry was modest compared to that of the vicar of St Patrick's, but well furnished as befitted a noble of the church. Matthew Lennon, a hard-nosed diplomat who had led his flock through the closing years of the infamous Penal laws, was known to have contacts at every level and in every situation, from the Court of St James to the local Seneschal's household. A network of Catholic servants, footmen, grooms and housemaids reported religiously to the bishop's agents on all manner of subjects, from the state of Henry Grattan's digestion to the peccadilloes of a leading peer. The bishop was one of the best-informed men in the country, and used his clandestine knowledge discreetly and to great effect. Moreover, he was a native of the parish of Kilbroney and had himself been educated in Paris, one of the thousands of young Irishmen who had fled their country to be educated there or at Salamanca, Antwerp or Rome. The revolution in France had the hierarchy in a quandary over the future of their continental nurseries, for by far the greatest percentage of Irish colleges lay in France, and the most celebrated of these was in Paris.

MacSorley, a nephew of the O'Neill of Clannaboy, one of the few surviving families of the old nobility which had remained loyal to Rome, was in accordance with his status properly received by the bishop. Captain Mercer, a man of influence, was greeted with the same courtesies, but declined to kiss the episcopal ring. The bishop listened to an outline of Mercer's plans for creating more commerce, and was impressed by the huge sums of money mentioned. He wished the captain every blessing on the success of his 'trading mission' but expressed grave reservations at the implied recognition of the authority of men who had imprisoned their king. Yet he stopped short of advising them not to take part in the mission. Accepting that his wishes would be, without doubt, disregarded, he pursued his own particular interest.

'I pray for the safety of our fellow-countrymen in the midst of such turmoil. I believe that so far God has saved our educational establishments from fire and sword.'

'As I understand it,' Mercer replied, 'there is nothing to be concerned about. The French, whatever their politics, are kind-ly disposed towards Irishmen. They'll leave your schools alone.'

'You may bring me back intelligence of this.' The bishop concluded the meeting.

As April drew to a close, Grace, escorted by Marcas Mac-Sorley, a deputation of merchants and two stout watchmen armed with pistols, departed on their mission to Paris. Thady did not go with them. He had no sooner stepped on the ship in Newry than he succumbed to seasickness and had had to be removed to the Neville's residence in High Street. Grace was unable to accompany him as an irate ship's captain was intent on sailing with the tide. She struggled to hold back tears as she watched the crestfallen figure on the dockside, lost among the small but enthusiastic crowd of cheering well-wishers.

The town band played a jaunty march as the ship was piloted down the narrow strait to Carlingford Lough. Through the lens of an eyeglass Grace watched the northern shore of the inlet slip by, places she knew so well but which, from the deck of Mercer's ship, looked tiny and vulnerable. The grey fort of Narrow Water still stood sentinel over this part of Iveagh, as if the MacAongus who built it had never departed. To the east was the growing town of Waring's Point, clustered around the small harbour dominated by the windmill. To the south lay the medieval town of Carling-ford, its castle almost hidden under a shroud of ivy. The eyes of the voyagers were drawn back to the northern shore and the whitewashed walls of Arno's Vale, its glass windows twinkling in the sun. Of Rostrevor village little could be seen, except for rising wisps of smoke among the woodland. Close to the shore, just on the edge of the oak forest, a sizeable plot of land had been cleared of trees to make way for what would soon be a huge edifice.

'What do you think of it?' she asked MacSorley. He was caught off guard by the question as he had been admiring, not the wooded shoulders of the Mournes, but the woman by his side.

'What are you referring to?' he asked.

'There, between the quay and the mountains. Dargan Butler's new home. You must have heard about it?' she said laughing. Grace had seen impressive mansions, but a house of such vast proportions in Rostrevor seemed to her too ludicrous. MacSorley was glad to see the coolness which surrounded Grace evaporate as a gust of salt wind from the Irish Sea sent her skirts billowing, and he felt his own spirits lift.

'Who knows,' he jested. 'We might be home in time for the inaugural ball.' He made an exaggerated bow, and for a moment their eyes met in understanding.

A little pilot boat, brown sails swelling, moved into position to guide the larger vessel down the deep channel and past the dangerous rocks and sandbanks at the bar. Within a short time, the Mournes were no more than a distant blur on the horizon.

The Blacksmith's Wedding

THE NEWRY GOODWIFE who had taken Thady O'Lochlainn in was most attentive and had a comfortable pallet made up in the kitchen for the old peasant, but Thady had only one aim in mind – to return home to Kilbroney as soon as possible. He had very little English and, without Grace by his side, felt alone and afraid, confined in a strange tall house in the midst of a noisy metropolis. When Tom Dunn borrowed Mercer's cart to bring him home the old man protested that he was well enough to walk, and that ten miles were nothing to a Kilbroney man, but his voice was weak and his pleas half-hearted. As the cart trundled out of Newry, Dunn was relieved to see that Thady had dozed off.

Eily's welcome was as warm as if he'd been away for twenty years, and she listened with tolerance to the story of his adventures, which would, she did not doubt, be well embroidered for the benefit of the Buller.

'I returned,' Thady explained to his curious neighbour, 'because I wished to be buried with my own folk, not with the fish.' The Buller understood the significance of such a desire, for a man was regarded as a stranger to the locality unless he had at least five generations before him buried in Kilbroney graveyard.

Johnny Fearon, after a winter of good nourishing food and the Widow's care, had ripened into a handsome young man. The only resources he had, unfortunately, were the muscles on his back and the brains in his head, of which, his aunt boasted, there were many. Yet Johnny himself was too glad to be free to worry overmuch about his future, and was content to spend his time renewing his acquaintance with his native soil.

Owen MacOwen undertook to reintroduce him to the finer rural pastimes, such as horseplay at the fair in Clonduff. They were a fine-looking pair, Johnny and Owen, and were it not for their lowly situations in life could have had their pick of the girls in the fairs. They were both in agreement that none compared with the comely Betsy Dunn, and this rivalry was a feature of their friendship.

Johnny Fearon enrolled himself as a pupil at Tom Dunn's hedge-school, trading a day's labour each week in payment. The mercantile expedition to Paris had fired his imagination; he was hungry to learn about the great and the wise, about princes and poets, but first he must learn to read. Johnny had picked up enough spoken English for everyday use in the gaolhouse, but he could neither read nor write. Owen, one of the least successful of all Dunn's scholars, tried his best to point out the folly of filling one's head with useless information, and offered himself as a model of one who scorned pen and paper. Such an example, however, made Johnny all the more determined to educate himself. Annie Dunn always had a sup of broth ready for the poorest of the scholars, believing that an empty stomach meant an empty mind, and Johnny never refused an invitation to Dunn's kitchen, which also provided an opportunity to admire Betsy at close quarters. He regretted the approach of the summer break, when the hedge-scholars were kept at home to help with the hay and crops, but he had high hopes of meeting Betsy again at the blacksmith's wedding.

The marriage of the blacksmith, Turlough MacCormac, was held on St John's eve, when Kilbroney celebrated mid-summer. Johnny and Owen joined the revellers at the forge. There was an eclectic attendance, for respectable farmers required the services of Master MacCormac as much as the ne'er-do-wells and paupers; and from the mountain, with a carefree disposition came the Dunns, Cobbler McChesney, the Widow Fearon, even the Buller and his ass. The O'Loch-lainns, however, had absented themselves, for Thady was still recovering from his abortive trip to France and was not of a mind to venture too far from home. Although keen to regale others with tales of his adventures, he swore that the next time he departed the Close would be feet first.

A bonfire of faggots and green wood sent sparks and acrid smoke into the summer air as the well-wishers gathered around. Especially welcome were a few strawmen in their traditional festive apparel of rags and rushes and bizarre masks; since no one knew their identity, it was assumed that they had come over from Hill Town for the drink. From their upstairs windows the village weavers' wives watched the outlandish antics of the new arrivals, suspicious of such heathen peasant ceremonies. They were the wives of skilled Scottish workers, attracted to County Down by good wages and employment prospects, and they kept themselves apart from the local women.

Johnny paid no attention to them; nor did he notice the

buxom bride and her stammering husband, nor the flirta-
tious glances he received from some of the young girls. His
interest was concentrated on a radiant Betsy. A chain of
daisies adorned her copper hair, and she laughed and talked
among her bevy of friends, appearing unconcerned by him
or the other young men. Owen, his hair still damp from an
involuntary dousing in the river, was unappreciative of
Betsy's floral adornment. 'You know, them dog daisies give
you a stuffed nose,' he informed his companion. But Johnny
had no fear of hayfever.

Giddyhead Magee the piper had died during the winter,
pipes in hand, at a wake in Clontafleece, and Turlough
MacCormac had been glad to acquire the services of Oran
O'Cassidy, the fiddler of the Clasha. The music began at a
steady measure, a few familiar planxties and hornpipes,
followed by some merry jigs. The tempo increased as drink-
emboldened dancers took the floor amidst rumours that the
weavers' wives had gone to alert the parish priest; but the
well-informed knew that Fr Mackey was not in residence, and
urged the fiddler to quicken his beat. Johnny, watching Betsy
dance, clutched at her arm as she stumbled in his direction,
and the fiddler struck up a reel. Round and round they spun,
Johnny's eyes aglow with every detail of Betsy's face, the pale
skin with its sprinkling of freckles, sparkling eyes and
upturned nose. He could not look away for he felt he would
lose his balance if he did, and he wondered if she felt the same
for him. The atmosphere around the bonfire was heady, but
the exhilaration of the dance came to an abrupt end among
shouts that the priest had arrived to chastise the sinful. Several
young couples dashed for the cover of the trees to continue
their revels in privacy, but Johnny was less decisive. Before he
could kiss his Betsy she had broken away to sit by the fiddler,
well chaperoned by two old crones, and was asking him to
play a sweet slow air.

As Johnny and Owen accompanied the Widow homewards the old woman prattled on about the merrymaking of her youth, which was, by her account, on a grander scale of debauchery than the trivial pursuits of the present age. Owen had been complimented by the attentions of three girls from Knockbarragh, and listened tolerantly to the Widow. Johnny said nothing, feeling the weight of rejection on his shoulders. He knew now for sure that Betsy Dunn had no interest in him, and wondered who it was that had put such a light in her eyes.

The Search for Sean O'Lochlainn

THE NEWRY DELEGATION found a city which at first sight did not appear to have changed much. The stench wafting from the Seine was much as MacSorley remembered it, and the clamour of the common folk going about their business was as strident as before. Their daily struggle to survive would continue, he reflected, in spite of the cataclysmic political changes.

They were not the only trade delegation to court the new government, but they were received almost immediately by a representative of General Robespierre. He graciously acknowledged their generous contribution to the city's coffers and presented a citation to the citizens of Newry on behalf of the citizens of France.

While negotiations continued on the supply of linen for military uniforms, MacSorley went to the north of the city to seek out some friends of his. He had offered to help Grace in her search for her brother but she had refused; he had been hurt by her sharp rebuff. He was disappointed to find that his old friends had moved home and, after a fruitless day's searching, he headed back to their lodgings. It occured to him that the city's apparent normality was superficial and that in reality many Parisians had been displaced during the turmoil of the revolution. He feared that Grace was doomed to even greater disappointment. She did not join the rest of the party for breakfast on the following morning and he excused himself from the table, fearing she was ill.

'You should let me help you. A woman on her own is not safe at such a time.' He stood in the doorway of Grace's bedchamber. Such familiarity arose from necessity, as their lodgings were small and cramped. Grace was bathing her face, which was pink and blistered from the city heat.

'I can manage on my own, thank you,' she said, reaching blindly for a towel. Seizing the opportunity, he lifted a cloth and dabbed her flushed cheeks. Her eyes were red and swollen, perhaps from the dust, but he guessed she had been weeping. Her body stiffened.

'I'll never find our Sean. No one can tell me where he has gone.'

'We'll find him, I promise you, we'll find him!' She looked into his eyes; words were cheap, she knew. Breaking away, she lifted a comb to dress her hair.

MacSorley stood back in the small room and studied his companion. Even in France she stood out among the women they had met, and the admiration of their hosts had aroused his jealousy. He longed to tell her how he felt, but so preoccupied was she with other matters that he dared not risk their friendship.

'Grace,' he began, and she turned around. 'Grace, wear your bonnet when you go out – it will protect you from the sun.'

She lifted a wide-brimmed straw hat and jammed it roughly on her head. 'Are you satisfied now?' she asked.

They made their way once more to the Rue du Cheval Vert, where the Irish College was situated. MacSorley had been a frequent visitor during his own student days, and spoke with the ancient concierge. Grace stood at some distance as the old man eyed her suspiciously. Eventually Marcas rejoined her.

'We must go in search of one James Coigley, a Louthman who shared Sean's lodging house. It seems he is still in the city. All the other seminarians have been evacuated to the country.'

'That man told me he had never heard of a Sean O'Lochlainn when I questioned him before,' Grace declared in annoyance.

'That, my dear, is his job. To protect his fledgling priests from voracious women.'

'How dare he? I told him Sean was my brother.'

'I'm sure he's heard that song before. It was only when I persuaded him that you were my new bride, keen to have Sean's blessing, that he relented.' He watched Grace's face contort in chagrin, but then she began to laugh.

'If I am so perilous, do you think they will allow me near James Coigley?' she said.

Young Coigley had remained behind after the upheavals to tend to the sick and wounded in one of the temporary hospitals which had been set up on the left bank of the Seine. His recollection of Sean was unmistakeable.

'A Downman; an argumentative type. Ah, he had a heart of gold.'

The priest's recollection of why Sean had left was vague, but he thought he had joined a missionary order, the Brothers of the Poor.

'And where can we find them?' asked MacSorley. Fr Coigley could not tell them.

'Nothing is as it used to be,' he shook his head sadly, 'so I'm unable to help you. May you find him safe and well.'

Further enquiries led them to the Abbey of St Joachim in a quiet avenue on the outskirts of the city. Alone among religious orders, the Brothers of the Poor had lived up to their name, and were consequently allowed to remain in their modest house, where there were no treasures worth taking. There, from an old blind abbot who knew or cared nothing of her appearance, Grace received a first-hand account of Sean's movements after he left the Irish College. But her delight was shortlived as the Abbé told her of her brother's mission to work among the poor in a distant colonial outpost.

'I fear, my daughter,' he continued sadly, 'that the ship on which he had been a passenger foundered on a reef near the island of Martinique, in the Caribbean Sea. For many weeks we waited and prayed for news, but, God help us, there were no survivors.'

'The bodies? Were they washed up?' asked MacSorley. Seeing Grace distressed he took her arm.

'There were some, I believe, but not that of our Irishman, the brave soul.'

Grace rose to her feet, her expression grave. There was silence in the room.

'I've come to the end of my journey then. Thank you, Father. You have been very kind to me,' she said.

'I'm sorry, child. Yet it is possible that a strong resourceful young man could have survived.'

'He might have been picked up by a passing ship,' MacSorley interrupted, 'or been washed ashore on some remote island. He may well be still alive,' the promise rushed from him, 'and if he is, I'll find him!' His words were brave, and Grace was glad of his strength as she wiped away her tears. He offered a straw of hope, and she chose to grasp it.

As they rode back to the city, MacSorley began to regret having lifted her expectations when, in reality, such hope was indeed frail. He himself had sailed the Caribbean in Mercer's ships, and knew only too well the dangers of shark-infested waters, pirate ships and warring natives, many of whom had good reason to hate the white man. He looked at her tenderly. She was clearly exhausted, yet fighting sleep. Now was not the time to tell her how much he cared for her; that would have to wait.

On the eve of their departure for Ireland, she thanked him for his friendship and his constancy. 'I'll never forget your kindness,' she said.

''Twas not kindness,' he replied gruffly, ''twas love.'

'Love?' She looked at him quizzically. 'Oh, Marcas, you know little of love. You are a very dear friend and you've lifted my heart during this difficult time, but please don't speak to me of love, for I've no love left in me.'

'You say I know little, and reject me so finally?' MacSorley's voice trembled. 'Look at me, Grace.' He grasped her shoulder, making her face him. 'I would never cause you pain. If that means I must leave you, then I will.'

'Marcas,' she stumbled over her words, angry at herself for misunderstanding his feelings. 'Forgive me, Marcas. I'm unworthy of you.'

MacSorley's temper softened and he relaxed his grip. 'I'll prove my love, Grace. I'll not return to Ireland until I do.'

A few weeks later, John Mercer saw the billowing sails of a ship on the bar at the entrance to the lough. He trained his eyeglass on the vessel and identified with satisfaction his personal ensign. Calling to Mistress Hanratty and Charlotte that he was riding to Newry post-haste, he pulled on his boots and hurried downstairs. Ignoring his daughter's demands that she accompany him, he set out, wondering if the mission to Paris had been successful and if his friends had returned safely. The lough was calm as a mirror and the little schooner, the swiftest in his fleet, made a pretty reflection in the water as it approached port.

A crowd gathered round as the passengers disembarked, one young member of the delegation sporting a French republican cockade in his hat, alongside a green one: the youths at the dockside gave him a hero's welcome. John Mercer cast his eyes around for the others. Grace O'Lochlainn came onto the gangway, her skin golden against her white collar.

'Mistress O'Lochlainn, the sea becomes you!' Mercier cried, arms extended in a warm welcome.

'Thank you,' she laughed, 'but dry land becomes me even more.'

'Where is MacSorley?' said Mercer jovially. 'Did he fall overboard, or did the mermaids spirit him away?'

'Dr MacSorley is not on the ship,' Grace answered. 'He has decided to stay in France. I think his services were needed at the hospital,' she finished vaguely.

'Just like MacSorley,' Captain Mercer threw his hands to heaven. 'He would have to get embroiled in something. Now, tell me, how were you received?'

Grace, however, would say little there on the quayside, but later, in the White Linen Hall, she answered the questions of the eager audience. The merchants of Newry listened agog to her first-hand account of the revolution and the impressions of her fellow delegates.

'And there was no shortage of Irishmen there; indeed, I

felt quite at home. Our Lord Edward Fitzgerald in particular has made a great contribution to the French cause.'

'But an aristocrat?' someone exclaimed, 'in Paris? Did he not fear for his life?'

'Citizen Fitzgerald? Not at all.'

To hear the son of a peer of the realm described as a common citizen surprised many.

'But will they trade with us?' asked one eminent merchant, who could not have cared if it was the devil himself he had to deal with.

'Yes, of course. They'll buy your linen – there's a whole new army to be fitted out. And they'll buy your glass...'

The Linen Hall assembly got down to business.

Some days later Grace went to visit Annie Dunn. She found her at a soapy tub before the fire, scrubbing a wriggling grandchild. Her son's wife, confined in the expectation of a new baby, had sent her troublesome two year old to his grandmother's home for a few days. Annie, who doted on all her grandchildren, was particularly fond of curly-haired Tom, whose angelic countenance belied an impish character.

'I see I have called at a bad time,' Grace apologised as she entered.

'Bad time? Why, I'm glad to have an extra pair of hands to hold him down.' Even as she spoke, little Tom scrambled out of the tub and sped towards the loft ladder.

'Oh no, my lad,' Grace intercepted the runaway. 'Back in the tub with you.'

A splash drenched her clothes as she struggled to put the slippery Tom into the tub. 'I never was half so wet crossing the ocean,' she laughed as Annie, exhausted by the effort, aimed a skite at the miscreant with her cloth. One final douse and he was on her knee, wrapped in a warm sheet.

'You wouldn't know him now if you'd seen the dirt of him an hour ago.' Within a short while, Tom was sleeping soundly, and Annie could at last question her friend about her exploits.

'The trade mission was highly successful,' Grace confirmed.

'Never mind the trade mission. I'm interested in how you got on with Dr MacSorley. Now, don't be giving me that look, Grace, I know you too well.'

'I'm just surprised that you ask me such a question,' Grace said cautiously.

'You mean he didn't speak with you about more personal matters? He's a more bashful man than I took him for. But he's right for you, Grace, right for you!'

'I need no advice, thank you.' Grace spoke sharply, then instantly regretted her answer. 'Forgive me, Annie, that was uncalled for.' She softened. 'Perhaps I do need advice.'

'You need somebody to listen to you, and here I am.'

'I got to know Marcas MacSorley during the voyage. He was very kind and the best of company.'

Annie beamed. The confines of an ocean-going ship were ideal for lovers. 'So you fell in love with him?'

'You of all people know, Annie, that I loved once – too deeply perhaps – and will never do so again. No one could ever take the place of Henry Valentine.'

'You deserve some happiness in life,' Annie remonstrated. 'Valentine brought you nothing but sorrow.'

'No, not just sorrow.' Here, by the cosy kitchen firelight, Grace could not convey the intensity of her feelings, the overwhelming love she had had for Henry. Love for her had never been cosy: it had been won in spite of everything – her class, her creed, her family. Not for her the comfort of children and grandchildren. Love had been a burning, intense pain which had left a scar on her heart. As she

110

looked into the fire, the wound still ached, but perhaps – just perhaps – less keenly than before.

Hutton

Newry, August 1792

THE PORT OF Newry was one of the busiest in Ireland, a teeming hive of activity, with a web of dark, dingy lanes spreading from the medieval town to the High Street. The sturdy old church of St Patrick stood on an outcrop of rock where the zealous saint once planted a copse of yew trees as a symbol of the town's submission to the new faith. There were few yew trees still surviving, though Christianity continued to thrive in its many forms.

'What was it Dean Swift said about this town: dirty streets, proud people? I'll hold you he wasn't far wrong. Dirty Lane is certainly well named,' Captain Mercer grumbled to his companion as they picked their way through a festering mass of refuse obstructing the route to Sugar Island. There, weatherbeaten ships from Jamaica and the Indies surrendered their cargoes of molasses to be distilled into rum. 'Island' was a misnomer, referring rather to a strip of land between the Clanrye River and the canal which carried the waters of

Carlingford Lough and the Irish Sea all the way inland to the River Bann and Lough Neagh. The first of its kind in the British Isles, the canal gave Newry a significant commercial advantage over its rivals. Merchants and manufacturers of linen, sugar, spirits, glass and many other commodities made Newry their base, reclaiming land along the canal and building fine townhouses and places of business as monuments to their growing prosperity.

John Mercer was in good spirits. He had made a complete recovery from his illness, a recovery which he attributed to the healing air of the Mournes and the lavish attention of Mistress Hanratty. Since the departure of Marcas MacSorley, almost two years ago now, Dr William Drennan had taken over his care, but had recently left Newry to move to a more lucrative city practice. Here, he claimed, he would make his fortune tending to the well-born rich, but it was more likely that the doctor's interest in the developing political situation had prompted his move. It was said that Drennan had become disillusioned by the Newry merchants, whose support of the French revolution was, he felt, inspired more by self-interest than political idealism.

Since the establishment of a republican government in France, the men of Newry had flexed their muscles in the face of the authorities, implying, too, that a revolt nearer to home might not only be possible but desirable. Republican hats were as common in Newry and Belfast as in Paris, and many men sported the new tricoloured cockade of red, white and blue.

John Mercer himself had profited considerably from his contact with the new government in Paris, and regularly sang the praises of France in the names of Liberty, Fraternity and Equality. His attitude had earned the opposition of the Newry Tories and the most influential landlords, including Savage Hall and Dargan Butler. Several notable churchmen also professed to being appalled by the secularism of the new order and their treatment of the French hierarchy. Bishop Lennon had condemned from the pulpit the recent seizure of church lands, and prayed that his beloved alma mater in the Rue du Cheval Vert would be spared.

Dunn and Mercer made their way along the wharves, leaving behind them the pungent odours of molasses and the potent rum which attracted the ne'er-do-wells and, in their wake, a number of abstentionist preachers. Ignoring the many calls to repent of their sins, the Kilbroney men passed the Butter Crane to where one of Mercer's smaller vessels was being loaded with casks of butter and linen bales, destined for the populous north-west of England. A sudden commotion was raised when two young stowaways were found among the provisions. On the intervention of Captain Mercer, the pair were saved a severe chastisement and dispatched with little more than a warning and a clip on the ear. Mercer laughed, remembering his own childhood dreams of running away to sea.

'I would say that the longing is there in every lad,' concurred Tom Dunn, 'but fortunately most of us grow out of it.'

'Some never do,' said Mercer. 'Take MacSorley, for example. I thought he would settle down, buy himself a farm somewhere and enjoy his old age. But where is he now? On a clipper heading for God knows where. That is the effect the sea has. Would you not agree that a man of his age should have had enough of it?'

Dunn refrained from comment. He sometimes wondered at what had passed between MacSorley and Grace while they were in France. The doctor's decision not to return had been unexpected, and Grace had been exceptionally discreet as to what had caused him to change his plans.

The shipbrokers and merchants of Newry faced many persistent and cunning enemies, not only on the high seas and oceans, but even on the busy shipping routes of their own Irish Sea. For many years the Isle of Man had been a favourite haunt of pirates and privateers, who found the linen ships of Newry a convenient prey. Accordingly, an understanding based on mutual self-interest had developed among the shipowners and merchants of the port. One such merchant had spotted Captain Mercer from his office window and scuttled down to intercept the pair. He held Mercer, with his views on the paramount importance of the safety of his crews, in the greatest respect, for he had seen too many grieving widows and destitute families and knew that the practices of some of the merchant seamen were cruel and greedy.

'Ahoy,' he called, 'Captain Mercer! Can you spare a moment?'

Mercer remembered him as one who had generously contributed towards the French campaign.

'I'm concerned,' the Newry man said, 'about a certain matter, and I thought you might advise me. It concerns an insurance policy which I bought from the Honourable Dargan Butler.'

Leaving the merchant with a few prudent words of advice, Captain Mercer and his companion crossed the river and made their way towards High Street and the old part of the town. Although many of the other old buildings, which had withstood the onslaught of Cromwell's armies more than a century before, were now displaying unmistakable signs of decay, the Pope's Head tavern into which they stepped was brightly lit and cheerful. Dunn ordered himself a hot rum while Mercer, having over-indulged on rich food the previous evening, requested a medicinal posset. "Twill purge your innards of all foul humours,' the landlord assured him. Heartened by the comradely aroma of tobacco, Dunn took a spark from the fire for his pipe, as a large passenger coach, the Cock o' the North, pulled up at the inn.

'This inn has a good reputation,' remarked Mercer, observing the awkward descent from the coach of a large matron, who spurned the assistance of one of the grooms.

'I have heard that this was once the best posting house in Ireland, but like many another establishment it rested on its laurels for too long. It has now some considerable opposition from the Hill Street inns. Not,' Dunn concluded, 'that there is anything the matter with this fine rum.'

The oak-beamed room was beginning to fill with weary passengers, and those who had travelled on outside seats moved to the hearth to ease the stiffness from their bones. The burly coachman was supervising the removal of baggage from his vehicle while a couple of grooms set about changing the horses. The matron was bewailing the state of her own baggage which, she maintained loudly, had been deliberately placed where it would bear the brunt of the weather during the journey from Belfast. The Seneschal, who, she declared, was married to her husband's cousin, would be sure to hear of this scurrilous deed.

'So will the rest of Newry,' muttered a stranger, settling into the seat beside Mercer. He introduced himself as Samuel Neilson from Belfast, then called over his travel companions, both Dubliners: John Keogh, a middle-aged merchant with a blunt edge to his speech, and a younger man with a more polished appearance, sharp eyes and an acquiline nose. His friends simply called him Hutton.

Tom Dunn casually appraised the newcomers. Neilson was the more talkative of the three, an amusing, lighthearted fellow, but as Mercer engaged them in conversation Dunn's mind was elsewhere. He wished that they could have assured the shipping merchant on the quays that he had placed himself in the hands of an honest broker. But, with a wife who could no longer control her own large fortune, he had no doubt that Dargan Butler was growing daily more greedy and ambitious.

'We have, I believe, a mutual acquaintance, Dr William Drennan,' Sam Neilson was saying. Dunn turned to ask how their old friend fared.

'Aha,' exclaimed Captain Mercer, 'a fine fellow, Drennan. I knew it would not be long before we heard from him.'

Hutton drained his tankard. 'You will not be surprised to learn that Drennan has been, eh, industrious since his arrival in Dublin.'

'We would expect no less of him,' Mercer smiled, 'and I look forward to the opportunity to hear some more of our friend's exploits.'

'This is Hutton's first visit to the area,' Sam Neilson remarked. 'He is recuperating from an illness, and is looking forward to a quiet convalescence in the mountain air.' Dunn took another look at the invalid. He was no medical authority, but as far as he could judge Hutton looked hale and hearty.

'I hope your recovery is as thorough as my friend's,' he indicated Mercer. 'He arrived three years ago and has not departed even yet, so well has he thrived.'

'I trust you would hope for a speedier recovery,' John Mercer opined.

'I certainly hope so,' replied Hutton. 'I have much work to do, and not much time to spare.'

A Newry lawyer, Patrick O'Hanlon, entered the inn just then. Neilson rose and excused the company.

'I hope we will meet again soon,' he said as they left with O'Hanlon.

Captain Mercer had faced the perils of both the oceans and hostile natives, but he would have preferred either to an encounter with a Newry schoolmistress. He had left this task until last.

'I'm afraid Charlotte is a most unsettling influence in the Academy,' Miss Stapleton spoke crisply.

'You mean she's got more in her head than the silly nonsense you teach to most lassies of her age.'

Miss Stapleton bristled visibly at this accusation. 'Captain Mercer,' she continued, 'I have heard Charlotte express opinions that no respectable young lady should ever hear, let alone voice!'

'What opinions, Charlotte?' His twelve year old stood in the corner, a disgusted expression on her face.

Miss Stapleton shook with rage. 'I am talking about politics! She is expressing opinions about politics!'

'Dear me, that is serious. Charlotte, please do not tell me that you are secretly a member of the Tory party?'

'Take her away, Captain Mercer, take her away from my school!'

'With the greatest of pleasure, Madam!'

Mercer's small open carriage awaited them down on the Mall, and an urchin was dispatched to pick up Charlotte's baggage from the school. But first John Mercer had another mission to fulfil, concerning John Hutton.

Hutton was pleased with his visit to Newry, feeling that here was fertile ground for the new movement, founded in Belfast the previous year and taking inspiration from the revolutionary fervour which had swept a corrupt French regime to its terrible doom. There was much sympathy for the French among the ordinary people of Ireland. Ever since the Treaty of Limerick, when the Wild Geese had fled to take up citizenship in France, relations between the two countries had been close and friendly, and France had for many generations been a haven for the persecuted. Since then, Irish eyes had often scanned the coast for the fleet which would bring deliverance, and even now Gallic ships slipped in and out of lonely Irish harbours with refugees of one sort or another: young men wishing to fight with the Irish Brigade of France; hopeful scholars, denied the opportunity to take their place at Trinity College because of their religion. Yet Ireland lacked a centralised movement. From Henry Grattan's Patriot party to the myriad secret societies which were synonymous with Irish rural life, there were so many different shades of opinion it seemed impossible that they could ever be united under a common banner. But on that hope the idealistic young man had pledged his future.

William Drennan had assured Hutton that they would be well received in Newry, and had supplied the names of O'Hanlon and other influential men who would be of assistance to them in their objective: to further the cause of the United Irishmen. Later that day a messenger presented himself at the inn with a message from Captain Mercer. He had arranged a dinner at Arno's Vale for the following week, and hoped that Master Hutton and his friends would do him the honour of attending.

The Maidservant

FANNY BUTLER LEFT her Newry bankers a most unhappy woman, with old Mr Fisher's words of warning ringing in her ears. Even though she realised by now that her marriage had been a dreadful mistake, still she could see no course other than to accede to Dargan's whim, although she knew in her heart she had just done something terribly foolish. She despised herself for her weakness; but still she loved him. Fanny had not thought it possible to love and hate with such intensity.

'If Grandfather Whitechurch were here, he would expect me to stand firm,' she muttered to herself. 'Perhaps, though, when the new house is completed, Dargan will feel more secure in his position. Maybe he will forget the other women.'

She had no one to stand by her, to advise or comfort her. Of late, Dargan had taken to taunting her cruelly with a familiar name: Grace. 'Grace O'Lochlainn,' she whispered. 'A woman I admired for her honesty and loyalty.'

A familiar sound disturbed her anguished thoughts. The fiddle music was sweet and plaintive, just as she had heard it in the woods. It was an old love song, the type that women might hum to themselves in the fields, but beautiful for all that. Fanny's appreciation of music was no less than that of any well-bred gentlewoman, but the primitive strains of the fiddler touched her as the concertos and canzonets of the German and Italian masters had never done. Here, in the busy town of Newry, it sounded both haunting and alien; a simple tune, with no sign of the player.

Intrigued that she might at last know the identity of the mysterious fiddler she made haste towards the source of the music. Turning expectantly into Hill Street she saw before her the usual begging urchins, an old street vendor and two robed clerics, but of the fiddler there was no sign.

Madam Hall, accompanied by a heavily burdened maid-servant, proceeded grandly down Hill Street towards Margaret Square, the attractive new centre of Newry. The main purpose of her visit was to call on the milliners, where fashionable bonnets could be made up at a fraction of the cost of their Dublin originals. She carried with her a copy of the latest London fashion gazette which revealed, with unquestionable authority, what the modish French exiles were wearing about town. Stopping to examine a pretty ribbon in a haberdashery window, she recognised a familiar figure whose peculiar behaviour was revealed in the shop's ample looking-glass.

'Fanny!' she called loudly, 'what on earth are you doing in there?'

A red-faced Fanny Butler straightened herself. Her efforts to avoid Bess Hall had been in vain. 'My bootlace,' she began lamely.

'And whatever have you done to your hair – and to your face?' She was astounded to see Fanny's fresh country complexion grotesquely painted and powdered like that of a back-street Newry whore. Her criticism ceased when she saw Fanny's palpable misery. The two stood in silence for some moments.

'We must have a talk,' Madam Hall said firmly, bustling her friend down the street. A little of Fanny's old spirit returned.

'I'm sorry,' she replied, not wishing to reveal her vulnerability, 'I have some important matters to attend to.' At that point, the threatening sky above opened in a downpour which emptied Margaret Square in seconds, and sent the ladies scurrying for the shelter of the nearest tea-room. The proprietress settled the breathless ladies in their place and instructed Madam Hall's unfortunate maid to wait outside and not to let the hatboxes get wet.

'Isn't it damp?' Fanny began with some understatement, but Bess was not to be deflected. She ordered hot tea and cakes, then turned to her friend.

'Now, my dear, what is this all about?'

Fanny heaved a sigh laden with resignation and defeat. 'I have been to see my banker.'

'Oh, Fanny,' Madam Hall's face lit up. 'I'm so pleased to hear that.'

'Really?' replied Fanny, 'I thought you considered such matters better placed in the hands of a man.'

'For the most part, yes. But in your case...'

'In my case?'

'Oh really!' The arrival of the waitress gave Bess time to get her thoughts in order.

'Isn't this nice? Sweet tea will do us the world of good. And you know, my dear Fanny, Savage and I always admired your pluck. Oh, you clumsy girl!'

A dollop of frangipane had settled on Madam Hall's cherry red overskirt. The trembling maid received a slap on the ear from her mistress, but her hasty attempts to remove the offending morsel only succeeded in making the stain worse. Furious at this embarrassment, the tea-room hostess dismissed her on the spot.

Fanny, forgetting her own troubles, was drawn to the unfortunate serving lass. She looked so forlorn, deep-set eyes peering from a fragile white face. Fanny hoped for a moment that the dismissal was simply an attempt to soothe the ruffles of Madam Hall, but the girl's despairing look told her otherwise. She decided to intervene.

Madam Hall smiled to see the sparkle return to her friend's eyes as she sprang to the girl's defence, calling into question the freshness of the frangipane and apportioning the blame to those who had prepared it. This was the Fanny Valentine of old! As they left the premises, Fanny had acquired a new servant, the tea-room was temporarily short of a maid, and Madam Hall was no wiser about the reason for her friend's visit to the bank.

'From where do you come, girl?'

'Lisnacree.'

'Lisnacree, Ma'am!' Fanny accepted bad manners from her equals, but not from servants.

'Your pardon, Ma'am, I wasn't thinking.'

Fanny wondered if she would regret having taken on such an uncouth country girl. No doubt the housekeeper would be able to find her some work in the scullery. She saw the girl was trembling.

'Are you cold?'

'No, Ma'am.'

'Have you a family?' The thought flashed across Fanny's mind that she might have allowed an unwed mother into her carriage, in which case she would have to get out immediately.

'I have a mother and sisters, Ma'am.'

'Are you not curious as to where we are travelling?'

'No, Ma'am. I'm just grateful to be getting away from Newry with my virtue still intact.'

Fanny smiled wryly. 'And do you think you'll be any safer in Kilbroney?' She watched in amusement as alarm spread across the maid's face. 'Oh, for heavens sake, girl, I was but jesting. What is your name, anyway?'

'Roisha, Ma'am. Roisha Fegan.'

'Fegan? Then you'll be quite at home in Kilbroney. I understand Fegan is a common peasant name.'

As the coach came to a halt outside Kilbroney House, Roisha gazed in awe. She remembered hiding among the trees as a child, watching elegantly attired folk come and go. She was already regretting having given her name to her new mistress; she had not intended to, but now the harm was done. In time, some people would realise that she was the daughter of mad Murtagh Fegan, and then there would be trouble. She swallowed hard as a groom tended to the carriage.

'Make yourself useful, lass,' called the groom, handing out Madam's fur-lined travel rug and foot bricks. He spoke in a friendly fashion and Roisha smiled timidly. Then her eyes were drawn to a handsome figure who had appeared on the steps of the house. He seemed to wish to talk urgently to the mistress, and had seized her arm in an awkward fashion. He seemed too young to be her husband and too old to be her son.

'Not here, Dargan, not now. The transaction was not as straightforward as you imagined,' the lady said.

Roisha stared, unaware that one in her lowly position was

124

not expected to witness such scenes. The man's face bore a furious expression.

'Who are they?' she asked the groom. He looked at her as if she were a fool.

'You'd best go round to the kitchen door and tell them Madam Butler hired you. Bella Morgan won't like it, but she'll have to put up with you.'

As she knocked on the back door, Roisha felt another wave of apprehension. What if Bella Morgan remembered her, and told everyone her father was a murderer in a lunatic asylum? Where would she be then?

'Liberty Boy'

JOHNNY FEARON WAS, older sages said, the spit of his grand-father Sean Fearon, save for his good teeth and black hair, which were a legacy from his mother's side. Johnny had laid out the shape of a small stone cabin for himself, much against the Widow's advice.

'A stone cot? And a chimney? Sure it would be grand, son, but you'll never meet the rent they'll be looking for. Make do with less until you're back on your feet,' she scolded. The Widow several times had faced eviction herself, and knew that any attempt to make a home more comfortable would only mean an increase in rent. Eventually, a visit from the agent to assess the potential of the new cabin persuaded Johnny to postpone his building plans. Crampsey, being of straightforward nature, lost no time about telling Johnny that he expected some personal reward for taking the trouble to set foot in such a God-forsaken hole, and Johnny, being no less blunt, suggested that feet of such dimensions as the agent's were more than a bishop could afford.

Instead of pursuing his building plans, he took pride in transforming the Widow's little patch from barren scrub to a verdant garden. This he did by hauling creels of shore weed over the mountains from the lough to Levallyclanowen. He had a strong back, another Fearon trait, and did not grumble at the weight of his burdens, thinking always ahead with dreams of the earth reborn and crops with a fighting chance of survival. As he waited for the land to bear forth, something even hard work could not hurry, he laboured for anyone who could pay him a few shillings. Tom Dunn's son, James, helped him get seasonal work at the mill, while Turlough MacCormac at the forge liked a man who was prepared to shoulder more than half his own weight. Then in August Tom Dunn asked Johnny to accompany three gentlemen, strangers from he knew not where, as they toured the south Down area. He told the lad that their mission was clandestine, but peaceful. Johnny's eyes grew wary.

'Secret, Master Dunn? I don't aim to find myself back in prison through association with a crowd of smugglers or swindlers. An honest man has nothing to be secretive about.'

Tom Dunn smiled at Johnny's lack of guile. 'Secrecy in this case is because they support a certain political cause. They don't wish to offend by antagonising their opponents.'

'And what are they, Whigs or Tories? For I've little time for either.' Master Dunn reassured Johnny that they were neither politicians nor ruffians, and asked him to make sure they did not stray where their purses would be lightened.

While Johnny's diligence earned him the admiration and respect of all his friends, there was undoubtedly some jealousy between him and Owen MacOwen, for Owen had always regarded the Widow as the nearest he had to living kin. The boys had come to blows, too, over young Betsy

Dunn, to the amusement of her father and to the distress of Annie who, on discovering them fighting in her yard, had quenched their ardour with a pail of slop water. Betsy was the object of a severe dressing down by the fireside that night, her mother warning her against behaviour which would set two such decent young men at each other's throats.

Mercurial as young men's friendships usually are, Owen's interest in Betsy soon declined, and Johnny eased the tension further by arriving at Leckan one evening with a load of wrack for MacOwen's plot. It was then that Owen confided to his friend his concern for the lovely maidservant at Kilbroney House.

The Reverend Bonaventure Whinehan rode up the valley with a sense of purpose. Fr Mackey, the parish priest, confined to bed with an unseasonal dose of coughing fever, had delegated to his subordinate full responsibility for the parish of Kilbroney until he was back on his feet again. Fr Whinehan, a man of inferior intellect but unrivalled arrogance, and blissfully unaware of his own shortcomings, thus became the temporary custodian of the ancient parish. That he was not a parish priest by now he put down to some inexplicable jealousy on the part of the Bishop of Dromore, who failed to recognise ability, piety and humility, qualities which the curate felt he possessed in abundance. Whinehan, however, never allowed his disgruntled feelings to show, always displaying a suitably obsequious manner before the episcopal chair.

The Feast of the Assumption had passed and the fields were full of toiling harvesters sweating under the summer sun. Young women worked alongside their menfolk, often, Whinehan grimly observed, with calves, arms and worse indecently exposed. There was, in his opinion, no greater sin than fleshly desire in its many forms, all of which he had dutifully and diligently researched in the confessional. He encouraged the more pious members of his flock to keep him informed of any misbehaviour which could lead to immorality. He believed that the common denominator in all cardinal sin was woman, and the archpriestess in his very own parish was undoubtedly the incubus of Upper Kilbroney, Grace O'Lochlainn. He had in his pocket a scribbled letter, anonymously delivered, but obviously penned by a well-intentioned person concerned that this woman was raising a child without the approval of the church, a claim which he was determined to investigate.

'I have been reliably informed that this child in your care has not been baptised into the church.' Fr Whinehan looked coldly from Thady to the little boy holding on to Grace's skirt.

'To be truthful, your Reverence, 'tis something I took for granted,' explained Thady, his tone hesitant and timorous before such authority.

'It should have been your first consideration,' the curate reproved him. Grace was unimpressed by his rudeness.

'In that case, we'll have him baptised now. Kneel down there, Michael, and I'll fill the pot with water. Do you need anything else?' She rolled up her sleeves purposefully.

'I fear that the sacraments are no trifling matter.' He gazed sternly at Grace. 'This child was reared in the blind darkness of paganism. He is unworthy of baptism, and is, I fear, a corrupting influence on the children you teach.'

'What are you talking about? How could a little boy corrupt anybody?'

'His soul has not yet been purged of original sin. Surely that is obvious? He must undergo a course of instruction.'

'I'm sure we can do that at home,' said Grace.

'No. You must take him to the cripple asylum in Newry.'

Eily looked uncomprehendingly from one to the other. '*Cad tá á rá aige?*' she asked, having no understanding of English. Grace began to translate, but the priest interrupted her sharply.

'We will converse in a civilised language or not at all,' he declared loftily, turning his back on the old woman.

'I understand your wishes,' Grace smiled sweetly, lapsing effortlessly into Greek, the core of Master Dunn's hedge-school curriculum.

Fr Whinehan's bald head turned rosy as he struggled with the archaic grammar; if there was one thing which horrified him more than an immoral woman, it was an educated one.

'There's no doubt about it,' Thady declared as the priest stormed off, dressing down his coat as he went, 'there goes a living saint; a man of God.'

'Saint?' cried Grace, unable to believe what her father was saying. 'Saint? How could you say such a thing?'

'You mark my words,' replied Thady, spitting into a pot, 'nobody could be that bad tempered unless he's wearing a hair shirt and cinders in his drawers. I tell you, girl, the man's a saint.'

That evening Grace looked apprehensively at Michael's tousled curls as he slept peacefully on his pallet, oblivious of the controversy stirring around him. She blessed herself, trying to ward off her vengeful feelings towards a priest of the church. Yet she knew that there was cause for worry, and it crossed her mind that someone must have pointed the curate in her direction. She dutifully began to instruct Michael from old Dean Pulleine's catechism, trying all the time to evade the intelligent child's questioning of some of the Church's most basic doctrine. In the end she told him that he had to learn to

130

recite the answers by heart or the bald-headed priest would try to take him away. She tried to make the subject more interesting for him by fashioning little charcoal drawings of scriptural scenes. She drew a Nativity scene, and was surprised when Michael added his own star over the manger.

'How did you know about the star?' she asked him, but the child just shrugged his shoulders.

In the following few weeks Grace noticed a decline in the number of pupils attending her class. It seemed Fr Whinehan was determined to make her pay for her opinions. Grace, proud of her independance, was reluctant to involve Dunn in her confrontation with the clergy, yet there were times when she tired of such conflict.

One evening after supping with her family, Grace left Michael asleep by the hearthside. 'I'll slip off home now,' she told Thady, 'and leave you in peace.' The old man answered with a grunt, and a mumbled instruction to keep to the track. Grace carried a small lantern she did not really need, for the moon was bright and the distance between their homes short; Michael wandered freely between her house and the Close, and regarded both dwellings as his home. She heard the approach of footsteps and then a shout, 'Grand evening, Mistress O'Lochlainn.' The Cobbler drew close, eyes glinting in his bearded face. A stick was flung over his back from which dangled a bag.

'Were you fishing?' she asked, for poachers enjoyed a moonlit night.

'Nay. Coneys,' he explained. 'Murren makes a good stew. Would you take one if I offered it?'

'Thank· you, no, I've had my supper,' Grace replied politely, reluctant to take the bite out of a poor man's mouth.

'At your age, Mistress, you should be settling down, for there's plenty I know of would offer you a roof over your head.'

As Grace let herself into her cabin, she laughed at what had amounted to a Kilbroney proposal of marriage. She had had many such overtures, all offered in the same oblique manner, as if on behalf of someone else. Marcas had not spoken in such a way. He had bluntly laid his feelings before her. More than that, he had proven his love by going away, and she wondered if she would ever see him again.

Hutton, Keogh and Neilson had spent a busy week, visiting the villages in the rural surrounds of Newry with their guide, Johnny Fearon. They learned at first hand of the many primitive political groups which had sprung up among the common people, especially the Defenders and their Protestant counterparts, the Peep o' Day Boys. Agrarian secret societies had long been a feature of country life. Most had been formed as pathetic instruments of revenge against the landlord classes, but these new organisations were very different. The customary oaths of brotherhood and secrecy now had new formulae, expressing vague political objectives. Crude as they were, they had this much in common with those of the French revolution: their goal was the emancipation of the common man.

The recent bloody clashes between the Peep o' Day Boys of Rathfriland and the local Defenders posed a particular challenge for Keogh and Hutton. Although both sides had suffered fatalities, it seemed evident that the Peep o' Day Boys had undoubtedly been the aggressors. Neilson suggested they adopt a balanced view so as to encourage dialogue, but Hutton would have none of it.

'From what I can see, the Defenders seem not to do anything worse than meet in large bodies and fire powder. Foolish, certainly, but not wicked.'

He was determined to make Rathfriland the central point of his itinerary, and assured the dubious Neilson that he would talk some sense into the men there. In no time at all, he insisted, the disparate groups would all be struggling together, with one common aim. Johnny Fearon listened to the conversation but said nothing. He wished them luck and blessed their innocence.

In spite of his misgivings, Johnny enjoyed listening to the man, and although he now knew his real name, it meant nothing to him. He shook his head when the Dublin man talked about politics. 'Don't tell me, Fearon,' Hutton had said to him, ''tis because you've no interest. You've more brains in your belly than the entire Tory party.'

During their excursion through County Down the strangers found most of the villages of lower Iveagh to be hospitable places, although they were glad to have a local man to translate where necessary. The Downmen had a turn of phrase all of their own; often when they said 'Nay!' they meant the opposite, but were just wary of appearing enthusiastic. They found that the name of Tom Dunn opened doors in the most remote mountain glens where folk had never heard of a war with France. Now they were coming to the town of Rathfriland, the ancient bastion of the MacAongus chieftans, now populated by some of the most hardened religious fundamentalists in the land. The inhabitants of the hilltop citadel looked over the valley of the young Bann river, and beyond it to the wild Mournes with their menacing population of dispossessed natives, seething to regain their ancient capital at the first opportunity. As Johnny led his companions into the town he turned to look back at the mountains.

'What they fear the most,' he explained, 'is what they can't see.' He had once shared his cell with a Rathfriland lad, and had tried to look at the mountains through his eyes. It was not hard to imagine the glint of steel amidst the bare rocks, or the glow of war torches in the dark nights. He could understand why the men of Rathfriland took no chances in the hostile and dangerous surroundings in which they found themselves, and why they had armed themselves to the teeth. Yet in spite of Johnny's warning, Hutton believed that Rathfriland need only listen to him speak and read his charter, and the settlers would realise that their natural allies were the Catholic peasants of south Down. Now as they completed the long uphill climb into the village, perspiring under the hot August sun, they observed a band of some one hundred and fifty 'Boys' drilling in a field of stubble.

'We will quench our thirst before we visit the rector,' Hutton decided, leading his mount in the direction of the village inn. The handsome market square, whose inn and houses had been built from the stones of the old castle, basked in the summer sun. Cooling draughts of porter were ordered and Hutton summoned the landlord to secure a night's accommodation.

'You're more than welcome,' the proprietor said with enthusiasm, while commenting on the uncommonly heavy weather for August. ''Twill take a good clap of thunder to clear the air,' he added, as though imparting some treasured secret.

'We noticed,' Hutton observed casually, 'some activity below the town. No portent of unhappy events, I hope?'

'In Rathfriland? Rest assured brethren,' the landlord continued in the same conspiratorial manner, 'that there is no better defended town in Ireland. And we need not depend on any constabulary or the militia to come from Newry.'

'But surely you are some distance from the coast and any enemy would have to traverse the mountains? What more defence do you need?' enquired Keogh guilelessly, lowering his draught. The landlord's bushy eyebrows twitched as he made to refill the tankards.

'The enemy, good brethren,' he muttered darkly, 'is from within.'

The visitors exchanged glances, for all knew who the 'enemy' was. The Rathfriland man's suspicions were aroused.

'Did ye come from far? I can usually tell by a man's speech from whither he hails.'

Johnny Fearon sensed danger immediately, but Keogh's tongue had been loosened by the excellent porter.

'Keogh is my name, a silk merchant of Dublin. John Keogh. And this...' He got no further, for the landlord's eyes had already begun to narrow.

'John Keogh, you tell me. John Keogh, of the infamous Catholic Committee? Out ye get the shower of ye, for I'll be damned if ye're welcome here, ye scoundrels!'

'Maybe if we'd had the opportunity to explain,' Hutton began as the party headed back down the hill, seen on their way by a jeering mob of townsmen.

'Explain what?' snapped Keogh.

The landlord had been right about one thing at least, for the heavens above them opened to announce a ferocious thunderstorm.

Dinner at Arno's Vale

MISTRESS HANRATTY COULD always rise to the occasion, no matter how exacting, but this time Captain Mercer was making quite outrageous demands.

'"Twenty for dinner," says he. "I know that 'twill be a squeeze in the dining room." "Squeeze?" says I...'

Nan the Spoon sat listening to the housekeeper's rambling, wondering what she was making such a fuss about. Her own family of fifteen resided comfortably in a cabin half the size of the Arno's Vale dining room.

John Mercer, no stranger to his own kitchen, interrupted the tirade. 'My dear Mistress Hanratty, you must forgive my lack of sensitivity. It is too much of a burden for your frail shoulders.'

His housekeeper, who had no intention of being cheated of her moment of glory, reassured him that she had overseen considerably grander affairs while in the employ of his predecessor, Colonel Ross. Her only concern was the comfort of the guests, for twenty would prove to be quite a crowd.

'Twenty, did I say?' he replied uneasily, as if calculating to himself. 'I really meant to say thirty – but only two or three will be staying the night. Two sittings. That should do it. We can run a few card tables in the parlour.'

'Could I not wait at the table, or stay with you while you receive your guests?'

'Once again and for the last time: no, Charlotte, no.'

'Please, Papa, please?'

'What am I to do with you?' said Captain Mercer in mock exasperation. 'Shall I send you to some French convent, where they will teach you to flutter a fan and curtsey and say your prayers?'

Charlotte looked horrified. She leapt from her seat at the breakfast table and darted to her father's side, chattering as she went. 'I already know my prayers, you can test me in any one of them! What is the use of saying them in French? And anyway what...'

'All right, you little vixen,' Mercer laughed, stopping her in full flow, 'you know I have no such intention. Not,' he was stern again, 'if you can prove to me that you can behave yourself here. I will find you another school, but you will have to be careful not to scandalise your next teacher. Keep your political opinions to yourself, and that way you will keep your head on your shoulders for longer.'

'But you are quite outspoken yourself, Papa,' said Charlotte.

'That is quite different. Now pass me the toast, if you please,' Mercer said, ending the argument.

Arno's Vale was as industrious as one of Mooney's beehives in preparation for Captain Mercer's dinner. It was an affair for

137

gentlemen only, he explained to a disappointed Charlotte, who had been looking forward to a glamorous display of evening attire. Most of her father's friends were dark-coated Dissenters and Quakers and the only fine plumage likely to be on display would be from Narcissus Batt, albeit in the over-decorative mode of the pre-revolution days.

Mistress Hanratty's main concern was the deployment of the extra staff engaged for the occasion, and although the kitchen was not quite her domain, Captain Mercer having hired a chef, she kept a dutiful eye out for any signs of indolence. There were rugs to be beaten, mattresses to be aired and any amount of white linen to be laundered for the Captain's house-guests. Game birds from the Batt plantation arrived by the score, along with freshly churned butter from Hill Town and sides of well-hung beef from the O'Neill herd.

'Good plain fare, and plenty of it, is what we require,' Mercer told his chef, dismissing his recipe for calves' hearts stuffed with minced lobster. 'Boiled ox tongues,' he requested, 'with plenty of strong mustard sauce.'

John Mercer studiously surveyed his guest list for the umpteenth time, for this was no ordinary social occasion. He had given the matter a great deal of thought since Drennan had sent a message from Dublin informing him of Hutton's visit, and advising him to handle the occasion with the utmost discretion. The member of parliament for Newry, Mr Isaac Corry, was in Dublin and unavailable, and it was just as well, thought Mercer, for the man was highly persuasive and as likely to oppose his principal guest as to support him. There were many Newry merchants and eminent gentlemen, including John Gordon of Templegowan; Andreas Boyd, who would take up as much room at the table as two men, but was an amusing fellow nonetheless; the Neville brothers, George and John; the Lowans, the Cochranes and others. His former physician's uncle, John O'Neill, head of the Clannaboy branch of the ancient clan, was the most senior of his guests. The old man had entertained him at his home, Bannvale House in Clonduff, during the previous week, in the open-handed style of the old nobility. There had been many a merry song and sad recitation that night, and Mercer himself had been coaxed into retelling some of his traveller's tales. O'Neill had toasted his absent nephew, Marcas MacSorley, wishing him a speedy and safe return to his native shore.

Mercer was well pleased with his guest list, including, as it did, men of differing political opinions, but all influential in their own spheres. He wondered how they would respond to Samuel Neilson of Belfast, and his companions from Dublin.

Charlotte was delighted to learn that she was to stay the night at Dunn's Hill: Betsy Dunn, although five years her senior, was an entertaining companion. Betsy had been soundly warned by her mother not to lead young Miss Mercer, a well-brought-up young lady, into any mischief. Mistress Hanratty delivered a similar warning to her charge as she set off late in the afternoon for Dunn's Hill.

Master Dunn, immaculately garbed in his best linen, was ready to depart for Arno's Vale as she arrived. The assembled females agreed that he looked very fine indeed with his remaining crop of grey hair combed neatly back and caught with a silk tie.

'Expect me home by daybreak,' he told his wife as he set off down the hill.

'Watch out for footpads,' called Anne, 'for if they see you looking so prosperous, they'll take it you have a full purse!' She pondered the figure of her husband for some moments. Despite his many assurances of love over the years, she could never, even to this day, understand why he had chosen her from among the many women who had found him attractive. She had been a good wife, mother and grandmother through the years and had done her best always to be by his side. Their two surviving sons were quiet, hardworking lads who took after their mother. James, the eldest, was a steady, good-natured fellow, married now and working as a clerk at Martin's Mill. The younger son, Harry, the scholar of the family, was a professor in a Belfast academic institution. Only Betsy was permanently at home, and she, of all of them, was most like her father. As she watched his horse disappear into the trees, Annie wondered again at her good fortune in being the wife of Tom Dunn. Then she returned to the house and called her family to supper.

Charlotte Mercer had not come to Dunn's Hill for a good night's sleep. Sitting up in bed as the moonlight streamed through the window, she nudged her bedmate.

'Tell me about your young man,' she whispered.

'Go to sleep, Charlotte. I have no such thing,' Betsy hissed, turning her back on her visitor.

'What? No young man? I will have many when I am your age.'

Betsy stretched over to retrieve her portion of the bedclothes.

'Ah, no,' Charlotte insisted. 'You must tell me. I cannot sleep. Not a wink, until you tell me.'

Betsy relented, not needing much persuasion.

'I have no young man,' she said coyly, 'but I have a faithful admirer. His name is Johnny.'

'Is he handsome? Will you marry him?'

'No, of course not. I love another,' Betsy said firmly.

Charlotte was thrilled to hear this. 'You love another? Who is he? Does he love you?'

'No, I'm afraid not.' Betsy's voice was wistful. 'He knows nothing about me. He is a fiddler and he lives on the Clasha, in a forest glade. He is beautiful and sad. I often go to the forest to listen to him play to his lost love, and imagine he is playing to me.' Betsy talked about the fiddler, Oran O'Cassidy, until the first dim ray of Sunday's dawn crept through the window. By then Charlotte was fast asleep.

'So your message fell on deaf ears in Rathfriland?' John Mercer sympathised. 'Don't be downhearted. If the Archangel Michael himself were to walk into that miserable town, someone would be sure to accuse him of having strayed from the path of righteousness.'

'We cannot expect to win every battle,' Hutton agreed.

'I trust we will be better received tonight,' Keogh remarked. Rostrevor, he felt, was as somnolent a village as any in Ireland, with its little clump of comfortable residences cluttered around a strong garrison. He had already become acquainted with Dargan Butler, whose name was associated with the most reactionary and anti-libertarian forces in the county. Yet experience had taught him that for every force there is a counter force, and he suspected the poor land surrounding the fat, cosy environs of the village was home to many folk who needed only to realise their strength.

Introductions were made as the guests began to arrive at Arno's Vale. There had been much curiosity as to the purpose of Mercer's summons, but as the reputation of his table was beyond criticism, few had refused the invitation. They were not to be disappointed: the chef had excelled himself. After Dr Moody, a Dissenting minister, said grace, the meal commenced. Within a few hours every appetite was satiated, and the guests sat back in a receptive mood. Captain Mercer rose to his feet and introduced Samuel Neilson and John Keogh, the leader of the Catholic Committee, whose aim was to achieve equal voting rights for the peasant population. A lively spate of whispering greeted this announcement, not all of it in agreement.

'Gentlemen,' continued Mercer. 'My next friend has come to this district with one aim in mind: to unite all those of us who believe in, and hope for, a better future for our land and an end to the trials and terrors of the past.' Glances were exchanged around the table. So many different interests were represented it was hard to conceive of a common cause: here was the Quaker shipowner, the Presbyterian banker, the Papist schoolmaster and the Protestant landlord.

Hutton rose to his feet, his voice vigorous and compelling.

'Gentlemen,' he began, 'I have something in common with each one of you here. I am the descendant of one of Oliver Cromwell's soldiers. My maternal grandfather was a sea captain, like my friend Mercer, in the East India trade; my father, a loyal adherent to the established faith, farmed the land in County Kildare. As for myself, I was called to the bar three years ago, having obtained my degree from Trinity College.' Murmurs of approval greeted this. 'I have, for reasons which I hope you will appreciate, been travelling under an assumed name. I am Theobald Wolfe Tone, and I am at your service.'

Tone's audience listened attentively as the young man continued. He spoke confidently, his eyes alighting on his listeners, eager to win them but careful not to antagonise. Yet he left them in no doubt that he, at least, believed passionately in the righteousness of his cause, and would not be deflected from his purpose. That was to establish the Brotherhood of United Irishmen in south Down.

The usual attendance at the Mass House was much augmented on this fourth Sunday of August. It included some of the travellers who had come to take the waters on the Feast of the Assumption, and those servants of visiting gentlefolk who were permitted to attend Sunday Mass. Mercer, a good host, had insisted on accompanying John

Keogh while Theobald Wolfe Tone attended simply out of curiosity. Neilson, the son of a Presbyterian minister, was directed towards the tiny meeting house at Drumreagh.

Tone felt heartened by the warm reception he had received at the previous night's dinner. He was glad he had spoken in restrained terms, for there had been those present who were not convinced of the benefits of having all men, irrespective of faith, possess the right to vote. They were most concerned by the sheer numerical strength of the peasant population and several had expressed reservations about placing power in the hands of a largely uneducated and uncultured body of people. Some, too, had been wary of furthering the cause of those who were loyal to the Pope of Rome before their king or country. But there was general agreement round Captain Mercer's table that something would have to be done, and soon.

Tone was not a religious man and as he walked into the Mass House hoped that the service would not be overly tedious. In his experience the Latin intoned in these rural parishes was usually incomprehensible. However, he was glad of the opportunity to meet the ordinary peasants, especially the old black-shawled women and the men who still retained memories of Mass rocks and Penal oppression. Some of them, he was sure, had made the most remarkable sacrifices to attend, perhaps walking many miles from early in the morning. He wished, not for the first time, that they would exert the same energies in a more fruitful direction, and depend less on their priests for guidance.

The alert eyes of Fr Whinehan had not failed to notice the three well-dressed gentlemen in the company of Tom Dunn. Such an opportunity was not to be wasted, so, abandoning the sermon he had prepared on the subject of lust and the recent lewd behaviour at the bleaching green, he cleared his throat and adopted a practised, pleading tone. The church needed more money, it seemed, and just as Christ had lived in poverty his flock must do likewise. Someone at the back of the church coughed loudly. Whinehan's monotonous voice droned on as the chapel grew more stuffy and smelly. Within a short while Tone had joined the ranks of those dozing off to sleep.

'I never heard anything so dull in my life,' he told an amused Tom Dunn after the ceremony. 'Do you have to listen to that every Sunday? If so, faith, I would not begrudge you your place in heaven.'

'If you think it is bad now, you should hear some of the Lenten dirges and chants. I would swear that they add an extra dozen saints to the litany from one year to the next!'

Dunn was anxious for Tone to visit his school before he left Kilbroney. His students, he hoped, would take inspiration from the great man and be among the first to make the open affirmation to the society. The gathering at the barn included Johnny Fearon, Owen MacOwen and young Hugh John MacVeigh. All well-motivated young men, he told Tone. Cobbler McChesney also attended, and, more welcome still, MacCormac the blacksmith. Thady and the Buller, their fighting spirit undimmed by old age, had come along to view the proceedings.

The first man to take the oath was vouched for by the Cobbler. Tone called the candidate forward, and was satisfied from his answers that he was well versed in the new creed.

'I, Oran O'Cassidy,' the fiddler began, thus becoming the first member of Tom Dunn's branch of the United Irishmen.

New Homes

DARGAN BUTLER PERUSED the architect's plans, noting that everything was in accordance with his instructions. The house, which would resemble Castletown in style if not scale, was situated between the sea and the flax meadow, much of which would have to be replaced by lawns.

'Of course,' enthused the architect, a dapper little man with well-trimmed whiskers, 'the setting, Sir, is everything. The grandeur of the mountains, the wildness of the sea – one can visualise the passage of savage corsairs, of Spanish galleons.'

'Spanish galleons? What the devil are you talking about?'

The house on the edge of the woods would be a country residence to equal those of the most powerful men in the land. It would be as grand as some of the English noble seats, and be built at a fraction of the cost with cheap local and migrant labour. In time, he hoped to have a son of his own to inherit the estate; not with his present wife, of course, but with a younger and more well-connected bride. His fortune had multiplied over the past few years, although there had been many a casualty on the way. One of the Newry shipping merchants was the latest, and although Butler had pretended a degree of sympathy to the now destitute mariner, he had not been averse to advising the distraught man that, had he been less charitable towards the poor of Newry, he would not now be joining their ranks.

Dargan was well pleased with the progress of his plans. He had thought that he might have some difficulty with Fanny, but in the end it had all been quite easy. The old fool nauseated him, but for the moment she had her uses. He had only to make love to her and any questions she had were silenced. It was, of course, a rather distasteful exercise, but if he closed his eyes and concentrated on the thought of Grace O'Lochlainn, it was tolerable. 'Grace': he would whisper her name, not caring what Fanny thought. He wished to possess Grace; he wanted her devotion. Most of all he longed to humiliate her, to make her want him.

Bella Morgan, the housekeeper, set about breaking in the new servant, Roisha Fegan. She found her irritating, with her woebegone expression; she often felt like slapping her, and often did. The mistress had acted in an extremely foolish manner in lifting such an urchin off the street and taking her into Kilbroney House, to be a temptation to the master. It was traditional among the Valentines to give employment to residents of the orphan asylum in Newry, who had been trained to obey orders and were not afraid of hard work. These girls from the Poorlands were a different matter, with their slovenly ways and lack of respect. Most of them barely understood English!

This girl's waxen skin and dark eyes had already attracted the attention of the grooms and menservants about the house, too, and Bella was in a quandary as to the safest position in which to place her. Not that she was in any way forward, but Bella, being an upright Christian, knew that sin must be nipped in the bud. Men, God help them, being of a higher order, were subject to more temptation from the devil.

Owen MacOwen delivered his barrel-load of sloes to the rear of Kilbroney House. He had been doing so for years, and Fanny Butler had given orders that he be given a bite to eat whenever he came. She considered him a wild man, a pathetic figure with delusions of grandeur, but yet deserving of Christian charity. Her late brother had renamed his townland but she knew the old name, *Leath Bhaile Clann Eoghan*, was still used by the local peasants. It would eventually fall out of use, and maybe the poor creature would settle down.

The scullery maid instructed him to come no further as he deposited the sloes at the kitchen door. The cook peeped into the barrel and pronounced the sloes to be of poor quality. She instructed the maid to put a couple of chicken carcasses and the remains of the bread pudding on a board for Fearon; she would have given him some coppers, too, she said, but for her conviction that he would go and drink it at Sammy Shields'.

Owen hid his resentment: he had other means of ensuring a fair payment for his labour and would bag a few ducks from the pond on his way home. In any case the real reason for his visit was the chance to see Roisha, and he waited as usual for her to appear behind the stables.

Before long a timid little face with frightened eyes peeped around the corner. A finger was raised in front of a tremulous mouth, imploring his silence. Owen listened, ears cocked. A few whinnies could be heard from the stables but there was no other sound.

'Roisha,' he whispered, 'don't be frightened. What ails you?'

'I'm scared, Owen. He knows who I am.'

'And I know who you are, too. Why should you worry about that braggart?' Roisha's eyes grew wide and round.

'Don't say that. He might hear you.'

'To the devil with him,' Owen said, taking her hands, 'I don't care if he hears me or not, Roisha Fegan.'

'Please, Owen,' Roisha tried to pull her hands away. 'He said he knew my father was in the asylum. He'll have me admitted there too if I don't...' She drew close in fright as hooves clattered outside the stable.

'Hurry,' she cried, ''tis the master.' Her caution was in vain as the black horse came through the doors. Dargan Butler saw them.

'My dear Roisha,' he drawled, 'misbehaving again? Such indiscretions must be punished. Don't you agree, my young friend?'

'Damn you, Dargan Butler,' Owen was defiant. 'Dare you lay a finger on this girl, and I'll see you in hell.'

Dargan Butler smiled. 'Lay a finger on a lunatic? Do you think I'm as mad as she?' Almost casually his whip lashed out. A trickle of blood traced a line down Owen's cheek. When the whip lashed out again he seized it and jerked it savagely. The surprised rider was pulled out of the saddle and fell sprawling in the stable muck.

'Come with me now,' Owen hissed to Roisha.

'I can't! I can't!' Roisha sobbed.

'You don't have the choice any more!' Owen cried as he grasped her hand and pulled her after him. As Dargan Butler's senses cleared he suppressed an urge to follow. He had other business to attend to now.

Owen surveyed his mountain eyrie despondently, comprehending for the first time the miserable quality of his life. The cows of the village lived in better style. He did not even have a hearthstone: the fire was in the middle of the cabin. Still, there was talk of them doing away with the hearth tax, and with a bit of help from Johnny it would not take him long to have a cot as good as Thady O'Lochlainn's. There was no shortage of stones on Leckan Mountain and maybe Johnny, kind soul that he was, would fashion him a stool or two.

The one thing of value in the cabin lay in broken, desolate shards: the remains of the old Staff of Saint Bronach, once a symbol of the abbess's authority. It had been handed down through generations of the MacOwens of Levallyclanowen. As he fingered the broken staff his thoughts were not on the medieval saint, but on the girl he had left with Annie Dunn. He had always intended to marry and to rebuild the old Healing House, his family home, but he could not return there now, at least not until he was sure that Dargan Butler would not come seeking revenge. His mountain retreat was safer.

As far as Roisha was concerned, he would marry her if she would have him. He wondered, though, how the O'Lochlainns would feel about the return of Murtagh Fegan's daughter. After all, there had been bad blood between the O'Lochlainns and Fegans in the past.

Owen MacOwen married his Roisha one month after she left Kilbroney House. Annie Dunn was relieved to see Owen happy for once, and pleased that the young girl had acquired such a gallant protecter. She had expected Betsy to be petulant at losing one of her train of admirers, but her daughter had seemed only mildly interested in the affair. The Widow was overjoyed, for she looked on Owen as one of her own.

Owen accompanied Roisha across the mountains to visit her mother in Lisnacree, where they were to marry. Brigid Fegan, old and worn before her time with the care of a fatherless family and two bedridden parents, reminded Owen that what Roisha wore on her back was all the dowry she would have, but the young man was undeterred. Of all the Fegan girls, a family noted for their good looks, Roisha was the loveliest.

The marriage took place without ceremony or style, and the couple returned to Levallyclanowen the same evening. If Roisha had not been so captivated with her husband she might have had reason to lament the poor dwelling which was to be her home, but so sweet was her happiness that she would have been content to live with Owen under the stars. Only one shadow lay across her world: Roisha was expecting Dargan Butler's child.

The Alehouse

THE WIDOW FEARON had a new spring to her step for now she was a woman of property with a stone hearth and a pig fattening for the winter, and all due to Johnny's hard work. There was no more devoted nephew in Kilbroney, she thought, and now she was in a position to help Johnny find prosperity.

As Johnny came whistling his way up the track, the Widow waited with gleaming eye to prepare him for a change in his circumstances. The young man had never felt so happy and carefree in his life, for although his courtship of Betsy Dunn was progressing but slowly, her mother had not yet kicked him out of the house, and that he considered a positive sign.

'Johnny, my lad, your days of hard toil are over!' the Widow announced as he reached her. He looked at his beaming aunt warily.

'What are you talking about?' he asked. 'Did you come

across a crock of gold or some poor creature's lost treasure?'

'The old boy in Tamnaharry. The one I gave my cure of gangrene.'

'Don't tell me your potion worked,' replied Johnny doubtfully. The widow's gangrene cure was the most evil-smelling concoction he had ever come across.

'Certainly it worked. He has skin as smooth as a baby's backside. He was so delighted with it he gave me this by way of saying thank you. Says he: "I can't give you money, in case I need it for my sons, but I'll give you something just as good." Well, Johnny, I needn't tell you that my first thoughts were: "You miserly old git, what harm would the loss of a few pence do you?" But God rest his soul, he was decent enough.'

'Soul? I thought you cured him?'

'Certainly I cured him, but he died all the same. When a man's time is spent on this earth, there's devil all I can do about it.'

Johnny looked carefully at the grubby document she proferred to him.

'I can't make this out. I can see the English words, but they make little sense to me. I'll ask Master Dunn.'

'I've already asked Master Dunn, *a chroí!* 'Tis a two-year lease on Sammy Shields' alehouse.'

'An alehouse? What in the name of God do I know about such places?'

'Now, Johnny, you won't be long learning, or you're no Fearon,' said the Widow.

The alehouse was a low stone house in need of rethatching, situated behind the lane which ran from the barrack green down to the river. It backed on to the village slaughterhouse, and had a regular clientele of local ne'er-do-wells. A door at each end of the house afforded a convenient exit when the military came visiting at a late hour, and the close proximity of the wood ensured a safe haven until morning. Johnny looked at the alehouse with considerable misgivings. He could see himself ladling out tankards of porter and strong brews; he could see his aunt exchanging banter with the woodmen and scutchers, but he could see no place for his Betsy and, he was sure, neither would her mother.

'I had thought a trade... I was always good with my hands, or so I've been told. I made a few coffins in gaol.'

'Coffins? There's no money in coffins, and above all people I should know. When times are poor they just drop you in the hole with barely a shroud to cover your arse. But no matter how bad things are, a body will always find the price of a drink. Sammy Shields, God rest his soul, would tell you that himself. And they say he pulled a very clean tooth.'

'He pulled teeth? Would I be expected to do that?' Johnny blanched.

'By the devil, it wouldn't cost me a thought.' The Widow's high spirits were remarked on by a couple of passing village women, who sniffed as they went past.

'Did you see the jealousy of them bitches?' she cackled. 'Come on in, Johnny. Between us, we'll make a start.'

The Widow took to her new profession like a maggot to an apple. Her midwifery practice in the country was taken over by one of the evicted Killowen women, who was good at the job even if her hands were always cold. The Widow returned to Levallyclanowen now and then to keep up her stock of herbs and potions. Johnny was back and forth regularly, for the Widow's field gave forth a supply of potatoes, turnips and onions and the produce of her still was hidden nearby. The poteen-still gave the Widow an edge over other establishments in Rostrevor, for although porter was the staple beverage, contraband liquor was also in demand.

Johnny found Tom Dunn unexpectedly supportive of his new venture, and the lawyer would occasionally call in for a drink himself. Mick the Fox was the most faithful of all the Widow's clientele, having been barred from every other establishment. The old woman, however, was quick to nip in the bud any sign of rowdy behaviour which would bring the wrath of the barrack and the priest down on their heads.

''Tis like a bloody prayer house,' Mick the Fox was overheard to remark.

'Prayer house? 'Tis well seen that you haven't set foot in one since you were christened,' retorted the Widow, whose hearing was legendary, 'and if you want to huff in the corner, away off somewhere else with you! Wouldn't old Minnie be proud to have a son thrown out of every alehouse from here to Hill Town.' Mick knew well that there were no other alehouses between here and Hill Town, but the invocation of his late, much respected mother's name had its desired effect, and he retired meekly to contemplation of the amber in his well-filled tankard.

The unexpected marriage of Owen to Roisha Fegan, 'a lovely wee girl if she'd smile now and then,' gave the Widow great pleasure. She remembered all the Fegan family with affection, and reminded the new bride that she had plenty of kin living up around Knockbarragh, quiet people that kept to themselves but would always look after their own blood. On the eve of the wedding in Lisnacree, she toasted Owen's health.

'Long life and many children to Clann Eoghan, and may its future be as glorious as its past,' she cried, filling the tankard of every man in the alehouse.

The Tutor

'IT WOULD ONLY be a temporary measure, of course, but I would be more than grateful if you would act as her tutor until I can make some more permanent arrangement.'

Captain Mercer had been wary of approaching Grace O'Lochlainn. All the females in his experience had been soft and compliant, like his late wife, or else fussy and particular like Mistress Hanratty. Grace had an aloof manner for a woman of peasant lineage and yet he knew she was very capable. Perhaps she is going to say no, he thought, almost with a sense of relief. He might be better off sending Charlotte to one of those boarding schools which would teach her the ladylike decorum in which she was so lacking.

All at once Grace smiled. 'I'd be delighted,' she replied. 'Charlotte is a very intelligent girl. It doesn't surprise me to hear of her adventures at the institution you describe. It must have seemed like a prison to her.'

'Ah, yes. You see her mother was French; a very refined lady.'

'But she is every inch your daughter too, and she hears you talk constantly of your exploits in faraway places. What else would you expect of her?'

'All a little exaggerated, I fear.' Mercer's doubts evaporated. Grace had grasped the situation perfectly.

Grace was pleased with the progress of her new pupil, but was even more impressed by the library at Arno's Vale. It included many more contemporary works, foremost among them a book which had become the Bible of liberation movements from France to America, *The Rights of Man* by Tom Paine. Since Wolfe Tone's visit it had become obligatory reading for his supporters, and those who were unable to read gathered around the literate in their midst to listen and to question. The new doctrines had been described by public officials as 'the whiskey of infidelity and treason', and influence was exerted to have the book denounced from the altar, but still people assembled in little groups to read and discuss these new and radical ideas.

At the beginning of December the Mercers moved to Dublin to join Charlotte's French grandmother and to visit other members of the Mercer family for the celebration of Christmas. The captain asked Grace if she would consider coming along as a companion for his daughter. Grace was touched by the invitation and would have accepted, had not the memory of visits to the capital city with Henry Valentine evoked such bittersweet memories.

'Please, Mistress Grace,' pleaded Charlotte. 'Think of all the concerts and assemblies you could go to, and my father would buy you lots and lots of nice new clothes.' That was all the persuasion Grace needed.

'Your offer is most kind, Captain Mercer, but I must

decline.' She smiled sweetly. Mercer felt something akin to relief. Clever women could be overpowering at times.

As winter settled in there was a considerable increase in the size of Tom Dunn's classes, and he was glad to have Grace's help. Most children attended the school from December until February: there was less work for them to do at home at that time and their parents knew that they would be warm and safe in Dunn's barn. Those who could paid a penny a week, while others brought turf or firewood. Attendance had increased because many families evicted from Killowen had moved up to the mountain areas where they could set up turf cabins without hindrance. The O'Lochlainns and other Upper Kilbroney families did not begrudge sharing the land's poor assets with the newcomers, and welcomed their new neighbours in whatever way they could. The Cobbler McChesney, visiting a tanner in Hill Town, reported the hiring fair busier than ever, an indication that families from further afield were also in distress.

The fishing folk regarded their migration as temporary, a last resort outside of the workhouse. Several of the men were forced to leave their wives and children and sleep rough under their boats along the shore so that they could avail of any fishing opportunities which presented themselves. Some set up makeshift camps at the water's edge during the dark nights, to wait for large ships beyond the bar in need of a pilot through the jagged reefs at the mouth of the lough. This hazardous occupation claimed a few victims every year and oarsmen's bodies were often washed up on the beaches of Cranfield and Greencastle, but the ocean-going captains were generous and there was always a shilling or two for the pilots. But many Killowen men opted to sell their boats in order to pay their fare from Waring's Point to Liverpool, where work, however hard or menial, would be found. All blamed their deprivation on the landlord, Dargan Butler.

A letter addressed to Grace arrived via one of Captain Mercer's ships which had put in at Waring's Point. Thady did not enquire too closely into its contents, but he noticed his daughter smile and blush like a young lass of sixteen. 'Twas a pity, he thought, that she had not encountered Dr MacSorley years ago, but what was past was past. Although Eily still harboured whimsical notions of Grace's finding a husband, it was Thady's opinion that at her age it was hardly worth getting married. But in truth, he did not want to lose her.

Grace rarely spoke of Marcas MacSorley. It was now two years since he had returned to sea, and this was the first letter Grace had received from him. The life he described was rich and varied, a tapestry of exotic placenames and strange customs. She read aloud to Thady, once a competent reader himself but now blinded by age.

'He says he is going to visit the tobacco isles. Maybe he'll bring you back the fill of your pipe.'

'What does he say about Sean?'

'Only that he's still keeping an eye out for him.'

'Read me the whole bit,' Thady cried impatiently, 'and don't you miss out on any.'

'For a man of your years, you've got a curious disposition.'

'Haven't I nothing else to do with it?'

Grace smiled as she returned the letter to her pocket.

In her cabin she pored over the letter by the light of a rush candle until she knew every inkspot on the pages. She had not wanted to raise her parents' hopes unnecessarily, but she had a feeling that her friend was one step nearer the end of his quest.

War with France

'I HEARD IT FROM the Darner that they've half of Kilcoo rounded up for hanging,' said McChesney in a dispassionate tone. The Cobbler was not given to exaggeration, but his information had come from Darner the pedlar who was never the most accurate source. They considered how to make a fair interpretation of the news.

'They most likely caught a couple of boys for thieving from the bleaching green,' the Buller suggested.

'In Kilcoo? What bleaching did they ever mount in Kilcoo?' replied Thady.

'Aye,' agreed the Cobbler, feeling that he'd said enough on the subject. 'Did you hear what they're asking for hoggets at Hill Town this week?'

The Buller was less willing to let a good story go to loss. Determined to find out more of the situation in Kilcoo he harnessed his ass and asked the Cobbler to accompany him down the mountain to the Widow Fearon's alehouse. The post-Easter period had seen an upsurge in customers, now free from their Lenten pledges, and the alehouse was full. The Buller was warmly greeted by the Widow who quickly cleared a place by the hearthside for him and his companion. Tom Dunn was sitting across from them, nursing a tankard of ale.

Those who knew Dunn well had detected a change in his spirit since the visit of Wolfe Tone. It was as though he had embarked on a course to which there was no happy conclusion, and no turning back. Thirty or forty years ago the situation had been in many ways simpler: generations of illiterate paupers had forgotten how to think for themselves and were content to allow the church do their thinking for them. It was different now. The hedge-schools, primitive though they were, had opened the eyes of the innocent and inspired hope in the hopeless. There was an air of confidence abroad, and many folk were quoting Tom Paine, not as a philosopher, but as a prophet.

The Buller was hungry for news. 'Master Dunn, tell us if 'tis true what they say.' The hum of conversation around them ceased.

''Twas the Defenders,' Dunn explained softly. 'According to *The Times*, sixty-eight have been hanged this past two months, and there will be more to follow. And that does not take account of the men who were transported, God preserve them.'

Johnny Fearon paled. He knew more than most about hanging, and the terror that accompanied it. He listened to the anti-government curses around him and said little, for he knew there was no mercy for political crime. Some of the men in the alehouse protested that if the men of Kilbroney were any good they would take up arms alongside their beleaguered brethren. The memory of the old Oak Boys was invoked, though wiser counsels recalled that the same lads had caused themselves more harm than they had ever inflicted on the authorities. One beardless youth, the worse for drink, declared loudly that he would proudly die on the scaffold in the cause of freedom, equality and the brotherhood. He received a half-hearted cheer.

Johnny grew more concerned. For that act of bravado alone the whole assembly could have been arrested, and to what purpose?

'I take it,' he said to the youth, 'that you've never seen a hanging? Dangling at the end of a foul-smelling rope is about the best of it. They watch till you're gasping for life, and the eyes roll in your head and your tongue begs for air until your face turns black. If you died then, Jesus Christ, you would have suffered your time in purgatory.'

'Johnny,' the Widow tried to intervene, but her nephew would not be stopped.

'They cut you down before you black out, or revive you if you have. Then they slash through your stomach; not to kill you, mind, but to pull out your bowels inch by inch and then to roast them in front of your face. You'd be glad enough when they finally grab your hair and hack your neck off. And then stick your head on a spike to be spat at and ridiculed until your wife or your mother, if she's brave enough, takes it down for burial. So think well before you raise your bare fists, for there was never yet a fair fight.'

The crowd were perplexed by Johnny's vehemence, for he was usually a quiet fellow, and turned to Tom Dunn for his opinion.

'What say you, Master Dunn?' someone asked. 'Do we listen to Johnny Fearon here, or is there a braver man amongst us? We play for high stakes.'

The old teacher stared sadly into his tankard and thought for some time before speaking.

'Not yet, lads,' he said gravely. 'We have to be sure that

161

the outcome will be worthy of the sacrifice.' He, too, had been surprised by the depth of young Fearon's feelings. But it was no harm, he told himself, to have a dissenting voice, for it was easy to get carried away with emotion. Many young men might die, he thought, and he would bear the responsibility.

Two months earlier, in February 1793, England had declared war on the Republic of France after the republicans had shocked Europe by executing the king and queen. William Pitt looked to his counterparts in the Irish parliament to take action to prevent their disaffected fellow countrymen from exploiting the situation in the enemy's favour, and a cautious Henry Grattan introduced the Catholic Relief Acts to ease the political tension. Tom Dunn had interpreted the situation for the Irish-speaking peasants, who were confused by the promises now being made to them.

'I would suggest to you,' he said to his students, 'that the vote is of little use to me when I cannot yet vote for a man of my choice.'

Now with the suppression of the Defenders came the formation of a new militia instituted by the Irish parliament. Its rank and file were to be drawn by ballot from among the peasantry. Hugh MacVeigh, White Matty's son, was one of the first to be drawn, much to the distress of his mother who depended on the boy as the family breadwinner. One of his cousins offered to go in his place and the two presented themselves at the recruiting office in Newry. But in spite of his cousin's offer, there was no question of Hugh's avoiding the call from king and country. The two boys were signed up and posted to Wexford. No one heard what became of them after that.

Johnny's outburst was misquoted and misunderstood all around the parish. The Widow, fretting over his predicament, bemoaned ever having taken over the alehouse. Johnny also regretted it, for although he liked the company and the conversation he preferred other work. Betsy now had little time for him, and he felt sure that it was because of the alehouse, for no respectable young woman would wish to be associated with such an establishment. They were not even making a worthwhile profit. He was on the point of abandoning the business when Tom Dunn asked him not to.

'I would prefer to work hard and sweat in the fields; anything just to be out in the open,' Johnny argued.

Dunn understood. The lad had spent so much of his life confined in a prison cell that to be smothered in the little alehouse was no doubt difficult for him, even more so now when he was being goaded for his views. Unlike most of the men of the Poorlands and many of the village residents, Johnny refused to take the oath which would place him under the banner of the United Irishmen. In spite of this, Dunn saw him as a couragous young man who was not afraid to speak his mind.

'With the times the way they are,' he said, 'we need to have a regular meeting place where folk can gather and talk without arousing suspicion.'

Johnny agreed to hold on a little longer.

Captain Mercer had been delighted at the success of Tone and Neilson's visit. Some of the local gentlemen had taken him to task for encouraging the expectations of the poor, but Tone had made many converts and had even won over some of the dissenting factions of south Down. Rostrevor, he had told Mercer, was just a black little Tory town, but there were enough good-hearted men in the surrounding countryside to redeem the whole of Kilbroney.

Shortly after Christmas Mercer met with him in a Dublin tavern, the Brazen Head. Tone was in the company of another gentleman, Lord Edward Fitzgerald, the younger son of the Duke of Leinster. The flamboyant aristocrat had just returned from France, where he had been fêted by the republican government as an honorary Frenchman, Citizen Fitzgerald. His subsequent dismissal from the British army had come as no surprise, but in spite of his family's embarrassment the young man continued to present himself as an unofficial French ambassador to Ireland.

A proud John Mercer received Lord Edward's thanks for the money he had raised to help the citizens of the new republic, and then France's unofficial ambassador invited the tavern to join him in the 'Marseillaise'.

'He is a good-hearted fellow,' Tone explained to Mercer after the party had been asked to leave, 'though I fear he lacks discretion. That is the aristocratic breeding in him; he does not feel the need to hold his tongue.'

Mercer made no reply. It seemed to him that the possibility of help from France was too perilous a subject to make light of. Lord Edward might have suffered dismissal from his post for his bravado, but poorer men would pay a much higher price.

Grace was glad to welcome the returning Mercers, remarking on the changes in Charlotte since she had last seen her.

'I would have left her with the family in Dublin, but she protested that no one can look after me quite so well, and I must confess,' remarked Captain Mercer tenderly, 'that she speaks the truth.' Grace thought he looked weary after his journey and did not hide her concern.

'I am glad to see you home,' she said. 'An excess of city air is not good for you.'

'No,' he agreed, 'especially for one who has spent most of

his life on the deck of a tallship.'

Grace had missed her visits to Arno's Vale. Even though she had been invited to use the library in the master's absence, Mistress Hanratty had clearly indicated her disapproval of this arrangement. Grace was well used to handling such censure, but she had more important matters with which to concern herself at this time. Money had always been scarce but now her financial position was quite precarious. The rents had been raised and her school pupils came weekly with excuses rather than pennies. In normal times, she would think about pleading her case with Fanny, although it had always been a matter of pride to her that she had never taken a penny of Valentine money. Now, if she did approach Kilbroney House, it would not be Henry's sister with whom she would have to contend.

Not the least of her worries was Michael. Fr Mackey, when he had heard about the visit from Bonaventure Whinehan, had exploded with indignation.

'That upstart,' he had protested, 'I'm glad to see the back of him. He certainly got no instruction from me.' He resolved to look into the matter to see exactly on whose instructions the curate had acted. Grace was relieved to know that this danger had been averted, but the feeling still remained that someone did not have Michael's best interests at heart.

Now that Grace was back in Captain Mercer's employment, she had a request of her own to make.

'Michael is hungry to learn. His companionship might amuse Charlotte and, although she is his senior, he is very bright and will not hold her back.' Captain Mercer assured Grace that he would be delighted to have the lad.

The door had been left ajar, allowing John Mercer the opportunity to examine the preoccupied faces of the children in the makeshift schoolroom. A shaft of sunlight fell on a table littered with books and paper. Charlotte was reading to Grace while the little boy practised his handwriting with a quill and ink, his face furrowed with concentration. He was already beginning to master this new implement.

Mercer looked at him closely, trying to determine the child's origins. On his travels he had met people of many different races, and was familiar with their different characteristics. Michael had abundant curly hair and a wide brow, yet his skin was not as dark as that of an African boy; he had the small mouth and nose of a European, yet his eyes were large and brown. Michael was of mixed race, he thought; the lad certainly had a fine blend of qualitites, too, he decided. Not wishing to disturb the class, he slipped quietly away.

Ambition

FANNY'S HAND TREMBLED as she sipped tea in Madam Hall's sitting room. 'Oh, for heaven's sake,' the mistress of Narrow Water said sharply, 'this really cannot go on. Tell me what is upsetting you, Fanny.'

'You must excuse me. I am wasting your time!' Fanny made to rise.

'Oh, sit down. It has something to do with your husband, hasn't it?'

The floods of tears which greeted this accusation confirmed Madam Hall's suspicions. Not for the first time she scolded herself for ever having led Fanny into such an unfortunate marriage. Of course it was common knowledge that Fanny was the world's worst judge of character; one had only to look at the way she let her late brother's mistress ingratiate her way into the house to see that. The Squire had done his best to warn her of the consequences, but it had been to no avail.

'Grace O'Lochlainn,' Madam Hall murmured, recalling those past times.

'You know then?' sobbed Fanny. 'Everybody knows!'

Madam Hall looked at the woman in exasperation. She had become a total travesty of herself in a few short years. Gone was the confident self-reliant businesswoman, and in her place was this miserable, fumbling, whingeing creature pathetically searching for her handkerchief.

'And what, my dear Fanny, am I supposed to know?'

'That Grace O'Lochlainn is now my husband's mistress.'

'Is that all?' Madam Hall almost laughed with relief. 'I was afraid you were going to tell me you were expecting a baby. So he has a mistress? All men do. How on earth could we ever satisfy them?'

'I don't care if he has twenty mistresses; he can have them if he must. But Grace? Grace is the last person I would have suspected. We were almost friends.'

'What a foolish notion, Fanny!' But even as she spoke Madam Hall entertained an unworthy but niggling doubt that the O'Lochlainn woman was a most unlikely mistress for Butler. Grace O'Lochlainn, loathe though she was to admit it, had always displayed some degree of principle.

'You may be mistaken, Fanny. I know many women who harbour suspicions against their husbands, and let me warn you,' she continued sternly, 'it is a self-fulfilling prophesy.'

'I would have her evicted,' sobbed Fanny, 'if I could.'

'Of course you can. I certainly would if I were you. And what's more, I would withhold his allowance.'

'I can't! I gave him complete control of my finances.'

Madam Hall reached for her smelling salts. 'Oh, Fanny,' she whispered, shocked by this revelation, 'what will you do?'

Dargan Butler despised the merchants of Newry. He hated those who had refused him credit in the early days, and now he swore vengeance on the bank manager and the lawyers who had tried to poison his wife's mind against him. His hostility included the Gentlemen's Lending Library, beside the now defunct theatre, which had declined to accept his membership. Yet he knew that his star was in the ascendant. The Francophile men of Newry had signed their own death warrants, and he would be the chief reveller at their grisly executions. England was now at war with France and the government would pay well for any information he might give them regarding the loyalty of this rebel town. In his mind's eye he pictured the erection of a gibbet in High Street. That would bring them to heel.

The new house was progressing splendidly and he was already considering how to build up his livestock. The old nags at the stable in Kilbroney House would have to go to grass to make way for some of the fashionable Arab stallions which were the hallmarks of a real gentleman. He had bought one such animal, which he called Saladin, a beautiful black horse with a mane like a silken veil. He left the stables now to ride down to Colonel Trevor, the commander of the local garrison who resided at the Crag. An expert on horseflesh, Trevor was only too glad to give his opinion on the thoroughbred, and even summoned his wife to admire it. Madam Trevor, disturbed from her embroidery frame, could only stand aside and gasp at the magnificent creature. Dargan Butler elegantly doffed his hat to the lady.

'Is he not handsome?' she sighed as he rode off. Her husband was less impressed.

'Why shouldn't he be with nothing to do save preen himself?' he remarked smartly. He had little time for Butler, but he did truly admire the horse. In the meantime, he was preoccupied with converting the old coachhouse behind the Crag into an arsenal. It would be of vital importance if the present threat to the security of the realm were to be tackled.

Dargan Butler cantered along the shore, observing a few old crones bent under rush panniers as they scavenged for pieces of flotsam and jetsam washed up by the sea. He made a mental note to prohibit such unsightly activities, just as he had stopped the practices of wrack gathering and shellfish harvesting. Such privileges had been taken for granted by the peasantry, and only their withdrawal for a year or so would make them appreciated. He did not yet feel in full control of his new horse, and wished to familiarise himself with its moods in privacy. The animal suddenly stumbled, whinnying in distress as a razorshell became embedded in a hoof. Butler led his mount off the shore and into the woods at Arno's Vale. He carefully extracted the shell, stroking the handsome neck to soothe the upset stallion. 'We may have to walk here, my beauty,' he said, and looking up, 'but a walk through the woods can be most diverting.'

Even from a distance he could recognise Grace O'Lochlainn. She was exquisite. Now and then she stooped to gather some wild flowers, all her movements lithesome and graceful as she filled her basket, soft tendrils of pale golden hair escaping from under her linen bonnet as she worked. Only the nervous pacing of the stallion alerted her to his presence.

'Squire Butler,' she bowed slightly.

'Mistress O'Lochlainn.' His return bow was more extravagant. 'This meeting was surely ordained by Heaven itself. My horse received a slight hoof injury while walking on the beach,' he explained, all the time observing her movement, her every expression. There was certainly no sign of fear, much less hostility. His boyish smile, he knew, could disarm even the most recalcitrant woman.

'An unfortunate accident,' she sympathised, 'but I've seen worse; it will soon heal.' With a slight nod of dismissal she

170

made to go, but he stepped in front of her, blocking her path.

'Please, Grace, do not be in such haste. Your company is so exhilarating and our encounters so infrequent. 'Tis a lovely evening...'

'Yes, it is, and I have some distance to walk before nightfall.'

'Ah, Grace, would that I could come with you. Nothing would give me greater pleasure.'

'You pay such pretty compliments, Squire Butler, but it is late and I really must be on my way.' She sidestepped neatly as he tried to detain her and within moments was lost in the trees. Had Butler's horse not needed attention, he might have followed her.

'Next time, Grace,' he called into the woods; 'until the next time.'

The Fiddler of the Clasha

'SHE'S FRETTING ABOUT something.' Annie Dunn, pegging out her laundry on a fine May morning, voiced her concern about her daughter.

'Our Betsy's moonstruck,' Tom Dunn replied as he struggled with a motherless calf. 'She must be pining for Owen, or maybe afraid of being left an unwed maid. You know how young girls are.'

'I do; indeed I used to be one,' replied Annie, 'but this is no simple caprice. She hasn't a word for Johnny, or any of the young men at the nightschool. I used to worry about her hoydenish ways, but now she's gone to the other extreme. I wish she would confide in me like she used to.'

'All young maids behave so from time to time. Too much religion does that.'

'And what makes you an authority on religion, let alone young maids? I think you make too light of the problem.' Annie was cross at her husband's dismissive manner. He gave a sigh of resignation.

'Annie, would you like me to talk to her? Where is she now?'

'I have no idea. I never seem to know where she is nowadays.'

'No doubt trying to escape her chores.' Dunn gave up on the calf and handed her over to his wife, who had a better way with young beasts.

'That's just what worries me,' insisted Annie. 'She was up before dawn, and all her work is done. Now that's not Betsy's form.'

There was activity around the barrack, Turlough MacCormac reported to Tom Dunn. Drilling on the village square had become more purposeful and organised.

MacCormac had cause to be wary, and made sure that a trustworthy lad kept watch while he was working at his craft. The forge by the river stood in a little woodland clearing not far from the alehouse. He had two sturdy young brothers, the stronger of whom worked with him and learned his trade, while the other worked at Martin's mill. Johnny Fearon helped out when work at the smithy was heavy, although of late MacCormac was reluctant to hire him. He was uncertain of Fearon's political inclinations and did not trust him, despite Tom Dunn's assurances. The fires of the brazier were always lit, day and night, for theirs was a busy forge. As sparks flew and the anvil rang, Turlough MacCormac, as well as mending spades and scythes, was fashioning pikes of the sturdiest iron.

Johnny Fearon was concerned about his neighbours. So full of hope were they, and so lacking in understanding of the ruthless nature of the state which they were defying. Often he felt like standing up and shouting to them: 'Be wary! Be cautious! Trust no one.' He knew how even steadfast friends could betray each other when the lure of gold was in the air. He wondered how many Kilbroney men would hold their tongues under the lash of the whip.

Tom Dunn stood by his pupil. 'It takes a man of courage to voice his honest doubt,' he said to the nightschool, 'for any fool or flatterer can follow the crowd. We need a cautious man in our midst. There are plenty of hotheads who would let anger get the better of their good sense.'

Johnny was glad to know that he was so well thought of, but he would have bartered any man's approval for a smile from Betsy Dunn, and wondered if she too had branded him a coward. She seemed to have little time for him now.

If Betsy had been aware of Johnny's feelings it would have made no odds to her, for she was still fascinated with Oran O'Cassidy. His violin, a shabby, battered instrument which looked as if it had been rescued from a fire, in his hands could produce the most beautiful music she had ever heard, and she never lost an opportunity to hear him play. He had become well known at fairs and street corners as far away as Dundalk on the other side of Cooley. Betsy heard that he had been approached by one of the Dundalk Gentlemen Fiddlers who had asked him to join their ranks and play at balls and country assemblies. Acceptance would have given him higher social status and better earnings, yet he refused the offer and remained in his little cabin on the Clasha. Betsy hoped that she had had some influence on this decision, but knew in her heart that the fiddler had other things than a simple red-haired girl on his mind.

The Clasha was a woodland glade some way below the mountain summit, on the south-facing slopes overlooking the lough. It had been known as a haven for outlaws and highwaymen during the oppressive Penal years, and on more than one occasion forest fires had been lit by the military to flush out their quarry. To the east of the Clasha an old quarry was cut into the mountainside, a treacherous drop for the unwary and a natural line of defence against intruders.

One evening, curious to know his rival, Johnny Fearon found himself following Betsy Dunn. She crossed the Owen-abwee and the flax meadow, heading towards the forested slopes of Slieve Ban. As she scrambled up the steep incline, securing her basket with her petticoats, Johnny wondered if her lover was some wild brigand or dangerous cut-throat who was in hiding from the law. It was then that he heard the music, a sweet sad melody.

'Why,' he exclaimed to himself, ''tis the fiddler O'Cassidy.' The fiddler had not been seen around Kilbroney during the winter, and his appearances at the fairs in Hill Town or Waring's Point had become infrequent. All assumed that he had moved on to more lucrative pastures as times were hard around Kilbroney.

All at once the fiddling stopped. Betsy remained perfectly still until again the music sounded and then walked forward as if entranced. Johnny retreated, a beaten man, pondering if he should tell Master Dunn, but thinking better of it. He would sink even lower in Betsy's eyes if he were to tell tales. Yet he still loved her and had her safety at heart. He remained hidden in the trees until she emerged again, her face aglow and her eyes sparkling.

Michael was an exemplary student, and he and Charlotte enjoyed sparring for the attention of Grace. Captain Mercer was amused by the little fellow and though intrigued by his background refrained from prying.

'I do not wish to see him upset,' Grace had explained. 'He had a very distressing time before he found us, and if he is to speak of it I would prefer that he does so of his own accord and in his own time.' John Mercer reluctantly agreed with her, although he would talk often in Michael's presence about distant lands he had visited to see if it would provoke some response in the boy.

As for Grace, she was glad of Michael and his little dog's company to and from Arno's Vale. When eventually Captain Mercer persuaded her to accept the loan of a pony, Michael loved the ride through Rostrevor, holding tightly to Grace and looking down at the envious local children. Some of them would call him names, but Grace would laugh at such insults and, after a while, so did Michael.

One evening riding homewards through the Arno's Vale woods she encountered Dargan Butler once more. He was mounted on his black stallion, a grand animal with a proud head and a well-groomed coat.

'Squire Butler,' she greeted him courteously, sensing that this was no chance encounter.

'Mistress Grace. I thought we might meet again.'

'I'm glad to see your horse has recovered from its injury. I'm sure you're keen to put it through its paces. I must not delay you.'

'I cannot stop thinking about you,' he said abruptly, tired of dalliance. This was a woman who would appreciate direct speech.

'But you can if you must,' she replied. 'And you must.'

'In such matters my heart rules my mind. I love you, Grace. I want you and I will have you.'

Grace felt Michael's arms grasping her tightly from behind; he buried his head in her back. She could see the desire in Butler's eyes and knew the danger of the situation. 'I am flattered,' she said. 'A man of your experience, so well travelled, must have met many beautiful women in his time.'

'But none like you, Grace. None with your fire, your passion!'

She smiled at him; he was both charming and dangerous, a heady combination. 'This is not the time to talk about such things,' she said, 'when we have company.'

Butler started when he noticed the clawing hands of the child. He raised his whip as if he would brush this irritant aside then, spurring his horse, he rode off without another word.

Grace wondered if it would be safer to return to Arno's Vale, but Michael was so distressed that she decided to ride homewards. When they reached Dunn's Hill, Grace dismounted and lifted Michael off the pony. He had not spoken since the encounter with Butler.

'I am afraid for both of you,' Tom Dunn said. 'He is a dangerous and reckless man.'

'But why was Michael so upset? He did not harm us or threaten us.'

'I think I can guess why,' Dunn was thoughtful, 'but perhaps we should wait until he is able to tell us himself.'

Dunn, having previously witnessed evidence of Dargan Butler's volatile nature, was unsure if Grace realised how precarious was their situation. He decided to pay a visit to Captain Mercer.

The next morning Michael refused to return to Arno's Vale.

'Leave him be,' coaxed Eily. 'I'm sure he's had enough of learning. As far as I can see he's best served without it.'

'Michael,' said Grace, trying to disguise her anxiety, 'what is troubling you? Can't you tell us?'

Eily cradled the little head to her bosom. 'The wee lad doesn't want to talk about it. And whatever it was, 'tis past now.'

Grace had abandoned any attempt to coax Michael further when a muffled voice said: ''Twas him. The Seigneur.'

'Who was it, Michael?' asked Grace, not understanding.

'The Seigneur who beat my mother.'

'Dargan Butler, the man with the black horse: is he the Seigneur?'

'Yes, he beat us and we ran away. Through the snow.' The little voice was quiet for a time.

'He beat my mother, often. She was screaming, but he kept on beating her.' A little sob came. 'I was the only one who could help her, but I hid because I was too afraid.'

'Now, now, a wee lad like yourself, Michael? You couldn't have helped her. Why, he might have beaten you too,' Grace tried to reassure him, upset at his distress.

'He did beat me, once only. That's when we left the house. It was dark and cold, but my mother kept telling me to ask for O'Lochlainn's. Even when she stopped, she made me go on. 'Twas all my fault.'

When Grace reached Arno's Vale, John Mercer had already heard about her encounter with Squire Butler.

'It was Dargan Butler who assaulted his mother,' Grace explained, her tone fierce. 'The poor boy recognised him.'

'Dunn had guessed as much,' said Mercer. 'He is worried that Michael is now in great danger.'

'For what reason? Surely he cannot pose a threat to Butler?' Grace asked.

'Now that the boy has identified him, there is no certainty as to what that blackguard will do. That is why he could not allow Johnny Fearon to stand trial. Michael would undoubtedly have recognised him. And it was he who put Whinehan the curate up to his mischief, you may be sure.'

'But who would take the word of a young blackamoor against an influential magistrate? It would never be taken seriously.'

'True, but you would never know what other dark secrets Michael might be keeping. They could be the downfall of an ambitious man. Grace, it may even have been because of Michael's presence that he has not come looking for you before. His position was too tenuous, but now he feels more secure.'

'I am not concerned for myself. I have my own ways of coping with his like. But I am worried now for Michael.'

'He must be kept out of Butler's way. It might be best for him to stay here at Arno's Vale.'

Grace considered the offer. 'I think he will insist on remaining with my father; the two are very close. And Michael has a habit of running away when he takes the notion, and can be very hard to catch – even if only to get his head scrubbed,' she added with a smile.

'But what about you, Grace? Would you stay here? We have ample room and you would be most comfortable and safe.'

Mistress Hanratty was concerned about the scandal this arrangement might cause to Mercer's good name, and made her opinion clear to the captain.

'Come now,' he reassured her, 'with you here as chaperone?'

'But her reputation,' the housekeeper protested.

'It is undeserved and certainly something we can live with.' Mercer held up his hand to signal that the discussion was at an end.

In spite of the captain's reassurances, Grace decided that she would prefer not to provoke another local scandal. She thanked Mercer for his offer, and assured him that she would continue to tutor Charlotte to the best of her ability. Captain Mercer accepted her decision, but not without regret.

More Evictions

OWEN MACOWEN HAD never been so content. Since his mother died he had lived in extreme poverty and relied on charitable neighbours for his food. He would not beg, but would insist on carrying out some chore in payment, for as the Widow often remarked to Eily O'Lochlainn, 'there was some oul' oddness on the mother's side' which made him act the way he did. Now with a wife to provide for, Owen laboured at the beetling mill, and in the evening would work hard to make his little home safe and secure for his Roisha. No one knew for sure when her baby was due, but by the size of her belly the Widow estimated that summer would see the new arrival. That it was not his child concerned him little. He loved his wife very much and it was her baby. He promised her that it would never be in need of a shirt for its back and would never go hungry. Through the cold evenings, Roisha would sit happily by the fireside fashioning little clothes from meal-bags.

After Easter Owen visited the abandoned Fox cabin in Knockbarragh across the mountain. The McVeighs had lived there for a time after their father had drowned, but had since been evicted; now, with young Hugh conscripted, the mother had brought the family north to take their chances at the hiring fairs. Owen's purpose was to retrieve the huge churn which Minnie the Fox had once taken from Kilbroney House and fashion it into a cradle.

The cabin, a damp little hovel built with sprouting sods, had almost been reclaimed by nature, with nettles and weeds growing from the floors, the walls and the roof. He approached the house quietly, for Fr Mackey the old parish priest resided near by, and he did not want to be accused of stealing. As he sneaked past the house, he heard a shout.

'Hello there, young Owen. Are you saying your prayers, like a good man?'

'Good day, Father. I was just looking to see if there was anything in the Fox cabin.'

'Nothing worth stealing, for sure. And what did you want, O last of Clann Eoghan?'

'Minnie had a big churn. I thought it would make a good cradle.'

'So there's good news on the way? Well done, lad. We'll have another MacOwen by Christmas!'

'It could be any day now, I'm thinking.'

As Owen rolled the churn homewards, the priest did some mental calculations regarding the date of Owen's wedding and his expectation of an early arrival. There was certainly some serious misdemeanour involved.

'Ah well,' he sighed, 'at least he's not slow when it comes to getting his breeches down.' The old priest had over the years developed a deep and flexible understanding of human frailty.

The young McChesneys and Murphys chortled and made

181

fun of Owen as he struggled homewards with his cumbersome burden.

'I'll tan your backsides when I catch up with you,' he warned crossly, but the children only laughed all the more.

'*Eoghan a chuinneog! Eoghan a chuinneog!*' they shouted. Wondering if the name 'Owen the Churn' would stick, his humiliation was complete when he arrived home to find Betsy Dunn and the Widow Fearon with another cradle, a gift from Annie Dunn. But his irritation was shortlived when he saw the occupant of the crib, a beautiful little black-eyed baby girl, the image of her mother.

From the front door of Tom Dunn's barn there was a good view of all the approaches from the village, and from the back door an escape route if necessary. Turlough MacCormac was an infrequent visitor to the nightschool, and when Cobbler McChesney spotted the blacksmith puffing up the hill at some considerable speed, the assembly sensed that something was wrong.

'Sit down and rest yourself for a minute,' said Dunn as the panting man tried to catch his breath. He had great respect for the smith and for the quality of his pikeheads. 'Now what news have you got for us?'

'They're talking about more conscription for the new militia. Old Colonel Trevor let it be known that he would round up at least fifty able-bodied men from this area.'

'I wouldn't have thought so,' said Dunn. 'They tend to take men from land where there is no other employ: from the west and such places. They need the labour for the flax here. Could you see old Trevor breaking his back at such toil, or Dargan Butler lifting his own harvest?' Some of the men laughed.

'Nevertheless,' said MacCormac, 'I tell only what I have heard. If it is true, we will soon know.'

Thady spoke at some length to Fr Mackey about Michael, emphasising his concern for the child's spiritual welfare. 'Think no more about it,' the old priest reassured him. 'He's a fine lad, and I've no doubt he'll make a great acolyte when he's older. He may even join the priesthood himself.'

In the corner, Eily's prayers became more fervent: one failed priest in the family was bad enough.

'Our main worry,' explained Thady, 'is that he may know too much about certain powerful people.'

'I take it you mean the blackguard in Kilbroney House? He has destroyed a good woman in Madam Valentine. And who would ever have thought to hear me say such about a Whitechurch? You may set your mind at rest for the moment, O'Lochlainn. Dargan Butler has gone to Dublin to debate the electoral laws. Not that he'll do much good for us, but at least he's out of the way for the time being.'

Grace O'Lochlainn was surprised when she was visited by the Agent Crampsey. The agent was a tiny man whose very large wife had borne him an even larger family, most of whom resided in the area. So busy was the notoriously henpecked Crampsey in setting up his children in lucrative positions that he tended to carry out his own duties in spurts, usually when Squire Butler required extra cash. He would then descend on unsuspecting tenants' cabins like a demon from hell, with two sons as sturdy bailiffs by his side. No one knew when Crampsey was likely to call, and it was with some annoyance that Grace opened her door to him just as she was laundering some personal items of underwear.

'Can I help you?' she enquired in the sharp tone she usually reserved for tardy scholars. The agent looked most anxious and apologetic.

'I beg your pardon, Mistress O'Lochlainn, but I am

required to deliver this.'

'What is it?' she demanded. Crampsey licked his lips nervously.

'An eviction notice, if you please, Ma'am.'

'They have only given me a week to leave,' Grace told Tom Dunn.

'But that is disgraceful; you are no ordinary tenant.' The lawyer paced around the kitchen until his wife told him to settle down.

'Perhaps,' Annie suggested, 'if you were to visit Madam Butler. After all, Grace, you and she used to be on such good terms.'

Grace glanced at her ruefully. 'That's the puzzle, Annie. 'Twas not Dargan Butler who ordered my eviction. 'Twas Fanny herself.'

'Really?' Annie was at a loss for words. Then she looked at Grace, a question in her eyes. 'After all, 'tis not as if you have given her any cause for annoyance, have you?'

'Not that I know of,' Grace shrugged. 'Certainly nothing passed between her husband and myself, in spite of his words. I would never have dreamt that Fanny would do such a thing.'

'You're going to have to call on her, Grace. Whatever has poisoned her mind, you are the only one who can set things to right.'

Reluctantly, Grace prepared to visit Fanny Butler. She was not looking forward to it, but could see no other option.

Madam Butler would not see anyone on estate matters in the master's absence, Grace was coldly informed by Mullan, the footman. Agent Crampsey would deal with her.

As she left the house, Grace wondered what had become of Bella Morgan, her old adversary. She had dreaded a confrontation with the gorgon who had been in the Valentine's service for many years, and was surprised to see Mullan usurping her position. The house had a rundown appearance, as all Squire Butler's efforts were now reserved for the magnificent new residence on the shores of the lough. A team of bailiffs was employed day and night to keep the local peasants at bay, all of which added to the already exaggerated rumours of marble staircases the length of the street and gold fountains which spat forth sweet wine.

In spite of the unhappy memories Grace retained of the old house, she was dismayed at the sight of the shabby lawns and neglected gardens, once Fanny's special pride. The house itself was unhappy, she decided, perhaps reflecting the feelings of its mistress. On impulse, Grace took a favourite old route through the orchards. To the south of the fruit trees were the beehives, and there Grace found the mistress of the house.

Fanny looked as though she had been weeping, and greeted Grace with little warmth.

'Why, Fanny,' asked Grace, 'why have you done this to me? To evict me after all these years?'

'I trusted you,' said Fanny, 'you of all people. I might have expected it of others, but I considered you worthy of friendship.' She began to weep softly.

'When have I been other than a friend?' asked Grace gently, upset at Fanny's distress. 'Let us go inside. Don't let anyone see you like this.'

'I don't care who sees me. How could you understand this? You will always be beautiful; age leaves no mark on you. That is why he pays you so much attention. How could you have betrayed me with my husband?'

Grace sat back in astonishment. 'You cannot believe that,' she protested. 'It is completely untrue.'

'Untrue? How can I think otherwise?'

185

Grace watched as the woman began to weep once more, her words of dismissal almost incoherent. She looked on helplessly before rising to leave. There would be no reasoning with Madam Butler in this state.

'Come All Ye Brave United Men'

IN THE YEARS which followed Wolfe Tone's visit, the membership of the United Irishmen grew from a small band of hopeful enthusiasts to a widespread movement. Freeholders and peasant cottiers, mariners and mill owners joined their ranks. Everywhere young men and old, and a few intrepid women, gathered in small groups to listen to the literate in their midst read Tom Paine's *The Rights of Man*.

The call for revolution was heard from the narrow streets of the town to the remote mountain valleys of the Mournes. In Newry, United volunteers paraded openly in the streets and attempts to curb their display met with a hostile reaction from the burghers of the town. Activity was more secret in the countryside, but every so often news arrived from Belfast warning men to have their weapons ready should they be suddenly summoned to arms. From Attical to Lisdrumgullion and from Ballybot to Barnmeen, folk met in lonely glens and poor cabins to assemble the armoury of a peasant militia.

At Dunn's barn men gathered in the evening to listen to the stirring words of their leader, who was enjoying a new confidence and sense of worth. In the fields above the barn, protected by the woods of Thunder Hill, they drilled with the spirit of men who knew that all over Ireland there were thousands marching.

'I heard from the Darner that the Pope of Rome sent a chest of gold to arm the Catholics,' Cobbler McChesney confided.

'Aye,' the Buller took a slow draw on his pipe, 'and 'twould suit him better if he would send a few decent sacks of seed praties.'

'The Pope? Would he know a pratie if he saw one?'

The Buller sometimes found the Cobbler a difficult conversationalist. 'Wheesht man, I'm talking about the Darner. The praties in the ground are hardly fit for pigs, and by the end of the summer they'll be no better.'

'Maybe if you put a bit of wrack on the lazybeds.' Thady O'Lochlainn was concerned for his old neighbour, whose swollen joints had made him more crotchety than usual.

'Wrack,' cried the Buller, wincing with the pain in his legs. 'And where the hell are we going to get wrack, with Butler closing off the shore? Unless we find a body,' he looked at Thady, 'fool enough to cart it over the mountain from Annalong.'

Cobbler McChesney gave Thady a look of warning. Another row with the old warrior was best avoided.

'Don't upset yourself. We'll all throw in together and that way there'll be enough praties to see the whole lot of us through.'

Owen MacOwen took his vows of secrecy seriously and refused to tell his wife what had been discussed at the nightschool. He had been a poor scholar in his youth, and if Roisha wondered at his sudden enthusiasm for learning, she kept her opinions to herself. If he was content, she was content.

One morning, after a hearty breakfast of oatmeal and whey, he went down to his work at the mill and found the gates locked. A small group of workers peered forlornly through the bars; no one knew what had happened. James Dunn, the master's son, walked towards them.

'There is no more work for us,' he told them. 'A glut on the market, they say.'

'I know what it is,' Owen said angrily, 'we're not growing good flax any more. No wonder they're turning back the bales.'

'At any rate,' James said sadly, 'there's nothing we can do about it.'

'I hear there were a couple of hundred at the Clonduff hiring fair last week,' commented one of the crowd. Others muttered about Dargan Butler turning one of the best flax meadows into a park for his own pleasure. Owen stared at the closed gates. Tomorrow he would seek work at the hiring fair, for he had a wife and child to support.

Some weeks later, Annie Dunn bade a tearful farewell to her son James, his wife and their children as they set off for a new life in America. She had pleaded with James to stay, to run the farm for his father, but he was adamant that he wanted a better life for his family.

'What is there here for them?' he argued. 'I could be called up at any moment and how would my wife manage on her own? I'm sorry, Mother, but I have no choice.'

The children kissed their grandmother and promised that one day they would return to see her. Tom shook his head sadly, torn between the loss of his son's family and the relief that they would soon be out of danger.

The departure of James Dunn for the port of Derry had a disturbing effect in the valley; it forced others to wonder if they would eventually join him in that land of plenty an ocean journey away.

Thady was distressed to learn of Grace's eviction and he insisted that she stay at the Close. Cobbler McChesney also graciously offered his home, but Grace refused him.

'Do you not think that you would be evicted too?'

'They'd hardly turn me out,' the Cobbler answered, 'for I pay the rent on time.'

'And have you a tenancy agreement?'

'I have.'

Grace admired McChesney's bravery, but as a widower with a young family she knew he was vulnerable. 'Do you have a written agreement?' The Cobbler shook his head. 'I thought not. A spit on the hand won't hold up in court, I'm afraid. If they really wanted to they could evict you as they pleased.'

The dejected Cobbler would have been only too willing to share his home and his bed with Grace, and he realised that such a distant hope might almost have become a reality but for that scrap of paper she had offered him, but which he had carelessly rejected.

'There is no alternative! You must make your home here,' Captain Mercer declared, 'and no one could be more welcome.'

Grace was of two minds about accepting the invitation, and it was only when she was assured that the leasehold agreement for Arno's Vale was airtight that she agreed to stay. Charlotte was delighted to hear that her tutor would be taking up residence with them, and even Mistress Hanratty was mollified by Grace's modest decorum and her fondness for young Charlotte. In the evening they sat by the fireside while John Mercer chatted about his overseas adventures. Grace was an appreciative listener who enjoyed his tales of India and the eastern lands. To his surprise she had a story or two of her own to tell, for she had travelled herself in former years, not on long ocean voyages but on cultural expeditions to Europe and to the Italian cities in particular. He laughed at her descriptions of the opera in Venice and the amorous antics of the city fathers.

'Faith, you have seen as much as I have, my dear, although maybe not the same things! Have you ever wished to travel again?'

'No,' she replied. 'It was magical when I was young, but not any more. There is so much to be done here.'

The Cobbler McChesney felt despondant as he turned over the thin Kilbroney sod. He would barely be able to feed his children during the coming winter. He looked across the field at his neighbour, the Buller. The old fellow had been getting very stiff of late and was barely able to look after himself. After spending a lifetime in the mountains, it seemed he now faced the workhouse. To compound the Cobbler's problems, his daughter, Murren, lay in a fever by the hearth. The familiar figure of the Widow Fearon lifted his heart as she appeared on the horizon.

'Murren, daughter,' he called, 'here's the Widow come to see you. She'll have you on your feet in no time!'

The Widow had returned to her cabin in Levallyclanowen some weeks previously. In truth, having had a taste of being a woman of consequence, she was content to return home. She was much in demand in the Poorlands, and when she heard the news of a sick child in the Cobbler's home she wasted no time about coming to her bedside. She brought with her the usual purges and poultices and a crock of whey, the only beverage which now passed her lips. She sat with Murren through two nights, cooling her brow with spring water scented with dried meadow blossoms, and crooning the lullabies that were older than any man or woman living. Round the hearth she hung weeds collected from mountain, bog and riverside, some of which the Cobbler recognised, some which he did not. Most important of all were the few shards of black wood with which she occasionally brushed the patient's lips. The other children gazed from the shadows with eyes wide, wondering if the Widow was a witch or a healer. She held up a black fragment.

'This is a most precious relic,' she said to them.

'The True Cross?' one of the boys said in awe. He had heard of such things in Master Dunn's class.

'In the name of the Jews, there's enough True Cross around here to build a bridge to Cooley,' replied the Widow. 'But this,' she kissed the shard, 'this is much more sacred. It's a relic of the Staff of Bronach, the saint who once walked on this very ground.'

'You mean she stood here in this cabin?'

'Now,' cautioned the Widow, ''tis hard to be exact about such things, but,' she sensed their disappointment, 'there are some who will swear that she walked on this very spot. Just where you have your feet, lad.'

The boy shifted uncomfortably, looking uneasily at the ground beneath him.

'And what was the staff?'

'Now, you heard me tell you often enough,' the Cobbler interrupted, worried his children would look stupid. 'The staff was the symbol of an abbess. The MacOwens, who are of her family, were stewards of the staff, until the bailiffs wrested it from them and smashed it to pieces.'

'And is that all that remains of it?' said a tiny voice from

192

the corner. All eyes went to the patient where she lay on the pallet.

The Widow stayed until she was sure the worst had passed and then she took her leave. 'Your Murren's a fine wee lassie, Mary take care of her! But she needs building up. Eggs and mutton broth and the like, if you want her this coming Easter.'

The Cobbler did not doubt her advice, but he did not know how he could provide such fare for his daughter.

'I still have my tools of trade and my skills,' he told the Buller. 'All I need is leather from the tanner, but I owe him for two hides.' It was clear to him that no relic, however potent, was going to solve his problems. Curing the sick was one thing; paying bills was another.

Roisha

THE BABY GIRL born to Roisha MacOwen was christened Dervilla after Owen's mother. She was a healthy, robust child from birth, and the Widow maintained that she had never seen a child with a hungrier appetite, a tighter grip or a stronger suck. In a world where many children did not survive infancy, the MacOwens were deemed to be blest with such a hardy little girl. On one thing the couple were agreed: this was their child, and the details of her conception were no one else's business.

After losing his job at the mill, Owen used his time to begin restoring the Healing House. Their little mountain booley on the slopes of Leckan was too damp for the baby, and although the MacOwens' old home was no more than a burned-out shell, it had strong stone walls. All it really needed, Roisha told her husband, was a roof, and it would not take him long to sort that out. Johnny Fearon and the Cobbler rallied around their neighbour, for there was good luck in the erection of a roof. The Buller, looking for his share of fortune, gave Owen the benefit of his advice, and a man of his seniority had plenty to give. Roisha herself, with the assistance of the Cobbler's children and little Michael of the Close, collected bundles of reeds from the bogs alongside the Owenabwee for the final thatching. Within a short time the MacOwens were back in residence. Owen hoped that by the time the Agent Crampsey found out about them, he would be able to pay the rent.

Grace had few personal possessions. A chest containing her books and clothing was transported down to Arno's Vale, and her good chair and table were gratefully accepted by the Cobbler, who assured Mistress O'Lochlainn that they would be well cared for. Her clock she offered to Thady, but he refused it, saying that measuring time at his age was worthless. In truth, he disliked anything which had associations with Grace's past life, although she assured him that the clock had been a gift from Fanny Valentine, not her brother.

'And 'tis a wonder then that she doesn't want it back as well as the house,' he grumbled.

Grace wished to visit Roisha Fegan in her new home, to reassure her that the O'Lochlainns at least were glad to see her back in Kilbroney. Roisha's father, Murtagh, had been responsible for the death of Eamonn O'Lochlainn, and although the wounds of grief were deep for Thady and his family they were nothing to the hurt, humiliation and guilt of the young Fegan daughters. They had had to watch as their father, a strong, brawny blacksmith, was led meekly away to end his life in an asylum, a house for the mad and the damaged.

Grace herself had lived in the Healing House for a short time and as she approached the old building she noticed the crudely re-thatched roof and the young pratie plants struggling to survive on the poor soil, small signs of rebirth in a house which had played host to tragedy. Night was slowly drawing in, and the moon which would guide her steps homewards was already peeping over the mountains of Cooley. A dim light shone from over the half-door.

'God save you, Mistress MacOwen,' called Grace, 'and a blessing on your house and all within.' Roisha MacOwen was preparing to feed her baby. She looked out warily at the visitor. She knew Mistress O'Lochlainn only by reputation and was unsure of how to greet such a lady.

'Come in and welcome,' she replied, mustering up the courtesy which would be expected from a bearer of the MacOwen name. The baby roared her disapproval of this interruption to her feed.

'Don't disturb yourself. I know that when there's a hungry child in the house, even King George must wait his turn,' Grace said, admiring the neatly swaddled bundle.

'He'd wait a long time before I'd let him cross my threshold,' Roisha smiled, put at ease by Grace's friendliness. 'Take a seat by the fire and don't mind me or the *leanbh*.' She eased a breast into the infant's greedy mouth and its howling was at once stifled. As peace returned Grace admired the little room, which was well swept and had a lamp suspended from a beam. There was scarcely a stick of furniture though, save for the two stools and a candle in the corner.

'You have plenty of light,' Grace remarked.

'I brought a good crock of seal oil from Lisnacree,' Roisha explained.

'I didn't know seals had such a use. You learn when you travel!'

'Aye. Lisnacree's not too far from here, but even there they have their ways. My grandfather was a great hand at skinning a seal and saving the grease. The skin makes a good lining for the cradle and keeps the rats at bay.'

'Rats? 'Twould be the brave rat that would step in here. I always heard that Saint Bronach put a blessing on the Healing House to keep out the vermin,' said Grace.

'You're not one to believe in such a yarn, Mistress O'Lochlainn,' Roisha chided as she eased her charge into a more comfortable position.

'No, but I can honestly say that I have never once seen a rat about the place.' Grace leaned forward to admire Roisha's baby. 'She certainly has the Fegan good looks and, God willing, the Fegan brains,' she said.

'She is a wee beauty,' Roisha agreed fondly. 'And to think that I said a novena for a boy. They say that a house of boys is a lucky house.'

'Now you are being superstitious,' said Grace. 'Wherever did you get such a notion?' She was silent for a while as Roisha rocked the baby.

'Your father often spoke of you with pride,' she said then. 'He had more affection for his girls than either he or they realised.'

Roisha looked up, her dark eyes heavy with sadness. 'You spoke with my father?' Grace nodded. 'You visited him in prison?' The last word came out like a sob.

'He sent for me,' Grace answered. 'Yes, I saw him many times. I was with him shortly before he died.'

'I did not know that,' whispered Roisha. 'He died suddenly in the end.'

'Aye, his brave heart gave up fighting. He's at peace now, God rest his soul. He's served his purgatory.'

'We never saw him in that place. My mother couldn't bring herself to visit him. Oh, she was always so busy, between the old folk and the young children; somebody was always ailing. She could have let me go to him, but she said I'd be better off forgetting all about him.' Roisha swallowed. 'I suppose you hated him,' she said, 'for what he did to Eamonn.'

'No, I did not hate him,' replied Grace. 'Poor Murtagh loved too much. He struck out blindly and impetuously, because he believed Eamonn responsible for his son's death.'

'And 'twas a foolish and cruel act.'

'Look at your child, Roisha. Would you kill for her?' said Grace, trying to help her understand her father's actions.

'Yes,' whispered Roisha distantly, 'for this child, I believe I would.'

Grace left the Healing House quietly, for little Dervilla had fallen asleep and her mother had also looked drowsy. As she followed the track towards O'Lochlainn's Close she pondered on the times she had visited poor Murtagh Fegan. They had both known what it was to be denied by their own families. Murtagh's remorse had never left him, and he had paid for his crime more surely than if he had been decently hanged. Roisha did not know of the dreadful conditions in which her father had been housed, chained to a post and fed like an animal from a trough. Grace thought of the peaceful domestic scene she had just left, and breathed a silent prayer for the soul of Murtagh Fegan, the blacksmith.

It was very much against her husband's wishes that Roisha MacOwen went into service as a wetnurse for Madam Trevor's grandson, Ben. Huttie Trevor, said Madam Trevor, had married a soldier who had been killed in battle long before his son was born. Roisha was probably the only woman in Kilbroney artless enough to believe this story, as Huttie was a well-known coquette who had compounded her crime by being a neglectful mother. She had bosoms like two fried eggs, incapable of producing even a droplet. Roisha had plenty of milk, and the more she fed the babies the fuller her breasts became.

The kitchen at the Crag was clean and warm, with gleaming copper pans and a smell of fresh laundry. Madam

Trevor always made sure the young wetnurse had a nourishing breakfast before feeding baby Ben. Dervilla, naturally, had to wait for her milk but, Madam Trevor observed with a smile, this was the natural law: a peasant baby should give way to her betters, and a female to a male.

Within a few months Ben was weaned onto nourishing goats' milk and Roisha's services as a wetnurse were no longer needed. When the poor potato harvest which the Buller had predicted materialised, Roisha began to fear for the health of her little daughter. Needing more work, she offered her services as a washerwoman, and every morning she trudged down from Levallyclanowen with Dervilla on her back to pick up washing from one of the Kilbroney lodging houses. She would join the other women, some of whom she remembered from her own childhood and most of whom looked old and worn beyond their years. With red chapped hands they rubbed and pummelled and washed in the rushing waters of the Owenabwee.

In the afternoons, Roisha called at the Crag for Madam Trevor's washing which was left in a basket by the scullery door. There was a cobbled yard behind the house, surrounded by a high wall topped with jagged iron spikes on one side. An L-shaped building with one studded door and a tiny iron-barred window completed the square. It was a dark, dismal place even on the sunniest days, and it always made Roisha feel nervous. She never lost time in lifting her basket and scurrying back down to the riverside to join her companions.

One evening after she had been to Madam Trevor's, the arsenal behind the Crag was raided. A gang of masked figures cudgelled the sentry on guard and forced an entry. Thankfully, Colonel Trevor told Dargan Butler, only a few dated muskets and some boxes of shot were in storage at the time, so the blackguards had got away with very little.

Butler was concerned that the raid might be a portent of things to come and sent an urgent request for more troopers. A company of Fencibles was sent from Newry with orders to recover the firearms stolen from the Crag armoury. Every cabin in every street and townland was ransacked but no weapons were found. The small groups who habitually gathered at corners and wells were told to disperse and the clientele of Sammy Shields' were closely questioned. Tom Dunn instructed all the United men under his command to say as little as possible and, at all costs, to avoid provocation. He kept a careful eye on the young hotheads in his charge.

Walking homewards one evening a few days after the raid, Johnny Fearon debated with himself about approaching Agent Crampsey to acquire a vacant farm tenancy. After all, as his aunt often remarked, it was high time he settled down with a wife. She reminded him that he had more to his name than the breeches he stood in, for he had thirty-five shillings put by. Johnny did not feel that money taken for ale was honestly earned. He did not object to taking money from Tom Dunn, who could afford it, nor from Mick the Fox, who deserved to lose it, but there was many a poor devil who came to the shebeen to drown his sorrows, and these pennies Johnny was loathe to take. He was lost in these thoughts when a cry roused him. Betsy Dunn was running down the hill towards him, skirts kilted, hair streaming in the wind.

'Johnny,' she cried, 'Johnny, the troopers are at the Healing House! You'll have to get Owen. The screams are terrible; there must be something awful happening.'

'You fetch Owen. I'll go to the Healing House myself.'

'Where is Owen?'

'He's down cutting rushes at the Owenabwee, below the Eel Hole.'

'I'll call him, then. And, Johnny, you take care, do you hear me now,' and Betsy was off again.

Johnny ran as fast as he could up the track past Dunn's Hill and over the beaten path leading to the Healing House. Shouts and whinnying horses warned him to take cover behind the ditch. As he did, the rumble of hooves came pounding along the track, then receded in the distance.

A distressing sight awaited him at the Healing House. The hurdle swayed on one hinge in the doorway and the window shutters were in splinters. He found Roisha MacOwen crouched by the well.

'Mistress MacOwen,' he cried, 'what have they done to you?' The girl screamed and shrank away from him.

'They pulled the skirts off me. They shamed me. I want to die.' Johnny had faced this situation before, with poor women prisoners abused by the warders, and his heart went out to Roisha.

'Look at me, Roisha,' he said quietly, taking a firm hold of her hand. 'They have not shamed you, only themselves. Are you badly hurt?' The calmness of his voice soothed her. She shook her head.

'No, only where I fell. I blooded my knees.'

Johnny examined the injuries with a practical hand, for he had learned some of the Widow's skills. 'There now,' he said, 'they're just scrapes. I'll draw some spring water and we'll get you cleaned up before Owen comes. Is the baby safe?'

'Yes,' she smiled wanly, regaining some confidence. 'She's from a tough breed.'

Johnny waited until Owen came. He looked at the wreckage in the kitchen and at Roisha, shivering amidst the debris, and struggled to contain his anger.

'Roisha!' he said fiercely, 'what have they done to you? Was the child harmed?' Roisha nodded towards the cradle and Owen bounded past her, lifting Dervilla in his arms. 'Thank God,' he breathed, 'you're both safe.' Johnny, satisfied that all was well, slipped quietly away.

Through her tears Roisha watched her husband and child. He was quick to anger and she dared not tell him the truth, for there was no knowing what foolish and impetuous act might follow. She bit her lip. The assault on her home had been no random act. The troopers had insisted that she had intimate knowledge of the Crag, having served in it, and knew what was stored there.

'Did they hurt you at all?' Owen asked. She shook her head. She was carrying Owen's child, and he deserved some peace of mind.

'They were looking for weapons,' she said. 'They've been to every house.'

'Weapons! As if we'd be foolish enough to hide them here.' Owen looked at the damage around him; another wrong to be avenged. At least now he had that hope, though Master Dunn had impressed on them how important it was to be patient, to wait for the day when the signal to rise would come.

'Owen,' Roisha said hesitantly. 'Owen, maybe we shouldn't stay here. We'll go back to the booley, up Leckan.'

'But it won't take me long to mend the damage here.'

'I know,' his wife answered, 'but up Leckan it would be safer; we would see them coming. I'm afraid they'll be back.'

MacOwen's face darkened. 'Dare they touch a hair of your head! If it was Butler put them up to this, I'll kill him yet.'

Correspondence

A CLATTER OF HOOVES on the cobbles announced the arrival of a dispatch rider from Newry with mail for John Mercer. Charlotte, in no mood for scholarly endeavour, abandoned her lessons and scampered outside.

Grace closed her books, resigned to the fact that Charlotte had a tendency to frivolity. She was more concerned with designing ballgowns than learning the elements of Euclid and her work was littered with illustrations of *outré* fashions. The latest, a picture of a child and her mother in matching gowns, lay unfinished on the leaf of the book from which Charlotte was meant to be reading. As she looked at it Grace's frown softened to a smile. The picture bore all the longing of a motherless child who had spent her life being moved from one home to the next.

'Mistress Grace, a letter for you,' Charlotte called. 'I wonder who sent it – it looks as though it has come from a long way away.' Grace recognised the writing of Marcas

MacSorley. As she broke the seal, Charlotte watched her expression turn from expectancy to joy, and then to apprehension.

'Grace,' she said, 'is it bad news?' Grace's eyes were bright with tears.

'No,' she answered. 'Not yet, at any rate.'

October was drawing to an end and the bleak mountainside above Kilbroney was a lonely place as Grace rode into the Close on John Mercer's dappled mare. She brought with her a plump chicken, a bag of oatmeal and sweet wine from Arno's Vale to keep the family company through *Oíche Shamhna*, as the mountain folk called Halloween. No one ever slept on the eve of All Saints, for doing so would provoke all kinds of mischievous behaviour from the brooneys and ghosts. Tom Dunn made a point of joining the company at the O'Lochlainns' on Holy Eve, for Annie disapproved of such superstition and dismissed it as a relic of the pagan past. Betsy, usually keen to accompany her father, had to be coaxed to join him.

'Go on then, the pair of you,' said Annie, 'and if you find you can't sleep over the next few nights, don't blame me.'

The Buller, crippled though he was, had not abandoned his nightly visits to the Close, although he relied now on the help of two sticks and the arm of young Michael. The Cobbler took care of the old man, and the Buller had regained some of the spirit for which he was renowned. Such was the air of growing expectation in the Poorlands that Thady and the Buller had vowed they would see in the next century together.

Grace had intended to leave the Close early in the evening, but was coaxed by her mother not to return to Arno's Vale in the half-light, however swift the mare. She did not need much persuasion, for childhood memories of headless phantoms and ghouls were daunting even to Grace's intelligent mind. More dangerous still was the flesh and blood landlord who, in spite of expectations, had not returned to Dublin for the winter sitting of parliament, but had remained to see the final touches added to his new residence.

Grace was welcomed by her old friends and neighbours as if she'd been twenty years in America, and she was touched by their warmth. As dusk settled in, more and more neighbours gathered in the Close to see the night through together. While Michael helped the Cobbler light the bonfire, Grace caught up with all the news she had missed while she had been at Arno's Vale, including the identity of a new tenant in her cabin; it was Martha Crampsey, the agent's aunt by marriage.

'A spy, undoubtedly,' declared the Buller.

'And why the hell would she spy on you,' asked Thady, 'for you never set foot out of your bed?'

'I still know more of what's going on around me than you do, Thady O'Lochlainn, for all your running up and down the mountain.' Grace smiled as the old sparring partners flexed themselves for an argument.

'Martha Crampsey?' said Tom Dunn. 'I know her. Her brother, Spendlove, was a preacher.'

'You think she's a spy, Master Dunn?' asked Johnny.

'Not at all, man, not at all. The Buller will be seeing spies under his bed next,' said Dunn.

The Buller's eyes narrowed as if considering the possibility. 'Do you mind her husband, Virgil Crampsey?' he enquired of the Master. 'He was some rooster. Always running to the barrack with rumour and hearsay.'

'I know him,' replied Dunn. 'He ran off with a Burren woman half his age, and left poor Martha to fend for herself. She's a God-fearing woman, and there'll be no more sinful behaviour in Kilbroney if she has her way.' Some ribald comments followed this remark, and the company, buoyed up by the Widow's root distillation and Captain Mercer's wine, were ready now to listen to the Buller's ghost stories.

As story followed story the knot of listeners huddled closer together in Thady's kitchen. Johnny could not believe his good fortune when a trembling Betsy Dunn squeezed close to him and, while the Widow petrified them with her terrible tales, his arm stole around her shoulder.

Grace went outside to sit for a time alone in the dark, gazing at the silver trail of the moon in the lough below. She had many things on her mind. After a while Tom Dunn joined her. He put his greatcloak around her shoulders.

'I didn't notice how cold it had become,' she said, thankful for the warmth. Tom drew at his pipe and sat down beside her.

'I received a letter from Dr MacSorley today.'

'Marcas? By all that's wonderful! When will he be home?'

Grace did not answer. Tom looked at her; she seemed thin and fragile in the gloomy air.

'And is there word of Sean?'

'Yes. Marcas has met him. He says he will bring him home if he can.' Her tone was dry, the words spoken without joy.

'Grace!' Tom jumped to his feet. 'Come, you must tell Thady!' He sat down again at once: if Thady did not know already, there must be bad news to come.

'No, Master Dunn, I daren't. I can't tell my father the truth. Sean is very ill and Marcas doesn't know if he will ever get better.' Tears welled in her eyes as she rose and returned to the cabin.

The young men and women danced round the bonfire until just before midnight. Only the foolhardy would remain under the stars after that time, and there were no fools in Kilbroney. The crowded little cabin made room for them as they came in. Little Michael squeezed through the throng and scrambled up the ladder to his pallet in the loft. He lay staring at the thatch. His memory was hazy, and only fleeting pictures of his past remained. Fires of sugar cane and baying hounds mingled with the sound of his mother sobbing. He tried to recall the image of her face, but found he could not. He pulled the fleece over his head and wept.

Next morning after Mass Grace returned to Arno's Vale and found Captain Mercer waiting for her anxiously. 'Grace,' he called, 'thank God you're safe. I was worried when you didn't come home.'

'It was Holy Eve,' she excused herself. 'My mother was in need of my company. She is very superstitious and gets nervous on nights like that.'

'Of course,' he said, his brow furrowed, 'I should have remembered.'

'No, 'tis I who must apologise for causing you to worry.' John Mercer sank into his favourite armchair. At this moment he looked frail and old, and she wondered if there was another reason for his annoyance.

'You should marry me, Grace. 'Tis time you were married,' he said, only half in jest.

'I know I should,' she smiled, 'although some would say it's hardly worth our while at our age.' She sat on the arm of his chair. 'And now tell me what's really on your mind.'

Mercer sighed. 'We never thought it would be easy, Grace, this great movement of ours. Perhaps history will judge us as lunatics, intoxicated by the notion that men can be enriched by their differences.'

'Has there been news from Dublin?'

'Yes, Drennan has been in touch. He says that one of our confederates, Jackson, has been charged with espionage – spying for the French. Anyone who has been in contact with him will also fall under suspicion.'

'William Jackson? We met him in Paris. I took him for an Englishman, but he told me he was of Irish descent.'

'That's him. A most unlikely rebel, but I know him of old. He was one of the leading French agents, totally devoted to the revolution.'

'In Paris he was in the company of a gentleman from London, a Monsieur Cockayne.'

'He was Jackson's close friend, and a British counter-spy.' Mercer turned to study her face, suddenly concerned. 'Did you talk with them for long, Grace? Can you remember anything of what was said?'

Grace pondered for some moments. Her encounter with Jackson was no more than a brief memory, but she could recall no indiscretion. 'Jackson was a small man, very courteous, but Cockayne, I think, dismissed me as a person of no consequence.'

'A grave misjudgement of you, Grace. Yet sometimes it is safer to be overlooked. We must be extremely cautious; many of our friends have taken flight, and the Society of United Irishmen, even the most eminent gentlemen, may no longer meet openly without fear of arrest.'

Grace was not disturbed. 'People like myself, Captain Mercer, have learned from the cradle the wisdom of listening much but saying little. It is the only way to survive.'

'If only we had all had that self-discipline.'

'Why, 'tis often not lack of discipline I would fear,' Grace replied, 'but simple greed.'

The Cobbler's sons were gasping with excitement as they ran towards the O'Lochlainn Close where their father was helping Thady mend a hole in the thatch. 'Look, Da!' they yelled, 'do you see what we've caught?'

'A hare.' The Cobbler reached down and dangled the animal by the ears. 'Why, 'tis a fine beast.'

208

'In the name of all that's holy!' exclaimed Thady, who had been offering unsolicited and unnecessary instructions to his patient neighbour. 'You'll bring seven years' bad luck on your house for killing a hare. They come down from the mountains at this time of year, and there's them that say they're looking for the stable of Bethlehem.'

'I never heard that one before,' said the Cobbler.

'Well you've heard it now,' answered Thady, 'and young cubs like yourselves can learn much by listening to your betters.'

'We didn't kill him,' said the breathless child. 'There was a net across the ditch between Paddy Kielty's field and the loanin. He was well dead before we got him.'

'You can't deny that, Thady,' beamed the Cobbler, planning his evening supper.

'And 'tis easy seen you weren't born and bred around here if you'd think of eating a hare. Hugh the Duke ate one the day he married and died of a choking fit. Besides, the only man around here who would net a hare is Mick the Fox, and I wouldn't cross him.'

The Cobbler, well used to being described as 'in-blown wrack' despite his many years in Kilbroney, was still sensitive about such matters. Neither did he wish a feud with Mick the Fox, who could be a vindictive enemy.

'Maybe we shouldn't eat him,' he said thoughtfully.

'But Da!'

'Houl' on boys, I know the perfect answer: we'll sell him. You can get good money for a big buck hare down in the village.'

Martha Crampsey, the new tenant of Grace's former home, sat astride her roof, battening down a few wisps of thatch. She was a big-boned woman with a long face and a wide mouth with good teeth. Her ample black hair was trapped within the confines of a linen bonnet and her skirts were kilted round her waist. As she worked she sang her favourite hymn, 'A Stronghold Sure,' in a resonant voice. There was a faint echo in the valley, an indication that her prayers were being heard.

Martha Crampsey's childless marriage had not been a happy one. Her brother, Spendlove Bushel, having first tried to dissuade her from marrying Virgil Crampsey, afterwards told her that she could not leave her philandering, violent husband, and that she would have to put up with his beatings just as her saviour had borne the cross. Martha's faith in God's mercy was restored when Virgil left with a young woman from the Burren and the cross was taken from her.

A deserted wife, however, was an embarrassment to the Crampseys, many of whom lived around Rostrevor in positions acquired for them by Agent Crampsey. When he suggested that she relinquish her little house on the square in favour of a mountain cabin he had not seriously expected her to accept, but was very relieved when she did. Martha was glad to get away from her meddlesome in-laws, and even the draughtiest booley at the top of Kilfeighan would have pleased her. She respected the folk of the Poorlands in spite of their outlandish ways and superstitious beliefs. Her command of Irish was poor but she was determined to learn; she attributed her brother Spendlove's lack of success around Kilbroney to his insistence on using English. It was a tragedy, she told him, that souls hungry for salvation heard the word of God only through the Pope's Latin or the King's English, and never through their own tongue.

As she dismounted from her precarious perch she momentarily lost her grip and slid painfully down the thatch. A pair of strong hands arrested her fall. Turning she saw the bearded face of the Cobbler and, unused to such close contact, stammered with embarrassment: 'Unhand me, Sir!'

The Cobbler ensured she was steady on the ground before relinquishing his hold. 'Would you like to buy a hare, Mistress?' he asked courteously. 'I have one here to sell.'

'A hare?' she said. 'No, thank you. But I'd be obliged if you would take your foot off my skirt.' The Cobbler took a step backwards.

'I'll away then,' he tipped his hat. 'Maybe they could use it at the inn.'

Martha was about to ask if his wife could not cook, but thought better of the question. 'I suppose you heard my singing,' she said, her evangelical spirit coming to the fore.

'Why, 'twas loud enough to wake the dead,' the Cobbler answered, adding quickly, 'but it was a lovely air.'

Martha soon found out that the Cobbler was widowed, had a sick child, and not a brass farthing to his name. He was just the kind of creature God wanted her to help.

'Come in here or I'll skelp your backside!' Eily O'Lochlainn shouted as she chased Michael round the yard, scattering the ducks in all directions.

'You can't catch me,' giggled the boy, evading Eily's flailing arms. Thady's croaking laughter brought on a fit of coughing.

'Now look at what you've done.' Eily stopped to pummel her husband's back. 'Cough it up there,' she scolded. Michael, repentant, came forward.

'I don't want my hair cut. 'Twill be too cold,' he said, his lower lip curling.

'I'm only going to trim the dangling bits. To keep them out of your dinner.'

'I can do that myself,' Michael protested.

'Leave the lad be, Eily,' Thady said. 'There's the divil all wrong with his hair; nothing that can't wait till after Christmas.'

'Sure what's the use of me worrying; all I'm good for is darning your hose and patching the seat of your breeches!'

'Oh, go on,' Thady relented. 'Sure you'll be in the height of the fashion now,' he consoled Michael. 'Grace tells me the Newry men are cropping their heads like the French.'

Thady hadn't been about much of late and relied on his daughter for tales of the outside world, but in the quiet of the dark evenings he often picked up the sound of a sharp voice shouting commands, a muffled drumbeat and the clash of steel against steel. Earlier in the year when the weather had been better, the Buller and Thady had been able to make their way across Ruaslieve to a glen where the United Irishmen trained and drilled. The youthful sentry knew them and allowed them to pass unhindered. It was a stirring sight: men from the townlands around Kilbroney marching in fours, some well shod, many barefoot; farmers' lads, cottiers and spalpeens alike, their heads high, following the drum. Some had guns, but most carried only pikes. There were many other groups like them in other parts of the mountains: Protestant, Papist and Dissenter all marching under the one banner. To Thady it was a sight at the one time beautiful and terrifying.

Fr Mackey had harsh words for those who imbibed anything stronger than buttermilk during Advent. His sermon was brief. He had jugged a hare in onions and coarse wine before Mass and was anxious to set it on the fire. Like his congregation he had fasted from midnight, and he looked forward to a satisfying lunch with plenty of praties and butter. By lucky chance he had come across the Cobbler on his way to the inn the previous evening and had purchased the hare from him for a few pence. 'I'll remember young Murren in my prayers,' he offered for good measure.

With these uplifting words, coins in his pocket and the

strictures against alcohol forgotten, the Cobbler payed a call on Sammy Shields' alehouse. There he found MacCormac the blacksmith, Tom Dunn and several others in earnest discussion.

'I saw the conscript lists,' MacCormac was saying. 'Ten from each parish.' He closed his eyes and recited names from Killowen, Moygannon, Knockbarragh, Reagh and the other townlands. 'Owen MacOwen was the last name on.'

'Owen, of all people.' Tom Dunn was pensive. 'He'll not leave his wife and child.'

Everyone agreed that Owen would not be a willing recruit.

'Whatever he thinks, he'll have to go all the same,' opined MacCormac. 'The war's going badly for them and they need more men.'

'Which means it's going well for the French.'

Johnny Fearon listened quietly, knowing that his opinions were likely to go unheeded. He drew Tom Dunn aside.

'Master Dunn. I know 'twill break Owen's heart to go. Poor Roisha, with a wee girl and another due. You'd nearly think they did it on purpose.'

'You could never be sure.' Dunn was unwilling to engage in speculation.

'I will join up in his place.' Johnny held his head up. 'I have no wife or children. No one will mourn me when I've gone.'

'I doubt that, Johnny; you'd be sorely missed. And anyhow, if you were to volunteer, they'd only take you both. Remember what happened with young MacVeigh.'

'And what if Owen doesn't want to go?'

'I'm sure Owen won't want to go.'

'Would they put him in gaol?'

'I fear they'd hang him.'

Tom Dunn's company was dealt another blow a few days later when news came that the Cobbler McChesney had been arrested for selling a hare, an offence against the game laws. The troopers had arrived in the early hours of the morning, causing great upset to the children. McChesney had been as shocked as anyone, as he had made no secret of the fact that he had a hare for sale.

The McChesney boys, remembering the talk about their new neighbour, Martha Crampsey, assumed that she had been behind the arrest and promptly went and threw stones at her house. The Buller and Thady, on hearing the commotion, came hobbling down to them.

'They've taken away our da,' cried the youngest child, 'for selling the hare. She told them about it.'

'Will you get a grip of yourselves, lads,' the Buller shouted, 'and leave the poor woman be. You'll only make matters worse; and remember, you have to share a well with her.'

The hot-headed McChesneys spilled out the story of their father's arrest. When she heard what they had to say, Martha Crampsey was almost as angry as the boys. The blame she laid firmly at the feet of the Agent Crampsey, her nephew-in-law.

'If I see him first, I'll douse him in clabber, so I will,' she promised the youngsters, who were now regretting their action. They offered to repair the damage they had caused, and Martha Crampsey graciously accepted their apologies, telling them she'd have oaten farls off the griddle by the time they'd finished.

Tom Dunn wondered why such an obsolete law had been enforced; it was a long time since anybody from Kilbroney had been gaoled for such a trivial crime. He suspected that this was part of the response to the raid on the arsenal, and that

214

there would be many more such incidents. He would have to warn his men to be careful.

'McChesney's in gaol,' he told his wife as she sat by the fire.

'Poor lad,' replied Annie, closing her eyes. Tom looked at her tenderly. She had been withdrawn since James and the grandchildren had left for America. The old spirit had gone and a malaise had come over her.

'I'll go over to Arno's Vale. Maybe Mercer will bail him out,' he said.

'What's the point,' Annie said quietly, 'there's no hope for us now. We'll be beaten before we even begin to fight.' Tom lifted a fleece rug and wrapped it round her shoulders. They were not getting any younger: he was nearing sixty years of age, and Annie was not far behind. Her face was thin and worn, and a mist clouded her once bright eyes. Yet she was still the wife he loved. He stoked up the fire, stooped to kiss her brow and then tiptoed out of the house.

Christmas in Kilbroney

T HE GENTLEMEN OF the Down Hunt and their ladies made merry after a successful day in the field. A minor outbreak of smallpox in the city had encouraged them to stay in the country until word came that it was safe to return to Dublin, and the ladies had risen to the challenge by organising a round of balls and assemblies to brighten up the dark evenings.

At Narrow Water chandeliers blazed with beeswax candles until the early hours of the morning. Savage Hall's home was modest compared to the country seats of the Annesleys and Nedhams, and was little more than a shack beside Dargan Butler's magnificent new house which would soon be ready for occupation, but such matters did not bother the Squire. He was content with a strong, well-fortified home, free of vermin and with chimneys which did not smoke. He could offer a decent table, with the best of imported wine and liquor, ostensibly from the merchants of

Newry but in fact from the smugglers of Hill Town. There was no use, he confided to his lady, in throwing good money after bad, for what was paid to the treasury only helped the good-for-nothings in Dublin Castle keep their own decanters full.

It was a cause of some chagrin to Madam Hall that Dargan Butler was now fully accepted into county society. She watched him sit with her guests, immaculate in snowy silken hose and polished slippers; his hairline, now receding slightly at the temples, added to his distinguished appearance.

'And just think of poor Fanny,' said Madam Hall to the Squire; 'she never goes anywhere now.'

Savage Hall knew Fanny Valentine's situation better than most, but felt it was largely her own fault that she had got herself into a mess. As for Butler, he had crossed all the right paths, met all the right people, spent Fanny's money in the right places. He was now one of the county's more influential landlords and, at present, considerations of national security had to take precedence over petty domestic situations.

The increase in secret societies and the veritable explosion of radical 'United Irishmen' was a cause of great concern to the landlords; they threatened agricultural production and disrupted trade and commerce. Squire Hall fumbled for his spectacles.

'Listen to this,' he said, holding up a copy of the *Northern Star*, a seditious Belfast newsheet. '"It is something more than ridiculous to see a set of country squires hot from the chase, flushed with wine, and still more intoxicated with an idle and imaginary idea of their own consequence!" What a nerve that Tone fellow has. Absolute cheek.' A murmur of disapproval circulated round the table along with the port. Dargan Butler's voice rose above the hubbub, urging his companions to take immediate action against the rebels.

'We can deal with the ordinary peasants,' a military man responded, 'but the simple people are easily led, and many have not the intellect to distinguish right from wrong.'

'They can distinguish a farthing from a groat all right,' glowered Hall.

'As I say, it is not the peasantry who are at the root of the problem but the merchants, the freeholders; lettered men, people of intellect. And there are very few Papists among their ranks.'

'So what do we do about it?' Dargan Butler shouted angrily. 'Are we to become figures of fun, lampooned by every street-corner ballad singer? And there is more than personal honour at stake: the nobility of France has paid dearly for lack of vigilance. Have you not heard the horrific tales of the Paris bloodbath?

'I have no doubt as to what must be done,' Butler finished heavily. 'These people are planning treason and they deserve the fate of traitors.'

When it was deemed safe for society to return to Dublin, Madam Hall breathed a sigh of relief: her carefully planned winter wardrobe would not be wasted on the county folk of Down. She had selected jolly colours of berry red, claret and mustard, packed a ballgown of turquoise and mauve and a fur-trimmed crimson riding attire. Some items in her wardrobe were of deepest blue, but no green was included for fear of encouraging the wrong element to believe they had her support.

Bess Hall did not concern herself with matters of state, the French war or the current agrarian unrest. Even if she did have an opinion on these topics it would be unlikely to carry much weight socially. She confined herself to worrying about her family, whether her eldest daughter would at long last find a beau or whether the younger girl might soon produce a son, and she worried about her friend.

She had tried very hard to persuade Fanny to accompany them to Dublin. Everyone else had given up on the eccentric woman; some were even of the opinion that she had inherited a family tendency to insanity from old Colonel Whitechurch. Many reasons were advanced for poor Fanny's behaviour: 'Her sex,' suggested the men; 'Her age,' whispered the women. It angered Madam Hall that no one remembered what a splendid person she had been before she married Dargan Butler. Butler was a rising star in the political sky, and no one was prepared to hinder his ascent.

Rostrevor's woods had changed from summer green to the vibrant shades of autumn and faded to the transparent grey of winter. The modest summer residences of gentlefolk along the shore were shuttered and boarded and in the village the lodging houses had closed for the winter. All spinning and weaving had stopped since the mill's closure and some of the scutchers and bleachers had upped and taken a boat for England. Those who expected poor relief from Kilbroney House were disappointed, but some were employed on the laying of a new road from the village square to Master Butler's new residence. It was never referred to as Madam Butler's, for it was no secret that Fanny did not wish to move from her family home.

The trees of the Kilbroney estate bore only a few ragged brown leaves as Dargan Butler's carriage came up the drive. The servants of Kilbroney House scurried to attend to the needs of their ill-humoured master, who was soon wallowing in a rose-scented tub and imbibing a hearty nightcap. He had things on his mind. A succession of expensive young mistresses and a few unlucky gambles had left him short of pocket, and the new house was turning out to be more expensive than expected. On the other hand, he was about to be appointed Surveyor General by the Viceroy, a sinecure which carried a substantial salary. As Surveyor General he would be charged with gathering intelligence on events in the county and reporting it to Dublin Castle. He thought he would look at what his neighbouring landlords had done to tackle the United Irishmen; he would perhaps question their resolve. He despised the sycophantic county gentlemen who had once looked down their noses at him.

Dargan Butler sank deeper into the tub, pondering. Rejected by his 'father', his childhood marred by his mother's promiscuity, he had been left in no doubt that his roots were far from aristocratic. Once a housemaid had called him the 'coachman's bastard'. Butler winced at the recollection. He had resolved from that moment to brook no insult, suffer no slur. He thought of Grace O'Lochlainn, a peasant woman, already used by Henry Valentine.

Owen MacOwen kissed his wife and bade her goodbye. Roisha was pregnant again and had been looking forward to presenting him with a little son, an heir to the MacOwen name. A name: so much to leave, yet so little. MacOwen had lost his home, his land, and was about to lose his freedom. On this bitter morning Roisha and the Widow watched the last of Clan Owen of Levallyclanowen leave his home, conscripted into the king's militia to fight for a cause in which he had no faith, against men with whom he had no quarrel.

Most lads of the Poorlands might accept such a call as a cross to be carried, but not Owen. He knew in his heart that he could not do what was asked of him. At Dunn's Hill he stopped to say goodbye to Master Dunn.

'The worst of it is we don't know where you will be sent or when we will see you again,' the old man said gravely.

'Maybe sooner than you think, Master Dunn.' Tom Dunn

looked closely at Owen. 'I know,' the conscript continued, 'of a man who hid out in Brennan's booley for months.'

An hour or so later Owen was crossing the mountains below the Clasha, on his way to Kilfeighan. It was best that Roisha did not know her husband had deserted even before joining up.

Tom Dunn watched Owen's departure. He had few fears now for this wild boy, reared by the people of the Poorlands; Owen would survive in the mountains for as long as he had to. Certainly his chances were better there than if he were on some foreign battlefield, fodder for enemy guns and ambitious generals. In the meantime, Tom would have to make sure that Roisha and her children were provided for.

He felt a sudden longing for companionship and rode to Arno's Vale where Mercer greeted him with warmth, enquiring after his family.

'His family?' Grace appeared smiling in the doorway. 'He has adopted half the mountainside.' She thought Dunn looked tired and careworn. Mercer bade him sit in by the fire.

'Kick off your boots there, man. Is your Annie in good health? And Betsy?'

'Both in fine fettle, thank God,' he gave the customary reply. Grace knew him too well, however.

'Is there anything wrong with Annie?' she asked bluntly. 'Does she miss James and the grandchildren?' Dunn was quiet for a moment.

'Yes, she misses her family. She says little, but she's pining all the same. I was going to send to the school in Belfast for Harry, the young lad, but she told me to leave him be. "He'll come to less harm where he is," she says. Annie's not herself anymore. Ach, she makes the bread and feeds the fowl like she always did, but she'll not fight, she'll not argue. She's not

221

even concerned about Betsy's comings and goings, and she used to have my heart broken on the subject.'

Grace knew how much Tom Dunn relied on his wife, and how important her support was to him in his long fight for justice. There was little she could say.

'Maybe when the winter turns and the days get longer she'll pick herself up.'

'That's what she would have said,' Dunn smiled. 'Maybe you're right, Grace.'

Mercer knew what it was to have an ailing wife and felt sorry for his friend. 'Will you partake of some lunch?' he invited. 'Mistress Hanratty's roasting a hare.'

'Oh, God: a thorny subject in Kilbroney,' Dunn laughed.

'This one was bartered from Mick the Fox who was found squatting in one of my fields. In return for the hare, I didn't kick his backside.'

'You should have kicked it good and hard,' Dunn said stoutly, 'for the cur deserves it. The poor Cobbler has had to pay for his sins.'

'You need not worry on that score. I sent a man to Newry to bail the Cobbler out. Seems he was prosecuted by the Down Hunt.'

'A poor man with starving children.' Dunn shook his head wearily. 'I couldn't raise the bail myself.'

'Why should you? Our comrades rallied round. Isn't that the meaning of fraternity: to stand by one another?'

The fiddler had left the Clasha. His music had not been heard for some time and there were rumours that he had joined up with some of the scutchers on their way to England. The Buller and Thady recalled how he had been the first man to take the oath in the summer of '92, when Wolfe Tone had visited. The Buller had commented then on the uselessness of a crossroads fiddler, but Tom Dunn had been adamant that every man's particular skill could be of use, and one who could lift the heart with his planxties and love songs or stir up passions with laments and marches was beyond price.

Betsy Dunn said little about the fiddler. She knew that her feelings for O'Cassidy had started as a girlish infatuation, yet there remained a deeper concern for him, fired by pity and compassion. On her last visit to the Clasha she had stood boldly outside O'Cassidy's hut, but he had refused to come out; had begged her to leave. Then the music started, painful, raw chords, so different from the lyrical lilting tunes that had first captured her heart. Now it anguished her to listen; the tears coursed down her face, her weeping a fitting descant to the ragged music. The music faded to a whisper and then, with one last dreadful jarring chord, stopped completely.

The Cobbler returned to Kilbroney a hero. He was over-whelmed by the generosity of the Newrymen who, having bailed him out of gaol, had sent him home with two guineas in his pocket. He had come via Ballyholland and the Bridge of Mayo into Hill Town, where he invested one of his guineas in leather from the tanner. He selected his material after considerable deliberation, wanting a hide that would mend twenty pairs of boots or more. He then purchased a large sack of oatmeal and, in a moment of extravagance, a fat rooster from the tanner's wife. She let him have it at a bargain price, partly in anticipation of his future custom but also because it had lost a wing in a fight. It was a good solid bird, nevertheless, and if the Cobbler's back was sore by the time he crossed the wasteland into Kilbroney, his step was lighter. He still had to face trial, but Captain Mercer had told him that he would most likely be fined, depending on the pleasure of the magistrate. If he faced Dargan Butler, though, a prison sentence would be more probable. He had heard of men being hanged for lesser offences, but had chosen to disregard this grim rumour for the time being. As he breathed again the air of Kilbroney and smelled the scent of heather, peat smoke and a hint of sea, he resolved that no one, not even Dargan Butler, would compel him to leave his home again.

Martha Crampsey obliged her neighbour and roasted the rooster on a spit over her own fire, attracting hungry faces from near and far. By the time the bird had been cooked and distributed, there were only bones left for the Cobbler to pick.

Christmas Eve in the Poorlands was observed by a fast, which was repeated by the more devout on St Stephen's Day. Fr Mackey went to great lengths to stress that the very young, the very old and the infirm were not obliged to undertake the fast, but it was understandable that those who were nearest to death were most inclined to earn as many indulgence as they could before leaving this world. Though there were some cabins where a piece of fat bacon enlivened the day's fare, for the great majority Christmas was no different from any other day of the year. If there was one comfort to be gained from it, it was that the child Jesus had at least been as poor as themselves.

An hour before midnight on Christmas Eve, the Cobbler brought Michael of the Close to the top of Leckan Mountain. They stood with the other men and boys in silence, listening. At the head of the valley many more ears were alert, including those of Thady and the Buller. On many a Christmas Eve they had climbed Leckan, but the time had come for younger, fitter men to uphold the tradition. From their well-chosen vantage point the two men watched the tiny flickering lights, the lanterns of families on their way to Mass, dim reflections of the star-studded sky.

Then from the distant west came the music, a mere echo at first, then louder and more triumphant: the call of wild horns saluting the infant king. They heard the sound in Fathom and Cooley, and then the men of the Kilbroney Poorlands raised the ancient ram's horn to their lips and blew with all their might. It was the battle cry of peace, the herald of a new beginning. From across the mountain in Kilfeighan came the answering call, and the strange, beautiful fanfare proclaimed to one and all the birth of Christ.

Captain Mercer and Charlotte attended morning eucharist at the parish church of St Paul's at the Crag field. The little church was modestly decorated with sprigs of holly, for the vicar abhorred high-church frippery. It was a draughty building, although hot bricks were always prepared for the main pews, a luxury for which many of the older ladies were grateful. They brought fur-lined rugs, too, for there was no predicting how long the sermon would last.

Fanny Butler had been some ten minutes late taking her seat in the Valentine family pew and had held up the start of the service; she was accompanied by her maid only. Agent Crampsey sat in the pew opposite her, taking note of the names of those who attended, or rather, those who did not. The vicar of Kilbroney strongly objected to this practice for, as he often remarked to John Mercer, he would prefer to think that his congregation was there by choice. The agent's 'Black Book' was a tradition dating back to the Penal years, when it was instituted by Fanny's ancestor, the Puritan Colonel Whitechurch, whose memory she revered.

The service was pleasant enough, if overly long. As the final seasonal hymn brought the ceremonies to a close, Madam Butler rose to leave, accepting the reverences of her old retainers. As she reached her carriage, a weatherbeaten gentleman of military bearing approached. He introduced himself as Captain John Mercer, mariner, of Arno's Vale, and asked permission to call on her to pay his respects.

Conclave in Belfast

THE ROAD BETWEEN Belfast and Newry was the smoothest in Ireland, or so claimed the coachman as he helped Grace O'Lochlainn board the Cock o' the North for the eight-hour journey to Belfast. Heavy rains in December and early January had made the Great Northern Road impassable, and abandoned vehicles and broken carriage wheels littered the highway. Gangs of bedraggled spalpeens and paupers from the workhouses were constrained to mend the worst of the potholes with picks and shovels in return for a few pence and a daily dish of soup.

Grace found the carriage comfortable and endeavoured to pass the time by reading, but the light was poor and the quality of the roads fell short of the coachman's claims. She abandoned her book, removed her spectacles and conversed briefly with her companions, one of whom was a convivial gentleman of ample girth with a repertoire of jests which kept Grace amused for a few miles. The gentleman, who professed to be a bishop, introduced his sister, a sniffling woman who ate candied sweetmeats and clearly disapproved of her brother's familiarity with strange women. Near Dromore, where the passengers usually refreshed themselves, the bishop's sister was overcome with travel sickness, no doubt due to a surfeit of candied pears, and was persuaded to rest at the inn for a day or two before resuming her journey. Grace had to suffer the lecherous advances of the bishop, free from the constraints of sisterly devotion. It was with no small relief that she alighted from the coach into the noisy welcome of Belfast town.

Grace had agreed to visit Belfast on behalf of Tom Dunn, whose wife's illness had compelled him to remain at home. She was delegated to speak on behalf of several south Down companies of the United Irishmen, and to listen to and bring back the views of other branches. As the society had grown, so also had prospered the various sectarian groups, suspicious of the concept of equality and unable to comprehend the notion of brotherhood. Yet in Antrim and Down, greed and self-interest had not yet sullied the revolutionary ideals of the United Irishmen. While the posturing Dublin society, boasting among its members the social elite, called for revolution, the cautious northern men of Ulster had organised themselves into cells and were prepared to wait, to change from within. As she met and exchanged experiences with delegates from other parts of the country, Grace worried about the young hotheads who talked of expelling the English and were spoiling for a fight.

Tom Dunn had written a brief note introducing Grace to Mary Anne McCracken, who welcomed the Kilbroney woman to her home, a cheerful, bustling house with children and callers constantly coming and going. Mary Anne was the sister of Henry Joy McCracken, one of Belfast's leading linen merchants, who had opened his doors to the revolutionary movement. Samuel Neilson and the Simms brothers, William and Robert, who owned a tannery, were regular callers, as was the ladies' favourite, the handsome Thomas Russell. A young organist from Armagh, Edward Bunting, lodged in the McCracken house.

Mary Anne sympathised with anyone who had to live in the country, especially in an outpost as remote as Kilbroney with its wild men and smokey cabins, and took Grace around Belfast, showing her how to find her way through the busy little lanes and entries. It was a vibrant throbbing town with a palpable air of pride and self-confidence. They passed burgher's wives in starched caps and aprons bustling about their business while choristers snaked across the cobbles towards Church Lane. Even the beggars were well shod and had a superior air about them, as if they'd turn their nose up at anything but the freshest crusts.

As they walked towards Hanover Quay the odours of tar, linseed, hemp and hides mingled in the air – the smell of prosperity. Acres of mud around the Long Bridge marked where the city was reclaiming the lough for its use. Several handsome vessels were moored in the deep channel along Chichester Quay. Pride of the fleet was the *Hibernia*, Henry Joy McCracken's beloved ship. It bore a crest of a harp surmounted by a crown, an emblem which had provoked the jeers of Wolfe Tone and his companions on one occasion.

'The *Hibernia*,' Grace voiced her admiration. 'She's beautiful, with or without the crown!'

'You should see her with sails unfurled on the high seas. She's like an angel in the water.'

They turned away from the docks to one of the missions where Mary Anne worked. Ports, she explained, attracted poor wretches from all parts of the globe, many suffering from scurvey or malnutrition. The goodwives of Belfast took pride in succouring them with nourishing food, at least while their ships were in port.

When she had time to herself Grace spent many hours browsing in the musty bookshops around the Linen Hall, recalling with affection old Makepeace Theophilous Agnew, a stout Presbyterian bookbinder who had befriended her family many years before, and protected them at the price of his own life.

In the evenings, the company would gather to dine and talk about the future of the 'Union Regiment', Tone's nickname for the corps of United Irishmen. Mary Anne McCracken did not believe in the women leaving the dining table with the port, for she counted herself the equal of the men. As the tide of political debate rose and fell around the table, Grace was wont to listen rather than speak, to learn rather than teach, but when she had something to say she did so with conviction. As the finest of Master Bunting's Irish airs floated through the McCracken house, it occurred to her, not for the first time, the responsibility they held in their hands, and the serious consequences to which this dining-room discussion could lead.

A fortnight after Grace's departure for Belfast, Annie Dunn died in her sleep. Tom Dunn's grief was tempered by relief that her suffering had come to an end: the apoplexy which had attacked her body had left her helpless and unable to speak and the best of the Widow's remedies had proved ineffectual. Even the physicians brought from Newry could only shake their heads and advise that she be bled and made as comfortable as possible. The Widow Fearon had then concocted a strong draught which eased her agitation and helped her sleep.

Harry, their youngest son, had been summoned to her bedside during her last week and had been in constant attendance. Harry, small and slight, with a scholarly air, was of all Dunn's children the most like his mother. Each night he would hold her hand and read her favourite psalms by the light of a rush candle, while Dunn stood helplessly in the doorway. He paid only lip service to religion, so the psalms had little meaning for him; the words of great love and faith could not easily pass his lips. Instead he fed the chickens, milked the cows and did all the daily household chores usually undertaken by Annie.

When she died, Tom Dunn, so often a source of comfort to others, found it hard to cry, although the pain of her loss lay like a cross upon his shoulders. Throughout his ordeal, Betsy stood by him, no longer a carefree girl but a woman who had tasted bitterness and drunk sorrow. The Widow laid Annie out 'as fine as a queen', for there was no woman more loved by the poor and disadvantaged than Annie Dunn. They came for three days and nights to the house to wake her and mourn her passing, and even Fr Mackey called to pay his respects. The parish priest's visit intensified the customary rumours of a deathbed conversion to Catholicism, but Annie Dunn had died as she lived, a staunch Presbyterian. Her burial was not according to Roman ritual, but she was laid to rest alongside the shrine of Saint Bronach, among the people she loved most.

Early in May, Tom Dunn joined Grace O'Lochlainn and some seventy other delegates at a rally of the northern United Irishmen in Belfast. They represented thousands of men throughout the north who waited for the word to rise. Heartened by the successes of their compatriots in the American colonies and in France, all believed that the tide of freedom was flowing and that their ship was as seaworthy as any.

Dunn had followed keenly the news of Jackson, the French agent, whose trial had become the talk of the country. His brief encounter with Grace and the trade delegation in Paris was no more than that, but such were the rumours circulating that even slight acquaintances of the man had been questioned by the authorities. Then some days before the Belfast rally a dispatch rider reached McCracken's house with news that Jackson had committed suicide before sentence could be passed. Dunn thought this would mean that the Newry brotherhood was no longer in danger of investigation, but he soon discovered that, far from subsiding, talk of Jackson could be heard at every street corner. Pamphlets and magazines were circulated describing every detail of the events and, in particular, Wolfe Tone's involvement with the French spy.

'This propaganda by the authorities is as sure a sign as any that the French are on the sea and ready to sail for Ireland,' the younger delegates remarked, but Sam Neilson received the same news with much greater caution.

'Tone would be well advised to keep out of harm's way,' he told Dunn as they entered the meeting room.

Despite the controversy the man from Bodenstown was given a heartwarming welcome from the delegates. He and his wife Matilda were treated to the best of northern hospitality, and there was even a collection to alleviate his personal debts. Dunn was delighted to renew his friendship with Tone, and joined him, Thomas Russell, Henry Joy McCracken and Sam Neilson in a climb to MacArt's Fort on the top of Cave Hill. They looked out over Belfast and its lough, and beyond to the green rolling drumlins of Down, the pearly mist above Lough Neagh framed by the distant mountains. There, on that heady spring evening, with the sun setting on a distant horizon, they pledged themselves anew to their cause. In the days that followed Dunn told Grace: 'I felt myself a young man again. It looked so simple standing there; this green land, peaceful and prosperous, laid out like a dream. It seemed to be there for the taking.' Grace was pleased to see her old mentor throwing himself into his political activities again. It would not heal the wounds of Annie's death, but at least it would divert him from his grief.

As the Belfast conference continued, debate raged as to the timing of the rebellion. No one doubted that it would come; the only question was when. The delegates from Newry declared themselves well armed and drilled, and were among the many who urged a speedy insurrection while the British army was still engaged with the French. Thomas Russell, speaking on behalf of the eager young men of Belfast, pointed to the popularity of the movement.

'The people are with us,' he insisted. 'Everywhere we go, they cheer the green cockade.' There was a wild feeling of celebration in the air. The conference voted that Wolfe Tone should sail for America. His mission: to inform the French minister of the strength of the United Irishmen and their readiness for battle. In the meantime the leaders were asked to return to their villages and townlands and advise the ranks to be patient, to wait just a little while longer.

The Return

T HE SHIP STRUGGLED into the port of Newry, storm-tossed and weatherbeaten, its cargo from the tropics, its sole passenger Dr Marcas MacSorley. He was glad to feel dry land beneath his feet. He dispatched a couple of brawny lads to the Pope's Head inn with his trunk and instructions to order a hearty breakfast for a hungry seafarer.

Newry had little changed in the years he had been away. The yeomenry corps appeared to have increased in number, and there were very many more redcoats on the streets than he remembered. At the corner of Hill Street a band of noisy youths had gathered to taunt the yeomen. The Newry rebels, he thought, must be in a strong position, for he could not remember such audacious behaviour going unpunished before. He turned towards Sugar Island, the name a curious reminder of the lands he had left behind him.

'MacSorley! Marcas MacSorley, after all these years. God

save you!' A small, shabbily dressed man raised his hat as he passed.

MacSorley took some moments to recognise Neville the merchant, one of his companions on the French expedition; he seemed so careworn and old. 'How have you been since I saw you last?' he asked.

'Not so good; like many of my comrades.' MacSorley listened to his old friend's story. 'It was Butler,' Neville finished bitterly. 'He reneged on my insurance policy. It was my own fault for trusting such a man, but it broke my wife's heart.' MacSorley shook his head. No, Newry had not changed.

Next morning a messenger boy delivered a hastily penned letter to Dr MacSorley, informing him that Captain John Mercer was aware of his arrival and urging him to return to Arno's Vale without delay. MacSorley was amused at his friend's lack of patience. He had looked forward for some months now to meeting his friends again, but as the time approached he grew more apprehensive of the welcome he would receive from the one he most dearly wished to see: Grace O'Lochlainn. Their parting in Paris had been cool, almost bitter. He should never have declared his love in such a way, he thought. Oh, she had listened courteously and her refusal had been gentle and honest, but he had found rejection hard to accept: rarely had he admitted his feelings so openly. It seemed that Grace regarded him as no more than a friend, a comrade-at-arms. Yet it was love for Grace which had sent him across the ocean to find her brother Sean, who had been no more than a name to him then. It was the same love which had brought him back. He had a long tale to tell, and he had hopes that the years might have changed Grace's feelings for him.

The woods around Rostrevor were verdant green and a

gentle breeze blew across the lough as MacSorley rode over the meadows towards Arno's Vale. A cowman bringing home the herd shouted a greeting to the stranger. MacSorley smiled as he thought of John Mercer, the old seadog who once swore he'd be buried at sea, now settled down in this pastoral idyll.

The welcome was all any returned mariner could hope for. Captain Mercer opened the pride of his cellar to celebrate the return of his friend. After Mistress Hanratty served supper they talked long into the evening by the fireside. They had much to discuss, for neither had been idle in the intervening years. Mercer brought his friend up to date on the events of the locality and talked sadly about the death of Annie Dunn and the distress this had brought upon Tom. The physician expressed his sorrow at the news, and then asked about Grace.

'How is she, John?' he asked. 'You say she lived here for a while, but what now?'

'Grace? She has become a woman of great influence. She is accompanying Tom Dunn to Belfast for an important conclave. Have no fears for her.'

'She has not married?'

'Married? Grace? I don't think any man would live up to her ideals. If you're looking for a wife, Marcas, find a nice young wench with a dowry.' As he spoke he realised he had discomfited his friend. 'Of course,' he continued, 'I may be wrong about Mistress O'Lochlainn, but she doesn't seem to have the manner of a mild little wife. If that's what you want,' he finished awkwardly. As he scrutinised Marcas's face he realised, with some misgivings, that a mild little woman was not at all what his friend had in mind.

MacSorley rode through Rostrevor in the early morning. An ass stood tethered under the old oaks in the square; the sound of a pump clanking suggested that the village was coming awake. MacSorley rode up past the Mass House towards Dunn's Hill. Master Dunn was still in Belfast, Mercer had told him, but Harry and Betsy would be at home. He had not forgotten the many kindnesses of Annie Dunn, and he wished to pay his respects to the family.

Betsy failed to recognise him at first and would not open the door to him. It had not occurred to MacSorley how much he had changed: his skin was sun-browned now, his beard abundant.

'Betsy, you should remember me! Many's the time I looked after you: Marcas MacSorley, your physician,' he said. She smiled then in recognition and invited him in. He remarked at the change in her. Since he had tended her fever in the winter of 1790 she had passed from childhood to womanhood. Her skin was pale, almost translucent, and there were dark shadows under her green eyes. The red hair which he remembered tumbling wildly over her shoulders was braided and constrained under a cap. He shook hands with her and Harry, sympathising on their bereavement; there was a sense of emptiness in the kitchen where Annie had presided for so long, and the young people seemed subdued. Then he asked Betsy if she was still breaking hearts and was rewarded with a laugh.

As he prepared to ride on his way, the girl ran after him.

'Dr MacSorley,' she said, 'I must talk with you. I dare not speak with anyone else.'

He wondered if it was some young maid's complaint, to be spoken of in riddles, but he could see that she was very troubled.

'Are you feeling poorly, Betsy?' he asked gently. Her face was grave as she wiped her hands on her apron. 'You need not be afraid to talk to me. There's nothing you could tell me I haven't heard before.'

'Dr MacSorley,' she blurted out, 'I want to talk to you about the fiddler of the Clasha.'

As Marcas listened to the girl's story, his interest grew. It seemed he would have to find the fiddler, but first he had another call to make.

An hour later MacSorley was enthroned by the hearthside at O'Lochlainn Close. Eily expelled a few scrawny chickens to the yard outside and joined Thady and his guest, feeling both apprehensive and curious. After the usual courtesies had been exchanged the doctor had asked to see Michael, saying that he had something important to tell them.

'He's away up the mountain with Pup. He's turned into a great lad, you know,' Thady told him.

'I asked,' Marcas explained, 'for this story partly concerns him. But maybe you should be the one to tell him, not me.'

'Go on.' Thady pulled on his pipe and sat forward, determined not to miss a word.

'I left France in '91 bound for the West Indies. I had promised your daughter I would try to find out the truth about Sean's disappearance,' he began.

'If he'd wanted to come home, he could have done so of his own accord.' Thady was cagey in his reaction. He had long ago given Sean up for dead, and any hint that he might still be alive only reawakened the old pain.

'No, Thady, it was not so simple for him. But hear my story and you'll understand.' The old couple listened, Eily's eyes wide with wonder as MacSorley described his voyage to the sugar isles, Thady interrupting occasionally with queries about crops and the price of tobacco.

'I spoke with some French Fathers at their mission on Martinique,' MacSorley continued. 'At first they were unable to help. The ship, the *Saint Clothilde*, had been lost and there were no survivors. They had said many Masses for the souls of the drowned, but, with the unpredictable winds and currents around the Windward Islands, it would not have been the first ship to be lost, and certainly not the last. Oh, they did suggest that he might have met the enviable death of a martyr at the hands of pagans, but otherwise had no further information to give.'

The tapping of a stick on the cobbles in the yard heralded the arrival of the Buller. The old man's shadow entered the cabin before him.

'God save you all! Any news from the north?' he enquired civilly, but was bade sit down and say naught else by Thady.

'The truth began to dawn when I suggested that this Irishman was one who would not stand idly by if martyrdom offered itself. Then they spoke of a troublemaker on the Isle of Tobano who had roused the slaves to revolt against the landowner.'

'That's our Sean,' cried Thady. 'What mischief did he stir up?'

'He had been washed ashore on Tobano and given succour by the workers on the sugar plantations. These plantations are evil places, worse even than the most evil estate in Ireland. The slaves' work is backbreaking, their food scarce, their conditions foul. Many die, and are replaced by fresh supplies of negroes from the Africas. They bring diseases with them, these poor slaves, diseases the white man has no defence against.

'Sean started a school on the island. He did much to ameliorate the conditions of the slaves. The productivity of the plantation improved as a result, it seems, and the owner, an elderly French exile, was pleased with Sean. Indeed, I believe they grew quite close.'

Marcas's listeners bent closer.

'Then the old man died. His nephew inherited the plantation and put a stop to the school, for he was only

238

interested in profiting from sugar and couldn't see why his fieldhands should need education.'

'So he and Sean fell out?'

'I'll say they did. And the lads that had become used to school took it badly when it was withdrawn. They aired their grievances hotly.'

'And Sean was stuck in the middle of it all.'

MacSorley nodded. He wondered if he should tell them the whole story but decided to leave the final part to Sean. There was one thing more he had to tell them.

'Mistress O'Lochlainn,' MacSorley turned to Eily, 'your son's a free man, and intends to come home soon. He will have much to add to the story, and no doubt he will tell you how he fell in love with a woman.'

'Holy God,' exclaimed the Buller with a mixture of shock and pleasure, 'a holy priest and a woman!'

'A good man, but a man for all that. The woman was very beautiful, the daughter of the old Seigneur and an African slave. Her name was Ruth, and she was Michael's mother.'

The Cobbler's Trial

THADY O'LOCHLAINN WOKE to the sound of Eily's prayers. Her usual litany had a lilt to it this morning, and the clatter of her brogues had the makings of a dance as she went about her chores. Thady cleared his throat and began pulling on his breeches. Michael and Pup were already up and about; the boy had been to the well for Eily. Michael knew there was something ado, for the old people were in better spirits than he had ever seen them.

Thady leaned over the half-door, recalling the news Marcas MacSorley had brought. It was hard to believe that Sean would soon be back in Kilbroney. Thady had once had four sons. Two he had lost to smallpox on one bitter night. The youngest, Eamonn, had survived a sickly childhood only to meet death in a tragic misunderstanding before he had reached manhood. When Sean had gone away, it had seemed that Thady's line would end with him. It was a lonely prospect for any man, that none of his name would follow him to turn the Kilbroney sod. Well, Fr Mackey could think what he liked about Sean's behaviour, but he would welcome his son with open arms. He did not believe that the old priest would be too hard on them, though, for Fr Mackey was a pragmatist.

He would have to tell Michael the news, of course; he might do that today. Young Michael had become his constant companion, minding the goats, lifting the turf and planting seed. The knowledge that Michael was his grandson could not have made Thady love him any more than he already did. The lad had learned his catechism, too, and to Fr Mackey's satisfaction, and the priest had lavished praise on Thady's good work. Grace had been the teacher, but Thady's encouragement and approval had played no small part.

Thady had not seen his daughter for some time, since she had gone to Belfast on business of Master Dunn's. He missed having Grace around, although young Betsy called regularly on her father's behalf to see if all was well at the Close and the Master also sent a lad up once a week to assist with any heavy work. But of Grace there was no word. The trouble with the lassie, he repeatedly told Eily, was that she was too wise for her own good.

'If she had a head on her like other women, she'd be at home rearing her childer, and be happy about it,' he would say.

The Cobbler was perturbed at the prospect of his approaching trial. Fr Mackey had offered to speak on his behalf and tell the court of the straitened circumstances which had prompted him to catch the hare. He would attest that he had not paid the Cobbler, but rather had made a donation towards the care of his needy family. Tom Dunn, however, had respectfully persuaded the priest that such evidence, no matter how sincerely presented, would not necessarily help the Cobbler.

The Cobbler felt bound to honour his bail, although many had advised him to up and run. He had begun to practise his trade again, with some success, and had worked long into the night mending boots. He had found some military-issue boots discarded at the back of the inn and with considerable skill had granted them a new lease of life. Canny buyers at Waring's Point, Hill Town and the Bridge of Mayo had recognised a good bargain and left the Cobbler with a tidy profit. Although his prospects were poor, the Cobbler continued to hope that he would he not be imprisoned. He planned to continue to build up his trade and, given time, pass on his skills with needle and awl to his children. As it was, they were clumsy of hand and likely to do the devil and all with anything that required even the slightest manual dexterity.

When he found out that the presiding magistrate was Dargan Butler, the Cobbler abandoned all hope.

'I'd sooner stand afore Pontius Pilate,' he said to Martha Crampsey, who had come to the courthouse to speak on the Cobbler's behalf.

'Any more such blasphemy and transportation is what you'll deserve,' she snapped.

'That's what I'll likely get, if the blackguard doesn't hang me first,' he said bitterly.

But the Honourable Dargan Butler, having listened to the charges, took a lenient view of the act. He saved his wrath for those who had bailed out the Cobbler, and warned of the perils of giving patronage to criminals. Poor men, he declared, were better treated in Ireland than anywhere in the world. He fined McChesney and ordered him to restitute the Down Hunt for the loss of the hare.

The Cobbler had been spared prison: he could hardly

believe it. But many people at the hearing were outraged at the magistrate's suggestion that this was fair treatment for the poor – that a cobbler should be forced to pay some of the richest men in the county for an animal which lived freely on the mountains and belonged to no one. Yet there was no denying that the outcome could have been more drastic by far, and McChesney was satisfied to be walking home a free man. He could not say whether it had been the prayers of Fr Mackey and Martha Crampsey or the Widow Fearon's dark incantations which had swung the balance in his favour, but it was hardest of all to believe Tom Dunn's suggestion that Butler might, after all, have some decency in him.

The Cobbler was blamed with having started the fight in the alehouse.

'How many hares did you sell this week, Fox?' he asked Mick the Fox sarcastically. Too late Johnny recognised the aggressive glaze in his eyes.

'Keep your voice down there, McChesney,' he said sharply, 'or you'll have the Night Patrol down on us.'

'And who are you to tell me to keep my voice down,' the Cobbler turned his attention to Johnny, 'a coward that wouldn't take the oath with the rest of us? A mealy-mouthed scoundrel that would take his comrades hard-earned shilling, and yet wouldn't stand shoulder to shoulder with us?' Johnny ignored the jibes, knowing the futility of this argument.

'You don't talk much, do you?' McChesney swallowed the last of his flagon.

'You may be sure he talks plenty in the right places,' Mick the Fox butted in.

'You'd know all about that yourself,' the Cobbler hissed at him.

Tom Dunn arrived to see the mêlée in full spate, the Fox's

nose already swollen and bloody. He sent a youth to fetch MacCormac from his forge, and the combination of his calm authority and the smith's burly shoulders persuaded the participants to abandon their reckless combat. Dunn was not satisfied until MacCormac had doused the bushy and befuddled heads of the Cobbler and Mick the Fox under the pump.

''Tis the uncertainty that has them on edge,' said the blacksmith after the pugilists had been sent home. His words troubled Tom Dunn, who worried that the discipline of which he had been so proud might break down as they waited for news from Belfast.

Dargan Butler had taken up residence in his new home, though it was as yet only partially complete. Already he was experiencing the boredom of one who, having achieved his goal, needs to look for another. A title, that mark of recognition by the establishment, had so far eluded him, and he wondered what gesture of loyalty he might make to the new Lord Deputy. He looked around him at the empty splendour of Butler House. His wife had refused to join him; further evidence of her eccentricity, he thought. In time he would want rid of her anyway. In the meantime, he had acquired the services of a new housekeeper whose talent in the bedchamber redeemed her lack of domestic flair. She was a passable antidote to the monotony of life in Rostrevor.

The devoted footman Mullan had followed his master from the Valentine family home to the new residence, but as only one wing was ready he found living conditions far from comfortable. Butler House was some distance from any other dwellings and at night had a ghostly character, with the wind whistling through the unfinished portion of the house. Idle talk about strange sounds and apparitions quickly spread around Rostrevor. Such rumours suited Dargan

Butler, for no band of burly guards could secure a house half as safely as a single ghost.

Fanny's life had undergone a transformation since she had made the acquaintance of John Mercer. The sea-captain's initial impression of her had proved to be correct: here was not a featherheaded hedonist like many of her peers, but rather a spirited, independent woman who, though deeply wounded, still had a spark of fight left in her. His friendship proved to be just the tonic she needed, and his shrewd advice helped to restore her confidence. The language of trade and commerce was something with which she was comfortable, and although socially and politically John Mercer and she were poles apart, they both agreed that trade and industry would lead to prosperity for all. They enjoyed talking together, though Fanny never talked about either of her marriages. Dargan's name was mentioned only in connection with her financial situation. She still feared her husband, but she now knew she had the means to stand up to him. For that she was more than willing to accept Captain Mercer's advice. With his help, the grip of Dargan Butler was gradually crumbling.

Grace's Ordeal

TRY AS HE might, Dargan Butler could not forget Grace. He had considered different ways of winning her favour after their encounter in the woods. It was unfortunate that the boy had been with her, although Dargan suspected he was too young and too simple-minded to remember the last time they had met. He hoped that news of his merciful judgement towards the thieving cobbler would reach her ears as quickly as other gossip spread around Kilbroney.

It was by fortunate chance then that on a brief visit to a discreet Belfast moneylender, Dargan met Grace again. A temporary gambling embarrassment had made necessary the trip and, keen to keep the consultation with the usurer as unobtrusive as possible, Dargan rapped sharply on a door near Pottinger's Entry. After some moments the door opened slowly and a respectful servant asked his name and if he had made an appointment. Before he had time to answer his attention was caught by the sight of a familiar form entering a nearby bookshop. After making a brief excuse, he crossed the street and stood by the shop window. Grace was engrossed in a leather-bound volume, her spectacles perched precariously at the end of her nose. She gasped when she saw him standing in the doorway and dropped her book in confusion. He bent to retrieve it, never once averting his gaze. She tried to pass him but he grabbed her wrist.

'You and I have unfinished business, Grace O'Lochlainn.'

'I have nothing to say to you. Please let me pass,' she said.

'Oh, but we have much to discuss. Particularly,' he said slowly, 'the matter of young Michael.'

Dargan hailed a hiring chaise and ordered the driver to take them to some picturesque spot which would please the lady. The driver noticed that the lady looked slightly distressed, but shrugged his shoulders: what went on between rich folk and their women was none of his business. He often took lovers to discreet woodland bowers north of the town, and this particular gentleman had slipped him twice the usual fare.

Dargan nodded to the coachman to take himself off. 'Find an alehouse and don't return sober,' he ordered. The driver did not need to be told twice. They were in an overgrown leafy lane, part of an old disused road. Grace sat stiffly in the coach.

'What do you want of Michael?' she asked, staring ahead. 'You know he cannot harm you.'

'Nor would I harm him. If I had so desired I could have hired a common cut-throat to take care of him.'

Grace did not flinch. 'Am I to thank you for that? You who tormented a poor woman, turning her out to face the winter's snow.' She spun around to face him.

'But, Grace,' he protested, 'you don't know the full story.

247

She was a murderess! They called her a sea witch, for she stabbed a poor sailor to death.' He took advantage of her startled look. 'You thought I would harm an innocent woman, did you? She was evil, Grace, very evil, and the world was well rid of her.'

'The laws of this country are strange and often cruel, but no one can be judged guilty until tried by judge and jury. Did this woman face a court?'

'My love, you have read too many books; this fellow Dunn has corrupted your mind with all his talk. Of course she was a murderess. She confessed her guilt to me.'

Grace thought of what Ruth must have suffered and for the first time she felt a chill of fear.

'If you threaten Michael, I will have him tell his story to the magistrates.'

'Really? The tale of a half-breed brat? Known only by a mob of ignorant peasants, a rabble of would-be revolutionaries? Well, think about this, Grace; think about what I could do to them. Dunn, MacOwen, your father. I could hang them all in the morning if I wished. Think about that: I hold the power of life and death.'

He took her face in his hands and forced his mouth against hers. He felt her heart beating wildly, with passion or fear, at that moment he did not care. 'You want me too,' he said hoarsely, 'I know you do. 'Tis in your eyes...'

Grace struggled ineffectually, pushing her assailant, trying to free herself as he tore at her skirts. He held her fiercely, willing her to surrender. With a sigh, Grace closed her eyes; her body relaxed and slowly her arms crept about his shoulders. He grew more ardent.

'I knew you wanted me, Grace! I have always known that we were made for one another, you and I.' He kissed her eyes and face, ripping open the strings of her bodice, tearing and clawing. He began to struggle with his breeches, panting with excitement, his passion aroused.

Grace seized her moment. She took a deep breath, gave one sharp push and sent her assailant headlong out of the carriage. She reached for the whip and lashed the startled horse. It bolted forward down the narrow, overgrown track.

'Don't let him catch me,' she prayed, not daring to look back. Never had she felt so disgusted, so sullied. The track became a little wider, and still she urged the snorting animal onward. Soon the track opened on to a crossroads and she reined in the horse. She stumbled along a laneway, hiding at the sound of approaching hooves. Finally she fell exhausted in the sheough by the side of the road. She lay through the night, shivering uncontrollably, but unable to drive herself forward.

The following morning a passing farmer's wife and her son had pity for the distressed woman and took her home with them. No woman, they told her, was safe on the roads nowadays. Later, in the privacy of a bedchamber, Grace bathed her bruised body over and over again and dressed herself in a borrowed gown. She pinned her hair back as tightly as she could and put on her reading spectacles. She swore to herself that never again would any man touch her.

The Churn

ROISHA MacOWEN WAS a deserter's wife, unworthy of parish charity, forced to fend for herself and her child and constantly harrassed by the troopers. The Healing House, without Owen, was a cold, unfriendly dwelling and during the long winter nights she often longed for the warmth of someone's kitchen. Once she went back to the Crag hoping that they would remember her and give her some work, out of charity for Dervilla, but Madam Trevor set the dogs on her. No respectable village wife would employ her, no matter how menial the task. Johnny Fearon, Tom Dunn and her neighbours helped her as best they could, but she was a reluctant mendicant. In return for a daily plate of potatoes she helped Master Dunn with the farmyard chores, but would take no payment from him: rumour had it that even Master Dunn was now finding it difficult to get by. She knew Owen would disapprove of her accepting charity from their neighbours, but he had left her with little alternative. That she was expecting another child made her predicament even more precarious. She longed for the return of Mistress O'Lochlainn.

Then, at the end of March, Owen arrived on her doorstep just as the light was fading. He carried a sack with a couple of woollen blankets and a linen shift for Dervilla. He had a side of bacon and a bottle of sweet wine, washed up, he told her, on the shore at Annalong. She wondered where he had obtained the other things, or the purseful of coins, but he assured her it was in payment for honest work. He kissed her tenderly, telling her how much he had missed her, and they lay entwined before a blazing fire. Roisha knew complete contentment that night. They talked about their future together, when the baby was born.

'We'll call him Donard, for my father,' said Owen.

'And Murtagh, for mine.'

'Two fine names. He'll be well served.' Owen told her he would take them to Liverpool, perhaps even America if he could raise the fare. They would have a great life there, he promised.

'But will they not catch up with you?'

'Not if I change my name,' he said firmly. She knew how much this would cost him. He was proud of his past, of who he was, but now he was ready to let go of that, to begin a new life for his young family.

'But not until after my son's birth,' said Owen softly. 'At least he'll be born in *Leath Bhaile Clann Eoghan*, wherever else life might take him.'

Later that night Owen left the house to visit the nightschool. On his return he said little to Roisha, other than to tell her not to worry about anything. When Dunn's rooster crowed on the following morning, Owen had gone.

The news that Owen MacOwen had avoided conscription had spread throughout the district, and other desperate young men had soon followed his example. After all, the tories and rapparees of old had hidden out in the Mournes for years without ever being brought to justice. Like them the outlaws moved from one refuge to the next, with a system of lookouts to scan the horizon for the tell-tale fleck of red that betrayed a soldier's uniform. The military employed undercover agents in the guise of straying travellers from time to time, but few ever came back from the hills. Many of the outlaws believed that it was only a matter of living under the stars until the day their fortunes would turn, the day the French would come. Like Owen, many were forced to turn to petty crime and highway robbery, but from those who had little they took nothing.

Dargan Butler was informed of the increasing problem of desertion by the commanding officer of the Loyal Fencibles. He was about to dismiss it as being outside his area of responsibility when he recognised a name on the officer's list: MacOwen. He remembered the ruffian who had intervened between him and a young maid at Kilbroney House. His tone changed. 'The rebels are clearly encouraging simple young peasants to desert, for whatever reason. I will personally see that these men are brought to justice,' he said briskly. This turn of events suited Butler. It gave him a chance to settle an old score and to demonstrate his loyalty and ability to the Lord Deputy.

They came looking for Owen MacOwen soon after dawn. It was mid-May. He had risked staying the night with Roisha, by then heavily pregnant, but had been alerted by an accidental discharge of shots further down the valley. He quickly kissed his wife and baby, reassuring Roisha that all would be well.

'Stay quiet and say nothing and they can't touch you,' he whispered before slipping off in the mist like a ghost, heading towards the woods at Thunder Hill. Despite his reassurances Roisha was sick with fright, remembering the troopers' last visit.

The mountain of Leckan loomed above her, great bare rock with heather, scrub and bracken on its southern slopes and, hidden to the west, the precipice of *Alt na Broc* where Owen's mother had met her death. She thought she might be safe back in the booley on Leckan now, and ignoring Owen's instructions she quickly dressed the baby and hurried towards the mountain.

Just a few stony ditches and sheoughs and a young stream separated the Healing House and the Widow Fearon's cabin. Johnny Fearon and his aunt were awakened by the shots. The Widow shouted to Johnny to get out and hide.

'Get up, you devil, they could be coming for you,' she cried, pulling him from his pallet. 'Now remember you're an honest man and you took no oath. Say nothing about the oath. Say you never heard of it,' she contradicted herself in her anxiety.

'What oath?' said Johnny.

'They'll flog you and make you say you did. Johnny, you would have been safer in gaol.' Johnny agreed that he would do well to make himself scarce. He looked out to see if the coast was clear and noticed black smoke drifting from the Healing House.

'By all that's sacred, that poor wee girl all alone in a burning house!'

He pulled on his coat and started across the field, the Widow hobbling after him. He caught sight of Roisha scrambling through the bracken with Dervilla in her arms and called to her. She did not hear him. Leaping over the ditches which separated them, he wrestled the crying child from her mother and tried to calm her.

'You're all right, girl,' he soothed her. 'I won't let them harm you.'

He took her arm to guide her to the safety of his aunt's cabin. As she turned, Roisha saw the thin spiral of smoke from the Healing House. She screamed once, her eyes wide and wild, her breath harsh, and wrenched herself from Johnny's grasp. She scrambled away from him, stumbling frantically over the rocks. In desperation Johnny rushed back to the Widow and pushed Dervilla into her arms as the shouts and clamour of the troopers rang across the fields. 'Mind the child,' he said. 'I'll try and stop the girl.'

Owen MacOwen could be expected to visit a pregnant wife now and then, so an early morning raid had seemed advisable. Dargan Butler had come in person to see the job done. A search of the house proved fruitless, but Butler was determined to show MacOwen and the other rebels that ignoring the muster-to-arms was a serious, treasonable misdemeanour. MacOwen had become a symbol of defiance among the mountain people; he had to be humiliated, and quickly. The sooner MacOwen swung from the hanging tree in Rostrevor, the sooner the rebels would realise that their cause was hopeless. Butler's restless stallion pranced and kicked as the troopers ransacked the Healing House.

'They were here but a few moments ago,' reported the sergeant. 'They might still be close.' Cursing in annoyance, Butler stood in the stirrups, scanning the horizon for any sign of the fugitives. In the pale glimmer of dawn his sharp eyes lighted on a lone figure struggling up the side of Leckan. Calling for the others to follow, he spurred his horse towards the mountain.

The pains of labour stabbed at Roisha as she reached the little booley which she had shared with Owen, but still she had not shaken off her pursuers. The only place to hide was in the large churn which Owen had carried on his back from Knockbarragh to make a cradle for her first child. As she squeezed into the large vessel the pains became more intense and she feared she would miscarry. Encased in darkness her fright and grief mingled together as she gripped her sides and willed the pains to stop. Then she heard the horse's hooves and the harsh voices from without and her despair was complete.

A young trooper entered the booley and heard the moans from inside the churn.

'He's in here,' he shouted breathlessly, rolling the churn out into the light. With one push he sent the big barrel rolling and spinning over the turf. Seeing the tragedy unfold, Johnny Fearon ran towards the precipice, ignoring the warning cries of the soldiers.

'Stop it!' he cried. ''Tis only a woman!'

A shot rang out and then another, hitting him in the arm and shoulder. The red morning sky swirled before his eyes as he lost conciousness.

The churn gathered momentum and reeled towards the precipice of *Alt na Broc*. The troopers' laughter stopped abruptly as they recognised the cries of a young woman, not an outlawed brigand. They rushed to catch the barrel, clutching hopelessly at its sides, but now it was moving too fast and slipped away from them. It struck a rock at the edge of the cliff and arced upwards for a moment, glinting in the sun which had appeared over the mountains, then fell with terrible speed down on the rocks below. There was a sickening crash and a single forlorn cry. The troopers looked at one another, shocked into utter silence.

Owen MacOwen watched the retreat of the troopers from the shelter of the woods. He had heard the shooting on

Leckan but hoped it had nothing to do with Roisha or the child. He crept through the bracken and ran towards the smouldering ruins of the Healing House.

'Roisha,' he cried, choking back his rising panic. He rushed over to the Widow's cabin. She held his daughter in her arms and could only point up the mountainside in answer to his frantic questions. Owen turned and saw the bloody body of Johnny Fearon being carried down the mountain. He climbed towards them.

'Johnny,' he shouted, 'where's Roisha?' Johnny could not speak, and the neighbours who had fetched him would not answer. Seeing something dreadful in their eyes he rushed on up the hill to the booley, and then he stopped. Fear and terrible memories drew him to the edge of *Alt na Broc*. Slowly he stepped to the cliff's edge and, as if in an old dream, looked over. Roisha's body lay on the rocks below, her eyes wide and staring.

The Rescue

FANNY BUTLER HAD heard that her husband was entertaining lavishly and frequently in Butler House. His guests were a pleasure-seeking set, the type that haunted the gaming dens and drinking salons of Dublin. They had probably decided to sojourn in the country only because they had run out of money of their own, she decided. It irked her to see such unworthy folk disporting themselves at her expense, but her dejection at the failure of her marriage had of late given way to anger. She felt angry that her friends had been proved right regarding her husband's character, and that her blindness to Dargan's faults had allowed him gain such power and cause her such misery. More and more she compared him to John Mercer, and in that light her husband seemed vain, shallow and dishonourable.

Madam Hall had expressed her unease at Fanny's developing friendship with Mercer, but her criticism was muted as she had initially given Dargan Butler her full approval and felt partly responsible for the consequences. As for Grace O'Lochlainn, Fanny had forgiven if not forgotten. Mercer had tried gallantly to defend the woman's honour, insisting that she was innocent of all charges, but Fanny was slow to believe this. Yet she had been fond of Grace and in her new circumstances could find it in her heart to forgive her.

Fanny was determined to reassert her authority in Kilbroney. Her first aim was to get the scutchers, spinners, weavers and bleachers back to work and to revive the flagging flax trade. She employed an eager new manager for the mill and instructed him to have things back in order as soon as possible, especially now when prices were good and still rising. On Mercer's advice, she was able to restrict Dargan Butler's access to her finances, although most of her reserves had already been frittered away by the rascal's extravagant tastes.

One morning, after leaving Newry's Linen Hall, where she had resumed her business activities, Fanny paid a call on the Gentlemen's Lending Library in Hill Street. Although clearly not a gentleman she was by virtue of her pedigree accepted as a member without demur. During her enforced absence from the world of commerce she had developed a taste for novels, and there was a small, discreet section reserved for reading material deemed suitable for the wives, daughters and sisters of members. The reading room was not busy – in truth it was more of a gentlemen's smoking chamber than a library – and while browsing among the shelves Fanny heard two officers from the Fencibles talking by the fire in hushed tones. She could not mistake certain familiar names she overheard.

Fanny went about her business of choosing a book, but she was puzzled by what she had just heard. Having no strong political views of her own, she found it hard to believe that others would put themselves at such risk for any cause. She was quite content to leave the government of Ireland in the hands of those who had always been at the helm: that there might be alternatives had never occurred to her. As she left the library Fanny's mind was on neither books nor business. Could John Mercer be in danger? Surely not. A man of such stature could not possibly be a rebel. She banished the thought from her mind, although she did resolve to relate the officers' words to him at their next meeting.

A lone rider galloped to Dunn's Hill under cover of darkness. His features were shadowed by a wide-brimmed travelling hat and his greatcloak stained with the dust of many byways. Dunn recognised the rider as a saddler, a trustworthy man of few words.

'Bide here a while, O'Hare, and quench your thirst,' he invited the horseman. 'There's supper enough for both of us.'

'I wish that I could,' replied O'Hare, 'but I've two more stops to make this night.'

'An hour won't make a farthing's worth of difference.'

'Russell said there was no time to be lost. It might be already too late. I had better be on my way.'

As the saddler disappeared into the night Dunn read the letter. It was information gathered from a young officer in the Fencibles who had taken the oath of the United Irishmen; it warned of men who faced arrest and interrogation, and heading the list was Captain John Mercer of Arno's Vale.

'They may come for you at any moment. Possibly at dawn. You had better go at once.'

'I knew this might happen sooner or later. But how do you know they're coming for me now?' John Mercer had just finished a handsome supper with Marcas MacSorley and had been looking forward to a game of backgammon when the unexpected arrival of Tom Dunn had sent Mistress Hanratty scuttling to the door.

'This source is reliable,' Dunn answered, and there was much anxiety in his voice. 'You must leave Arno's Vale tonight. Mind my advice, John, and may heaven take care of you. Now I must go.' He rode off: there were other men to warn and Mercer at least had the means to save himself.

'I'm afraid we'll have to postpone our game,' Mercer said wryly to MacSorley.

'This may be a false alarm. What evidence can they hold against you?' said the doctor. Mercer shook his head.

'In times like this they might not need any. Somehow I thought that our strength of numbers would be my protection.'

'But since there are so many others,' MacSorley pressed, 'why would they single you out?'

'Perhaps I have been careless,' Mercer replied. 'But this I know: I cannot allow them to interrogate me. Under torture, heaven only knows what I would say.'

MacSorley looked sadly at his old friend. He had become every inch the country squire, with his cattle and milch cows, and had grown settled and content after years of travel. Mercer seemed to sense his friend's thoughts.

'Don't worry about me,' he said to MacSorley. ''Tis time I was back sailing the high seas again. I suppose I was never destined to be a farmer.' Captain Mercer summoned Mistress Hanratty to his side and gave her some instructions. 'I'm not going to get my head chopped off, for goodness sake,' he reassured the weeping housekeeper. For all her scolding, he had grown quite fond of her.

'Where will you go?' she asked him.

'Somewhere with plenty of fish and maybe a palm tree or two for shelter. What more could I want?' Mistress Hanratty, though, was in no mood for jests: her own future was now far from assured. 'I will explain later, but first of all,' continued Mercer, 'I must say goodbye to an old friend. Will you pack Charlotte's clothes for me?' He drew MacSorley aside as he left the house.

'My ship leaves for Jamaica tomorrow on the evening tide, and I'll be on it.'

'But they'll be watching the docks.'

'Perhaps not. They won't have procured a warrant yet.'

'Will they wait for such formalities?'

'I'll board her out past the bar, if need be. Do you want to join us?'

MacSorley drew a deep breath, recalling their many adventures at sea. 'No, my friend, not this time. I've travelled enough these last few years. I'm staying here.'

Mercer rode across the shore. The tide was out, and a few little girls searching for oysters in the moonlight ran off at the sight of the horseman. Mercer was sorry he'd scared them: 'A distressful country,' he said to himself. At the mouth of the Owenabwee he turned in towards Kilbroney House.

Fanny heard furtive whispers and murmurs in the hallway as she prepared for bed, and came to the top of the stairs.

'He's insisting on seeing you, Madam,' a frightened maid called. 'Will I get the grooms?'

'No need for that,' a familiar voice shouted. ''Tis only myself, Mistress Fanny. I had to see you before I left.'

'Captain Mercer!' cried Fanny, running down the stairs. The captain was dressed for travel. She sensed he was in danger. 'What can I do to help you?' she asked.

Mercer was not at home when a party of troopers arrived to escort him to Newry. A nervous Mistress Hanratty informed them that he had gone away on business and would not be back for some time. They searched the house and left with some documents in an unidentifiable language, which might or might not have been the incriminating French.

Next morning Madam Butler called on Charlotte Mercer to invite her for a ride in her carriage, and directed the coachman to Newry. Fisher, her banker, asked her to reconsider the orders she gave him, but she assured him that her mind was made up and, leaving his office, she rejoined Charlotte in the carriage.

Charlotte had been frightened by the events of the previous night but, having been reared on tales of travel and adventure, was now looking forward to the prospect of a sea voyage. It had been arranged that Fanny would take the girl to the ship so as not to arouse suspicion. She was known by the merchants of Newry and no one would pass any remarks if they saw her near the ship. The yeomen patrolling the docks paid little attention to the carriage of a lady of quality. For Fanny, who had lived so much in recent years between drawing rooms and herbaceous borders, this was the adventure of a lifetime.

John Mercer put thoughts of a peaceful life on the shores of Carlingford Lough behind him and looked ahead to the balmier climes of the island of Jamaica, where he owned a small plantation. He could live like a king in exile, yet his heart was sore at the thought of leaving his comrades at a time when every man counted; he had little hope of ever returning. He said as much to Marcas MacSorley as they rode over the hills to Newry.

They left their horses on the outskirts of the town and took a route through the winding back-streets, through the Shambles and down Dirty Lane towards his offices. Two soldiers paced the main street in front of the building as he furtively opened the safe in his office. The three clerks did not appear to notice anything amiss, and continued quietly with their work.

'We risk too much coming here.' MacSorley watched the street below. He was anxious that Mercer should go quickly.

'Do you think I'd leave all this for the rascals?' Mercer emptied his safe of deeds, banknotes and other documents and packed them into an oilskin bag. 'As for these, I can only take what we can carry.' He dug into a chest of sovereigns and ordered MacSorley to do likewise. Then he summoned the clerks and told them to distribute the rest of the gold among themselves and the other staff. The senior of the three seemed to understand his master's situation and promised to carry on as if nothing untoward had happened.

'I think 'tis safe now.' MacSorley saw that the two redcoats had moved on. They slipped out and quickly mingled with the crowds in Hill Street, but a cry went up behind them.

'There he is!' a rough voice shouted and within seconds they were surrounded by troopers.

'John Mercer, East India merchant? You are under arrest.'

'And what is the charge?'

'High treason.' The words were like a death sentence.

Mercer spoke in a loud voice, desperately seeking a way out. A small crowd had began to gather round them.

'I regret I am not yet able to accompany you. I have some remaining business to transact.' He spoke with authority in his voice. The soldiers looked at him uneasily. They were used to apprehending drunks and ne'er-do-wells, not men of substance.

'Whatever your business is, it will have to wait,' the sergeant said sharply. The street was growing more and more crowded and the crowd's mood was angry. The sergeant ordered his men to clear a path down the middle of Hill Street, shouting urgently to the crowd to stand back.

'Ye blackguards,' a shout came, 'ye took Mad George's shilling and now ye're selling a decent man!' Insults were hurled as the crowd grew louder and more brazen.

'Get back,' the sergeant yelled, but his voice was lost in the clamour. From the adjoining streets canal workers, dockers and shop owners were spilling into Hill Street. Word spread like wildfire that a leader of the United Irishmen had been arrested. The soldiers were young and inexperienced, overpowered by the sheer weight of numbers surrounding them; they surrendered their weapons without much of a struggle. Cheers rent the air as the guns were taken from them and several frightened young troopers were doused in the canal. Others lost themselves in the crowd, hurriedly shedding their uniforms.

A great roar went up as John Mercer was lifted shoulder high and chaired the length of the street and down to the Butter Crane where his ship was moored. MacSorley watched him disappear as the tumult continued, the crowd dancing and playing with discarded military hats.

'God speed, my friend,' said Marcas MacSorley, and allowed himself a smile of relief.

Retribution

TOM DUNN NODDED over his books. For a change they were not the works of the modern political philosophers: he had read too much of them in recent years. In front of him rested the books he had loved in his youth: Ovid and Virgil, Horace and Homer. A dim rush candle burned low beside a stack of blank writing paper, an ink-pot and a few Flemish quills, pared and ready; behind them lay some yellow tomes bound in flaking goatskin. Dunn had once been a wealthier man, a lawyer and freeholder, but now only his farm and his small library remained. The books, fragile with age and mould, looked as though they would crumble at the slightest touch, but these he would not exchange for a sack of Spanish gold.

As his white head drooped in half-slumber, he dreamed of times past; of how, as a young man, he had inherited the hedge-school from a learned scholar, a graduate of Douai, one of a hardy breed who had braved the worst of the Penal years. He recalled the gnarled hands which had passed him the treasured volumes and with them responsibility for educating the young of the Poorlands, the tattered and demoralised remnants of a beaten race. They had survived the worst excesses of the Penal years, the massacres and carnage of the Williamite wars and the misery that followed. Down through the years Dunn had become their champion, listening to their griefs and sorrows, defending them against hostile magistrates, and now, finally, he would lead them in battle. He had taught them in the woods, by the shore, even out on the mountain with sentries posted to warn of enemies approaching, but his favoured place had been the ruins of the little medieval monastery of Kilbroney which for him represented the Ireland of the past, a land of scholars and of sanctuary. There he had taught the young O'Lochlainns, Fegans and Fearons, MacArtains and MacCormacs, fathers, sons and grandsons.

As his memories drifted on he dreamed of hazy summer evenings when his young scholars, weary from the harvest, laughed and joked on the sward at Dunn's Hill. Many were thin and ragged, with lice-ridden hair falling over their slates, but all were hungry to learn, to be more than slaves and servants, the role ordained for them by history. Most of the cleverest boys had left. There was no future for them in Kilbroney, but at least they arrived in Liverpool, Glasgow, even Boston and Philadelphia, knowing their letters. To the four corners of the earth they had travelled, free of mind and soul, having fought against the ignorance that might have been their destiny. Those who chose to stay at home faced a greater challenge, but when the call to arms came, not one of his scholars would march forth in blind obedience at the command of some foreign general. Because the time of the free man had come, they would go of their own choice.

As the moon began to wane in the sky, he dreamed on:

Achilles, the little fellows' hero, who had inspired many a spirited fight; Mount Parnassus, shrouded in dead bracken and stained with the blood of mother and child; and finally he dreamed of Thermopylae and of three hundred wretched beggars who had held out against the army of a great empire, pikes frail as barley stems as they died, one by one.

The hum of the crickets in the hearth did not rouse him from his reverie, nor did the morning birdsong. It was the hand of his daughter on his shoulder which woke him.

'Father,' chided Betsy, 'you've been sitting up all night. You'll die of exhaustion if you go on like this.'

'There is so much to be done, child,' he shook his head, 'so much yet to learn.'

'Learn?' asked Betsy, 'And what have you to know that you haven't already forgotten?'

Tom smiled wanly. Education to him meant comprehending his own limitations, realising all the knowledge which had passed him by.

'This new world we talk about,' he mused, still red-eyed and sleepy, 'is it only the other side of the mountain, or is it still a lifetime's journey away?'

'Let me get the fire going and I'll put a bit of bacon on the griddle,' Betsy said practically.

'That was your mother's answer to everything: fill your stomach, and the devil may care what fills your head.'

'You're overtired. Let Harry and myself take care of things for a while. You get into bed and have a good rest.' Betsy knew that there was as much a chance of her father going to bed as there was of Squire Hall joining the rebels. As she sliced through a blackened side of bacon she wondered if she should mention Johnny Fearon's injuries to her father, but thought better of it: there was no sense in adding to his worries. She knew what she must do herself.

Roisha MacOwen lay below the precipice, her face peaceful in death. Her neighbours stood guard at a distance, some standing sentry on the heights of Leckan. Owen knelt by Roisha's side in tears of despair. His remorse was beyond meaning. He had been too proud to join the army, but had he done so they would not have come for him, and his Roisha would be alive now. No one could comfort him. Fr Mackey said some words over the body, but they meant nothing to Owen.

'I want to bury her here.' The words were a hoarse whisper.

'But, MacOwen,' the priest protested, 'this is not consecrated ground.'

'Well, consecrate it then. This is MacOwen land and the MacOwens will lie here.'

A warning shout was heard from the sentries and Owen was hurried away. By the time the soldiers arrived, Roisha MacOwen had been buried where she died, guarded by the mountains of Levallyclanowen.

The Widow's cures failed to help Johnny. His right arm had been shattered and his other wounds were beginning to fester. She could only watch and cool his brow. The nephew who had tried so hard to make a decent life for himself was slipping away from her, and she could not bring him back. Betsy Dunn had called and sat by his bedside, although he didn't seem to know she was there, and Martha Crampsey had brought sheets of fresh white linen for his bed and strips to bind his wounds. Everyone wanted to help Johnny, for the Widow's sake as well as his own. His courage had been acknowledged even by those who had accused him of cowardice and the Cobbler McChesney, in particular, had not been able to lift his head for shame. Yet he came, cap in hand, and asked the Widow's forgiveness.

'Don't fret yourself, son,' she reassured him. 'I know 'twas the drink talking, not yourself.' The Widow had all but given up hope of Johnny's recovery when Marcas MacSorley arrived on horseback from Arno's Vale. Betsy had asked him to come. The Widow had removed the lead fragments cleanly, but the deep wounds had become septic. The physician's voice was calm and soothing as he gently examined his patient, but the injuries to Johnny's arm made him shake his head. He turned to the Widow and Betsy.

'We may be able to save him, but the means will be extreme and desperate. We must cauterise the wounds to halt any further infection.' He looked again at Johnny's shattered limb. 'His right arm will have to be amputated. We have no choice,' he said, forestalling their protests. The Widow shrieked and almost fainted. The old woman had tended flogged men and watched women die in labour, but Johnny was her own kin and his agony was hers also.

'I shall give him a draught to dampen the pain,' the doctor continued, 'but I fear it will be very great, and we will need help to hold him.' Turlough MacCormac was summoned, while Martha Crampsey persuaded the distressed Widow to go home with her for a few hours. The Cobbler was ordered to kindle a good fire and melt down pitch to cauterise the wounds. Then he, Harry Dunn and the blacksmith held Johnny down while MacSorley burned the festering sores.

The next operation was martialled by MacCormac, who grouped the men around the pallet. He ordered an ashen-faced Harry Dunn to leave, and the young man, more at home with books than with crude surgery, was happy to comply. In spite of his weakness, Johnny struggled hard, his eyes bulging with pain and fear. A leather belt was placed between the patient's teeth and the blacksmith, with a swift decisive stroke, hacked his arm off at the elbow where the bones joined. The stub was quickly thrust into hot pitch and Johnny, mercifully, slipped into oblivion.

Moll McIntyre, the gamekeeper's widow, had strayed deep into the woods collecting faggots. A lively, intelligent woman in her youth, she was now in the age of dotage and growing more infantile every day. The vicar's wife, remembering past services to the church, treated her with kindness, but few others had any time for her constant prattling. She amused the village children with her warnings of the ghost in Butler House, and their mothers, while sympathetic towards a woman who once worked alongside themselves, would now throw her a few crusts and bid her begone from their doors.

Mistress McIntyre knew for sure there was a ghost. She had seen him. She was not afraid of him because he had spoken to her gently, soothingly. He was the ghost of a musician. He had played the violin before King Solomon and even Brian Boru. Not many spoke to her in such a way. The voices around her were usually harsh and intimidating; the ghost's voice was sweet and sad. As she picked her way through the trees she crooned a rhyme from her childhood. The woods in spring were soft and gentle, a place where she liked to wander. All at once the sound of baying hounds was upon her and the raucous horn of the hunter broke in on her peace. She retreated into the thicket to hide until the riders had passed by. It was then she noticed an upturned face in the ferns, still and pale amidst the new growth of spring.

No one paid heed to the ramblings of old Widow McIntyre as she hobbled up the lane towards the barrack. The women had gathered around the pump to exchange gossip, and a chambermaid from the Crag had everyone's attention.

'He's away. Left her altogether. A young boy, they say, not even a woman. Madam Trevor says she'll scald him if she ever catches him.'

'There was always an oddness about the rascal.'

Failing to get the women's attention, the Widow McIntye threw a military jabot caked in blood at their feet. The women recoiled from her.

The barrack sergeant was alerted and an immediate search of the woods ordered, for old Widow McIntyre was unable to say precisely where she had found the jabot. Some time later a young trooper called his comrades over. In the thicket lay the body of Colonel Trevor. He had been piked to death.

For several days after the rescue of John Mercer, Newry and the surrounding countryside were placed under strict curfew. The murder of Colonel Trevor added to the military's anger, and there were daily reports of beatings and floggings.

News of Colonel Trevor's death spread quickly through the Poorlands, and though there were some who said he was the greatest rascal who ever wore a coat and fully deserved his fate, more felt it to be a brutal act, one which would provoke the wrath of the authorities. It was more than a decade since the infamous Captain Walls had brought terror to Kilbroney in his relentless pursuit of two outlaws, and the expectation of another such visitation caused alarm among the poor.

Harry Dunn told Johnny that a wheeled scaffold had been set on the square, foreby the barrack. A division of Fencibles had been billeted around the village and were regularly patrolling the streets in a display of strength. Several local men had been taken in for questioning and it was expected that the intention was to make an example of one of them.

'What's to be done?' asked Johnny. 'Who is for the scaffold?'

'My father says there's nothing we can do, not yet,' said Harry. 'He says that if we were to fight now we'd be massacred, and the rest of the country would be betrayed. He says we have to hold tight.'

'Could it be 'tis just an act on their part, a gesture to show they mean business.'

'I'm going down to the village, Johnny, to show them I don't fear their scaffolds.' Harry's young face was pale and drawn and Johnny felt sympathy for the scholar, drawn from his books into a conflict which was not to his liking.

'I'll come with you. Help me with my coat.'

'Are you fit to be abroad?'

'I still have my legs under me,' his friend replied as he eased one arm into a coat-sleeve. Together they walked to Rostrevor, the stub of Johnny's arm swathed in rough bandages. It was still very painful, and there were some who maintained that the ache of his lost arm would never leave him. Betsy came to the door as they passed Dunn's Hill, and she winced when she saw the stub. Johnny saw her flinch and turned away, his heart sore. She was now even further beyond his reach.

As the pair arrived in the centre of the village, a crowd had gathered round the scaffold, an ugly stark creation of blackened wood and iron. A whisper went round the crowd that an execution was imminent, but the identity of the condemned man was still uncertain. Could it be Turlough MacCormac or perhaps Mick the Fox, both of whom had been publicly flogged?

The crowd hushed as a prisoner was led out with a sturdy trooper on either side. Although his hands were bound and his feet shackled, he looked at the crowd without guilt or shame.

'Who is it?' asked Harry Dunn, his eyesight poor from years of study. At that moment his father rode up to join him, shaking his head.

'I've been to see Squire Hall. He says there's no point in appealing the sentence. He's pleaded guilty to Trevor's murder.'

272

The drumroll began as the prisoner was led on to the scaffold, his gait stiff. The rope was placed over his head and he looked for the last time towards the mountains, the land of his ancestors and his own broken dreams.

'God's curse on all of you,' he said coldly. Then the last of the ancient Clan Owen of Levallyclanowen, hereditary Keepers of the Staff of Bronach, was dispatched to eternity.

The Fiddler's Lament

O RAN O'CASSIDY HUDDLED under some beams abandoned among the masonry of Dargan Butler's unfinished house. He knew he was dying; although in no pain, he could feel his life and his passion ebbing. His fiddle rested by his side, as it had done all his days. He hoped they would bury it with him, if they buried him at all. Once he had played the music of the masters – Corelli and Vivaldi, Geminiani and Giordani – but he had not touched his fiddle for a long time now.

He had come down from the Clasha to kill Dargan Butler, but he knew he would never fulfil his plans. Many times he had planned in his mind to cut through Butler's saddle-girth or poison his food, but he had never been able to bring himself to carry out these things. Oran O'Cassidy feared his God and loved his fellow man, and the canker of bitterness in his heart had not yet destroyed him. He remembered the prayers of his mother, chanted night after interminable night in a windswept hovel overlooking the Atlantic, in hope of his father's safe return. As the storm raged and the waves thundered around their home, his mother's litany had brought comfort: the constant Pater Nosters and Aves intermingled with older, stranger invocations to saints never heard of in Rome. Now, all these years of grief later, he recited the prayers to himself once again, as if he were a child. His tongue was numb, his throat dry and parched.

In the distance he could hear the merriment of the hunting party, fiddles playing worthless catches and glees. Their triviality angered him. Such a jangle was not music. It was the tawdry souless strain of those who lived in mediocrity, who were strangers to the sacredness of love, the beauty of excellence or the fire of intense grief. He had known all three, deeply and vividly. He lifted his violin once more and blew the dust away gently, as if with a kiss. He held it close to his breast, a companion in life and death. Then, with care, he set it once more on his shoulder and slowly lifted the bow.

Dargan Butler dropped his fork and fumbled around for it under the table. He was growing tired of his companions, claiming to be from county families, calling themselves aristocrats; the devil only knew what they were, for he had never examined their pedigrees. 'I must be getting old,' he said to himself. The glitter of his life had begun to wane and his plans to go awry. His wife had left him. It was almost laughable that his plain, frumpish wife should desert him and run away with a sailor. But not only had she sailed away to Satan-knows-where with a traitor, she had taken almost every penny with her. He could not sell Kilbroney House, which was entailed, and the other houses and land she had already mortgaged. Neither could he marry again, at least not for years. He had served his country well, and now here he was in a half-finished mansion inhabited by rats and ghosts. He had packed his back-street mistress off to Newry after some items of value had disappeared, and now his most trusted servant, Mullan, had also left without notice. He did not care about the Newry woman, who had been vulgar and coarse, but he felt let down by Mullan. Had the cur no loyalty at all?

Yet surpassing by far his anger towards the servant was his hurt at his rejection by Grace O'Lochlainn. He could not understand why she did not love him. All women did, for a time anyway. Why didn't she care for him, instead of humiliating him in such a way? He cursed himself for having mentioned the dark woman. Had he played his cards differently, she might have melted into his arms, for they were two of a kind. Even now he yearned for her.

Dargan's companions were planning some new diversions.

'Come on, Butler, let's have a bit of sport. A midnight gallop across the shore: I'll wager you won't be back first!' The sniggering and coaxing of a few new ladies hired from Newry left him unmoved. Looking at their crude, sneering faces, his temper broke.

'Damn the lot of you to hell!' he yelled, disgusted at them and at himself. This outburst was greeted by a howl of laughter, and the wheezy violins led a merry party out towards the stables. Dargan Butler was left on his own.

'Grace,' he whispered to himself, 'Grace O'Lochlainn.' If she had loved him, things could have been different. With such a mistress his home could have become a centre of elegance instead of a squalid pleasure house. He stumbled to the front door and shouted abuse after his friends, then sat on the steps listening to the waves lapping the beach. The moon left a trail of silver on the lough as it rose over the Cooley mountain; a land of ancient myth, the resting place of Fionn MacCumhall and the battleground of Cuchullain lay right on his threshold. Above the sigh of the night breeze and the gentle splash of the waves came the sound of a violin playing somewhere in the darkness.

The noise was faint at first, but grew stronger, a tortured raucous tone resonating through the building. It was coming from the west wing, as if a lament for his failure to complete it. He doubted if he would ever have the money to finish the house as he had intended, and he had certainly lost the hunger for it. He moved towards to the source of the sound, feeling a whisper of fear, but still compelled onwards.

'Who's there?' he shouted. The sound stopped.

'Answer me, I say, or I'll set the dogs on you!'

A faint voice spoke from the darkness. 'Nothing you would do can harm me now.'

'What are you, a phantom?' asked Dargan sarcastically. 'Show yourself to me!'

'I am no phantom. I am Oran O'Cassidy, who once played the violin. I played for rich and poor, for old and young, and all who heard me were the better for listening.'

'Your name means nothing to me. I've never heard your music.' Butler's tone was contemptuous.

'That was your misfortune.'

Butler stepped forward into a pool of moonlight which spilled through the window. 'I've had enough of this. Come out of those shadows, you scoundrel. What have you to do with me?'

The fiddler paused before continuing. His breath was short and his voice weak. 'You destroyed a woman I loved. The happiness I had in my life, you took from me. I speak of Ruth, the dark woman.'

Dargan Butler felt a sudden chill. 'Ruth? You accuse me wrongly. I did not kill her.'

'You might as well have run her through with your sword; she died at your hand. Did you love her?'

'Me? Love a black stray with a bastard trailing behind her?' Dargan Butler disdained the very idea.

'Yet you took her away from me!' The fiddler's voice was suddenly vigorous. 'We were happy together. We travelled the roads and the laneways, we crossed mountains and rivers together, and everywhere our strange appearance mattered not, for people loved my music and her dancing.'

'Your memory does not serve you well. You say nothing of

277

the stonings and beatings. Don't think I did not see the bruises and welts on her body. Her beauty was well flawed by the time I had her.'

'Yes,' the fiddler's voice dropped to a whisper, 'we met cruelty too. I protected her as best I could, but there were always those who would hurt her. She trusted me to look after her.'

'Yet she chose to come to me.' Dargan shrugged. 'She was only a woman, you know.'

'Had she any choice? Tell me that!'

Butler grew uneasy. 'Did you know Ruth was a murderess? She killed an honest sailor. The woman you say you loved was surely no angel of virtue.'

The fiddler's voice cracked in anger. 'She killed to defend herself and the child. You knew it was not murder, yet you threatened to expose her, to see her hanged and have her child taken away.'

'I would not have betrayed her secret,' Dargan protested. 'Why should I become embroiled in a murder, a man in my position?' His mind went to the evening in Newry, not long after his marriage, when he had chanced upon a beautiful dark woman dancing in the lamplight to the music of a violin. 'It had to be her,' he told the fiddler. 'I knew by the fear in her eyes that she was the dark witch the sailors talked about, but I looked after her for a while, set her up in a room of her own.'

'You deceived her and then imprisoned her with your blackmail, and in the end you threw her out.' O'Cassidy's voice was hoarse.

'In the end I did throw her out. She was changing. She had lost her looks and there was a rancid air about her.'

'You might as well have killed her yourself!'

'Why should I have troubled myself in such a way? I knew she was ill and she was of no more use to me.' Butler was already weary of the conversation. He listened to the sound of the fiddler sobbing and felt no pity. 'You wasted your love on such a woman.'

The sobbing stopped and the fiddler hobbled towards him, his breathing heavy and laboured. Oran O'Cassidy stepped into the moonlight, and a horrified Dargan Butler knew his Nemesis.

'A leper,' he cried in sudden understanding, his hands creeping towards his own face, touching, wondering, fearing.

'God help me, Butler. In a few years you also will be like me. See if any poor woman will love you then. Choose the wild mountains, as I did, or rot in a leper asylum!'

Dargan Butler staggered back to his house, retching at the horror of what he had just seen. He would never forget the fiddler's face, the empty chasm where a nose should have been, the festering sore of a mouth, the deformed fingers. He felt a growing dread at the realisation that Ruth had been the harbinger of the disease. The many times he had lain with her had left his fate in no doubt. He cursed her memory.

He watched his house-guests return across the beach, full of brandy and hilarity, unaware and uncaring of his agony. He turned his back on the house and roused a weary stable lad, ordering him to saddle his horse. The hounds bayed at the disturbance, straining at their leashes. On hearing the clank of the stable door the magnificent Saladin whinnied and snorted, his eyes flashing silver, his coat almost blue in the moonlight. Dargan Butler mounted and thrashed the stallion's hindquarters; he bucked and reared angrily before breaking into a reckless gallop across the strand.

A small band of poachers fishing the river ran under the bridge when they heard the thunder of the animal and a pair of lovers in the woods were almost mown down by his hooves. One of the weavers, working late, saw the horse's mane flash past, and swore to his wife it was the devil incarnate. The steed galloped over meadows and fields of flax and barley, clearing ditches and hedgerows with great leaps, his hooves churning through cottiers' potato patches, crushing young saplings underfoot, out onto the Poorlands' bracken, heather and rocks. The few mountain dwellers who were still awake heard the pounding hooves and prayed for the dawn.

Dargan Butler barely noticed the Healing House as he passed, or the Widow's small cot. The face of the fiddler haunted him, urging him on and on, his horse foaming now and panting fearfully. Leckan was bathed in moonlight as the animal galloped upwards. Despair and disgust overcame Butler. What were all his plans worth now? His friends were worthless, and he had wronged so many. Grace loathed him. There could be no peace in his life.

He spurred Saladin and, with a final anguished cry, rode him across the rocks. With one mighty leap over the precipice, horse and rider tumbled to their deaths on the grave of Roisha MacOwen.

As soon as the bodies were discovered early the following morning, horse and rider were consigned together to a lone mountain grave by the men of the Poorlands. After Owen's execution, further blame and retribution might have followed had Butler's corpse been found. A hurried prayer was said by the gravediggers, but neither cross nor stone was set to mark the mound.

Two men died that night, the squire and the fiddler. Dargan Butler was unloved and unmourned, but in a cabin by the sea in far-off Donegal, an old woman, deep in prayer, threw her head back, keening and lamenting the death of Oran O'Cassidy the fiddler, her son.

Dervilla

MARCAS MACSORLEY WATCHED as a small clipper, sails unfurled, glided down Carlingford Lough, past the bar and out to sea. Every departing ship reminded him of Mercer's flight to safety. His friend had been lucky; the euphoria of the Newry people was shortlived as a detachment of the 22nd Light Dragoons soon restored order in the town. The authorities had been cautious and there were no further arrests, but many of the more prominent United Irishmen had hired themselves bodyguards, while others had gone into hiding. There had been considerable embarrassment following the spontaneous demonstration of strength by the Newry men, and the authorities were loathe to provoke such an exhibition of defiance again without adequate military strength to enforce their control. The war with France had reached a critical stage and troops could not be spared for the streets of provincial Irish towns.

It was now several months since Mercer's departure.

MacSorley had not seen Grace O'Lochlainn since his return to Ireland and his disappointment was intense. He had been told by Tom Dunn that she was his emissary in Belfast, yet when he had travelled up to Belfast and called at McCracken's house no one would say where she had gone. He had considered discussing his intentions with Thady, but his reticence as always restrained him. Mercer had told him of Grace's eviction and he was angered to think that she had been victimised in such a way. Arno's Vale was his now: he had bought it from Fanny Butler. It would be a worthy home for Grace, if she wished.

Johnny Fearon came to see him. Poor Johnny had recovered physically from his ordeal, but the loss of Owen and his wife had caused him much grief.

'If they had only let him be, he would have been content to work in the mill and grow a few praties. He didn't ask for much out of life.'

'There are many more like him, unfortunately.' MacSorley offered little consolation.

'No,' said Johnny, 'to me there was only one MacOwen. I mind when they let me out of gaol, his was the first face I saw this side of Ruaslieve.'

'I mind that time well myself. The snow was as bad as I ever saw and I had to spend the night on Dunn's Hill.'

'Owen and I used to chase the same women and bet on the same roosters at Hill Town. He was easy roused, but he'd give you the shirt off his back.'

'If I remember rightly,' said the doctor, 'you nearly came to fisticuffs at your first meeting.'

Johnny smiled at the memory. 'Aye. He would have hung me there and then had there been a tree in Kilbroney that could take the weight. Well, neither of us had ever seen the like of her before, and there she was, dead in the Widow's cot, Lord rest her soul.'

'The dark woman,' mused MacSorley.

'Wasn't she the unfortunate woman ever to set foot in

Ireland,' said Johnny. ''Tis ironic to think of someone choosing to come here when so many would sell their souls to get away. I wish I could.'

Marcas could not remember seeing Johnny so downhearted. There was no shortage of limbless beggars in Ireland, but Johnny, he thought, should be stout-hearted enough to overcome his disability. After all, he still had one good arm.

Leaving the coach at Hill Town, Grace O'Lochlainn gathered her baggage about her and set off to walk over the mountains to Kilbroney. It was a familiar journey, and she had a spring in her step as she drew nearer to home. 'I have been far too long in towns,' she told herself as she breathed the fresh mountain air. On stopping to quench her thirst at Kielty's well, she heard about the disappearance of Dargan Butler from the woman of the house. She did not rejoice at the news, but she was relieved that Michael and herself were no longer in danger from him. The memory of the assault she had consigned to the darker recesses of her mind.

Michael ran to meet the solitary figure struggling across the mountain from Clonduff, laden with bags containing books and paper, a cut of bacon and some tobacco for Thady. He chattered continuously, about how his father would be home soon and work he had done with Thady all summer, the new tricks he had taught Pup. How he has grown, she thought, as she watched the boy run and skip ahead of her to alert Thady.

'What kept you away so long?' Thady scolded her fondly. 'Sure you could have found us all dead in our beds.'

'Is your cough that bad?' Grace bantered, looking at him keenly. She had to admit he looked quite well.

'Never mind the cough. Damn the bit of harm it ever did anybody. Did you bring me something to put in my pipe?'

Eily appeared in the doorway. She was bent almost double and her face was wrinkled and puckered.

'Sean! Is that you? Are you home yet?' She seemed confused.

283

'Don't mind her,' Thady explained softly, 'she's beginning to dote.' Speaking more slowly he turned to Eily. ''Tis not Sean; 'tis only Grace.'

'Is she left that man yet?'

'Don't mind her, girleen,' the old man said to Grace. 'If it wasn't for Michael and myself to keep an eye on her, she'd have the house burned down. Isn't it lucky I'm still strong and in good health?'

'Here's a pouch of your tobacco,' said Grace, affection in her voice. 'I'd say you've earned it.' She smiled at the delight in the old man's eyes as he inspected the tobacco, rubbing it between finger and thumb and sniffing it.

'Michael has grown. He was talking about his father coming home, but I could make no sense of it.'

'Ah, his father,' said Thady. 'Sit down, daughter, and listen to my news. Sean is indeed coming home.'

As Grace listened her face flooded with joy. 'Why,' she cried, ''twill be like the old days again.'

'I doubt it,' replied Thady. 'Old days never come back, and who'd want them to? We've MacSorley to thank for saving Sean, God bless the man.'

Grace made up a bed for herself in the byre, a small cramped cabin in the corner of the Close. In the summer, with clean straw on the floor, it was not the worst place to be, and her beloved grandmother had lived there until she died. She thought again of Marcas who had surely proven his love for her. She pulled her shawl tightly around her shoulders. She did not feel she could return such devotion.

The following morning as she washed her clothes in the mountain stream her attention was drawn to a wisp of smoke from the home she had been forced to leave. She spread her washing over a bush to dry and allowed her curiosity persuade her to take a walk down the valley. As she approached the house she saw that it was neat and well kept, and the thatch looked as if it had been tended by a fine comb. A woman appeared at the doorway holding a child. Grace had met Martha Crampsey only briefly before and greeted her formally. She was asked to kindly step into the house, if it pleased her to do so.

'Did you come about the child?' asked Martha in a conspiratorial tone. Seeing Grace's puzzled expression she explained further. 'Wee Dervilla, poor Roisha's baby.' The child, a winsome, curly headed little girl, looked up at Grace.

'Come here, my little love.' Grace held her arms out to the child.

'We're hiding her,' Martha continued to whisper as if there were a spy at the window, 'since the mother was killed. She goes from one house to the next, for fear of the Poor Law men.' Grace understood only too well how the children of executed criminals were spirited off to the workhouse or sold into labour, and were often never heard of again.

'She has a grandmother, Brigid Fegan, living in Lisnacree. I'm sure she would want to take the child,' said Grace. She watched Dervilla playing with a kitten by the hearth. She was certainly the image of Roisha's people.

'We didn't know what was the best thing to do. Lisnacree's a long walk for a child. I'm glad you're back,' sighed Martha, pouring Grace some tea. She was happy to relinquish responsibility.

The following morning Grace called at Dunn's Hill. She had some matters concerning Belfast to discuss with Tom, and was anxious to hear his account of the events of the past few months.

'You'll have heard about the return of Marcas MacSorley,' said Tom.

'Yes. His news about Sean has put new life into my father. My mother,' Grace continued sadly, 'seems very confused, but perhaps that is only to be expected at her age.'

'She'll pick up when she has Sean back. Marcas could not have done more for you, Grace. Did you know he has bought

Arno's Vale from Fanny Butler? He must intend to stay here.'

'I wish him long life and health in it,' answered Grace. 'He is keeping well, I take it?'

'He is,' Dunn answered, 'but wanting, I'd say, for a bit of company.'

'He should get himself a dog.' Grace instantly regretted her harsh words. No one deserved happiness more than Marcas MacSorley, yet she felt it could not be with her. Tom looked at her closely but decided not to pursue the matter any further.

Grace turned to the subject of Dervilla, the MacOwen baby, and Tom agreed that the proper thing to do was to return the child to Lisnacree. He offered the use of his cart.

'I'll have it back before nightfall,' Grace assured him.

True to her word, she stepped into Dunn's kitchen just as the evening sun sank behind the mountains. She carried Dervilla in her arms, fast asleep. Grace herself looked exhausted. Master Dunn and Harry had just sat down to eat, and Betsy was ladling out their supper.

'Come in, Grace,' called Betsy. 'Sit down and sup with us. You must be starving.' Betsy pulled a stool up to the table and placed a steaming bowl before her guest, while Grace explained tiredly the events of the day.

'Brigid wouldn't take her. She said she'd be better off in the workhouse.' Poor Brigid Fegan was worn out by a lifetime of child rearing without the support of a husband. A new grandchild would have been too much for her.

'What will become of the child now?' asked Betsy.

'I'll take care of her myself,' said Grace, 'for I couldn't put Murtagh Fegan's grandchild in the workhouse. I suppose you could say she's mine now.'

Before returning to the Close, Grace went with Betsy and Dervilla to visit Roisha's grave. Betsy placed a reed cross on the mound, as was the custom. Dervilla struggled free of Grace's hold and scampered over the grave, unaware of its significance. As Grace whispered a silent prayer, recalling Roisha's gentle face, her eyes kept straying to the other, larger mound where lay the remains of a horse and rider. She found herself praying for the soul of Dargan Butler, a pretender to greatness and power, lord now of nothing but a lonely cairn beneath the bare cliff.

Grace picked the child up and hugged her tightly.

'You'll never know, *a chroí*, that both your parents lie here,' Grace murmured softly. She wondered if Roisha had told anyone else that Dargan Butler was Dervilla's true father. It was a truth which was best left buried in the mountainside.

'It's getting cold,' she shivered. 'We'd best be heading for home.' Her next task would be to find a home for the pair of them. Dervilla might have chosen a new mother more wisely, she thought. The light was fading over Levallyclanowen and a chill wind from the north swirled around her skirts as they scrambled homewards over the heather. Grace thought she could hear strange sounds in her ears, she knew not from where, like the scud of thundering hooves.

Sean

L ATE IN SEPTEMBER, a traveller neared the end of his long
journey. The pilgrimage which had taken him first to
France and from there to more distant lands was over.

Sean O'Lochlainn had arrived in Belfast on a cotton ship and
secured food and a bed in a seaman's mission near Chichester
Quay. He had gone to St Mary's, a handsome Catholic chapel
recently endowed by the townsmen for their Papist brethren, to
give thanks for his safe voyage. He introduced himself to the
parish priest who heard his confession and then submitted
himself to three days fasting and abstinence before attending
Mass on the feast of Michaelmas. He felt the better for his
penance, knowing that a merciful God had forgiven him his
broken vows.

Next day he set off on foot through the farmlands of north
Down, savouring the familiar stench of retting flax and the low
rumble of beetling mills. He spent the night in a small inn to the
west of Downpatrick. There was much industry in the fields of
the north of the county, but as he drew further south the pristine

stone cottages gave way to poorer peat dwellings, though they were often neatly limewashed and proudly kept. He saw women and children gleaning the barley and passed the time of day with the workers in the fields. People were wary of strangers and, although willing to be hospitable to a returned wanderer, were circumspect in expressing opinions about anything other than the weather or current market prices. There was much activity on the highways, but the byways and country paths were quiet, and the first familiar face he encountered was on a narrow pad some way north of Kilcoo. The years had added inches to the Darner's girth, but the coat and hat were still the same.

'God save you, pedlar, and how are the folk of Clonduff behaving?' Sean saluted the approaching vehicle. The Darner reined in his nag and squinted closely at the stranger. The broadly built man in his forties, well burned by the sun and with a black eye-patch, had the look of a buccaneer.

'If you've come to rob me you're wasting your time,' said the Darner. 'The woman that sold me these eggs took every last farthing.' He looked again, trying to put a name to the face before him.

'The last time I saw you, 'twas yourself lightened my purse,' said Sean grinning.

'In the name of the Pope, it wouldn't be yourself, Sean O'Lochlainn?' cried the Darner, recognising him all at once. 'We took it you were dead and buried long ago – on a desert isle, they said.'

'Well, if so, I'm back from the grave.' Sean felt pleased at the pedlar's recognition.

'If you have a shilling in your purse, there's an inn around the corner with porter that can't be bested,' suggested the Darner civilly. He looked forward to hearing what Thady's son had been up to this past ten years, for although many people left the Poorlands, few ever returned. News was money in the pedlar's trade. Sean O'Lochlainn must have some reason for coming home, and a bellyful of porter would soon loosen his tongue.

One or two drinks later the Darner had gleaned little from Sean, but the Kilbroney man had learned about every death, birth, wedding and adulterous misdemeanour that had taken place since he left. The watchful eyes of the landlord had rarely left the stranger, and eventually he called O'Lochlainn aside.

'I take it by the number of questions you're asking that you're a stranger to these parts.'

'Not a stranger, Sir. I've been away, but I was born in Kilbroney, and 'tis there I will go when I've slaked my thirst.'

'You're more than welcome to a drink,' the landlord assured him, 'but there are many here who have reason to fear unfamiliar faces. Now take my advice and don't let that old fool prattle on any longer. Drink up and be on your way.'

The Darner was about to start on the tale of Virgil Crampsey's embarrassing disease, but Sean felt that the innkeeper had been talking good sense.

'Sit down, lad,' ordered the Darner. 'You're away that long, what difference will a few hours make?'

'All the difference in the world to an old man waiting for his son. And to a son waiting for his father!' Sean threw back the dregs of his flagon in one gulp and wiped his mouth clean with the back of his hand; then he took his leave, thanking the Darner for his company.

Sean resumed his journey a little disturbed by the landlord's warning. The Darner just had a loose tongue, he reasoned, and nothing would annoy the taciturn Kilkoo men as much.

The route through the mountains held certain perils for the unwary, but Sean had walked them since he was a boy and felt safer there than in any city street. He passed the Priest's Mountain, its bleak rockface crowned with an altar stone which now only the mountain goats and ravens visited. Sean had once been bitter and resentful of the suffering which the Mass Rock symbolised, but he had seen lands where the degradation of slavery was rampant, and recognised now that tyranny was not confined to Ireland alone. Indeed, having worshipped in a fine new church, the first such he had seen in Ireland, he felt that perhaps change was at hand. He climbed the mountain to pray for the souls of the worshippers of old, and prayed, too, for the people of other lands who experienced the darkness of oppression.

Sean crossed the march ditch between the parishes of Clonduff and Kilbroney. The woods on the slopes of the Rostrevor mountains were tawny with shades of autumn and the evening sun lay low where the lough narrowed. It was a peaceful, somnolent scene, a haven of tranquility to warm the heart of any homecoming wanderer. Sean wondered if his son would remember him, for Michael had been barely four years old when they had last been together. He had been a manly little lad, comforting his crying mother. Since then Sean had known the hell of loneliness and despair, and had it not been for MacSorley he might never have returned to Ireland. The news of Ruth's death had almost crushed him, but MacSorley had persuaded him to come home and be a father to his boy.

As he stopped to shake a pebble from his boot the plaintive bleating of wild mountain goats reminded him of his childhood, herding the goats with Grace and their brothers. His mouth watered at the thought of a bowl of steaming praties washed down by goats' milk, and he lengthened his stride. He had almost reached home. After all these long years and weary miles, he could hardly believe it.

Eily was pottering among the ducks when she saw him come, the spit of her Thady when he was in his prime, but a shade darker of skin. She gave a strangled cry.

'What is it, Mother?' Grace called from the house where she was kneading oatbread.

'Sean,' stammered Eily, finding her voice. ''Tis our Sean come home to us at last!'

Grace ran outside, tears of gladness streaming down her face, and threw her arms around Sean's neck. Eily followed, a little bewildered: so many times they had told her that she was wrong, that Sean would not be back. She was almost afraid to touch him.

'Sean, 'tis yourself, *a chroí?*' she whispered hoarsely.

'Yes, 'tis myself.' Sean embraced her carefully, for she looked fragile enough to break. Then he looked hopefully around. 'Michael? I thought he might be here.' There was a longing in his voice.

'He's helping his grandfather with the praties.' Sean was off in leaps and bounds towards the low field.

His reunion with Michael was joyful. 'You've grown so tall.' He stood back to look at the boy. 'They've been feeding you well.' His heart was aching as he looked at the sweet face which reminded him so much of the woman he had loved and lost.

'Plenty of praties and buttermilk,' sniffed Thady happily. He did not embrace Sean, for Kilbroney men were not given to such demonstrations of affection, but he offered his son a draw on his pipe, the warmest compliment he could give anyone.

There was no fatted calf, but Sean's homecoming was all he had ever hoped it would be. There was so much to tell and more to learn as they sat around the hearth over *maegh*, the mountain goat's buttermilk, and a dish piled high with floury potatoes. Michael clung to his father's side, chattering continually about his new home and his friends and all the things he wanted to show the homecomer before bedtime.

Sean laughed. 'I declare that boy speaks Irish as well as

any Hill Town merchant.'

'And why shouldn't it be so?' demanded Thady. 'Grace will tell you his Latin is just as good.'

'Wasn't I a smart scholar in my own day?' Sean reminded him humorously. He began to enquire about his neighbours and friends. He listened quietly as his father told him of the death of Annie Dunn and the hanging of Owen MacOwen.

'Sad news indeed. Did anything good happen while I was away? Is the Buller still alive?'

'There's many a year left in the old villain. He still has time to learn a few manners,' said Thady. Sean laughed. Some things never changed, especially the simple ones.

'I take it you were talking with Dr MacSorley? But for him I probably wouldn't be here at all.' Grace, clattering at the hearthside pans, came to sit by him.

'He told us something of your escapades,' said the old man, 'but don't think that excuses you from telling your own story.' Thady took a pull at his pipe, newly filled with a twist of tobacco carried in oilskin all the way across the Atlantic.

'Tell me about yourself, Grace. I'm surprised you're not married and in your own house by now. MacSorley had a brave notion of you as far as I could tell.'

'Is that a fact?' Thady shook his head, by now beyond surprise at anything involving his daughter. 'I doubt that she'll marry any man now, her and the age of her. God knows, 'tis not as if I didn't encourage her in the right direction many's a time. She's a great wee woman, though, thon sister of yours. Goes on men's business to Belfast for Master Dunn, and is highly respected among the best of folk.'

'Such compliments, Father, I'm overwhelmed!' laughed Grace. She was not going to be stung into comment on her personal business.

'Sure we have the best of men right here in Kilbroney,'

chuckled Sean. 'Maybe Grace should stay at home more often.'

'Now 'twould take a man and a half for our Grace, for she wouldn't put up with any oul' fool.'

'Like I put up with you,' snapped Eily from the corner. 'I told you that smoking would set you off spluttering and coughing again.'

'Do you see now what I've suffered all these years,' Thady whispered out of the corner of his mouth.

'Yes, you're as holy as St Joseph,' replied his son.

'If he'd had to live in this house, he'd be no saint.' There was a sparkle in the old man's eyes as he spoke.

They talked into the long hours of the night, comprehension slowly dawning on Thady. He understood at last why his son had left the priesthood, and the compunction that had driven him to work among those enslaved in chains. Now and then his gaze strayed to the tousled head of his grandson, who had fallen asleep by the hearth beside Pup. At last, at Eily's insistence, they knelt to say their prayers: tonight, of all nights, there was much to be thankful for.

'Tomorrow evening, after the work's done, we'll send word to Master Dunn and the two of us'll dander down to the Buller's. Then you can tell him everything you've told me, for otherwise he'd brand me a liar or a drunkard.'

The next morning, Sean helped Michael and Thady with the rest of the praties. Thady was approaching his seventy-seventh year which, even among the long-lived Kilbroney men, was considered a great age, and he still gathered his own potatoes and cut his own peat with the help of Michael and the Cobbler. Sean remarked on the changes in the landscape. There were more mountain dwellers than before, and a scattering of new cabins had sprung up on the other bank of the Owenabwee. Even the poorest bogland held lazybeds of praties. Some plots had been abandoned, leaving the shadow of potato beds on top of the soil.

'The fishermen, the McVeighs, settled there,' Thady explained, 'the folk that used to live along the shore near the quay. Sure I knew they couldn't grow a blade of grass on that windy gap, but, God help them, they were desperate.'

'And where are they now?'

'One of the lads went with the militia, to Wexford, I believe. The others went to England or Kilkeel or somewhere.' Thady had only a vague notion of the world outside Kilbroney.

Grace had left early that morning with Dervilla.

'She comes and goes as she pleases, but I'd say she's away to break the news to Master Dunn.' Grace did indeed call on the Dunns but her mission was more significant than that. Now that Sean had returned, she and Dervilla would look for a new home.

In the evening, friends and neighbours gathered round the Buller's fireside to hear Sean's story. It was a fine night and the firelight spilled on to the sward outside where Michael and the Cobbler's boys were playing. Thady, Grace, the Cobbler, the Dunns, the Widow Fearon and Johnny were all in attendance. Even Martha Crampsey, seeing the gathering from her window, had come to see what was going on. Sean barely recognised the Buller, now all but bedridden with not a tooth left in his head. The old fellow wept and held out swathed hands to Sean.

'God bless you and you're grown into a fine lump of a man,' he exclaimed. The Widow cared for the Buller now, saying that it suited her to mind the old blackguard, and she stayed by his side from first light until evening, going home each night in deference to local opinion. Fr Mackey would not approve of any arrangement which encouraged improper behaviour or, just as bad, a rumour of such.

'Damn all the improper behaviour I'm fit for,' the Buller had told the priest angrily, 'and me that can hardly manage to fill the pisspot any more.' Sean laughed at the Buller's tale. But although the Buller was still the best *seanachie* in Kilbroney, tonight all were eager to hear the story Sean O'Lochlainn had to tell.

'I begrudged the dirt and filth of the Valentine's quarry that cost me the sight of my eye,' he began. 'No matter how hard I worked and how much sweat I spilled, I still felt little more than a beggar. Master Dunn had shown me worlds I'd never have imagined; they were but pages in books, but I knew they were out there somewhere. I read of cathedrals, but the Mass House was the most I ever saw. I read of music makers, and yet all I had heard were the pipes or the whistle.'

'Now is that all that made you leave Kilbroney?' asked the Cobbler, thinking to himself that the pipes made grand music.

Sean shook his head. 'No, there was more to it than that. I would have stayed but for Eamonn.' There was silence in the cabin; time had eased but not banished the memory. Grace's eyes softened as she crossed herself. Thady looked into the embers of the fire, remembering his fair-headed son.

'When Eamonn died, I thought it was my task to take his place and be a priest. The day I left Kilbroney I was sad at the parting with my own folk, but stirred by the adventure that lay before me.'

'But, son, you're not a priest, are you?' asked the Widow, trying to clarify his status. If he was, they were all being too familiar.

'No, Widow Fearon, I was never ordained. I was too old and I couldn't accept the rule the way the younger men could.' Tom Dunn smiled to himself, for he had never known Sean to accept authority at any age. He listened as Sean described the kindness of the missionary fathers and how they had allowed him to join one of their missions to the Caribbean islands as a lay worker.

'The people of those lands had much to give. They knew of herbs and medicines which could cure many of our ills. They were skilful with their hands, respectful of each other, but the white man who came did not wish to learn from them. He wanted only to steal, to take by force of arms. He built plantations, enslaving the local people and bringing in thousands of Africans, young men and women. I'll tell you, we thought we were bad, but the suffering of these people was beyond description.'

His story was interrupted by the sound of an approaching horseman. Johnny Fearon was sent to investigate.

''Tis only Dr MacSorley,' he announced. As Sean rose to clasp the doctor's hand a respectful hush fell on the room. 'Come on in,' called the Buller, telling the Cobbler to pour a mouthful of liquor for the newcomer and MacSorley to find himself space to sit down. The old man, impatient to hear the rest of the story, bade Sean continue.

'You know, don't you,' said Sean, 'that were it not for Marcas I would be a dead man this day. 'Twas he sought me out at a time when I had abandoned all hope.'

MacSorley cleared his throat with poteen and related his role in the story. 'When I first found Sean he was working in an isolated colony. He was very ill, and I feared at that moment that my search had been futile. I wrote to Grace and told her that I didn't expect her brother to live.'

'Why didn't she tell me?' cried Thady.

'And what would she have said? Would it have comforted you to know that your son was dying?' said MacSorley. 'In truth,' he continued, 'the sickness was one which I had seen before, and I had had some success with treating mariners on

Mercer's ships. Yet I don't think it was my medicines which cured O'Lochlainn, rather it was this which gave him hope.' He held up a small wooden shard, blackened with age.

'This was given to me by Mistress Grace when we parted in Paris.' The woman turned from the shadows to meet his eyes. He smiled at her. 'You knew just how much it would mean to Sean – a relic of his homeland.'

Sean returned to his story. 'The sickness had killed many: some died after years of illness, others lasted only a few weeks. That was why I sent Ruth and Michael to Ireland, to escape the plague that had fallen on us. She was the most beautiful woman I had ever seen, in any of the lands I had visited, and I loved her dearly. Ruth was the daughter of a slave and the old Seigneur. My memories of that time still hurt, so happy were we when Michael was born. Yet our hopes crumbled when the Seigneur died and sickness struck the island, a disease against which the people had no defence. In fear for Ruth and the child, I took them to the port and put them on the first ship which was going to Ireland, a sugar boat bound for Cork. I hoped that she would eventually find Kilbroney and that my family would take care of her.'

Many of those present recalled the face in the snow. Ruth had come so far, yet had never reached her goal.

'It was my intention to follow them as soon as my work could be taken on by someone else, but some weeks later I fell ill. I had contracted leprosy.'

The following evening Tom Dunn visited Arno's Vale. He had a few questions to put to Marcas MacSorley.

'You know more about this than Sean. Did Ruth have leprosy?'

MacSorley did not reply immediately. Such was the ignorance and fear of the disease that many people panicked at the mere mention of the name.

'I was fairly sure at the time she was a leper. I saw the signs on her body and wondered if this could be so. But it was only much later – in recent weeks, in fact – that the fiddler confirmed my fears.'

'O'Cassidy?'

'The poor devil must have loved Ruth as fiercely as did Sean. He looked after her, fed her, clothed her, all the way from Cork. He kept her away from people, for she knew herself the consequences should her ague be discovered. Then Dargan Butler coaxed her away from the fiddler, how I do not know. He told me he blamed Butler for her death, as surely as if he had twisted a knife in her heart.'

'So that's why O'Cassidy came to Rostrevor. I had often wondered why a fine musician would want to stay in such a remote place.'

'He wished revenge on Butler, but soon discovered that leprosy had taken its hold on him.' MacSorley shook his head in pity. 'Such a curse to a musician; the fingers gradually losing their sensitivity and feeling, the hands becoming weak. That is why he lived in the Clasha, keeping out of other folk's way and shunning all company. Your Betsy was good to him, leaving him baskets of food when he needed it, bless her kind young heart.'

Tom Dunn paled. 'Betsy! Could she have come in contact with the disease?'

'No. He stayed well away from her at all times,' MacSorley answered firmly. 'The strain of the disease is erratic. It might only harm one in fifty and most people, like Sean, will recover. The poor fiddler's illness was fatal; alas, his constitution was frail. I saw him before he died, at Betsy's request. He was a pitiful sight, and too near the end for me to be of any help. All he wished was to be left to die on his own. He confronted Dargan Butler, I believe. He told me that he would not rest unless he did so. Butler may have had

299

the disease, too; he would have contracted it from Ruth.'

'So Butler may have taken his own life,' mused Dunn. 'When faced with the prospect of disfigurement and ruin, he rode to his death.'

'I believe that such was in his mind. The ironic thing is, he would probably have recovered given care and treatment.'

Tom Dunn had nothing to add. He trusted his friend's judgement and tried to cast aside his fears for Betsy, which were more deeply rooted than he cared to admit. Even the most rational man might be afraid of the scourge of leprosy.

Fanny's Legacy

WINTER WAS APPROACHING and the pains were bad in Thady's chest. He sat by the hearth, waiting for his boys to come home. Sean carried into the cabin a sack of oatmeal purchased from the Darner.

'What news from him?' asked the old man.

'He says there's a lot of fighting going on in Armagh, a place called the Diamond. Catholics fighting Protestants, Peep o' Day Boys against Defenders.'

'What are they about?' cried Thady. 'Surely we're supposed to be fighting alongside each other now?'

'I don't know,' Sean replied, 'but the Darner says that a lot of folk are suspicious of their neighbours even after drilling beside them for years.'

Thady remembered the many summer evenings he had watched the youths training, himself and the Buller. 'Twould be a shame, he thought, if it were all for naught, that weavers and scutchers and bleachers would turn on each other.

'Poor Master Dunn,' he said as Sean threw some turf on the fire. 'Him that said we were all the one.' He dozed off, but woke to find Sean brushing down his coat.

'Are you going somewhere?'

'I'm only going to get McChesney to fashion a right strong pair of boots for Michael.'

'Tell me, son, do you think the lad's happy here?'

'And why wouldn't he be?'

'Do you not think maybe he pines for his own country? It's not that I don't think the sun rises and sets on him, for he's a great wee lad, but I want what's best for him and nothing less.'

'Michael O'Lochlainn is in his own country,' said Sean.

The Agent Crampsey was under strict instructions from Madam Butler's attorney to administer her estate fairly. However, his own family had grown so large that he had by now secured for them every possible sinecure in the parish, so he did not consider it beyond his brief to increase the rents, by a small increment only, in order to feed, clothe and educate the next generation of young Crampseys. The new Butler House had been meticulously looted, and if Crampsey knew the whereabouts of some of the more valuable pieces of furniture he kept his own council. A poor vagrant family from Armagh had occupied the shell for a few days until informed that the last inhabitant, a poor fiddler, had been a leper. They had hastily vacated the premises, and, in due course, it was put to the torch by local ruffians.

The farmers in Cooley watched the rising flames reflected in the waters of the lough; even shepherds on the hills at Fathom and oyster fishers at Waring's Point could see the red glow. And the fishing families in the Poorlands, who had been evicted to oblige Dargan Butler's vanity, packed up their few belongings and set out to rebuild their shattered homes.

A nervous Crampsey was obliged to ride up to Grace O'Lochlainn in the Close to deliver a letter from his employer. The tides of fortune were turning once again in Mistress O'Lochlainn's favour. When Crampsey had first taken up his position on the Kilbroney estate, he had to his astonishment found himself answering to this peasant woman. Crampsey had never been sure of her standing. She was educated to a preposterous degree for a woman, much less a peasant woman, and Crampsey, who liked a trouble-free life, simply avoided her as much as possible. Yet she had often sought him out to complain about the rents levied on the 'squalid peat hovels' as she called the quite adequate mountain dwellings, and quoted the law as freely as Mick the Fox swallowed porter.

During the years of Dargan Butler's supremacy, Grace's influence had declined, but now, it seemed, she was about to regain if not surpass her previous position. For Madam Butler, in her wisdom, had decided to bestow upon Grace the tenancy of Kilbroney House.

Though the gift would only last until a more permanent arrangement could be made with a distant English cousin, who would eventually inherit the place, the news quickly spread among the goodwives of Rostrevor and several voiced their disapproval to the vicar. The rewards of sin, they told him, should not be the tenancy of the Big House. Their ire increased when the vicar remarked that no one was more worthy of such a tribute than the woman who had devoted her life to helping the poor. The poor, however, were sceptical too, although some, like Mick the Fox, were quick to claim a kinship with Grace which they had hitherto denied.

Grace herself was the least surprised by the invitation to reside in the Big House. She had, after all, been housekeeper there for many years, and was not as much in awe of the place as were her neighbours. By all accounts the building had become very shabby and run down in recent years as Butler House had flourished: it was not as if Fanny had been in a position to sell it to one of her county friends. Yet had she not been in such dire need of a home for herself and Dervilla, Grace might well have refused the offer.

Thady had no such doubts as to what she should do. 'After throwing you out on the mountain with neither roof nor hearth, do you not think she owes you a bit of shelter for the winter?'

Tom Dunn added his own advice. 'Accept the offer, Grace. I feel that we may all be under surveillance now, and the privacy of such a house will give you more freedom to come and go. With the authority of Kilbroney House behind you, you'll be in less danger.'

Grace accepted his reasoning and the following morning, not without misgivings, escorted Dervilla down the valley towards her new home.

Madam Hall supervised the packing for parliament winter in Dublin with her usual attention to detail. The influx into London of French aristocratic refugees had raised the fashion stakes in the first city of the empire, and Dublin ladies felt compelled to meet London's standards. Bess Hall was determined not to be labelled a dowdy northerner.

She looked forward to meeting old cronies and was particularly eager to see the Ulick Butlers again. The disappearance of Dargan Butler had caused a considerable stir. Narcy Nedham and a couple of young bucks had been spending a weekend at Butler's new residence when he had disappeared, and all were completely baffled as to his whereabouts. Savage Hall had been characteristically unsympathetic. 'Damn good riddance,' he had remarked, with the suggestion that the man had sailed off to the south seas in search of his wife or, at least, her moneybags.

'Couldn't stand being made look a cuckold!' crowed the Squire. 'Anyway, he owes money everywhere – craftsmen, traders, the whole shebang. Looks bad, y'know.'

Reports that he had departed on his favourite horse gave credence to the theory that Butler had absconded in fear of his creditors. His disappearance had caused disquiet among his former associates and companions, but he had not been in their ranks for very long and there was little real sense of loss.

Some weeks later a letter from Fanny was delivered to Madam Hall's Dublin residence. It told her only that she was alive, ecstatically happy and had no intention of returning to Ireland. The estate incomes, she told the astonished Madam Hall, were to be paid to Fisher, her banker, and he had instructions for their further disposal.

'She says she's in love again,' the mistress of Narrow Water told Madam Ulick Butler as they endured an obscure Italian opera in the Crow Street Theatre. Beside them Dr Butler was snoring with more volume than the tenor on stage. His wife rolled her eyes to heaven.

'Love, indeed; if I thought that love mattered, I would have left this old bore long ago. It's Fanny's time of life,' Madam Butler opined. 'It affects some women that way. They call it the curse of Eve.'

Madam Hall, feeling nauseous at the overpowering odour from Dr Butler's breath, agreed that Eve had yet another indiscretion to answer for.

The flood of gossip concerning the fate of 'poor Fanny Valentine' dwindled to a trickle as more up-to-date society scandals seized the attention of the upper classes. The new Lord Deputy, Lord Camden, presided over the winter's social engagements, but amidst the gaiety and frivolity of Dublin Castle, disquiet over the possibility of a French invasion was mounting. The intentions of the new French Directory were not yet obvious, but the parliamentarians, Whigs and Tories alike, had been disturbed by the way a neighbouring country had beheaded its king and divested itself of all the most aristocratic and influential families. Christian men of many denominations professed shock at the reported closure of churches. Worst of all, the dissolute rabble which had taken control was defeating the armies and navies of Europe, and seemed unstoppable.

The Member for Newry, Isaac Corry, had been appointed Surveyor General of Ordinance, a sinecure which placed him directly under the patronage of the Lord Deputy. Corry had been a prominent 'Patriot', a comrade of Henry Grattan's, and when the news that he had given his allegiance to the Tories filtered back to Newry there was disappointment among the radicals and murmurs of betrayal. Savage Hall's fellow county gentlemen demanded new powers to deal with the growing insubordination of the peasantry and an indemnity act was passed giving the local magistrates a free hand in dealing with any trouble, from wheresoever it came. It was widely agreed among the powerful that such stern measures were now crucial. It was also felt that conflict was inevitable.

Betsy's Choice

THE MEN OF Kilbroney continued to meet in Tom Dunn's barn long into the winter nights. Three times a week they drilled in the Knockbarragh wasteland or on the mountains above Kilfeighan. It was better if the weather was rough, for wind and rain masked the clash of steel. The drill sergeant, a native of Dromara and a veteran of the Irish Brigade, came once a week from over the mountain. He served a wide area of south Down and did not like to be kept waiting. MacCormac the blacksmith, the quartermaster for Kilbroney, made sure all were well armed for the occasion, and pike heads were maintained in meticulous condition. He had also stolen a number of firearms, abandoned when Fanny Valentine left Kilbroney House; some were relics from the Cromwellian wars, but MacCormac was as good a gunsmith as he was at shoeing horses, and all would be put to use.

'When the day comes for the fight,' he told Tom Dunn, 'we'll be as well armed as any in the country.'

'I trust in heaven it won't come to a battle, or if it does, that it will be quick and there will be little blood spilled,' replied Dunn. He believed, as many did, that the militia, those who did not come over to the rebels' side, would lay down their arms when confronted by the sheer weight of numbers opposing them. Such was the optimism of the men of the Poorlands.

The Widow Fearon's lease on Sammy Shields' alehouse had expired and a new tenant had acquired the licence. The same clientele continued to give him their custom, but Dunn's orders were that matters concerning the 'Union Men' were not to be discussed outside his barn, and especially not in the alehouse. The scuffle between the Cobbler and Mick the Fox had been a warning to all of them, and it was understood that the next man to provoke such a row would be severely disciplined.

The numbers volunteering to join the United Irishmen grew steadily; the execution of Owen MacOwen had actually encouraged membership. Dunn greatly regretted the death of Oran O'Cassidy, their first volunteer. His body had been found by one of the Crampsey boys while exploring – Dunn suspected looting – Butler House. The fiddle lying by the side of the corpse had been the only clue to his identity. All had stood back in fear of the ravaged features until Marcas MacSorley arrived and shamed them all, lifting the poor body in his arms and cradling it to show he was not afraid of the disease. They had buried O'Cassidy in Kilbroney, and his comrades-at-arms had paid their respects. Betsy said little, for her grieving had given way to relief that the fiddler's suffering was no more. All who had heard him play agreed that no sweeter music had ever sounded in Kilbroney.

Johnny Fearon pondered his future. The prospect of marriage to Betsy had been remote to begin with, but now it seemed totally beyond reach. With his right arm no more than a withered stump he could not provide for any woman, let alone Betsy who had been so well reared. Yet she did not seem to be in any hurry to find a spouse. He spent much of his time at Arno's Vale performing light tasks for Marcas MacSorley and helping him with the herd, for the doctor's knowledge of animal husbandry was negligible.

'I know Betsy has no interest in me, indeed, why should she? She can't even bear to look at me any more,' he told a sympathetic MacSorley one evening.

'The butt of a limb's no pretty sight,' said MacSorley, 'but maybe she winced because she knows how badly you still hurt.'

Johnny disagreed. 'She's no milksop. She'll probably end up wed to some soldier.'

'Tom Dunn's daughter? That is rather unlikely, I think.' MacSorley decided it was time he intervened; perhaps Johnny's romantic aspirations might prove more fruitful than his own.

Harry Dunn, now teaching in the town, had taken lodgings in Newry's Dirty Lane. The walls of the medieval Cistercian abbey had crumbled, leaving the beggars and vagrants without their traditional shelter but providing masonry for a new school for the poor children of Newry. Harry, a townsman at heart, had been among the first to volunteer his services. Betsy, therefore, found herself looking after the farm, for her father was becoming daily more preoccupied with political developments. The Cobbler's lads did the heavy work while she managed the finances, sending beasts to market and buying seed. Johnny Fearon she had not seen since Sean O'Lochlainn's arrival, and she felt hurt by his abandonment of her. He had been a pillar of strength during the dark days of Annie's illness, and she had grown to trust and admire him. He held sincere beliefs on the futility of pikes and guns, and although most of his neighbours disagreed with him, not one could ever again brand him a coward. Betsy knew that she had more to worry about than Johnny's attentions, but she had to confess that the winter passed slowly without him.

The snows came early in February, not long after the feast of Saint Brigid. For a time there was but a sprinkling of snow over Slieve Bawn and the Cooley mountains; then, just as it seemed that spring was in the air, the blizzard struck. The Cobbler's boys were stranded in Upper Kilbroney, leaving Betsy with no help. Struggling to feed the beasts and break the ice on their drinking water, she saw skies heavy with more snow and remembered, with a shiver, that there was a hole in the thatch. She was milking the cow when she heard Johnny's voice calling her. She groaned inwardly for her clothes were filthy, her nose red with the cold, her knuckles raw and her appearance uncomely. Pulling her apron off, she flattened down her overskirt, mustering as much dignity as she could.

'God save you, Mistress Betsy.' Johnny stood with cap in hand. 'I brought the linament for your father.'

'Linament? What does he want with linament?'

He held up a jar. 'Dr MacSorley asked me to bring it.'

'He's in the barn.' She caught sight of her reflection in the water pail and was annoyed by what she saw. 'It would suit him better to get the thatch mended,' she said brusquely, turning her back on Johnny and bustling noisily about her tasks.

'Why do you not even look at me?' Johnny said suddenly, his voice full of pain. She was still. 'I see it in your eyes every time you are near me. We used to be friends, you and I. Does my mutilation offend you so much? Am I such a cripple that you cannot bear to see me? I'm still the same man I was.' He turned to leave.

'Oh, Johnny, Johnny, 'twas never so,' cried Betsy. 'I thought you had abandoned me. How could you ever think such a thing?' Johnny stopped, his silhouette dark in the doorway. Her words had caught him unawares.

'I'd better bring your father his linament,' he said.

He found Master Dunn bent over his books in the barn, oblivious of the cold.

'Are you sure it wasn't for another body?' He squinted at the jar he had received from Johnny.

'I'm sure it was for you.'

'Well, I'll take it off you anyway. Maybe I'll need it yet. How's your arm? No, your left one. The other won't hold a pen.'

'I've never tried to write with my left hand. I don't know if I could.'

'Don't think about it too long, just get on the job. You've plenty of brains, Johnny, and 'twould be a shame to see them wasted.' Johnny's silence was disbelieving.

'A child of five years old can learn, and so can you.' Dunn lifted his quill and continued with his work.

Johnny excused himself and returned to the house. Learning to write again was very far from his mind at that moment. Betsy was still in the kitchen.

'Do you want me to do anything before I go, Betsy?' he asked.

'Would you look at the thatch?' she said. 'Though I doubt there's much can be done while there's snow on the roof.' Her composure had returned.

'I could patch the hole under the rafters. It would hold for a while.'

'That would be very kind. I'll give you a hand with the ladder.'

Johnny failed to mend the hole, though he tried valiantly. In the end Betsy fixed it herself, following his instructions from below. They laughed and joked so that she nearly tipped off the ladder. An hour later Johnny was drinking hot ale by the fireside and Betsy was sitting by his feet. They talked of the past years and of his first appearance in Dunn's Hill.

'Do you mind that time? The snow was as bad as it is now.'

'And you were under arrest.'

'I was going to make a bolt for it for fear they'd hang me.'

'You wouldn't have escaped the Cobbler.'

'Oh, I would if I'd wanted to. But I didn't want to; not after I saw you.'

The clock ticked in the corner, the only sound to be heard as they sat in companionable silence. She wondered if he was going to stroke her hair or take her hand or kiss her, but he did not, even when she moved closer. A voice called from the yard.

'Are you all right, Betsy? 'Tis myself, McChesney. I'll feed the sow for you.'

Betsy knew how hard it would be to recreate this mood, and she dared not let the moment slip by.

'Johnny,' she turned towards him. 'Would you marry me?'

The Cobbler, having performed his good deed, had looked forward to the hospitality of the house, but quickly realised he was intruding. Instead he went over to the barn to pay his respects to Master Dunn.

Betrayal

TOM DUNN WAS unsettled by the news he was hearing. Vagrants and migrant families travelling through Kilbroney carried tales of skirmishing between Catholic and Protestant in Armagh of a type unheard of for many decades. At first he thought the rumours an exaggeration of domestic disputes, but the stories continued.

As the sectarian fighting in Armagh grew more intense, Dunn heard talk of an Orange Society, a new group which held no truck with liberal writings but rather claimed to take their inspiration from the Bible. He feared above all else the useless attrition of brethren who were divided only by a few theological beliefs and superstitious fears. He himself had been born a Protestant, baptised a Catholic, and married to a Presbyterian. He and his Annie had lived peaceably together for forty years, and if they had had the odd disagreement, it was certainly not about religion.

Early in March, just after the snow had cleared, he asked

Grace to visit Belfast once more on his behalf, to hear the news first hand from Russell and McCracken. He hoped, after all, that the Armagh riots were confined to that area, and that the wise and tolerant people of Belfast would pay them no heed. Grace could see that the master's habitual optimism had dimmed of late. She thought this mainly due to the approach of old age without the company of Annie, and she voiced her concern for him. He walked now with a limp, yet steadfastly refused the aid of a stick.

'You've been taking too much on your shoulders,' she said.

'I'll take as much as I can bear,' he answered, 'and when the time comes for me to lay down my burden, I must be sure that there'll be somebody to pick it up.'

Grace was, for the first time, reluctant to go away, for she hated the thought of leaving little Dervilla. She did not intend to loiter in Belfast, but to complete her business and return home as soon as possible.

'Our Betsy'll take care of Dervilla,' Dunn reassured her. 'She'll come to no harm.' Grace had no worries on that score, but still felt lonely as she walked across the wasteland to Clonduff.

A mail coach went once a week from the Eight Mile Bridge to Ballynahinch, and from thence to Belfast. It was filled to capacity with passengers, and Grace had to squeeze in among eight mildly inebriated bucks who had sojourned for the duration of the bad weather in the cosy inn of Hill Town. As many again hung on to the outside of the coach, and the heavily armed outriders implied that the highwaymen of Down were also back in business after the recent snows. The roads were difficult and uncomfortable, and on one occasion she had to help push the coach out of a sheough. She was in an extreme state of exasperation by the time they alighted in the darkness at the corner of Shambles Street.

A watchman called the hour of nine o'clock as she looked for familiar faces among the crowd. Some of her fellow passengers went to seek refuge in a nearby inn, and the street soon emptied. A single lamp guttered overhead to light the shadowy streets. Cold and tired, she was about to seek a room at the inn when the McCracken's carriage pulled up and a burly driver called her name. As the wheels trundled over the cobbles, Grace, exhausted, almost drifted to sleep. She sat up with a start as the carriage came to a halt, loud angry voices sounding from without. Her hand reached for a small dagger which she carried since the incident with Dargan Butler. The door opened and a bearded face ordered her out.

'Who are you?' she demanded. 'What right have you to stop me?'

The face withdrew to consult with the other voices, then reappeared. 'Out you get, woman,' he said tersely.

Concealing her knife, Grace looked out at a redcoat patrol, their muskets primed. The groom nervously clutched at the reins as Grace climbed down from the vehicle, resigned to a delay.

In the early hours of the following morning an anxious Mary Anne McCracken heard the arrival of the carriage.

'They seemed to be looking for something, I don't know what.' Grace's clothes were soaked through and her skin was blue with cold. Henry Joy McCracken was not in town, and his sister knew that the authorities regarded him with suspicion; the carriage had been stopped and searched before. She wondered if they were aware of Grace O'Lochlainn's role as a courier and emissary for the United men of south Down.

'They were certainly curious, and asked me many questions, over and over again, but fortunately I had no papers or documents on my person,' she told Mary Anne. 'I surely lead a charmed life.'

She met Thomas Russell who felt that the Armagh tragedy would not be repeated in Belfast, if only because the number of Papists residing in the town was very small. She also gathered scraps of information concerning Wolfe Tone's overtures to the French. When she arrived back at Dunn's Hill some days later, she asked Dunn if their discussion might wait: she felt feverish and exhausted after her journey. Dunn agreed that she did not look well and wished to send for Dr MacSorley, but so extreme was Grace's opposition that he did not dare. Instead he sent one of the Cobbler's boys in search of Sean O'Lochlainn.

All through the night Grace tossed and turned, and Sean dared not leave her side, but in the morning the fever appeared to have broken. She woke to find Sean sleeping in a chair by her bed.

'Poor Sean,' she said softly, touching his arm, 'did I keep you from your night's rest?' Sean woke with a start. The room, a bright airy bedroom as big as Thady's cabin, was cold.

'You need somebody living here with you,' he said as he set about kindling a fire in the grate. 'This house would hold the folk of three townlands and still have room for more. Are you not afraid all by yourself?'

'When I lived here before,' she reminded him, 'there were many weeks when I might as well have been alone. It doesn't bother me at all; anyway, I have Dervilla for company.'

'Why don't you rent out rooms or take in lodgers? If the barrack knew you were on your own here, they'd be billeting soldiers on you. Now how would you like that?'

'Let them do what they want,' she replied. 'This isn't my home. I'm only here because it was offered to me for a while and I had nowhere else to go.'

'Poor old Grace.' They both laughed, for Kilbroney House had once seemed as inaccessible as the seventh heaven. 'I'll keep a corner for you in my cabin when I have it built. If you need it, that is. 'Tis my guess that you won't.' Grace tried to rise, but she was still weak and she slumped back against the pillows.

'You're badly shook, although, I'll grant you, better looking than last night. You'll have to stop all this rushing around or it will wear you to the ground. Leave the serious business to the menfolk,' said her brother.

'I'll feel better once I've had some sleep; all I need is a bit of rest.'

'I'll go for Dr MacSorley just in case.'

Grace shook her head. 'I don't want to see him.'

'Don't you like the man? I thought he was a right good fellow. He certainly looked after me well.'

'I don't want to see him,' she repeated firmly, 'not now.'

A few days later Grace was on her feet again and asking for Dervilla to be brought to Kilbroney House. Sean was relieved to see some of the colour back in her cheeks, and broached the subject of MacSorley once more.

'Marcas MacSorley went half way around the world looking for me, all on your account. Surely you owe him some courtesy.'

'I owe him kindness, but that's all. I don't owe what I cannot give.'

'Haven't you been through enough, Grace? You're only hurting yourself, for I'm sure the man loves you deeply.'

'You, of all people, should know by now that the greater the love, the greater the grief.'

'That is a risk I have taken once and I would gladly take again. Isn't that what life is for? To love and to allow yourself to be loved?'

Sean decided he would fetch MacSorley himself. He knew she was not indifferent towards the doctor, and her bitter words had made this even more apparent.

That evening MacSorley called on Grace. He enquired about her symptoms and examined her, his demeanour detached and cool. He assured her that she would be well again, given plenty of rest and an ample diet. The sun was low in the sky as she sat by the light of a long window, the rest of the room in shadow. He stood looking at her for some time. She had changed little since their first meeting. He set his professional veneer aside and stepped towards her.

'Grace,' he said softly, 'look at me. Haven't we been through enough, you and I, these past years?'

She gazed at the sinking sun, her expression distant. 'Yes, Marcas, and could we stand any more? We both have so many secrets in our past, so much we cannot say.'

'To hell with our pasts.' He stood up angrily. 'Neither of us are young any more. Of course we have secrets. Can we not start again? I love you, Grace O'Lochlainn, and I've loved you since that first day I saw you stumbling through the snow at Dunn's Hill.' His voice became low. 'Stay with me, Grace; be my wife. We can build a new life together.'

Grace shook her head. 'Marcas, you know I care for you deeply. But love? I've been hurt too much before.'

He heard despair in her voice. Reaching out, he traced her cheek with a gentle hand. 'I'll never hurt you, Grace; allow yourself to love me and we'll never part, I swear.' He kissed her then, the evening sun setting a carpet of gold at their feet. His quest, his search for her, which had carried him through such pain and toil, seemed complete at last. He held her closely and for a while they were still. Grace broke the silence which had settled over them.

'Yes, Marcas, I do love you. Admitting it has been hard,

and I greatly fear what will come of it. It seems that misfortune follows me and those who love me.'

'All who loved you will have been the better for it. Henry Valentine's death was untimely, but what would his life have been worth without you? Do you think he would have exchanged your love for a few more lonely years?' He kissed her again. In time his love would heal her pain.

Betsy Dunn married Johnny Fearon in the Mass House soon after Easter. The Widow was too upset to attend, having been so overcome with happiness at Johnny's good fortune that she had come out in an unpleasant rash. She had, however, felt sufficiently well to drink the lad's good health on the previous evening. He was the finest lad that had ever walked out of Kilbroney, she declared to all who would listen, and even the Buller had to concur that Johnny was a 'right wee *garsún*'. The Widow had dressed her patient with great care for the occasion, insisting that the Buller wear his coat, with a new patch in the tail, and he surprised everyone by coming to sit at the door to enjoy the spring air and watch the diversions. His resurrection was naturally attributed to the healing well of Kilbroney, whose water was reputed to carry a potent cure. Not all would benefit from its powers for other factors were important, such as attendance at the sacraments and substantial donations to the coffers of the church. Since the Buller had fulfilled neither of these latter requirements, the cure was deemed all the more miraculous, a sure sign of God's benevolence and forgiveness. 'I feel so well,' the old man said, 'that I'm only sorry I didn't jump in altogether,' a sentiment the other imbibers did not share.

The Cobbler, Grace O'Lochlainn and Marcas MacSorley joined the bride's father to witness the short marriage ceremony conducted by Fr Mackey. There was no shortage of well-wishers and callers to the feast at Dunn's Hill, among them a couple of strawboys who each claimed a dance with the bride. After the celebrations Johnny proudly took his bride to his cabin below Leckan. It was not as fine as her old home on Dunn's Hill but Betsy did not mind, for she had taken her feather bed with her and no other furniture was necessary. As for Johnny, his spirits were high; the loss of an arm would not prevent him from reading and learning, and he had a mind to be a teacher like Tom Dunn. In that way he hoped to repay some small part of the debt he owed to his old master.

Thady O'Lochlainn was overjoyed to hear that his daughter had at last agreed to marry Marcas MacSorley.

'I hope now there'll be no more call for you to go running to Belfast and the like.' Grace smiled at her father.

'They're not pleasure trips,' she explained. 'I go only on business of Master Dunn's. He's not fit to travel far himself.'

''Tis time he found somebody else. Master Dunn will understand you're nearly a married woman now.'

'No one knows his affairs as well as I do. Who else could he send, if not me? He stood by me when I needed support, Father, and I'll not desert him now.'

Towards the end of the summer Grace received a letter from Fanny Valentine. There was no traceable address; the notepaper was headed only 'Jamaica'. Grace read her words with mounting pleasure. Fanny, without doubt, was blissfully happy. Taking Dervilla by the hand, Grace rushed up to Dunn's Hill to tell Tom Dunn the news.

'A school! Master Dunn, of all things, she wants to endow a new school for the Poorlands children.'

'I see Mercer's steady hand in this,' Dunn smiled in delight. 'I wonder where they are now?'

'If Captain Mercer is facing a capital charge in Ireland, I cannot blame them for being discreet.' Nor did Tom Dunn:

he had heard of fugitives being captured in strange and distant places, even from ships boarded by officers of the crown in search of traitors.

'Johnny could be the teacher. He's well trained by now and he'll be glad of the living,' began Grace, 'and the children, a warm dry schoolhouse...'

Dunn watched with amusement as Grace talked animatedly of her plans for the future, all the while hugging Roisha MacOwen's child. Dervilla was struggling to get free, yet Grace held on, seemingly unaware of the child's struggles.

'Dervilla,' Dunn whispered conspiratorily, gently disengaging her, 'come on and we'll feed the wee chicks.' The child placed a chubby, trusting hand in his, straining towards the chicks in the yard. He scooped some meal from a sack and sprinkled it into Dervilla's apron pocket, and she scampered around the yard sending the chickens fluttering in all directions. Dunn turned back to Grace and addressed her in a serious tone.

'McCracken's messenger was intercepted south of Ballynahinch. He's been taken to Downpatrick for questioning.'

'The saddler? I hope he can hold his tongue,' said Grace, her good mood evaporating.

'He wouldn't betray us, but I wish I could say the same about other folk.'

Grace was startled by the implication. Could there be a traitor in their midst?

'Gold,' Dunn continued bitterly. 'As ever before, they're offering gold for information. Someone will be tempted, for sure.' He sat down and rubbed his chin. 'It only takes one greedy man.'

Grace took his hands in hers. 'One informer alone can do little damage to us. Isn't that the strength of our movement: the web of cells, no one knowing too much?'

Dunn shook his head despondently. 'I wish I could be so

easily persuaded.'

'Let me go to Belfast again. I will speak with McCracken myself.'

''Tis too dangerous for you now. You've travelled so often before. I'll send MacCormac.'

'MacCormac would be too easily missed.'

'Then MacSorley could go in your place. He'd be glad to do so.'

'No!' Grace was alarmed. 'I would not have him endangered. He has endured enough because of me. Besides, he would not know where to go or what to ask. I'll go this time and be back before you know.'

Grace was to leave home many times during the next few months on Master Dunn's behalf, each journey more crucial than the last. She was more watchful than before, for now there was danger all around her. Her deepening involvement in a perilous political movement grieved Marcas, as her reluctance to talk about her meetings angered him. He refused to accept her explanation that her silence was for the safety of them all. As Grace became more deeply embroiled in the affairs of the United Irishmen, MacSorley went to see friends in Dublin, a cloud of uncertainty hanging over their plans.

In October she was summoned to a secret conclave of the Down Committee of the United Irishmen. A provincial representative was there to address the meeting. There was a sense of expectancy in the air as he rose to speak.

'I am here to tell you,' his voice was tense, 'that a French invasion is nigh. It is time to ready your pikes and guns.'

A hush fell on the group for some moments. Then the silence burst asunder as the delegates rose to their feet cheering, clasping their comrades' handshakes, embracing.

Catholics had dreamt of this redemption by the French for decades; Protestants drew a parallel now with the victorious expedition of William of Orange. The British militia did not seem a formidable obstacle and there were only 15,000 regular troops and yeomanry, many of whom had taken the United oath.

In December the French sailed for Bantry Bay with 15,000 troops under the command of General Hoche. By Christmas Eve nineteen ships were off Bere Island, ready to land, and on the deck of the *Indomitable* was Theobald Wolfe Tone.

Disarmament

'THE FRENCH ARE on their way!' Word spread through the streets of Dundalk as runners carried the news to Newry and from there to the townlands of Down. 'The French are on the sea!'

Throughout the north, men had waited impatiently for word of the French, but now that it had come it was confusing and told of defeat and desolation. Only half the numbers intended had landed; many had drowned in the wild winter storms. The invasion had failed.

Yet the men of the north continued to drill and recruit, and mountain and valley rang to the sound of thousands of marching feet, for now they said the French were indeed serious and would return. Wolfe Tone, now a general in the French army, sent word that a new invasion fleet was being prepared with the help of a new ally, the Dutch Republic. But the Bantry expedition had served to warn the government of the extreme peril of their situation, and in March General Lake imposed martial law. He gave instructions that Ulster was to be disarmed.

It was a bloody disarmament, with Newry and south Down being singled out for the most ferocious treatment. The 22nd Light Dragoons and the infamous Ancient Britons swept through the villages and townlands in a frenzy of brutality, burning cabins and slaughtering the inhabitants. In Newry men were hanged on the flimsiest evidence from the gallows newly erected below St Patrick's church. Townspeople fled to safety in the surrounding hills and were butchered as they ran. The county gentry were appalled at the undisciplined savagery unleashed on both innocent and guilty, and Squire Hall was among those who complained to General Lake. The county gentry's sensibilities were of no concern to the general, whose aim was a military victory, and the campaign continued. There was no time for the United Irishmen to mobilise. Such a concentration of force in one area had taken the rebel leadership completely by surprise.

Marcas MacSorley sat alone in a Dublin tavern, contemplating his future. He was torn between joining the crew of an ocean-going tallship and returning to Arno's Vale. He had heard snatches of conversation from other patrons in the tavern, news of martial law and disarmament in the north. Such things, he felt, were inevitable; much as he sympathised with the rebel cause, he could see no hope of its ever succeeding. He had witnessed the uprisings of the oppressed in other lands and knew that their victories were rare. And it was the poor who suffered most in the end, despite the good intentions of the libertarians.

As he stared into his tankard a former patient, a stout banker, passed by his table. He recognised the doctor and raised his hat, commenting civilly on the weather.

'From which end of the north do you hail now?' the

banker enquired.

'From County Down, Sir.' MacSorley was courteous, but not keen on idle conversation.

'And weren't you the wise man to leave County Down just when you did! My courier arrived this day with the most dreadful tidings of burnings and lootings. He says that Newry is in bedlam, with even respectable folk taking to the hills and the woods for safety. What's the country coming to, I ask myself? In my young day every man had his place and knew his place. This doctrine of equality, why, 'tis against God's law.'

MacSorley could listen no further. 'You must excuse me, I have business to attend to,' he said brusquely. He paid his bill and hurried off to find the next stage coach going to Newry. To his dismay no coaches were in operation during the present emergency, so he asked to have a horse made ready. As he made his way back to his lodgings, all around him were ladies shopping, delivery boys about their business, gentlemen saluting each other from sedan chairs: none seemed too worried about their countrymen in the north.

Within a short time he was riding up the Great North Road. He spent the night in a busy Drogheda inn and set out again at first light, stopping only to refresh his horse. Everyone he met carried similar stories, of trouble and despair in the north, and MacSorley was several times advised to turn back. The streets of Dundalk were empty save for a few patrolling yeomen and barking dogs; by evening he had crossed the Gap o' the North. He was halted by a troop of Ancient Britons who had set up camp at Cloghogue. This was wild terrain, country which the rapparees had considered their own, and Marcas wondered at the foolhardiness of the soldiers. Nevertheless, he greeted them civilly, for they were young men, far from home, little more than children emboldened by their uniforms and weapons. He wondered if they were acting under orders, for there did not appear to be an officer in their company.

'From whence did you come?'

'Dublin.'

'Where are you bound?'

'Arno's Vale in the parish of Kilbroney.'

'And what is your mission?'

'I am a physician returning to my practice, for I hear there may be grave need of my services.'

An hour or so later, MacSorley was allowed to proceed on his way, his purse considerably lighter. He had not relished the thought of travelling unarmed, so had paid a further sum for the return of his confiscated pistol. Everywhere along the route he saw the signs of turmoil: torched hovels smouldering, furniture and cooking utensils abandoned by the wayside, people dispersed along the road. He skirted the town of Newry, not wishing to be delayed any further. It was late in the evening by the time he reached Arno's Vale. He was relieved to see Mistress Hanratty safe and well. The old woman threw her arms around him as if he were a long lost son.

'I knew you'd come back. I knew you wouldn't desert us!' she sobbed. All the others, she explained, had fled in panic to the mountains, but she had stood her ground to look after the house.

'Did the troopers call here?' he asked.

'No, they didn't bother us at all.' Her voice dropped. 'Once they had Master Dunn, they were satisfied.'

The sentry on guard at the nightschool had been surprised by the speed of the redcoats who came swarming up Dunn's Hill towards the barn. His belated shouts alerted the assembly within and, in accordance with their drill, they escaped by the back door and scattered into the darkness.

The older men headed for the oak forest where plentiful cover was available; the faster young lads raced towards the mountains. But the alarm had been too late. Many were brought down by gunfire, and Tom Dunn was captured with ease.

The house and barn were searched but no arms were found: the blacksmith had secured a safer hiding place for the cache. The soldiers did not torch the buildings in the way they had destroyed more humble homes; they searched for documents, perhaps letters or roll books, but found none.

'Never mind the books,' an officer decided finally. 'We have our witness. He'll supply us with all the names we want.'

The flogging of Tom Dunn terrified the people of the Poorlands. They had believed that their champion was immune from prosecution, that somehow he would always outwit his adversaries. The spectacle of the old hedge-school master, bloodied and beaten and paraded on the village square for all to see, was a shocking sight, and sent many young boys and men into hiding. All over Kilbroney women prayed and wept for the man who had taught them, defended them, loved even the poorest of them. He would not talk, they whispered among themselves; to save his life, he would not betray them.

Grace selected one of Fanny Valentine's abandoned gowns, a deep blue riding-skirt with matching bonnet. Fanny was short and some adjustments had to be made so she could wear it with confidence. The barrack had a new commanding officer recently installed in the wake of Colonel Trevor's murder. If she were to present herself to him as the mistress of the Big House she had to be suitably dressed. The vicar of Kilbroney had advised her of this tactic when his own intervention on behalf of Master Dunn had failed.

She rode slowly to the barrack, bracing herself for the

encounter. The last time she had stepped past the gate, nearly twenty years earlier, had been as prisoner of the notorious Captain Walls, an ambitious career officer who had won his spurs quelling rebelliousness in Kilbroney. She had been arrested for treasonable activities, and only the intervention of Squire Hall had saved her from the most severe punishment. She was escorted to the colonel's quarters where a young officer, recognising a lady of quality, rose courteously to greet her.

'Please be seated, Madam.'

'Thank you, young man, but I prefer to stand.'

'Can I be of any service, Madam?'

'I wish to pay bail for Master Dunn's release.' Grace held her breath. She had only the money advanced by Fisher for the schoolhouse, and it might not be enough.

'Thomas Dunn has been arrested in accordance with the Insurrection Act. He must remain here until he has answered questions to our satisfaction,' said the officer, surprised at the request. What would such a grand lady have to do with a scurrilous radical?

'He is just an old man.'

'He is a rebel, Madam, and has been inciting the peasants. You, of course, may not be aware of that fact.'

'He has not been charged with anything yet, let alone found guilty.' Grace spoke with some confidence; her knowledge of the law might yet prove her mentor's salvation. The young officer looked uncertain for a moment.

'Thomas Dunn will be charged shortly with taking and administering an illegal oath,' spoke a voice from the shadows. 'I'm afraid, Mistress Grace, no sureties of yours can be accepted under the circumstances.'

Despair came over Grace as she recognised the voice across the years. 'No,' she whispered, 'it cannot be you, not after all this time!'

'I always had a feeling we would meet again,' smiled Colonel Walls, stepping into view. 'Our paths were fated to cross, don't you think?'

Walls! She felt the room grow cold. Walls, old adversary of Tom Dunn, who in the past had had her thrown in prison. He had flogged her father and hanged innocent men. A cruel, ambitious man without pity or mercy. She knew now that all hope had gone.

Marcas MacSorley knelt by the old man's side in the darkness of the prison. Dunn's eyes glistened with pain and his breath was short.

'You must take Grace away at once. She is in very great danger: they could arrest her at any moment.'

'She won't leave while you're here. You mean so much to her.'

'Yes,' spoke Dunn. His voice was weak and hoarse. 'She has a loyal heart. When I needed her most she stood by me, travelling all those lonely roads, risking her life. She deserves loyalty too.'

'I blame myself. I should never have left her.'

Dunn took his arm urgently, for he knew he had little time left.

'Marcas, Grace will forgive you! But heed my warning: she and the others are in very great danger.'

'But what of yourself, Tom? How can we help you?'

'I've had a long life, and my Annie is gone before me. I can see no escape for myself, and in truth I don't care. But I fear Grace has betrayed herself by coming to speak on my behalf.'

MacSorley took the old man's hand. 'I promise you, Tom, I'll do all in my power to save her, and if we're spared I will love and cherish her as you would have wished me to.'

Dunn smiled bleakly, his eyes brimming with tears.

'Take this, Tom,' MacSorley produced a small phial, 'it will make you drowsy and ease the pain.'

'I dare not! God knows what I might say if I didn't have my wits about me.'

Marcas realised that old Dunn was right. Helplessly, he turned his back on the suffering man.

'Oh, God help us, Tom! You, of all people...'

The clanking of bolts announced the return of the guards.

'Marcas, tell Grace I loved her also,' Tom whispered as the physician departed. MacSorley nodded but he could not speak. He knew he had talked to Master Dunn for the last time.

Betsy kept a silent vigil by the barrack in the company of Martha Crampsey and some local women. Such were the terrible stories of torture, of floggings and pitchcaps, that she had pleaded with Johnny to go into hiding for fear that he too would be arrested. She did not know when she would see him again and already she missed him terribly. Their baby was due in the winter; Martha was going to take her to Newry to stay with her brother Harry, so that she would have his company when her time came. That would be best for everyone, she was sure. The baby would have warmth and attention, and Johnny would be glad to know they were safe and well. As she waited under the barrack walls she was still hopeful that her father would be released, for life without him was beyond her imagining.

When the soldiers came to arrest Grace she was already gone. After seeing Colonel Walls she knew that she was in peril herself. She had left the barrack with no appearance of haste, but once home she bundled Dervilla into warm clothes and quietly led the horse towards the forest, hushing the excited child. Slipping through the trees, they climbed further up the mountain, every so often stopping to listen, in fear of being tracked. Above them lay the Clasha where the fiddler had lived. As the light began to dim, Grace wondered if it would be safe to continue, for the mountains above Rostrevor were full of hidden bogholes and gullies. At one stage she stopped, sure that she was being pursued.

'Who is there?' she called, trying to keep her voice calm. Through the dusk a slight figure approached. He had only one arm.

'Mistress Grace,' he said, ''tis good to see you safe.'

Johnny Fearon was a welcome sight. He had taken shelter in the Rostrevor woods, reluctant to wander too far from home. Taking the reins, he guided them through the forest and out to the clearing above the trees. It was cold beyond belief on the mountain during the night, and Dervilla whimpered and cried. Grace wrapped her cloak around the child, hugging her close, trying her best to soothe her and keep her warm until, exhausted, the little girl fell asleep.

A crescent moon shed little light over the Kilbroney valley as Johnny and his charges crossed the fallow and descended towards the Owenabwee. Pup barked as they approached the Close and at once Sean and young Michael appeared, armed with pitchfork and sickle.

'Who goes there?' growled Sean.

''Tis Johnny Fearon. Shut your mouth now or you'll wake the child. Grace and Dervilla are with me.'

Sean took Dervilla, crumpled up like a little rabbit, and carried her inside. Grace lay down beside her, for she too was exhausted. Johnny sat by the fire, whispering to Sean. The significance of Colonel Walls' command was not lost on the older man.

'She's in grave danger. You were right to bring her here, but she must leave with the dawn; the troopers will be here next.'

When morning broke Sean roused Grace from sleep. Dervilla was still deep in slumber, and Grace tenderly tucked the fleece around her. Sean would mind the child until it was safe for her to return. Grace kissed her father and mother goodbye. Both were very old and had seen many partings: this was as bitter as any. Thady was coughing badly and could say little.

'You'll be back by Christmas,' said Thady, hiding tears. 'We'll kill the rooster then. Away you go now and don't look back, for 'tis bad luck if you do.'

Grace could not afford to loiter. She had a full purse, the precious money for the school, but it weighed heavily in her pocket. She handed it to Johnny.

'That's for the new school,' she said. 'You'll see to that, I know, for you have the skill.' Then she pulled Eily's greatshawl round her and set off with her basket over the wasteland towards Clonduff. Her horse she left for Sean. As she walked she did not dwell on the sorrows of the past but on dreams of the future. She would be back, of that she was sure, for she still had her health and her wits about her. At the crest of the hill she disregarded her father's advice, as she had done often before, and turned for a last look on the valley of Kilbroney. She breathed a prayer for Master Dunn and for her family; a sinner's prayer, she knew, but perhaps those were the most graciously regarded of all.

She saw a horseman, still distant but coming towards her at speed. The open heath afforded no shelter and she had little option but to continue as though unconcerned, an ordinary peasant woman about her business. The sound of the hooves grew closer, closer, then halted just behind her.

'Go back, Marcas,' she said. 'You'll be needed in Kilbroney.'

'A physician is needed everywhere he goes.'

'You should stay with Master Dunn.'

'I can do nothing for him,' Marcas said firmly. 'His only wish is that I stand by you.'

'You place yourself in danger, walking with me.'

'Danger? Grace, of all people, you have been the most perilous to me. Yet I love you still.'

'Our dreams of a better world, Marcas,' Grace's voice scarcely rose above a whisper, 'they were all for nothing.' Despair clouded her eyes. 'And Master Dunn, facing such torment.'

'He is prepared for death,' Marcas said, 'and will die nobly.'

He reached for her then, an offering of hope in a time of heartache.

Thady poured buttermilk on his champ. The French could come and go as they liked, but he still had seed to put into the ground. It was hard for him to get his breath now, but as long as he had legs under him he could dander down to the Buller's to talk about the wrongs and rights of the world. Leastwise, he could listen while the Buller talked, Thady being the only man alive who could understand a word he said since he had lost his teeth. Sean and Michael were already out in the fields and it was quiet without them, but there was damn all wrong with a bit of quiet now and then. He had lived too long and seen too much to be worried by the latest scare. Grace would be all right. She would come back. His children always found their way back to Kilbroney.

Postscript

THE MEN OF Down, armed with pikes and with green cockades in their hats made a final, desperate stand against the King's troops at Ballynahinch on 12 June 1798. With their defeat, the rebellion in the north was over. Tom Dunn, unable to lead his company, had remained imprisoned since the disarmament of south Down the previous year. He received 260 lashes of the 'cat' before Squire Hall intervened on his behalf and secured his release. He died of his wounds on 2 August 1798, just four days before the final ill-fated French expedition sailed for Ireland under the command of General Humbert. There are many local legends concerning Tom Dunn and generations of Kilbroney people have learned the words attributed to him: 'What will it avail me to gain a few short years by betraying my comrades who have stood by me through the good times and the bad?' Each year on the anniversary of his death flowers are laid on his grave, just below the ruins of the church where he taught his hedge-school scholars.

All long-established communities have their ghosts, manifestations of the past which are so close we can feel them, in the woods, on the mountainside, in the meadow. Local historian John Joe Parr, who now owns Dunn's farm, records claims from people who have heard the repeated crack of a whip from the fields above the barn around the anniversary of Tom Dunn's death. According to local tradition, the arm of the soldier who wielded the whip withered. The barn with two doors which housed the hedge-school still stands on Dunn's Hill.

The grave of Owen MacOwen's wife and 'The Trooper's Bed', where a man of uncertain identity and his horse are buried, lies between Leckan Mor and Leckan Beg mountains. Local people tell that the scud of a horse's hooves may be heard on stormy nights; in the evening sun the rocks look as if they are stained with blood.

According to the Register of John Swayne, Archbishop of Armagh between 1418 and 1439, one 'Gyllabrony Mckewyn' was granted custody of the Staff of St Bronach, with all the privileges which that entailed, in 1428. According to one legend, St Bronach was herself a daughter of Clann Eoghan. The Staff, or baculus, has disappeared without trace.